THE WITCH ROADS

ALSO BY KATE ELLIOTT

Black Wolves
The Golden Key
(with Melanie Rawn and
Jennifer Roberson)
The Labyrinth Gate
The Very Best of Kate Elliott
(collection)
Servant Mage
The Keeper's Six

THE COURT OF FIVES TRILOGY
Court of Fives
Poisoned Blade
Buried Heart

THE SPIRITWALKER TRILOGY
Cold Magic
Cold Fire
Cold Steel

THE CROSSROADS TRILOGY
Spirit Gate
Shadow Gate
Traitors' Gate

THE CROWN OF STARS SERIES
King's Dragon
Prince of Dogs
The Burning Stone
Child of Flame
The Gathering Storm
In the Ruins
Crown of Stars

THE NOVELS OF THE JARAN
Jaran
An Earthly Crown
His Conquering Sword
The Law of Becoming

THE HIGHROAD TRILOGY
A Passage of Stars
Revolution's Shore
The Price of Ransom

THE SUN CHRONICLES
Unconquerable Sun
Furious Heaven

THE
WITCH
ROADS

KATE ELLIOTT

TOR

TOR PUBLISHING GROUP

NEW YORK

THE WITCH ROADS

Copyright © 2025 by Katrina Elliott

A Tor Book
Published by Tom Doherty Associates / Tor Publishing Group
120 Broadway
New York, NY 10271

www.torpublishinggroup.com

Tor® is a registered trademark of Macmillan Publishing Group, LLC.

Library of Congress Cataloging-in-Publication Data

Names: Elliott, Kate, 1958– author.
Title: The witch roads / Kate Elliott.
Description: First edition. | New York : Tor, Tor Publishing Group, 2025. |
Series: The witch roads ; 1
Identifiers: LCCN 2024060860 | ISBN 9781250338617 (hardcover) |
ISBN 9781250338624 (ebook)
Subjects: LCGFT: Fantasy fiction. | Action and adventure fiction. | Novels.
Classification: LCC PS3555.L5917 W58 2025 | DDC 813/.54—dc23/eng/20250108
LC record available at https://lccn.loc.gov/2024060860

Our books may be purchased in bulk for promotional, educational, or business use.
Please contact your local bookseller or the Macmillan Corporate and
Premium Sales Department at 1-800-221-7945, extension 5442,
or by email at MacmillanSpecialMarkets@macmillan.com.

First Edition: 2025

Printed in the United States of America

0 9 8 7 6 5 4 3 2 1

The Witch Roads duology is the book that reignited my love of writing during a rough period when I wondered if I should just quit.

I therefore dedicate it to all who persevere even as it may seem easier to give up.

Never give up.

I hope that you, that we, that all of us, find the will and heart to keep going.

THE WITCH ROADS

1

ON ORDINARY LANES AND BEHIND UNPROTECTED WALLS

ONE HUNDRED AND thirty years after the Pall tore deadly rifts through the Tranquil Empire, it is still prudent to avoid walking abroad at night. Even people holding official tokens that permit them to travel on the safety of the imperial roads will halt before the sun sets. These tokens allow them to lodge at an imperial hostel protected by a split in the road. But many people—most people—have no choice but to walk about their lives on ordinary lanes and sleep behind unprotected walls.

The Shield of Peace and Prosperity so forcefully promised by the empire's founders has, it turns out, only ever sheltered some, not all. This is exactly what the holy venerables of the Heart Temple predicted at the dawn of the empire, to no avail.

Three hundred years ago, these temple theurgists and custodians wrote uncompromising tracts condemning imperial ambition. They spoke out in village plazas and city markets. They warned against the consolidation of power into the hands of a single military clan.

In answer, the newly appointed imperial censors burned their pamphlets as treasonous. The imperial sentinels accused the venerables of sorcery and burned them as witches. The imperial engineers sealed their bones into the great roads that link together the growing empire and facilitate the swift movement of its armies.

After the rising of the Spore-laden Pall in the reign of the ill-fated Azalea Emperor, it was soon discovered that the imperial roads repelled the Pall and its deadly Spore. The imperial archivists sent out official dispatches proclaiming that it was the harmonious and honorable magic wielded by the reconstituted imperial theurgists, in cooperation with the imperial wardens, that protected the roads against the Pall's malign influence.

Yet a tradition persists among the common people that the interred bones of the old venerables were infused with a holy power and it is the relics of those condemned as "witches" that have kept the roads safe. Even after all this time, the murdered venerables are said to still watch over the humble and the weak, the menial and the forgotten. Or so it is whispered, where the authorities cannot hear.

A passage censored from *The Official's Handbook of the Empire*
as compiled by Luviara, theurgist, working at the behest of
the Inner Chamber of the Heart Temple

2

THE DEPUTY COURIER

It was early autumn, warm enough in the late afternoon that Elen and her nephew had taken off their long jackets, rolled them up, and tied them atop their packs. They tramped through the rugged Moonrise Hills on a path she knew well because every month for the last ten years she had walked the same route. She was a circuit courier for the local intendant, delivering messages, decrees, news, personal letters, contracts, warrants, and a copy of the imperial gazette to highland villages and hamlets that could only be reached on foot or by griffin scout. Griffins were out of reach for a humble deputy courier, but Elen had two good feet and was grateful for them.

"What are you smiling about?" grumbled Kem with the graceless bad temper of a cranky adolescent. "I have a blister. You said these boots would be broken in by the end of the circuit. And I'm hungry. How soon will we get home?"

"Tomorrow."

"Tomorrow?" He shaded his eyes and peered toward the setting sun as it spread a golden glow along the ridgeline that marked the edge of the hills. A knob of rock rising from the ridge was the best-known landmark, easy to spot. "There's the lookout! We can't be more than three hours from home."

She didn't need to check her official's pocket watch to judge the sky. Birds were gathering, flocking toward roosting spots. "It'll be dark in an hour."

"Twilight lasts a while beyond that. It wouldn't be so far to home, just another hour or two past the lookout. The trail is wide and chalky, so it's easy to see. It's almost full moon, so there'll be enough light."

"No."

"But—"

"No."

His voice got tighter and grouchier. "For one thing, Palls don't rise during the week of the full moon."

"A Pall is not what I'm worried about."

"Joef told me there's been no sighting of Spore in ten years, not anywhere near Orledder Halt or in this region of the hills."

"All the more reason to assume it could happen at any time."

"But—"

"How many nos do you need? I haven't forgotten when you were two years old. I can say no all day and night long and not break a sweat." She grinned.

"Ugh. Why are you always so cheerful?"

"It's a passage spell."

"A passage spell? I've never heard of that." His tone blended skepticism and curiosity.

"The grumpier you are, the more cheerful I become. It *passes* your grumpy energy across to me and I transform it into bright flowers and sunny days." She laughed at his eye-rolling.

"You're awful," he said as he fought not to smile. But then his shoulders sagged.

"What is it?" she asked, gently now.

"I know you got permission to bring me on the full circuit to give me a taste of courier duty. I know I have to make a decision. I know I have to Declare for something. But . . . half the month you walk your assigned circuit, and half the month you work in Map Hall at the Residence. Doesn't it get to be a grind, every month leaving at the new moon and returning at the full moon, walking at the same pace on the same path, seeing the same people over and over every year?"

"Having shelter, food, and a worthy purpose is never a grind. It might seem tedious to you, but I'd rather have had fewer shocks in my early life and more uneventful days like we've been fortunate to have, living in the Halt."

His right hand strayed to touch the faded green ribbon that tied back his long, glossy hair. The ribbon had been his mother's. She, too, had had unusually beautiful hair of a dark reddish-gold quite unlike the black hair most common in the empire. Although, she'd been more vain of it than Kem ever was.

The sting of losing Aoving would never fade and never heal. *Never ever*, thought Elen fiercely. But they had escaped, and had many good years before the accident. That they'd had so many good years considering where they'd started was a miracle worth cherishing every single day she woke up missing her sister. And she had the keeping of this wonderful if sometimes grumpy child, a responsibility that mattered more than anything in the world.

"I tell you what, Captain No. You have to make up your own mind whether you want to Declare as a courier. Or whatever profession you are eligible for. But today, I can give you a little taste of the unexpected and the slightly risky. We'll camp at Three Spires."

He cast her a shocked look, then a second and a third, like his head was stuck on a chain of disbelief he kept pulling. She wanted to laugh but knew when to stop. The ribbon touch had been a sure sign he was getting heart-tired, so she'd follow his lead. But he was still a youth, eager to hear about the most frightfully appalling things.

"Joef says Three Spires is haunted by the shade of a wicked sorcerer-king who wielded a hideous power that leached the life right out of anything the sorcerer touched," he said, sounding gleeful.

She chuckled. "Joef has a most amazing storehouse of tales and rumors."

"His aunt *is* the intendant's archivist."

"And the local gossip, with a finger in every bowl of porridge. Nourishing, but to be taken with a grain of salt. It's safe to shelter in the Spires overnight as long as we follow the rules. What are the rules?"

He reeled it off by rote, barely listening to himself. "'Don't get distracted or sloppy. No shortcuts. Stick to the routine. Stay calm.' Isn't that all just the same thing?"

"Is it?"

He sighed dramatically. He was brimful of sighs these days, the closer he got to the decision he'd have to make. "Declaration Week starts tomorrow! How do I decide? I can't be a midwife like Mama, even though I know she wanted that for me. And I'm glad you had me come along on a full circuit. But I don't want to be a courier. I'm sorry."

"My blessed child, my hope for you is that you can be safe, not that you do what you think I want you to do. You like to work with your hands. You could apprentice to an artisan, like . . . I don't know . . . old Seladwin would be a good person to learn from and work with. You'd never lack for customers. She needs someone to take over her shop since she has no heirs."

"I'm not going to apprentice to the cobbler! I don't want to make shoes all my life."

"Well-made boots are a gift of human ingenuity and skill. Never forget it."

He glanced at his boots, the first footgear he had ever possessed that hadn't been handed down to him. A pair of new boots was a traditional gift for a youth as they Declared for a profession and thus the path and status they would follow throughout their life. "You told me so, didn't you? That I should wear my old boots and break these in afterward. I really do have a blister."

"Blisters hurt a lot, as I know all too well. We're almost there. There's a spring in the courtyard between the three towers. You can wash your feet and put on dry socks. That'll help."

"You know what I like about you?"

"I'm afraid to ask."

"You never say 'I told you so.' Not like Mama always did."

"Your mama had her own monsters to fight. And she did gloat a bit, didn't she, when she was right? It's funny how I miss that about her."

He fiddled with the ribbon.

They walked in silence, feet crunching on the rocky path. Elen kept the pace brisk as the sun sank toward Lancer's Ridge. Shadows crept down the slope like reaching hands. The wind began to flag. The overwhelming scent of autumn grass was softened by a faint fragrance of rose oil, so brief that, as soon as she registered the smell, it was gone, a phantom. It was only a memory of a similar hike into twilight, long ago, and the shock that had followed. She rubbed her right forearm, caught herself doing it, and stopped before Kem had a chance to notice and wonder.

A white post carved of holystone marked the turnoff to Three Spires. A seam of chalk guided them along a track that curved around and along the rocky slope. At a cairn, the track forked. One branch ascended steeply to the southern edge of the hill where three stone towers clustered together. From this distance, the slender spires looked more like huge stone spears than towers.

The Spires stood on the edge of a striking promontory. Their summits overlooked a long valley that extended southeast. The imperial histories claimed the towers had been built by the first Tranquil emperor as a fort, the location chosen for its view, and were later abandoned. Every local knew the story was ridiculous because the towers were far older than the empire. They weren't even built with the same materials and techniques as imperial buildings.

The other branch of the track descended into the valley, to a cluster of ramshackle cottages and rough sheds ringed by a water-filled ditch. The village's buildings were barely visible in the deep shad-

ows pooled at the base of the promontory's cliff. Any other traveler caught out at dusk would have overnighted in the hamlet. Elen
ought to have done so, but she really didn't want to have to deal with
the awkward encounter she wouldn't be able to avoid if they went
there. She excused her reluctance by reveling in Kem's awed stare
as they climbed the final stretch toward the towers. The last light
of the sun shimmered along the smooth walls, rippling like water
because of an unknown magic woven into the towers that no one
living today could name, much less shape to their will. Reflexively,
she touched her forearm.

"Did you hurt yourself?" Kem asked, sharp as ever.

"My old injury that aches sometimes," she said, which was enough
of the truth.

His expression scrunched up as he eyed her. He was about to ask
another question when they heard the thump of hurried footsteps
from below.

A breathless shout caught at their backs. "Courier! Good Deputy,
if you will! Pray attend us!"

So much for her attempt to escape a meeting she should have
known was inevitable. She sighed, halted, and turned.

3

A THIRD PRESENCE

Three individuals came up the path behind them. The first was a huffing-and-puffing elder aiding himself with a pair of walking sticks. The second was a farmer, a man about Elen's own age, early thirties. The scrawny youth at the rear carried a bow and a quiver of arrows whose points were carved from scavenged holystone. Not that arrows would help if there was a Spore irruption, but it was better than no protection at all.

"Is that you, fair Elen, Honored Courier?" the farmer called in a wheedling tone that made her cringe. She did her best not to judge him harshly for the awkward way he fawned and flattered. He didn't know any other way to speak to imperial officials, even one so inconsequential as a local intendant's deputy courier. "We thought we'd missed you on your return from this month's circuit. What a shame that would have been! I've a plea to make to you!"

Seeing that she'd stopped, the trio hastened their climb.

Kem snickered. "You think he's going to ask again if you'll marry him? Be a mother to his motherless brood? How many children did he sire on that poor woman before she died of exhaustion?"

"Let's not be unkind to a person who knew no other road for her life. It isn't me he's enamored of. It's what I represent. Something he's never had."

"What's that?"

"Enough to eat more days than not. I know what it's like to wake up hungry and go to bed even hungrier."

"Mama used to say exactly that when I wouldn't eat my beets. But she never would say more when I asked why you two got so hungry."

"I expect she didn't care to relate the details." She fixed a smile to her face, the politely noncommittal one she brandished to good effect together with her facility for names, titles, and proper address. "Elder Marsilion. Tiller Urnesso. Deputy Sentinel Willomo. I greet you under the Shield of the Empire's Benevolent Cloak. It is late. I fear you will be caught out after dark beyond your moat. No need to follow me. Best to return to your homes."

Marsilion replied first, as was his right as an elder. "When Urnesso spotted you on the hill, we thought you would shelter with us for the night. Yet you turned in this direction at the cairn. Surely you cannot intend to—" He indicated the three towers with a trembling hand. "Moon-bright is a dangerous time at the Spires. Haunts emerge from the moon's malign shadow."

"Have you seen a haunt yourself, Elder? Have any of you encountered one?"

"Oh, no, no, no, not me, Deputy Courier. We never come up here, nor walk beyond our moat at night. But my granfa' told me, he did. Said when he were young, he lost a friend to a haunt. The lad went to the Spires on a dare one moon-bright night. Came walking down at dawn with a different set to his face and a stranger's eyes. Walked right past his family as if he didn't know them and never returned home again."

"Yes, I've heard about your granfa's story."

"You have?" he asked, startled.

"Indeed I have." She hadn't, but Elen was a cheerful liar. It wasn't that she thought lying was good but that she'd learned when a certain kind of lie oiled a string that would otherwise ravel into a knot. Sometimes people simply would not listen. It wasn't that she faulted them for closing their ears to answers they didn't want to hear or couldn't understand or were afraid of. But there were times it was pointless to argue or try to persuade, so she'd stopped trying. "After that incident, wardens set a warding circle inside the central courtyard to keep out the haunts, protected by a holystone pavement."

The elder nodded wisely, although his eyes creased with uncertainty. "Yes, it's true there is holystone inside. I've seen it."

Urnesso smiled, an expression more desperate than cheerful. "But you would honor us with your presence, if we might host you overnight, Deputy Courier. It would be our honor and duty."

"It's just not possible, Tiller," she replied in a pleasant tone, making sure to use his title instead of his name. "Inspecting the Spires is part of my rounds for the intendant. Each season I make sure the warding is still intact. It's just turned autumn, so I must shelter there overnight and refuse your kind invitation."

Studying Urnesso's hopeful expression, she accepted that she was using lies to fend off a proposal he would keep pressing because he didn't know what else to do, who else to ask, how else to manage when he had to toil in marginally yielding fields all day among a scatter of five households, none of whom could quite feed themselves on the valley's agriculturally impoverished land. One of his children had died last winter of an illness the little one had been too malnourished to survive. Kem had forgotten, but Elen didn't forget what she saw in this hamlet and in the hill villages. She did what she could, and she lied when she had to. Lies were how she and Aoving had survived. Truth was better. Truth was what you aimed for when you drew your bow in life. But truth could so swiftly kill people who had no one to protect them, and she was glad to be alive.

"Here." She swung down her pack and pulled from it the goat-meat sausage, the round of salted cheese, and the small sack of oats they'd been given that morning at a hamlet whose livestock had prospered on the slopes over the summer. "You'd be doing us a favor to take this off our hands and share it among your families. It will lighten our load."

Kem's eyes got round as he opened his mouth to protest. She gave him a hard stare until he snapped his lips closed and took a step back with a huff of displeasure. Willomo shyly looked Kem up and down in surprise, puzzled gaze lingering too long on Kem's chest. Realizing he was staring rudely, the lad blushed and looked away. Kem bit his lip, annoyed and flushed. He was a surging wind funnel of emotion these days, not that she blamed him, given everything he was going through. At his age she'd never had the luxury, and she was glad he did, even when it made him tiresome to deal with.

"Best we all get on our way, Elder," she went on, knowing they would have to let her go. "Sun's setting. You've got a longer walk than I have. Peace of the night to you, Elder. Tiller. Deputy Sentinel."

She beckoned to Kem and, without waiting for an answer, headed on up the track. It was rude, according to the custom of the villages, but fully in keeping with the perquisites of an imperial official, even one so humble as a deputy courier.

After one hundred steps she risked a glance back to make sure the others had taken the food. Of course they had. Urnesso lagged behind as if wondering if she would change her mind, not that she had ever given him an opportunity to ask again, not after the first time.

Abruptly Kem said, "It's selfish of him to think you would marry a poor tiller from a ragged hamlet that can't even feed itself. And give up being a courier, if the intendant would even allow it."

"Hard to say what any of us would do in his situation. I've been asking around."

"Asking around?"

"In the hill villages. Sometimes a person loses their kin or their home, or a stray relative from a distant village turns up and no one knows what to do with them. Can't turn them out, but can't feed them. There might be someone for whom Urnesso's situation would be a hopeful change."

"You're the one who just said none of them ever have enough to eat."

"He'd do better with a second pair of adult hands in his household to share the work. Who's to say it couldn't get better, in that case?"

"But not you, Aunt?" He slid a look her way, testing.

"Not me. I'm sorry for him, but I'm not sorry for refusing to be the one he's looking for."

"You're the sunniest person I know," he said with a considering tilt of his head, "but then I think you are also the most merciless."

She laughed. "You ever tried sitting on bare rock, under a hot sun, for an entire cloudless day, without water?"

"No." Another sharp look. "Have you?"

"Think it over. Now hush. Once we reach the promontory, no talk."

"No talk? What does that mean?"

"Haunts are attracted to the sound of voices."

"Haunts?" He cast a newly apprehensive glance toward the towers as the path began to level off. They'd reached the top of the slope. "There's really a haunt there?"

"Do you doubt Joef?" she said, stifling a laugh.

"I don't know. Joef tells all kinds of stories and says they're true. Is it safe for us?"

"As safe as anything in this world, which means it isn't safe."

"What about the wardens and the circle of warding?"

"There is a circle of holystone pavement. I don't know if it was put there by imperial wardens, or if it's always been there since the towers were first built. Stay inside its boundaries, and no restless soul can touch you."

"So there *is* a haunt in the Spires?" he demanded.

"There's a presence, although I couldn't say what. A haunt is as good a name as any."

"How do you know?" His mouth twisted. "Never mind. Of course you know every single little thing along this circuit."

"I doubt I do, but not for want of trying. There's something I want you to see, something beautiful in the towers you can't see anywhere else, except maybe in another set of Spires like these."

"There are other Spires? In other places?"

"Why would this be the only one?"

"I don't know. I could ask Joef, but he doesn't have access to the surveyor maps." He paused before asking, "Why are surveyor maps locked away from the archivists?"

"Up-to-date maps are for the use of the empire's armies, not for its historians."

"Oh. Huh. The same way you can't share the information you hear in Map Hall."

"That's right. While it's true an intendant is the chief magistrate and justiciar for an intendancy, it's really a military position. Keeping the peace locally and supervising scouts, surveyors, couriers, and I suppose spies, although I don't know about spies. Maybe only the palace has charge of spies. And never say I said that to you. It could get us both in trouble."

He nodded. "Do you think Elder Marsilion's story is true? About the haunt who possessed the youth?"

She smiled. "We'll be fine as long as you do what I tell you for once. To start with, *no talking*."

He opened his mouth, paused, and shut it. They shared an easy grin.

He was such a good boy. She loved him so ferociously, for himself, first of all, and also for everything her beloved Aoving had gone through without losing the brilliance of a loving if fragile heart.

The moon hung fat and bright, a sliver away from being full, and appearing as a gauzy pearl suspended low in the east in the darkening heavens. No clouds marred the sky's depths. The first stars hadn't yet appeared. Rock pigeons crooned, although she couldn't see them.

They picked their way up the slope toward the point of the promontory. The rocky ground was spotted with fragrant clumps of creeping juniper and straggling clusters of woolly speedwell. Partway across, the vegetation ended as if a line had been drawn. The promontory narrowed until it was barely more than an arm's span wide, a dangerous ridge path. Kem didn't falter as he followed her.

The perilous path led between an aisle of stone guardians who faced each other, in pairs. In most old tales, the statues were said to be all that remained of the dread armies of the wicked sorcerer-kings, petrified at the instant of a vast blasting spell that had wiped the sorcerer-kings from the world forever. Joef's aunt favored the old poems, mostly fragments, that called these statues "the Shorn," selfless volunteers who had offered to stand guard for eternity to make sure the sorcerer-kings never returned. Or maybe they were just decorative statues of incomparable appearance. Certainly the sculptors had lavishly depicted people of striking power, heroic warriors. Some were carved with armor or tabards and some with bared torsos, the better to display their musculature. But it was their heads that grabbed attention, because most bore the heads of beasts.

The beast heads were not fully animal but something blended, as if magic had fused the intelligence and beauty and power inherent in each animal to make each soldier stronger with the attributes of their guardian beast. A ram-headed man in lamellar armor. A tigerish woman wearing a headdress woven of stylized wheat and barley. A fierce rat soldier, eager to attack. A proud eagle-faced person whose seeming cape was really its folded wings.

Kem's breathing tightened. It wasn't only the lifelike nature of the guardians that troubled him, as if they might open their eyes at any moment and move to block the path.

Yet worse than that, to either side and mere steps beyond the statues, the ground dropped away into sheer cliffs. It was dangerously windy up here on the promontory. The sense of being one slip away from plummeting to death was palpable. That alone was enough to make it seem an invisible haunt prowled alongside, breathing down their necks, a third presence who might act on a whim to animate one of the stone guardians to push a trespasser over the edge. Such a malicious haunt might follow intruders inside the towers, might slide their shadow into an unsuspecting lad's body to steal it for their own ends, as an escape from the ruins into the world beyond.

That was an unpleasant thought. The elder's story was one she'd not heard before today, as if it were a shameful secret he'd not wanted anyone outside the family to know. She shivered, although maybe the sudden chill that engulfed her came from a cold gust of wind.

Kem touched her arm to reassure her, although she'd not said a word.

The last pair of stone guardians had startlingly beautiful humanlike faces, as if humans were just another type of beast—and weren't they, after all? Still, seeing human faces on the statues was a bit comforting, right up until the eye dropped to the severed head each held in its hands. One cradled the exquisitely carved head of a sharp-snouted dragon with a knifelike crest and gemstone eyes. The other held the head of a young man, mouth wide as if he had stiffened into stone as he screamed for help that would never come.

4

The Holystone Pavement

Past the narrowed ridge path and its stone guardians, the promontory widened into a flat area about two hundred paces across, a blunt, prow-like point high above the valley. Cliffs plunged away on all sides except the narrow ridge path that connected the promontory to the main rise of the hillside.

It was on this windswept little plateau that the unknown and long-forgotten builders had constructed three towers in a triangular formation, linked by three connecting walls to create a walled compound. The towers rose about sixty ells, measuring arm to shoulder, and were impossibly slender and yet nevertheless enduringly stable. The connecting walls were about twice Elen's height, with no crack of age or erosion on the smooth surface. Along two sides the walls rose directly from the promontory's cliff face. The third wall faced the statues. The path Elen and Kem were walking ended at a stone staircase.

These steps ascended to an arched opening set midway up the wall. None of the spires had an external door, so this opening was the only way inside the triangular compound. No physical gate was set into the door-like opening. Maybe that was because life had been peaceful in ancient days and no one had feared attackers or thieves, or maybe it was because the always-open gate was a lure to entice the unwary into a trap.

There was no way to know. Whoever had built this place was long gone before the empire; of that, she was sure. Elen respected the potency of haunts, but she did not fear them the way she prudently feared the threat of a steel blade held in the hand of a brutal soldier or a barbed whip by a cruel overseer.

She went up the stairs first and made space on the landing, beneath the arch, for Kem to stand beside her. The interior was an enclosed, triangular courtyard with a holystone-lined pool at the center, within a circle of holystone pavement. Beyond the pavement, the courtyard's ground was bare rock except for three holystone paths that led from the circle to the closed doors of each spire.

She indicated the holystone, and Kem nodded, understanding this pavement was the warding she'd mentioned. But he didn't look at the pavement for long. Instead, his gaze sped upward along the spires. The towers were linked at the top by an elaborate and magnificent scaffolding. It extended out from the crown of each spire to form a delicate three-way bridge. The bridges met on a central platform that seemed suspended in the air directly above the pool. By some magic, perhaps the last remnants of wicked sorcery, the scaffolding couldn't be discerned from the outside, so it was spectacular both because of its ornate construction and its unexpected presence.

Kem choked back a garbled sound as he stared up at this architectural marvel. Elen delighted in watching his face shine with excitement. After a few moments, aware of incoming night, she tapped him on the arm.

They descended into the courtyard via a ramp that sloped from the opening down to the ground. Scraps of vegetation and dead bugs lay scattered on the rock where the wind had blown them. The holystone pavement remained pristine, as if it had been swept that morning. It was darker inside the courtyard than outside because of the shadows. As stars blinked into view overhead she guided him onto the pavement and set down her pack.

"You can speak here," she said, "but do not leave the circle. There's a basin where you can wash your feet. Not in the spring. It's pure-water."

"As if I would pollute a pure-water spring!" he said indignantly as he shrugged off his pack. Sitting on the pavement, he unlaced the boots and tugged them off, and finally peeled off his socks with grimaces and gasps. "Oh! Ow! Ah!"

His feet had indeed gotten a few blisters; not many, but two had rubbed raw and were now oozing. Poor lad.

Elen grabbed up a hallow-wood bucket stored next to the rim of the pool. After dipping it into the softly burbling spring, she carried it over to a wood trough, poured the water in, and let half of it flow into a wash basin. After they'd both washed their hands and faces, Kem bathed his feet with gasps of pain. He scrounged in his pack for a vial of gelatinous wax-leaf oil. As he smeared the oil on the blisters, his gasps were succeeded by sighs of relief as the ointment soothed some of the pain. She handed him a small brush. He began to clean their boots of the day's dust and grime.

Couriers before her time had built fires in a crude stone hearth set against the outer curve of the pavement. She sat cross-legged as she arranged kindling she'd stored here months ago, and lit a fire with her tinder box. While she waited for the water to boil, she noted in her logbook the encounter with the elder and the gift of the food, as well as their stopover in the Spires for the night, listed as "seasonal inspection, autumn, Year Eighteen of the Magnolia Emperor."

When the water boiled in her little copper kettle, she brewed a single cup of precious Eloquent Flower Tea in the small iron pot in which she'd intended to cook up a tasty sausage and cheese porridge for their supper. Her stomach growled.

"This will take the edge of hunger off," she said, handing the cup to Kem.

"I don't mind." He sipped at the tea, then drained the whole cup in one thirsty gulp. "I haven't had this tea before. It's sweet."

"I save it for special occasions."

"I'm not sure I like it." He yawned. "That was the longest day's walk yet. What are you going to show me?" He gestured toward the scaffolding above. "What is that? How does it stay up? Do the tower doors ever open? Are there stairs?"

"We have to wait until the moon reaches zenith. Go ahead and take a nap now. I'll wake you."

"Aren't you tired?"

"Not yet."

"Guess you're used to it. I'm glad you let me walk with you for the full route this time. It really does help me realize I don't want to Declare for courier any more than I want to be a cobbler. Does anyone know? Is it just me who doesn't know?"

"You're finding your way."

"But I'm not allowed to put it off any longer. Why does it have to be seventeen? It used to feel like the day would never come, that I still had time to think it over, and now it's so rushed. If I don't Declare this week, then I'll get assigned. Maybe that would be better. Just go with what the justiciar's office sticks me with."

"How do you mean?"

He shook his shoulders the way he used to when he was small and frustrated over a trouble he couldn't fix. "The things I want, I can't have. To join an imperial order as anything but a menial you have to be Manor-born. Well, sure, it's true the calligraphers are open to anyone, but we never had enough coin to buy me the training I'd need to qualify. That wouldn't be so bad. Writing up contracts in beautiful letters."

She raised her eyebrows. This was the first time he'd mentioned aspiring to the Imperial Order of Calligraphers. "Maybe, but if you think a deputy courier's rounds are boring, then I have to wonder if you'd find such painstaking work tedious after a month. By then it would be too late, the die cast, and your life settled."

"It's not how it happened with you and Mama," he murmured peevishly. "You didn't even grow up here. You made a place for yourselves after the normal age for Declaration. Why can't I explore and try out more things before I have to settle down?"

"Our circumstances were unusual. It's only because we arrived in Orledder Halt in the midst of a virulent Spore irruption. We had useful skills when the locals desperately needed help. That's why we were invited to stay. Otherwise, two women and a toddler-in-arms would have been granted the customary three nights of hospitality and then required to move on."

He'd heard the story before, of course. But now he asked, "Do you ever wish you could have kept traveling? Seen more of the empire?"

She shut her eyes, swallowing a spike of pain and terror. Surely the past could not catch up to them. What did the past care about humble Orledder Halt and its unimportant inhabitants? "I'm content here, Kem. So was your mama. Her especially. I like being a courier. She was a good midwife. People respected her."

He wiped his eyes. "I wish I could be what she was, like she wanted me to be. But I can't."

"I know." She rested a hand on his hair. "You are who you are. And I love you for it. She did too."

"Did she?" he said in a low voice.

"She didn't always know how to show it. You know that."

"I know." He sighed with youthful despair. "Joef is going to Declare as an archivist and take his training from the order at Ilvewind Cross. He said I could come with him and try for a menial's position there. He says the archivists aren't as rank-rigid as the wardens and engineers. He says sometimes the Imperial Order of Archivists raises up promising menials to become novices. But Ilvewind Cross is so far away and so big, and has so many people. And what if they kept me as a menial all my life, sweeping the floors and cleaning the privies? I'd rather be a cobbler. But there's nothing else. Nothing, nothing, nothing."

"Be patient." She paused, eyeing him.

He yawned hugely as the tincture's relaxing properties took hold.

"It'll sort out," she said soothingly, needing him to succumb to his weariness instead of fighting to stay awake.

"I hope so." His eyelids fluttered.

None too soon. He lay down, pillowing his head on an arm, just as the rim of the moon topped the eastern wall. Within a few breaths, he fell asleep.

Elen set the kettle on the hearthstone and rose, settling her stance firmly on the pavement. She stood patiently watching the light and shadow shift as the moon rose like a lamp being slowly lifted until it was high enough to illuminate the depths of the courtyard. Moonlight spread fractured tendrils down the inner walls, creeping toward the ground. Where the delicate light lanced through the darkness, the shadows around it rippled. They seemed to take on substance and, like water, flowed along the walls. There was danger, and yet beauty, too. Life was so fragile that she chose to embrace the beauty she found even when it skirted alongside menace. She braced herself.

A harsh, grinding scrape of stone against stone sounded from beyond the opening that led outside, coming slowly closer. A dark shape loomed into view within the archway, as if one of the statues had dragged its weight down the path and up the stairs. Yet the physical statue could not pass through the opening.

The swirling shadows met the presence, seeped into it, filled it as wine fills an empty cup, and at the same time lightened it as if turning stone into mist. A whispery body formed—darker than night and dusted with the magic of the silent moon. Almost a person, but no longer stone and yet not embodied in flesh.

The figure descended the ramp with a brisk but soundless stride, approached the circle, and halted a few paces back from the pavement's gleaming edge. The haunt was beautiful, wearing a lithe shape and comely humanlike features very like those of the statue that had been holding the head of a dragon. Was the beast's head meant to represent his prey or his hidden heart, who could know? Elen saw him as a man, but she had no idea what manner of being he really was or how dangerous he might be.

She held still. Some said if you didn't move, haunts couldn't see you. But he saw her. Slowly, as with the sweet taste of hazard, he smiled.

5

THE HAUNT

His smile was barbed with a mix of peril, charm, and irony. Yet could a haunt even feel emotion? Surely they were caught between the fragility of the living and the permanence of the dead—if death was permanent for stone guardians, however they came about. Elder Marsilion's disturbing story suggested it might not be.

"I recognize you." His voice was silken, and his tone coolly amused.

"How can that be?" she asked easily. The holystone pavement protected her and Kem, and the boy was further made safe by being asleep. "You've never shown yourself to me, nor have you and I ever spoken."

"Perhaps not in so many words. I have sensed your presence before this night, arriving and departing with the same fleeting touch as a bird on the wing. You are one of those who walk the land in a ceaseless cycle. What is it you are called?"

She knew better than to give her name to a haunt. "I am a deputy courier, it's true."

"Yes, that's right," he said in a tone of satisfaction. "I suspect you have heard my whispers, for why else do you stand here awaiting me?"

"I have felt a presence before, it's true. But never to see or hear, much less speak! I don't understand how you could have felt my comings and goings. Human lives are so brief. To stone, they must seem like a speck of dust blown past by the wind, too small and ephemeral to be noticed."

"I felt your presence because you are like me."

An uneasiness flickered in her heart. "How do you mean?"

"You know what I mean."

She shook her head, tempted to laugh but too wise to do so. Yet the pavement's protection made her bold. "Ah, I see. You don't know what you mean and hope to unwind some secret from my tongue. Lure me into your reach. It won't work, not on me. Yet I wonder. Perhaps, years ago, a local man listened to a haunt and took a step too far at the wrong time."

"Perhaps one did, although that was not my doing."

"Did it really happen? Did one of your kind—the other human-faced statue, perhaps—possess a youth and walk away inside his body? Can a haunt like you take over the body of a person like me?"

His shadowy eyes glittered as with sparks. "Do you want to find out?"

She smiled back, meeting him blade for blade. "I want an answer."

His gaze widened as if she had surprised him. A flash of unfathomable emotion stirred in his face, and after a drawn-out pause he spoke, with reluctance. "Not without consent. And the passage is intended to be only temporary."

"That's what I would say if I were intending something more permanent," she said with a scoffing chuckle, "but it was a good try. Why are you really here, this night, if you have glimpsed me before, yet never manifested like this?"

He cocked his head to one side, gaze sliding past her to the walls and up the length of a spire to the sky. Stars kindled one by one, although it was hard to see them because the moon was so bright. "A voice has called to me."

"Not my voice!" But he was no longer listening to her.

"Strange to hear the life-eating knell after all this time. I had hoped never to hear the knell of sorcery again." His words disturbed her more than everything that had gone before. All at once, a thickening sense of dread and expectation gathered, as if a web were about to be cast around the world that would tighten by degrees until it strangled all life.

"Are you a sorcerer?" she whispered, and was immediately sorry the dreadful term had passed her lips, lest he smite her for guessing the truth.

He went on as if she'd not spoken. "But it's odd, for there's a messy, scattered tone to its resonance. Almost more a hiss rising like steam through the cracks in the lid of a pot."

"Steam through cracks? That's a mundane comparison for words that sound so ominous."

His gaze dropped to pierce her as with the point of a claw. Almost, she took a step back, but she stopped herself before she showed any such weakness.

"You would be less entertained if you understood the danger," he said harshly. "But I fear that those who walk the lands now have forgotten all that passed before."

"Before when?"

"Before the Shivering Tide and the Hollow Wind. Before the Spear-Driven Storm cut away the bones and sinews of our lives to defeat our enemy. It was the only way to save what we could, and to leave a remnant to guard our descendants."

"None of those things mean anything to me."

"Can it be the distance of time has so thoroughly erased the truth from the memories of our descendants?"

"If a 'shivering tide' and 'hollow wind' happened, they must have taken place long ago, in a land very different from this one. In these days we are ruled by the Tranquil Empire. The witch roads—the imperial roads, I mean—and their wardens protect us from the Pall and its Spore. The imperial army roots out bandits and thieves, and keeps the land safe from the Sea Wolves and the Blood Wolves. The imperial magistrates provide aid to those who suffer during famine, winter storms and summer fires, floods, tempests, avalanches, and a host of other natural disasters. The justiciars enforce the law. The Heart Temple and its healers nurse those who become sick and open the way for the dying. Theurgists do the palace's bidding. As for the rest of the dangers that plague and harm folk day to day, they are of the commonplace kind."

His gaze sharpened with a sardonic flash of interest. "The commonplace kind?"

"How people treat each other. Greed. Anger. Lust. Envy. Pride. The desire for power. The urge to be violent." She could not restrain herself from a remark meant to tweak his cool confidence. "But perhaps the noble and resplendent people of ancient days never suffered from such ordinary vices."

He laughed with a palpable sense of delight. "I would never claim such virtue for myself. I'm neither so foolish nor so conceited. Although not all those who once knew me would agree on that!"

She winced, because people who could laugh at themselves were her weakness; she trusted them too swiftly, as she'd learned at a cost. Wasn't that the danger of haunts? They were alluring precisely because they weren't alive and yet entangled their victims within an insinuating presence that knew where to strike where the heart was most susceptible.

What if, by some magic beyond her ken, the haunt became alive, as she and all those who walked on the earth defined living? When she thought of the beast's head that had been cradled in the statue's arms, she wondered if he was even human.

She rubbed her itching forearm, realized she had done it, and braced herself for what he would say next, he who saw too much.

"I do not know this Tranquil Empire. *Tranquil.* Ha! Such a claim must be purposefully misleading. Or perhaps it acts in the manner of a comforting threat. Rulers love to speak in ways that make their power seem benign."

She smiled in agreement, caught herself doing it, and realized the haunt was far more dangerous even than he had at first seemed. But he wasn't focused on her, not as prey. She got the impression he was talking through the situation as he tried to figure it out, like a man waking from a profound sleep and trying to remember where he was and how he had gotten there.

"Blood Wolves. Sea Wolves. A veritable feast of enemies! Joy to the warriors who race in bold pursuit! As for the other, every temple is a heart, and every heart a temple, so perhaps, Deputy Courier, you speak in deliberate riddles to confuse me."

"I do not!" she objected too quickly.

Abruptly he raised a hand to ask for silence. He took a step back, chin tilting up, eyes narrowing as he listened.

A spear-thrust of dread lodged in her chest. Elen held her breath as she, too, listened.

A tone as of a dissolving bell spilled outward, growing ever more ragged at its edges until she heard as from an impossible distance a noise that might have been the hiss of rising steam or perhaps the rumble of a storm blowing in from beyond the horizon.

"I hear an echo of the Shivering Tide and the Hollow Wind," he said hoarsely. "Just as the elders feared. This is ill-omened, indeed. I must investigate what it means."

"What does it mean?"

He examined the walls as if he hoped to discover the means to break whatever magical leash kept him bound to the promontory. Then he turned his gaze on her, like pools of darkness too deep to fathom.

His voice fell heavy, sonorous, a command expecting compliance.

"I call upon the law of passage."

"I don't know what the law of passage is."

"Can it be we sacrificed ourselves with the best of intentions and yet now will fail because no one remembers?" He touched a hand to his eyes as at a pain he could not reach, and though she knew better than to trust a haunt, the gesture made her wish she could help him.

"What is the law of passage?" she asked gently.

He lowered his hand to examine her closely. Was there magic in the shadow of his eyes? The dangerous allure of his presence? "To investigate what this means, I need to go north. Yet I can no longer walk in the world as I am, shorn of the body I once had."

"And here I am, headed south," she retorted, for there it was: the haunt's beguiling and deadly request. She hastily added, "With people expecting me."

"Then let me borrow the youth who sleeps beside you."

A pain in her heart flickered. She had been right not to trust any haunt, even so briefly. Yet, ridiculously, it still hurt a trifle.

He went on smoothly, encouragingly. "You need only wake him, so that I might ask. I give my word of honor I will return the young one unharmed when I am done with my investigation, according to the law of passage."

She snapped in a rage, "I think not! You can't have him!"

His smile mocked her. "It's not really up to you, is it? The choice is his. But I suppose that is why you drugged him, to make the decision on his behalf. I understand the urge to protect those we love when there is nothing else we can do in the face of an implacable world. You would do better to help me—"

"No!"

"—yet fear not, fierce one. The moon has reached the net, and I can manifest here no longer. So be it."

The faint tolling faded. In its wake, a fragrance of rose oil wafted in the air so strong it made Elen's eyes sting. She blinked. The scent vanished.

The haunt was gone.

She stood alone on the pavement under the gleam of the moon, Kem dozing beside her.

6

THE MOON-BRIGHT MIRAGE

Although Elen hadn't noticed time passing, the moon had climbed all the way up the sky, nearing its zenith. Moonlight shone through the lacework scaffolding. Was the scaffolding the "net" that the haunt had mentioned? For whatever reason, the lacework through which the moonlight now filtered had dispersed the magic that allowed a haunt to enter the courtyard. She looked down at her shaking hands and realized she was completely unbalanced, almost dizzy. It was terrifying to wonder if she was losing her toughness, the agility that allowed her to cope with anything and everything life threw at her.

But she'd brought Kem here for a reason, and she cursed sure wasn't going to let any haunt throw her off balance. They had only enough time as it would take the moon to cross above the scaffolding.

She nudged Kem, shaking his shoulder. He sat up with a loud, waking snort that made her jump and then laugh out of sheer nerves. He'd always been a fast and alert waker, a useful trait. But then, horribly, she wondered if the haunt had managed to get inside Kem anyway, had been able to cross the holystone pavement and slide into his sleeping body.

The youth's gaze flew up to where the moon had risen high enough to appear inside the halo made by the scaffolding. "Oh hey! Look! Wow! Wow!"

As her trembling subsided, Elen was able to smile. "Yes, it's beautiful."

He stared in awestruck delight, gaze tracking along the three hanging bridges and down the length of one of the spires back to the ground. The knobless doors set into the outer wall of each spire had curled back like a spring leaf.

He jumped to his feet. "The doors are open! Are we . . . are we going up?" he cried in a tone of choked excitement.

After her encounter with the haunt, she should say no. But they'd come this far. She'd promised, and she meant to keep as many promises to him as she could. By the end of the month, his life's trajectory would diverge from hers in ways she could not predict or control. As long as they stayed on holystone, the haunt could not touch them, wherever it had gone.

"Do you want to go up?"

The wild grin that split his face eased her. For the first year after his mother's death, he hadn't smiled once. "We can, really?" He pressed a hand to his chest as if to clutch his agitated heart.

"Yes. But we have to hurry. The doors remain open only for as long as the moon tracks across the central platform." She grabbed his arm as he took a step toward the edge of the circle. "Steady, Captain Reckless. Stay on the holystone. Walk behind me."

He panted with excitement as he followed her. She walked out along the spoke-like path that led to the spire standing at the very tip of the promontory. The span of pavement was narrow, more like a beam laid onto the rock. As they made their way outward, a resonance hummed beneath their feet, into Elen's bones, throbbing along her arm, though she gritted her teeth and ignored the pain. She thought the path had something of a beam's structural importance, that just as there were three bridges above there had to be three paths below because of the triangular nature of the compound.

She was no theurgist, but she often crouched at the edge of campfires and listened to the talk of the people she sometimes escorted from one place to another at the behest of the intendant. Once, she had witnessed two theurgists arguing. One had said, "Magic knits the world." The other had said, "Magic is knitted into the world." Then the evening's meal of roasted grouse and charred leeks had been ready and they'd eaten instead of continuing their debate.

She'd wanted to ask what they meant, but it wasn't the place of a deputy courier to ask questions of imperial officials, only to obey their commands. Yet she often thought about that exchange.

The interior of the spire was entirely taken up by a spiral staircase. As they ascended, winding around and back around, the movement became dizzying, the stairs like a screw turning and turning, lifting as they climbed. She counted each step, 108 in all.

The staircase ended in another tiny landing. The curved wall had peeled back to create a door. Beyond it stretched a delicate bridge that seemed spun out of shining metal lacework. No more than an arm's-span wide, the walkway was bounded by a railing along either side. It led to the central platform. From the spire's door, it really did look as if the platform was a huge and very thin silver-wire disk floating on the air ten stories above the ground with only the three bridges giving it any support.

"How does it stay up?" Kem whispered, clutching the side of the opening as he stared. "Is it safe?"

"I'm pretty sure Three Spires is a lot older than the empire. This place hasn't fallen down yet. Do you want to come?"

He rubbed his face nervously. But when she stepped onto the bridge, he followed, matching her steps as if he feared one step out of rhythm would send him plunging over the edge to a messy death. For such a fragile-looking span, the bridge felt absolutely solid beneath her boots. Magic, she thought, whether it was the mover or the moved. Everything in its pattern, connections like the netlike filament layers of fungus and rot that permeated the soil, unseen by those who only looked at the surface of things.

Spore, too, she thought, her fingers cold where they gripped the ropelike railing. A rose-oil scent almost always presaged a Spore irruption. Its warning burned in her arm.

Don't get distracted.

Every person's stride was a different length, but like all couriers she had trained herself to the imperial stride as a measure of distance. Thirty-six steps to the central platform, which was itself thirty-six steps across. An insubstantial dome rose over the platform, a lattice woven of mist rather than actual metal. As she stepped off the bridge, tendrils brushed at her face like a spider's web briefly felt and then lost. The disk rang softly beneath her feet as she stepped onto it. It felt solid, but she could see right through, down to the ground below, as if it existed in two places at once: here, in this world and yet, somehow, in another.

Not surprisingly, Kem hesitated. It was a big step to take. So she grasped his wrist as she had so many times grasped his mother's when Aoving couldn't bear to take one more step but to stop would have meant death or worse.

She led him to the center. Here, the silvery wire was laced tightly together to create a raised plinth. She tugged him up with her, took his shoulders in her hands, and turned him to face toward the promontory's point. From up here, well above the compound's walls, they could easily see past the leading spire and out over the valley, its sides bounded by the Moonrise Hills to the east and Lancer's Ridge to the west. The valley ran in what the locals called the heartward direction because southeast led toward the heartland of the empire.

She had seen the valley in daylight many times. So had Kem, most recently when he'd been part of a rock-clearing corvee sent by the intendant to clear more of the rugged valley floor in an attempt to create more fields for the locals. Although the valley had a decent stream running through it, the land remained stubbornly infertile, and its crop yields were consistently poor from year to year. Beyond the straggling fields stretched miles and miles of thorny scrub and copses of prickly poison-sap trees.

Seen through the moon-glamoured lattice, it was like looking onto a different land. She and Kem did not see the rocky fields and sparse pastureland and ragged terraces farmed and herded by the likes of Tiller Urnesso and Elder Marsilion. Instead, they saw a ghostly apparition in place of the valley they knew, a forest city whose mighty trees were spanned by lacework bridges like the one they had just crossed. Spires glowing under moonlight, and terraced gardens decorated by fountains held fabric pavilions whose banners rippled in an unfelt wind. Streets brimmed so full with carriages and carts and people moving about that they seemed like rivers in flood, all of it shadow, not real.

Kem's body shook as he recoiled a step, slamming backward into her. He would have knocked her off the plinth, but she'd braced herself, knowing the sight of this otherworldly landscape would come as a shock to him. So it had the first time for her, when her predecessor had brought her up at moon-bright, years ago, while training her in the route and her responsibilities.

This is our couriers' secret, Firiol had told her. *Most folk fear this place, but we couriers know the Spires can offer shelter if treated with caution and respect.*

He believed the Spires were the remains of benign Old Ones, a peaceful folk now lost to the world, their last fastnesses abandoned. He'd never mentioned haunts to her, or wicked sorcerer-kings, but he had said there were sometimes whispers in the night, and she'd heard them too. What the magic of the ghostly landscape meant, he had not known, nor did he guess.

"What is that place? What does it mean?" Kem whispered.

Even she, who had seen so much, and who had even seen this before, struggled to keep her voice steady. The wondrous vision never became less astonishing or intimidating. "I don't know. Maybe it is a vision of the distant past, a place that once was. Maybe it is a vision of the future, of something that will become. Maybe it is a remnant of sorcery, a sorcerer's whim woven into this lattice. An indulgence that has never faded."

"Why?"

"Why do people have whims and fancies? You tell me, eater of every honey cake in the house."

"But they taste so good," he said as he recovered from the shock. "This illusion doesn't look wicked. Does it look wicked to you?"

"It looks alive, doesn't it? A city we can't touch because it is only shadow and light."

"I've never seen a city. Have you?"

"The intendant once traveled to the Peaceful Essence of the Divine Tranquility on the Heart Rock of the Empire."

"Can't we just call it the capital city?"

She elbowed him lightly. "A deputy courier must not be heard using such a disrespectful term. The intendant wrote a poem about it afterward. 'There is no end to the flow of the waters of this life, by sun and by moon, by dark and by light, by dawn and by dusk, the avenues pulse and beat, for we are the blood in the veins of the empire, always moving and never at rest.'"

Shadow and light poured up and down the valley within the hazy night, never at rest. The moon kept on its path, as the moon must, traveling west across the zenith. It neared the edge of the circle created by the scaffolding.

"We have to get down to the pavement before the moon leaves the lacework," she said quietly. "But you mustn't tell anyone what I've shown you, Kem. Not even Joef. Promise me."

He nodded gravely. "I promise, on my honor and in my mother's memory."

7

THE SOLE FRAGILE DEFENSE

DURING THE REIGN of the beloved third emperor, known as the Peony Emperor, the crown prince drank once too often from the cup of suspicion. When the emperor died, the crown prince inherited as the Honeysuckle Emperor. Most of her siblings died of one accident or another in quick succession. Those who survived were locked into a special wing of the imperial compound built for this purpose.

The Honeysuckle Emperor had a younger brother by the same mother. As a courtesy to her benevolent and respected mother she put out one of the brother's eyes to make him ineligible to rule and placed him in charge of the newly expanded Imperial Order of Wardens. Afterward, by means of these wardens, she spread her vines throughout the empire so she might hear or see any whisper of treason against the Tranquil Throne.

For this reason, the commonplace expression "the all-seeing eye" is both a reminder of the first prince-warden of the order as well as a threatening figure of speech.

In the great Bedrock cities, the scions of the Manors walk secure in the knowledge that all those who support the imperial palace are protected by a skein of watchful enforcers.

In the market and industrial towns, known variously as Rings or Crosses, mayors, manufacturers, guild-folk, and merchants scramble to place their younger children in the Imperial Order of Wardens, hoping to nurture a friendly ear within its complex web.

In the Halts that provide havens along the roads, appointed intendants sit with nervous smiles at their desks, never sure who among their entourage may be a spy recording their every transaction.

Even prosperous Moat villages must welcome young justiciars for three-year terms of office, not knowing who is there to gain administrative experience and who is an agent seeking to uncover conspirators, malcontents, and fugitives.

Only in the lowly Hedge or Ditch hamlets do folk rarely concern themselves with wardens, as wardens rarely have reason to go there.

Wardens are the guardians of the imperial roads, the lifeblood of the empire that connects all the outlying provinces with the heartland. It is the couriers who walk the unprotected hillside paths and lowland lanes and who are therefore, in the countryside beyond the reach of the roads, the sole fragile defense against the Pall and its deadly Spore.

From *The Official's Handbook of the Empire* as compiled by
Luviara, theurgist, working at the behest of the
Inner Chamber of the Heart Temple

8

◆━━◆

THE SPORE

In the dawn twilight, Elen and Kem shouldered their packs and set out from the Spires. The promontory lay eerily quiet. There was no rumbling wind, only the whisper of an exhausted breeze. When they reached the statues, Elen halted. Kem gave her a puzzled look but said nothing, remembering her warning from the night before.

She examined the statue that held the head of a dragon. It was difficult to truly know a face woven out of shadows, but she was certain the haunt had shared these features: a long, well-made face with deep-set eyes that the sculptor had lined with a hint of humor. The eyes of the beast cradled in the statue's arms had the same expression, maybe even the same eyes: ready to laugh, and yet made wary by a spark of surprise. The surprise of getting one's head cut off? *I should have known that was coming,* the beast's wry gaze seemed to say.

Such a statue, old before the empire, ought to be pitted by erosion and overgrown with lichen and moss, but its curves and folds and intricately rendered strands of long hair were as pristine as if it had been set on its plinth yesterday. She reached out, thinking to run a hand down the statue's bare right arm just to see if it was as smooth as it had looked in the glamor of moonlight. At Kem's gasp, she caught herself. Touching the statue, however tempting, seemed like borrowing trouble. She'd never touched the statues before, or even thought to do so. Was the haunt whispering to her still? Best to get moving.

With a shake of her head she set off walking, faster now, needing to get away from the encounter, from the Spires, from the stirring of pain in her heart. From the memory of that fading bell tone that rang like a warning she didn't understand. Her forearm itched. Her back crawled as if the statue's gaze watched them go, willing her to return. She determinedly did not look back. She was good at not looking back.

They descended from the heights, past the cairn, and took the turn that led up a long, gentle slope toward the crest of Lancer's Ridge. Their feet crunched on the lane's chalk surface. Yellowing grass and clusters of late-blooming spiny-throat grew along the ground, not offering much in the way of grazing, except for goats. A morning breeze spun autumn's chaff in the air. A hawk circled above.

They passed the ruins of a village where a white pine grew. Stepping stones made a path across a dry streambed that ran merrily during the spring rains. The chalk path ran for a while below the ridgetop, alongside the outlines of old summer pastures. Here and there the broken wood railings of corrals stood as a reminder of a time when horses were still raised here, before the rising of the Pall.

Past the last of the rotting fences, about fifty paces downslope from the lane on a level terrace of abandoned field, lay a sprawl of giant bones. Kem glanced that way nervously and as quickly away, as if just looking at the bones could kill him. Everyone she had ever escorted on this route did the same. But with a youth's impetuous change of heart, he grinned as he looked ahead along the path. He pointed toward the knob of rock atop the ridge that marked the lookout. She let him run ahead while she slowed her steps, studying the ground for any signs of disturbance between the lane and the bones. Nothing obvious marked the tough grass and clumps of scrubby bushes, but she'd been on edge since her encounter with the haunt. Instinct nudged her. Her skin prickled as if it sensed a texture in the air that wasn't meant to be there. A bell's reverberating tone. The rose-oil scent. Were they warnings of an imminent irruption, or just her imagination?

Couriers walked their routes every month. In their own way, couriers were as crucial to knitting together the empire as Manor-born administrators, wardens, and surveyors, even if, unlike these exalted officials, couriers were humbly born people who happened to be hardy, clever, and bold enough to do the work. The most dangerous part of a courier's work was not walking alone on long, lonely routes, winter and summer—it was keeping an eye open for glimmers of Spore, whose caps and blooms could erupt anywhere, at any time. It was having the tools and the training to eradicate the first signs of an irruption before its tendrils took hold in living tissue and burst like seedpods to inundate a surrounding area.

She left the lane and walked toward the bone pile, careful where she set her feet. About twenty paces from the bones, she set down her pack on a flat slab of rock grown thick with lichen and pitted with water erosion. A flash of movement startled her, but it was just a field mouse that had taken shelter against the rock, equally surprised by her arrival. It scuttled off into the undergrowth, freezing in the shade to stare at her with black eyes. Its fur was a smooth golden-brown, untouched by any sign of sickly corruption. As she took off her jacket, the mouse vanished into the bushes.

She draped the jacket across the rock. Then she checked her goat-skin gloves for signs of wear that might expose bare skin. That was the first lesson couriers-in-training learned: Never get sloppy. Sloppy meant you were dead, or worse than dead.

One of the reasons couriers were assigned to the same routes for years at a time was so they learned the lay of their landscape. People who knew the land well could thereby catch Spore-sign so early they could dispatch it on their own even though they carried only the most basic of magical weapons. From the pack she extracted a courier's Spore-killing tools: a vial of salt spirits suspended in liquid form by means of a theurgist's spell, and an obsidian dagger. It wasn't much, but it was better than nothing, part of every courier's standard kit together with a weather-proof dispatch pouch, a pocket watch, a spyglass and a magnifying glass, a steel-tipped walking staff, a pair of boots, an oilcloth jacket, a seal of office, and a transmission log.

Unlike every other courier in the empire, Elen carried something more. Something no human was meant to have. Something that would condemn her to death by burning, should the administrative apparatus of the empire ever find out. Something that maybe a haunt could perceive, even if no humans could, not unless they saw it with their own eyes.

She looked up the ridge. Kem was almost at the lookout, so not only was he out of range if a Spore-burst took her, but he was too far away to see her as anything but a tiny and thus indistinct figure in the distance. She pulled up her sleeve to expose the lower part of her right forearm, revealing the tip of a ropy scar that ran all the way up her arm. She was as prepared as she could ever be.

To begin with, she paced a slow circle around the jumble of bones, keeping her distance, looking for anything different from what she'd seen last month. Any sign that might tickle her brain.

"Jumble" was the wrong word for the bone pile. Two monstrously sized rib cages like passageways crossed each other to create a cruci-form architecture. The skeletal structure's clean lines and orderly spacing were a marvel, even beautiful, if beauty could be measured out of death. Natural rib cages would have long since fallen apart, but these were no longer natural.

Smaller skeletal remains lay inside. Perhaps they were the bones of creatures the two leviathans had devoured before they'd collapsed and died. Perhaps they were the remains of people and animals foolish enough to wander beneath the ribs at the wrong time.

The bone pile had been in this place for so long that no one alive remembered what kind of creatures these were. Local wisdom claimed two sarpa had fought each other to death, but she'd seen the bones of sarpa and these lacked the skeletal remains of wings. It was more likely the host bodies had been warped and wildly transfigured by the baneful vapors of the Pall. The now-monstrous dead might once have been as human as she was. If she still was human, she thought, rubbing the scar on her forearm. Recalling what the haunt had said.

Kem's lively shout of delight carried across the distance as he reached the lookout. How she loved him, the way he was exuberant about things and so eager to learn, when he wasn't being cranky. She ignored his voice. He knew better than to follow her close to where Spore might lie hidden. He'd wait up there, enjoying the view, until she joined him.

She circled the bone pile the regulation three times, twice sunwise and the third time counter-sun to make sure she'd not missed any glistening wisp or pale root or glassy mushroom germinating outward from the bones. From the outside it looked exactly as it had last month. But looks could be deceiving, as she well knew.

Her predecessors had cleared a track through the bones. This trail ran beneath the arches of the larger rib cage and took two separate, elongated loops out and back through the crosswise rib cage, keeping boots clear of stray bones. The ribs were of a vast circumference. She and five friends, side by side, could stand up beneath them, not that they'd tried. Griffins weren't this large, and anyway griffins had the semi-hollow bones of flying creatures. In the old tales told by traveling peddlers and itinerant scribes, the sorcerer-kings had conquered the world on the backs of gigantic monsters. Or they themselves had been the giant monsters. The way the fragmentary scraps of old poems were phrased left it a bit unclear.

If not sarpa, then perhaps these two leviathans had begun their lives as common serpents, twisting along the earth. Or perhaps they had been gracefully slender dragons, with legs and wings and breath of fire. Breath of fire would come in handy when Spore germinated from quiet bones or forgotten tombs. Maybe that's how the ancient people had kept the Pall at bay, or maybe the Pall hadn't existed in those days lost to time and memory. Maybe magic could spoil and become rotten, but if the historians were anything to go by, only theurgy was safe, while sorcery had always been poisonous.

Had the haunt once ridden to war on the back of a dragon amid a host of warriors who were all as beautiful as he was?

She hammered down on her wandering thoughts, the constant allure of how brutal and horrific, and yet also strange and fabulous, the world could be. *Don't get distracted. Eyes on the dirt from which danger erupts without warning.*

Her boots were her best possession. Steel-reinforced toes pointed south where she stood at the center of the crossed rib cages, the holy heart of its cruciform, its shadows curling over her body. Had she made the second loop or just the first one? She remembered walking the first loop, which included a little wooden bridge of three steps set over a protruding bone. A perusal of scuff marks didn't tell her for sure if she'd walked the second looped path yet. Nor could she recall if she'd examined the tuft of sedge that grew by a scatter of moss-covered stones.

She paced carefully along the second loop, angry that she'd lost focus so badly. Something was wrong. A taste in the air, a sense of disorder, a throbbing in her arm. No birds feeding. No insects a-wing or crawling along the ground. Too quiet. A prickle of instinct crawled up her back as she reached the scatter of stones.

The sedge's spiky white flowers caught her eye. It should not be blooming this late in the season.

Elen's chest tightened with apprehension as her attention sharpened. She knelt an arm's length from the tuft. A scent like rose oil drifted from the conical flowers.

She heard a faint scrabbling noise. She turned her head slowly, careful not to move any other part of her. A mouse—the same mouse?— sniffed closer along the scuffed track. The mouse was so intent on the attractive smell that it seemed not to notice her. She scraped her boot against the ground to scare it away. The mouse froze, then darted sideways behind one of the stones. Best to make haste before more wild creatures nosed too close, drawn by the scent.

With her left arm she prodded with the obsidian knife at the nearest blooming stalk. The flower recoiled from the blade, dissolving into a mist-like wisp with a snarling face.

All the flowers shuddered as in sympathy. Their cones began to flow sluggishly downward, becoming vapory threads that wound around the stalks and toward the ground.

Spore!

Another deputy courier would have run for their life, back to the Halt to give an urgent report so a surveyor could be sent out. But catching an early irruption still grounded in a plant was the easiest time to eradicate it, although potentially deadly. She scooted back an arm's length to give herself time to track the threads to their source. Spore had to be killed at the source.

The mouse darted out from behind the stone and, in a haze of compulsion, raced toward the sweet vapor. She slapped a hand down to trap it, but missed. The mouse dashed straight into the sedge's quivering branches.

One of the tiny, ghostly faces oozed outward with an elongating tongue. This leering appendage caught the mouse's ear, wrapping around it. The mouse spasmed, its feet scrabbling against the ground as it tried to flee. It was too late. Its corrupted ear twisted into a bloody claw that groped downward to shove a fresh-grown white talon into its own eye. More threads flowed from the sedge, eager to stake a claim in the animal's living vigor. Plants were rich food, but a Spore's favored prey must always be a mobile animal, so as to quickly spread the corruption. The mouse's head was already distorting, growing two more heads like fruiting pods eager to expand and burst. The mouse went rigid, its desperate struggle fading as the Spore devoured its brain.

She had to act fast. It was a good thing Kem wasn't here to see.

She set her gloved right hand on the ground, palm flat, and woke the viper in her heart.

A sensation of burning cold started deep in her chest, like a coil unraveling around her heart. The feeling was not precisely pain and yet not pleasure, so intense it raised tears in her eyes. The sleeve of her shirt rippled as if a thick strand of icy wire was being drawn the length of her arm toward her wrist. The tip of the scar bubbled, swelling. A pale snake's head solidified into view. The white viper slithered out of her arm, tail popping free as it undulated off her skin and onto the dirt. Its body shimmered with a cold so sharp it glittered. Its tongue flicked out, tasting the air. It, too, was a predator.

Eagerly, the viper glided to the thick base of the sedge cluster. As the mouse convulsed, being eaten from the inside out by the Spore, the viper sank its fangs into the mouse's hindquarters. With a sound like suction, it inhaled the mouse. At the same time, its venom dissolved the skin, muscle, and bone of the writhing animal, turning it into a kind of melting sludge that shifted shape—claws, faces, snouts, snapping maws—as the threads of Spore tried and failed to escape. A few wisps reached the ground just as the mouse was fully consumed, and the wisps probed as if in pursuit of its lost prey. When they found no trace of it, they surged toward Elen's life force.

Flowing Spore could not move as fast as the viper because the cold radiated by its body slowed the wisps to a crawl. One by one it devoured them, until they were all gone. No trace remained of the doomed mouse. The stalks of the sedge withered, flaking away into dust.

The viper circled the dead tuft three times, then shoved its nose persistently at one spot.

Elen dug with the tip of the obsidian blade to reveal the shiny cap of a pale mushroom-like growth. Uncovered, it smelled strongly of the sweet rose oil that had attracted the poor mouse to its doom. She unstoppered the vial of salt spirit and poured it onto the irruption. The spirit sizzled as the salt spell took effect to chew through the Spore. It did not die quietly; there came a keening in the air that cut like claws against her ears, but left no visible mark. The cap blackened into ash, and a horrific stench hit her nostrils.

"Aunt Elen."

She jolted back, terrified that Kem had followed her. That he had seen the viper.

But he wasn't there. No one was there. The ghostly murmur was the Pall's last desperate attempt at survival.

The stench faded. The viper nosed forward, sticking its head into the hole left behind by the now-dissolved mushroom cap. When the viper retreated, there was nothing left, not even the ashy grit. The snake circled the dead sedge three more times before lifting its head and tasting the air with its tongue. Its spiky tail lashed the ground, leaving gouges as if marking its victory.

The Spore was gone.

9

THREE WELL-SPRUNG CARRIAGES

As Elen reached the lookout, Kem turned to greet her. His dust-streaked face was alight, grinning, excited.

"There's a caravan on the road, coming from the direction of Ilvewind Cross. Do you think they came especially for our Declaration Week festivities? Joef says that in the days before the Pall there used to be traveling fairs that would set up to help a Moat or Halt celebrate—" He broke off as he looked at her closely, brow furrowing with concern. "You all right? You look kind of gray and weird."

She wiped beads of sweat off her forehead. "Just tired," she lied.

Her arm still hurt, but the chills that always set in as the viper returned into her body were beginning to subside. She'd jogged part of the way up the last steep slope to heat herself up.

"You didn't get much sleep last night," he observed sagely, then elbowed her as he waggled his expressive eyebrows. "Were you watching for the haunt? What if it was a handsome soldier, like that one who was part of the escort for the cohort of imperial engineers who came out last year to try to clear the road?"

She sighed wearily, rubbing her arm.

He made a face. "I'm sorry. You do look tired. We're almost home. Look at that! Look!"

He gestured westward with a grand sweep of his arm. From atop the ridge, they had a magnificent view over the lowlands: the imperial road cutting straight across the countryside, the river looping and curving, fields and woodland and hawks gliding over autumn-gold meadows while ponds and irrigation canals gleamed under the morning sun.

Orledder Halt was always the first thing Elen really focused on, because of its distinctive shape, easy to discern from this height and at this distance. The elevated road split into two roads that curved outward and, after about a mile, converged back into a single road. This split created an island of ground, a "halt" for travelers, protected by the road from Pall and Spore alike.

The lively Sul River passed beneath the split roads via culverts, flowed through the Halt as its main source of water, and wound away into the southwest where eventually its waters would flow on through East Latch Pall and Sunset Province all the way to the western ocean.

Up here on the lookout they were too far away to pick out individual streets or houses, but the solidity of the Halt's dense buildings was a welcome sight. They were almost home.

Beyond the Halt, fields clustered close on either side of the elevated roadway and grew sparser the more distant those fields were from the safety of the road. The locals had begun to push their fields and orchards farther out with each passing year. There were more mouths to feed and less Spore to disrupt people's lives, to remind them of the danger. Soon they began to believe the danger wasn't real.

Elen didn't look forward to writing her incident report for the intendant, in triplicate—one for Orledder Halt's archive, one for the provincial governor's archive at Ilvewind Cross, and one for the palace archives. Was the Spore related to the appearance of the haunt? She didn't think so. Such a mushroom growth would have been slumbering in the ground for months before breaking out into the living sedge. But what had triggered the irruption? Maybe she had it the wrong way round. What if the haunt had appeared *because* an irruption so close to the Spires had disturbed its mysterious slumber?

"Look!" Kem tugged on her arm. "*Look!* What is that, coming up behind the caravan?"

She removed her spyglass from her pack. From this distance, she saw the caravan as a column of tiny vehicles moving north on the road, but no detail. She set the scope to her eye and adjusted its lens. The road sprang closer.

"What do you see? What do you see?"

She spoke without taking the spyglass from her eye. "The caravan is flying the flag of the Imperial Order of Conveyers. There are one, two, three . . . *six* cargo wagons. They're all marked with the banner of the imperial engineers."

"The engineers! Do you think they're finally sending the new equipment they need to clear the avalanche? We've waited so long."

Two additional cargo wagons and two covered passenger wagons flew the Merchants' Guild flag. Cat-sized watch-wolverns with wings furled braced themselves on little platforms set atop poles sticking up from the fore and rear wagons, ready to take flight if given the order by the caravan master. Ordinary folk, carrying packs or leading laden donkeys, stuck close beside the road, on the grassy verge, grateful for the protection of the Shield Guild even if such hangers-on weren't officially part of the caravan. Messenger dogs trotted calmly along, tongues lolling.

The caravan was accompanied by outriders under the banner of a licensed Shield Guild. By its green stripe, this one had been hired out of Ilvewind Cross for the trip. Guard lynxes ranged up and down the caravan's length, with three-horned, three-eyed swalters astride. One of the lynxes loped forward, drawing Elen's eye ahead of the leading wagon to a group of riders out in front.

"Can I look?" Kem bounced up and down in excitement.

"Wait."

A flutter of panic turned her stomach as she realized three of the riders were mounted on elks, but nothing about their faces or posture looked familiar. The avalanche that had closed the road beyond the Halt had blocked the route that ran to Flat Pall and Woodfall Province beyond. This meant that folk from the eastern region of Woodfall Province who were wishing to trade in the Orledder region had to make a long detour west and south through Sunset Province and then north and east again via Ilvewind Cross to come back around this way—unless this group had come directly from the heartland. Yet if they had, it would mean the leader of the elk-riding contingent didn't know the road north of here was no longer passable through Grinder's Cut. But the reports detailing the damage the avalanche had caused had been sent out last year, along with a list of the dead and the missing. Aoving's name among them, of course. Any caravan passing through Ilvewind Cross would have gotten the report, so there was no reason for anyone returning to Woodfall Province to ride past Orledder Halt. It couldn't be them. It couldn't be *him*.

"There! Do you see it?" Kem nudged her arm, throwing off her view.

She lowered the glass. He pointed south of the caravan.

She set the spyglass back to her eye and tracked south along the road. Three well-sprung carriages were coming up fast, overtaking the plodding caravan. Each had a driver with an armed warden beside them. The rear carriage, with crates and boxes lashed to the top and back, was pulled by four sleek bronze aurochs. These creatures, constructed by theurgists, were infused with a magic that allowed them to run for an entire day. The middle carriage also carried luggage on its roof, lashed tightly. It was pulled by four golden horses whose bodies gleamed under the sun as if they had been polished this morning. The carriage in front bore no luggage on its roof, only a single chest tied onto the back riding board between a pair of menials holding on to a rail. Like the other carriages, its blue exterior was painted with the stylized "eye" of the Imperial Order of Wardens. This carriage was pulled by four obsidian panthers, as big as the horses, loping at speed in eerie synchrony.

Elen stared, stuck on this vision out of sheer astonishment.

"Can't I see? *Please?*" Kem jostled her impatiently, and her view swung away from the road.

Made speechless by the sight of panthers, she handed him the spyglass.

From the lookout it was easy to see how the carriages had gained on the slower-moving caravan. The caravan's wagons began lurching to one side, making haste to give room for the party racing up from behind. Kem peered through the scope, shoulders tight as he tried to get his focus.

"What are those . . . big cats?" he said, scope still stuck to his right eye.

"Imperial panthers. I believe."

He lowered the scope to frown at her. "Joef says only the emperor and princes born in the Flower Court hold the right to travel in carriages pulled by imperial panthers."

"So I've heard. I thought it was just a story. But that means . . ." She trailed off, then shook herself. "Here, give me that back. We'd better get down to the Residence."

They started walking down the ridge along a switchback trail, Elen setting a brisk pace.

"Means what?" Kem asked.

"Means Orledder Halt is being visited by the prince-warden. The intendant never said anything to me or the other deputies about such an important state visit. Which might mean he doesn't know they're coming. We'd better hurry."

They tramped down the ridge in silence. For a while, the curve of a hill blocked the view, and then they reached the lowland plain. They hurried through woodland, crossed streams, skirted several outlying gardens, where poorer folk took their chances at growing crops on land not taxed by the intendant. Kem rubbed his stomach.

"You all right?" Elen asked, wondering if the tea she'd drugged him with last night might have upset his stomach, but she couldn't say that directly.

"Early cramps," he said. "Like Mama used to get the day before her blood. I don't know why I couldn't be more like you, never getting cramps, and not like Mama."

"And I don't know why I couldn't have long, thick, glossy, beautiful hair like yours and your mama's instead of this rat's nest of curls. Choose your poison, my boy."

A flash of vivid clothing moved amid the trees on the path ahead. A moment later, Joef jogged into view. Seeing them, he halted, waiting bent over with hands on knees to catch his breath. When they reached him, he straightened, still flushed.

"Whew! I thought you'd be down last night. Do I have news for you!"

"Like what?" said Kem, with a heavy-handed attempt at being casual. "A visit from the prince-warden?"

"You saw from the lookout! No fair! I wanted to surprise you!"

Joef was a tall lad, stocky, strong, excitable, and mostly good-natured except for a tendency to gossip. Learned from his aunt, who had raised him. He'd also learned how to wheedle because his aunt could be convinced to slip the two boys extra sweet rolls or apple dumplings if they flattered her enough.

"Auntie, couldn't Kem come with me? If we run, we can climb up and watch the dignitaries arrive through the lattice of the attic archives. No one will see us up there. I've never seen a prince!"

"Has anyone in this Halt ever seen a prince?" Elen asked.

"Have you?" asked Kem suspiciously.

"I have not, or not that I know. Maybe a prince in disguise, like in the tales."

Kem snorted. "A noble bandit? A peddler spy? No, no, I've got it. An actor in one of the traveling troupes."

Joef turned his big, soft gaze on Elen. "Please, Deputy Courier. You're always so understanding."

She waggled a scolding finger at him. "Auntie works better on me. Yes, go ahead."

Joef grinned, unabashed.

"Don't let anyone spot you," she added. "The intendant won't want people caught spying."

"No one will see us!" Joef retorted indignantly.

"Thank you!" Kem cried.

They sped off with the lightness of youth.

10

A SWIRLING RIOT OF ACTIVITY

Elen walked after them at her usual steady stride. She caught glimpses of the boys as they raced past coppiced trees, charged across Handler's Bridge where it arched over Sulwine Stream, and last as they scrambled via the shortcut along the lee of the Boulders.

She puzzled over the unexpected turn of events. Why would the prince-warden come now? The catastrophic avalanche had occurred almost two years ago, after a series of unusually bad storms. Torrential rains had destabilized the steep slopes along the outer rim-land of the long canyon known as Grinder's Cut. Debris had buried most of Olludia Halt, including the village's Heart Temple where Aoving had happened to have been midwifing a woman in labor. A few survivors had been dug out of the rubble, but yet another storm followed hard upon the previous one and brought additional rocks crashing down.

The terrible event had blocked the road in an area called Five Bridges, for the five impressively engineered bridges that made the crossing possible. No local detour was available because of the depth and rugged nature of the canyon and a low-lying stream of Pall that had long ago settled onto the canyon floor, running parallel to the Winding Thread River. The avalanche had brought to a stop the long-distance traffic that ran through Orledder Intendancy, across Grinder's Cut, and on to the Vigil tower planted on the southern shore of Flat Pall. The blocked road was a significant inconvenience for the imperial administration and especially for merchants, since the road across Flat Pall was the most direct connection between the heartland and Woodfall Province with its resources of tin, hops, furs, hallow-wood groves, and a unique pottery tradition prized throughout the empire for a glossy green glaze. While it was true that two other imperial roads ran from the heartland into the western provinces, only one of those swung north with a spur that went all the way into the western region of Woodfall Province. To travel via the western route took months.

Elen rubbed her arm, caught herself doing it, and picked up her pace, newly anxious. She oughtn't to have let Kem go on alone, not with such doings in town and a caravan incoming as well.

Riders on elks . . .

No, it couldn't be, not after all this time. Lord Duenn couldn't have found them.

How she and Aoving had cherished their years of freedom in Orledder Halt! Aoving had found a measure of peace she'd never before known and had become a respected midwife. Elen had taken on the duties of a deputy courier as well as the sturdy cottage, and the rations of grain and oil, that went with it. Even so, after Aoving's death she might have moved on, just to be safe, but she hadn't because of Kem. Orledder was the only home her nephew remembered. He was at peace here, where people knew and liked and accepted him. She could not take that away from him.

Yet how safe could anyone really be in this Pall-ridden world?

She considered the caravan she and Kem had seen approaching. Wagons flying the banner of the imperial engineers were good news. The locals had been waiting for months for equipment and a better way to clear the blocked road without triggering yet more avalanches, as the first attempts to clear the road had done. Maybe the matter had become important enough for a prince-warden to provide oversight. But why would the wardens be involved, when clearing debris off the physical roadbed and making necessary repairs was the responsibility of the engineers? That didn't make any sense.

The intendant had once told her that many of the decisions made in the imperial palace and its three advisory councils were for reasons that had more to do with princes and their in-laws jockeying for status within the palace hierarchy than with what would be best for the empire's people. Then, having spoken, he had looked scared, and had opened all the doors and windows of his office to make sure no "shadow wardens" had been listening outside. He knew Elen wasn't a spy because he and Aoving were the only people in all the world who knew about the viper. The intendant owed her his life because of the viper, and she owed hers to his discretion.

She passed the Boulders, climbing the steps up and over and then down onto the flat fields and neatly spaced orchards that surrounded the Halt. As always, she scanned the landscape for signs of Spore. This close to the Halt it was the job of a surveyor to ceaselessly patrol the land for telltale signs, so the weight of duty was lighter for her here than when she was on her circuit of the Moonrise Hills.

Her path met a cart track that paralleled the course of the Sul. It was a pleasant walk of about a mile to the earthworks. To the north of the river stood an old sarpa pen with its bronze-plated roof, but in ten years at the Halt she'd never seen a sarpa, much less one landing here to take a rest in its sandpit. Still, Halts were required by imperial law to maintain both a sarpa pen and a griffin mews.

At the earthworks, two canals branched off, one on either bank of the river. She passed the fenced-off oval of the burning ground and crossed the bridge over the northern canal.

The canals created a square moat all the way around the Halt, enclosing a great deal of useful farmland within the moat's boundaries. There were also clusters of houses for people who could not get a license to live inside the road-ringed Halt itself. This time of year, the tidy gardens of the outer ward were mostly stripped, being readied for winter, with the quince still too green to harvest.

Folk waved or called out greetings. The intendant's deputy couriers were well known in Orledder Intendancy, its Halt, and the surrounding villages and hamlets. People often paid Elen in produce or goods to take a private message or personal contract into the hills along with her official messages. Such transactions were how she had afforded new Declaration boots for Kem instead of the cast-offs he'd worn all his childhood.

Now, as she waved and called back, she thought of the Spore at the bone pile and what it would mean for the community. Would the news frighten people? Or would they refuse to believe her, since no one had witnessed the irruption except her? Did the locals truly trust her or did they still see her as an outsider? Was Aoving's death along with those of the others who had died in the avalanche enough to make Elen a local? Was it enough that she had spilled her heart's blood—her sister—in this soil? Or was she fated never to have a true home or community, she who did not know who had birthed her or what people she came from? She who from her earliest memories as a child had only Aoving, through so many terrible years.

She reached the entry ramp, where Hilsit and Emmar were on duty. Festival wreaths hung on the open gates in honor of Declaration Week, now begun. The grinning sentinels greeted her with forearm bumps, a badge of belonging that meant as much to them as the embroidered spear badges sewn to their uniforms to mark their place in the imperial order.

Hilsit said, "Those two lads came running through like they heard the last sweet rolls were about to go into someone else's mouth. Say, is it true the prince-warden is coming, like the boys said? You know anything about that?"

"You tell me."

Emmar said, "Approach horn blew already. Five blasts! Never heard five blasts before! We won't see a thing from down here, more's the pity."

"I'll tell you all about it afterward," said Elen, "but the likes of us won't be allowed into hall or temple if an imperial prince is in residence, so we can just make up whatever story we want."

"You think the prince will be handsome?" said Emmar with his shyest grin. "I like a handsome fellow."

"A prince is always a handsome man or a beautiful woman, unless they are a beautiful man or a handsome woman, if the taleteller likes that story better."

They laughed companionably, even though it was probably the next thing to treason to speak disrespectfully about the exalted imperial clan.

"Go on, go on," they said, opening the inner gate that gave access to the ramp. The four ramps were the only way into the Halt, unless a person could hold their breath for long enough to swim through the submerged culverts that channeled the river under the road. Ramps were necessary because, at a Halt, the road's foundation was built as tall as a defensive wall, making the town safe both from incursions of the Pall and from attack by brigands or traitors.

She headed up the ramp, bracing herself as she approached the magic-infused roadway that ran along the top. It was commonplace for people to pause at the top to survey the densely built environs of the inner Halt. But she sped up, running across the wide roadway with her pack thumping against her back. Each footfall spun a prickling sensation of heat up her legs, like lightning trying to reach her heart—to reach the viper, coiling tight in rigid alarm. The protection offered by the soles of her boots, together with her leaping strides, made the contact bearable. Then she was across and had to pause, panting, hands on her thighs, on the blessedly inert inner East Ramp. The discomfort had already faded; all that lingered was the memory, and she had plenty of experience in folding up memory and setting it aside where it could not plague her.

By force of habit, her gaze lifted to survey the town, with its neat division into four quarters set around a central plaza. The so-called imperial quarter, with the intendant's Residence, was a swirling riot of activity, as they desperately readied for the imminent arrival of the imperial carriages.

She hustled down East Ramp. After showing her token at Copper Gate, she made her way into the imperial quarter past stables and barracks and the practice arena to the Residence. Folk wearing formal festival garb came running to take up parade places in the assembly plaza that fronted the Residence's entry portico. Menials were scrambling to sweep and polish the marble stairs and scrub the statues of the emperors that lined the portico. A cartload of flower necklaces sat beside the portico, where the intendant's daughter nervously selected appropriate blooms for each statue.

Elen cut around to the administrative wing with its six doors, one for each rank of official. The door sentinels did not check her token; they were distracted, every face gripped with anxiety and excitement. The corridors were empty but she heard a buzz of talk from the far end of the wing, where it opened into an audience chamber. She cut through a courtyard and entered Map Hall, shared by imperial surveyors and intendancy couriers.

The hall, with its tables, storage drawers, and desks, had been abandoned in haste: an ink pot uncapped, a chart book left open with a pair of polished stones holding down its thick pages, a stack of message scrolls awaiting delivery spilled onto the floor and one crushed from being stepped on. The morning tea service, just poured into a selection of tea bowls, sat with the liquid cooling. She grabbed a bowl and gulped down the spicy brew, then drained a second, glad of the burn in her dry throat. She'd killed Spore before, but for some reason the tiny, leering faces snarling at her from the sedge kept flashing in her mind's eye, malicious and taunting, as if they knew something she did not. But Spore wasn't intelligent, nor was the Pall. It was just a malignant poison.

Past Map Hall, a covered walkway led across an enclosed herb garden. On the other side of the garden stood the rear entrance into the intendant's official chambers. Normally there was a sentinel posted here, but the sentinel was gone and the door left unlocked. A shocking breach of security at any moment, and worse with a prince about to arrive.

She turned the latch and eased the door open, listening. Footsteps came running. A hand grabbed the door, and it was flung wide. A short sword, point quivering, blocked her way.

"It's just me, Deputy Courier Elen," she said, hands raised but body poised to dodge sideways out of range.

The sword's point was abruptly lowered.

"Elen! Thanks to the Tranquil Heavens it's you and not someone else! I got left past my break and I had to piss so badly." The sentinel—Ujin—panted with relief. "We're a flock of headless chickens! We had no warning. No time to prepare. Did you know the prince-warden was coming?"

She exhaled as she collected herself, arms lowering. "I've been gone fourteen days, so this is news to me. I've got to see the intendant. Right now."

"He's making ready for the imperial visit." Ujin waved to indicate the length of a dim corridor whose thick earth walls had no windows. He gave her a look, wise to expression and tone. "You've got bad news."

She had one breath to make a decision, but she was used to making up her mind fast. People had to know, because everyone was at risk. "I killed a small irruption of Spore inside the bone pile on Lancer's Ridge. It was fresh, only a single cap. It hadn't spread. Get the word out. The captain should increase the number and frequency of surveyor patrols into the Moonrise Hills."

"Oh, by the Pale Blight, I'd begun to hope we were clear of infestations."

Elen waved a hand in acknowledgment and headed down the corridor at a jog. She had to reach the intendant before the prince-warden's party arrived, or her news might get lost, with deadly consequences.

The walls of the corridor were lined with locked doors to the intendancy storerooms. The door at the end of the corridor let into the Residency offices. Voices were chattering frantically in the rooms beyond. She took the menials' passage and clicked the door into the intendant's private sanctum, rang the handbell, and entered. There were four people in the room: the intendant, his interlocutor, his valet, and a sentinel at the far door.

The intendant turned in the direction of the bell. He wore his formal festival robes, stiff and uncomfortable. He looked flushed, the contrast notable against his age-whitened hair. His valet pressed a handkerchief to his brow to dab away sweat.

Seeing her, he blinked as if confusion had overtaken his mind. "Elen? Why are you here?"

"Intendant." She crossed her arms on her chest and bowed, reminding him they were not speaking in private and must adhere to the formalities of the occasion. "With apologies, I must speak."

"Come on then, hurry, I can't linger here," he snapped, then winced and added, "Forgive my short temper. I'm all worked into a lather."

Without waiting for her answer, he nodded to his interlocutor, who gestured to the sentinel to open the door. Elen hurried after them. The sentinel gave her a worried nod before closing the door at her back. She followed the intendant and his attendants across a council room with its big table, then through the informal receiving room, and finally past double doors into the main audience hall. Most of the household staff and many attendants and officials from the imperial quarter had gathered in their festival best, lining the walls, standing in restless silence.

The intendant mounted the dais and sank down on his chair of office. The intendant's chair was stationed one step below a copy of the imperial throne, whose presence in every provincial hall reminded the empire's subjects of the all-encompassing presence of the emperor in their lives. The intendant raised his hands as if to cover his face with nervous exhaustion, then recalled his audience and lowered his arms. Everyone stared but no one spoke. They were nervous too. No one wanted a visit from any member of the imperial palace, and especially not from the all-seeing eye. It was best to remain out of sight and thus out of mind.

Elen had wanted to do this in private, but the chance had never come. She knelt on one knee before the dais and addressed herself to the interlocutor. "With the intendant's permission, I request permission to speak directly to the intendant."

It took the intendant several breaths to reply, as if he had to return from away down a long distance. Finally, his attention fixed on her. With a sigh, he nodded.

"Of course. Go on."

"At Lancer's Ridge—"

Five rapid horn blasts interrupted her.

11

Of Course He Was Handsome

From outside, a piercing whoop of excitement broke apart to become the thunderous clattering of an arrival, more horns, and ecstatic cheers. The sentinels standing at the far doors looked toward the intendant. Before he could give the command to open them, the doors were flung open from the outside.

The first people who appeared were dressed in the lichen-dyed purple worn by the menials who toiled in the service of the palace and its imperial offices, each wearing a knit cap to cover their hair. They hustled in carrying rolled-up carpets, which they unrolled to create a golden walkway down the middle of the hall.

At their heels came four wardens dressed in indigo tabards. All carried strung bows, and they scanned the hall before arranging themselves so as to be able to shoot anyone who looked threatening.

A white-haired woman followed. She wore practical traveling garb dyed a drab reddish brown, pinned with the embroidered four-chambered badge of a Heart Temple theurgist. All theurgists were bound in service, like menials, to the palace. She also held an interlocutor's staff, which meant she was serving as the speaker for the prince.

Finally, three more wardens appeared on the threshold.

The last carpet, still unrolling, bumped Elen's leg.

A menial exclaimed impatiently, "Move aside! Move aside!" and slapped at her with a fly whisk. She jumped up, startled by the sting of its leather cords.

The intendant hissed, "Beside my chair."

Elen scrambled up to take a place to his right, behind his interlocutor. Two of the wardens at the door veered outward to walk on the tile floor, leaving the prince to approach alone atop the golden carpets.

Of course he was handsome, with pleasing, symmetrical features and the healthy look of a person who has always had enough to eat and has never once had to shovel out a trench stinking with feces, urine, vomit, maggots, and worms. She tried to imagine him knee-deep in shit and had to bite down on a smile. A mere deputy courier must not appear disrespectful in the presence of an emperor's blessed—and blessedly attractive!—offspring.

He walked with the confidence of a person who trained every day in the arts that imperial princes must excel at. Judging by his imperious scowl, he expected others to know he did indeed excel. But his good looks and arrogance weren't what struck her most about him.

He was just so incredibly well turned out. His garments fit as if tailored for him, and they had been. Such clothes would have been spun from the highest grade of thread, sewn in the imperial workshops, finished by the most skilled crafts-folk. The braided hem of his knee-length riding jacket glittered with delicate gold thread in the shape of lidless eyes. A badge to mark his status as a prince born in the Flower Court adorned his jacket, over the heart. The embroidered floral trim of the high neckline sat perfectly along his elegant neck. His hair was elaborately braided in multiple strands, each decorated with carved jewels, and the braids pulled back into a pony's tail and left to dangle like a fly whisk hanging from the back of his head. It was hard not to laugh but she knew better, and regardless would never do anything to embarrass or shame the intendant.

The theurgist-turned-interlocutor reached the dais and halted. Raising the staff to get the attention of the gathered people, she spoke in a penetrating voice that easily filled the hall.

"His Highness Gevulin, Prince-Warden of the Imperial Order of Wardens, Exalted General of the All-Seeing Eye, Captain of a Thousand, Adept of the Bow and the Spear, Conqueror of the Ten Peaks Race, Eloquent Grace of the Wind Dance, Artist of the Brush and Virtuoso of the Pen, Master of the Lyre and Preeminent Bard of the Twelve Cycles and the Three Hundred and Sixty Poems of the Glorious Founder, Prince of the Third Estate and Guardian of the Absinthe Grove, born into the Flower Court on the knees of the Elegant Consort in Whose Honor the Lily Emperor of Blessed Memory Instituted the Feast of Sweet Pipes and Contrapuntal Song—"

How long was this astounding recital going to go on? Elen had never heard the like before, but of course, she'd never been in the same room as an imperial prince.

"—Last of the Court-Born Princes Born of the Lily Emperor's Resplendent Seed—"

Elen stifled a giggle by biting hard on her lower lip.

"—His Highness Gevulin, He That Is All That Is Modest and Humble in Demeanor Bowing Before the Righteous Might and Magnificent Wisdom of the Magnolia Emperor His Blessed Elder Sister Whom He Serves as Do All Imperial Subjects. May the Heart of the Tranquil Empire and the Strength of its Emperor shine unto All Eternity beneath the Implacable Mercy and Gracious Justice of the Heavens. So do I, Luviara, interlocutor in service to the palace and theurgist dedicated to the Heart Temple, declare before all who are assembled here."

The intendant slid out of his chair to kneel. Everyone in the hall except for the prince's attendants knelt as well. It must be imperial protocol, Elen thought as she settled onto her knees. In his office the intendant had a copy of the ten-volume edition of *Imperial Rites and Courtesies,* but she'd never read it, even though he made his library available to his staff. It had seemed staggeringly unlikely she would ever see a member of the imperial household in person, much less have them mount the dais not a body's length from her. The prince examined the empty throne as if considering whether to sit in the only seat in the hall truly worthy of his eminence. Yet for any person except the emperor to sit on the throne would be to announce open rebellion against the empire; everyone knew that from *The Five Scoundrels Who Were Each Worse Than the One Before.*

The prince then considered the intendant's chair of office. He pressed his fingers to his eyes as if the sight of the plain cushion on the seat of the plain wood chair hurt him physically, then heaved a sigh so heavy Elen felt it burden her shoulders with its weight of displeasure. With a wince of distaste, he sat in the intendant's chair, forcing the old man to shuffle hastily aside on his knees. When Elen put out a hand to steady the intendant, one of the imperial menials flicked at her hand with a fly whisk, another stinging snap. The intendant flashed Elen a warning gaze, and she gritted her teeth, removed her hand, and lowered her eyes.

The prince spoke, his tone cultured, his accent precise in its heartland diction, no emotion in his voice except for a sheen of contempt.

"I am surprised, Intendant. I was told you are a Karis Manor official who has prospered for many years in service to the empire. Yet this sorry welcome is all you can manage."

Since the prince had addressed him directly, the intendant was allowed to reply directly. "The fault is mine, Your Highness. I humbly offer no excuse for the fact we were taken by surprise."

"Messages were sent!" The prince raised a hand, and the theurgist-interlocutor stepped forward. "Luviara, were messages not sent?"

The woman's gaze flickered with an expression Elen could not read. Alarm? Shame? Fear?

"Messages were sent," agreed the theurgist, again with that flicker of the eyes. Not a lie, Elen thought. Something else was going on. Maybe it wasn't fear or shame. Maybe it was mischief. Or malice.

The intendant glanced between the prince and the theurgist. As nervous as the old man had been, he calmed now. He'd seen a splinter, some manner of disjunction between what the prince was asking and what the theurgist was saying, and if anyone could manipulate a splinter to his advantage, it was the intendant.

"Please assure His Exalted Highness that Orledder Halt received no message to warn us of his arrival," said the intendant. "Had we known, all would have been in readiness."

The sheen of arrogance could not disguise a deeper intelligence in the prince's gaze. He was not a stupid man, even if he didn't seem to be able to hear anything he didn't want to know. "Besides the messengers sent by road, I also sent a griffin scout to alert each stage of my coming. The scout delivered his message at Ilvewind Cross. Are you saying the scout did not land here?"

The intendant bowed. "No griffin scout landed here. Perhaps Orledder Halt was deemed too unimportant, Your Highness."

The prince rubbed his forehead as if he was getting a headache. "I do not need a missing griffin scout on top of every other delay," he muttered to himself. Yet he looked up decisively, a man of action who knows his commands will be obeyed immediately. "Very well. A bath and a meal. Afterward, we shall go on. We must depart in haste to reach our destination with the speed given to us by the grace of the High Heavens."

The sooner gone, the better, Elen thought, careful to keep her expression bland.

The intendant carefully addressed the theurgist and her interlocutor's staff. "Worthy Luviara, may I humbly ask His Highness what destination I may assist him to reach?"

The prince jumped in with the impatience of a person who cannot believe he is surrounded by so much incompetence. "Can you not read, Intendant? The messages we sent ahead clearly state we are bound for Far Boundary Vigil. In case you are not conversant with the map of the empire, this Vigil stands on the northern border of Woodfall Province at the edge of Far Boundary Pall."

"Your Highness, my most abject apologies, but as I have already stated, this office received no messages of any kind, no griffin scout, no warning of your arrival. Furthermore, no traveling party can reach Far Boundary Vigil by this route."

"Of course they can! This is the most direct and fastest route!"

"Normally it is, yes. Unfortunately, the imperial road north of here was blocked by an avalanche two years ago."

The prince had a well-shaped mouth of the sort folk might swoon over were he an actor in a traveling troupe speaking words of love to a shy suitor. His sneer made his mouth ugly. "I was warned about this by my sister Prince Astaylin, Exalted General of the Corps of Imperial Engineers. She assured me messages had been sent and assurances received. If she'd heard the way was not clear, she would have told me. Who are you, Intendant, to say otherwise? Do you call a Prince of the Third Estate a liar?"

"I do not, Your Highness," said the intendant, eyebrows raising. He did not look at his valet or at Elen, two people he sometimes shared his honest thoughts with.

The theurgist's mouth twitched, but Elen could not read her expression. Something was afoot.

The prince rattled on obliviously. "Escort me at once to the imperial bathing chamber. Afterward have ready a suitable meal that can be taken quickly." He pulled out a jewel-studded pocket watch. "We depart in one hour."

12

A Gambit to Ruin Him

Elen had never seen the inside of the imperial suite. At every Halt, an entire wing of rooms in the imperial quarter was set aside in case any member of the inner palace were to pass through. According to Joef's aunt, the last time the suite had been opened was fourteen years ago, a few months before Elen and Aoving had walked into Orledder thinking they would stay in the Halt overnight before moving on. The visitor then had been merely an official of the second rank in the palace censorate, not even a prince.

As he had not been dismissed, the intendant was required to escort the prince as if he were himself a menial. In the hierarchy of the imperial administration, he was. The local interlocutor stayed behind. An intendant's interlocutor hadn't enough status to speak on behalf of a prince.

To Elen's surprise, Cariol, the intendant's valet, beckoned her to come along. She'd never expected to see the inside of the imperial wing, and she had a distrust of enclosed inner wings of highborn compounds, which could be prisons as much as they could be palaces. But she didn't protest or try to slink away. She had to let the intendant know about the Spore as soon as possible. Every delay felt like another spine in her throat. The viper slept, untroubled by her agitation. Eating the Spore had satiated it, although it could wake again in a heartbeat if she needed it. She did not want to need it.

Also, she was curious.

The imperial wing did not disappoint. As with the intendant's Residence, the arrangement led from outer public rooms to inner private sanctums. Each was more spectacularly decorated than the last with lovely floral set pieces, as well as wall paintings featuring ethereal clouds amid tree-dappled peaks, and hungry panthers tearing apart their grateful prey.

The imperial bathing chamber lay beyond the sleeping platforms and next to an enclosed courtyard with a cistern and bamboo water pipes. Every Halt had a local bathhouse for residents, a marketplace bathhouse for travelers, and a Residency bathhouse for the intendant's quarter, all clean, well-kept, but plain. The imperial chamber was so luxuriously furnished that its walls and floor glittered where sunlight poured through open doors and windows. There was a soaking tub, tiled with lapis lazuli and other precious stones. Next to it, tiled steps descended into a square basin fitted with a hallow-wood bench and drains.

The prince's personal attendants had arrived before him. Two—a young man and a young woman—were dressed in richly embroidered robes, their attractive faces enhanced by cosmetics, their bodies scented with perfume. They directed two menials. One of the menials was an unusually tall, big, broad person who set down a large, iron-strapped trunk as if it were as light as feathers. The other was a small, nimble-handed woman who began unpacking fragrant oils and soaps, a bone scraper, a soft brush, and folded towels. Certainly, a prince would not allow a towel that had touched another body to sully his own.

As he entered, the two attendants swept forward to fuss over him. Their manner was so gracious and pleasing that Elen assumed they had to be concubines. They would be of a lesser rank of intimate companion, the sort a prince took along for journeys, as opposed to the sort who, presumably, never set foot outside the palace's Flower Court.

The intendant halted by the door with Cariol, Elen, and theurgist-interlocutor Luviara behind him. No one in the prince's retinue spoke to the intendant, much less took any notice of Elen and Cariol. The prince did not speak at all, as if expecting his people to comprehend his desires without any effort on his part. He halted at the edge of the steps down into the big basin and extended his arms out to either side.

So swiftly it took Elen by surprise, the concubines stripped off his clothing, every piece of it, leaving him naked in a room filled with clothed people. His attendants did not find it unusual; they didn't even look toward the people standing by the door. Elen was surprised the prince seemed unaware of the presence of strangers in this bathing place, but perhaps in the palace the highborn commonly received visitors in any state of dress given that his retinue kept their gazes fixed on the prince without any sense that his nakedness was a forbidden sight. She could not help but stare.

A prince he might be, but he had buttocks like any other person, a part of the body Elen always found delightfully absurd. In fairness, from this angle, she had to admit the prince's muscular legs looked like those of a person who could indeed have conquered the ten peaks, whatever they were, and been proclaimed eloquently graceful.

Maybe he had danced up and down the ten peaks with the ease of wind. Equally muscular arms and sculpted shoulders suggested he was an adept soldier too. Weren't princes required to be adept soldiers, or at least trained as if they were? Except for the hair on his head, his body had been shaved smooth, as they were rumored to do in the palace.

The concubines each took an arm and escorted him down the steps. There he stood while they washed, scraped, and brushed him from top to toe in a remarkably intimate and surprisingly thorough manner, leaving not a scrap of him untouched. The intendant and his companions had all turned their gazes to the floor, but Elen watched with amazement. Why not? The world was harsh. Beauty should be appreciated when it appeared! A gorgeous sunset. A perfectly baked loaf of bread. A soaring hawk. A warm-hearted laugh. An exquisite body. Sadly, the prince did not get an erection; his mind seemed to be on other things than the attendants' hands and the soap and the washing.

Next to her, the theurgist made a tiny noise, a soft clearing of the throat barely enough to get Elen's attention. She glanced that way, and the old woman met her gaze and winked. *Winked!*

A spark of shared amusement leaped between them, a deep instinct signaling that one stranger has found another who is like them in temperament or guile or outlook, an intangible essence they both grasp and recognize in a heartbeat. The theurgist had been ogling him too, and there was no one to notice because all of the prince's attendants were focused on him as the centerpiece of their lives. The theurgist, Elen, the intendant, and his valet were as taken for granted as the walls.

The wardens had remained outside, on guard. No refreshing bath for them! Imperial menials scurried to and from the courtyard bringing hot and cold water for rinsing while others brushed clean the prince's trousers and jacket. The whole procedure was an intricate dance accomplished in a third of an hour. Astounding! Elen couldn't wait to describe the entire scene to Kem, who would laugh himself sick. Not to Joef, though. That boy was a gossip, and he'd tell his aunt, and that august woman would tell *just one friend* and then it would be all over the Halt and the consequences of Elen's insufficiently respectful behavior and insolent commentary would crash onto the intendant.

After being dried with towels, the prince waited with the same patience—or expectation—as his concubines clad him in a fresh set of undergarments. The trousers and long jacket were fastened with buttons and loops.

Bodies vanished so quickly. Beneath clothing. Under the roaring assault of an avalanche, like Aoving.

Or into the hideous tendrils of irrupting Spore, like the intendant's elder daughter. That poor young woman had been devoured and distorted into an eight-limbed, six-eyed, and four-mouthed shrilling monstrosity while meanwhile Elen had dragged the frantic father across a moat to safety. Seeing the horror unfold, he'd lost all reason and sense and had tried to fling himself into the Spore to rescue his beloved child even though anyone and everyone knew it was too late. On that awful morning, fifteen years ago, she'd been the only person willing to risk herself to save him. Her rescue of the intendant had given her, Aoving, and Kem an opportunity to make a new home in Orledder Halt. But the memory of his howling grief still haunted her.

She shut her eyes, shutting out the past, only to be elbowed by the theurgist in warning. Prince Gevulin was on his way out of the chamber. Elen followed at the end of the line as, again, the palace servants made no objection to her presence. They seemed not to see her.

The procession proceeded to the imperial dining hall, where a repast had been laid out. The concubines brought instruments on which they played "The River's Lost Love" with great facility.

The intendant's younger daughter served the prince herself, offering whatever delicacies the Residence cook had managed to produce on short notice to tempt the palate of a prince. His Highness gave neither compliments nor complaints, merely ate some things and passed the rest on to his wardens. At least he recognized they needed nourishment to continue at such a pace. Elen hoped the concubines and menials would get something to eat too, somewhere and somehow.

Once he finished eating, the music ended. He rose, flipping out his sleeves.

The intendant said to the theurgist, "May it please His Highness if there is any information I can impart to His Highness with respect to the road ahead."

The prince answered scornfully, "I have all the information I need."

He strode from the room, the concubines and menials scurrying after him.

The theurgist set a jade token on the table. "In thanks for your efforts," she said to the intendant's daughter. "You are a relation of the intendant, I must suppose, but not his spouse, since you wear a widow's badge."

"I am his daughter. My spouse died in the east, fighting against the Blood Wolves, so I returned home."

"May the High Heavens grant you peace."

"You honor me." Uliana was shy and uncertain. She glanced at her father for permission to pick up the token. When he nodded, she took it into her hand as gingerly as if it might burn her.

The theurgist studied this exchange with a keen interest that reminded Elen of a crow examining a trove of shiny objects with a covetous eye. But once the token was picked up, the theurgist did not wait. Accompanied by the last remaining warden, she strode out into the wake of the prince's entourage.

"Intendant," Elen said quietly, hoping to catch his attention, but he was already out the door, following the prince with his own modest retinue. Elen tagged along at the end of the line, and, again, no one stopped her. She was relieved the wardens were departing so quickly. The memory of Spore drove her onward. It was just so unbelievably frustrating that she hadn't yet been able to tell the intendant, and all because of an unwanted imperial visitor who didn't even have anything useful to offer.

Prince Gevulin moved with such haste that, by the time the intendant reached the assembly plaza, His Highness had already vanished into the carriage pulled by the obsidian panthers. The concubines climbed into the carriage pulled by the golden horses. The menials scrambled to the third carriage as the wardens took their places on drivers' benches, running boards, and roofs.

A horn blew. Bells clanged. The assembled people bowed as the carriages rolled out of the plaza. Residents and travelers alike had lined the central roadway through the Halt. Many rang handbells as the procession clattered past. The carriages rolled up the northern ramp onto the main road that ran north.

The intendant stood on the portico with his usual attendants. He did not say a word until the last bells had quieted and a final five-fold horn blast signaled that the prince's party had left the Halt behind. Uliana stood at her father's side, wringing her hands.

The head chatelaine of the Residence hurried up, looking harried and flushed.

"You may speak," said the intendant, not waiting for his inter-locutor.

"What now, my lord? What's going to happen when the prince reaches the first avalanche? How can the prince not know the road is impassable? The imperial engineers have been working on the blockage for almost two years!"

The old man stroked his beard, as he did when he was particularly unhappy. "This is how jockeying for position in the palace happens. Prince Astaylin wears the title of Exalted General of the Imperial Engineers, so she must know of the situation here. This, I guarantee. Therefore, if I have to propose an explanation, I must wonder if Prince Astaylin may have deliberately lied to Prince Gevulin. Prince Astaylin is also a prince of the Third Estate. Indeed, she and Gevulin are the only princes who hold that exalted rank, and only the crown prince stands above them. So if Prince Astaylin sees Prince Gevulin as a rival, it would make sense that she chooses to impede him, according to the battles fought inside the palace."

"He does have quite a list of accomplishments," Elen murmured. "Conqueror of the Ten Peaks. What are the ten peaks?" Uliana looked at her with alarm, surprised to hear her speak without permission. Elen hastily addressed the intendant's young interlocutor as if she had meant to all along. "If I may present my question, with your gracious assistance, Worthy Venwith."

The intendant raised a hand to forestall Venwith's reply. "The deputy courier makes the correct point. I've seen Prince Gevulin's name on the official festival thanksgivings that are read out every year, but I've not had any gossip come my way about him. He's young to be named as prince-warden. It might be brilliance on his part. It might be a grab for power and influence by the Elegant Consort and her kin, if she is in favor with the emperor. Or it might be that giving him an exalted rank so early was a gambit to ruin him."

"How so, Honored Father?" asked Uliana.

"By giving him authority beyond what he can command, in the hope he will fail. If he is competent enough that failure isn't assured, then his rivals might have decided to concoct this flagrant ploy to make him look bad, or to prevent him from accomplishing whatever task he's been assigned. About which, you'll note, he has told us nothing except that he is going to Far Boundary Vigil. I do know my map of the empire," he added with a faintly insulted air, "and I know perfectly well that Far Boundary Vigil stands at the end of the imperial road, on the northern edge of the empire."

"Wasn't there once an imperial province north of there?" Uliana asked.

"The Pall took it, covered all of it. Far Boundary Vigil might as well be the end of the world."

So the empire believes, Elen thought, but she said nothing. It was the secret she and Aoving had kept.

Uliana twisted her fingers together nervously as she addressed her father. "We've heard no alarming news from the north. No uprising, no plague, no famine, no large-scale irruption, no raids."

"Yes. Even with the road blocked, we'd have heard if there were a crisis in Farledder Intendancy or Woodfall Province that threatens the peace of the empire. That's why it strikes me as odd that the prince is headed north in such haste and with such determination. There's nothing to draw a prince-warden's attention. Not that I know of. Secret emergencies like this concern me. If there is a struggle inside the palace, I'd prefer to stay out of it."

"What shall we do, then?" Uliana looked even more alarmed. She loved her father, and feared for him. Her spouse had not died fighting against the Blood Wolves, as Elen had learned by listening from corners and blending in with the walls. Through no fault of his own, the man had gotten caught on the wrong side of a quarrel between two princes of the Fourth Estate and had paid with his life. His downfall had indeed happened at the eastern border of the empire, far from here, but his death in combat was a convenient fiction. So much of the world rolled on lies, like carriages running along roads built on the bones of those who warned against the misuse of power.

The valet, the chatelaine, the young interlocutor, the daughter: all looked at the intendant. He scanned the plaza where folk were waiting to get their orders. Every person in the Halt knew the road north was blocked, that there was no way around it. Grinder's Cut was a huge, unnatural chasm and escarpment that cut multiple gashes across the landscape, creating a jagged canyon that could not be crossed for a hundred or more miles in either direction except on this branch of the imperial road.

Or by taking a little-known, rugged, and dangerous backcountry path through the Moonrise Hills. On foot.

"We have to make ready for his return," said the intendant.

"Tomorrow?" asked the chatelaine.

"Alas, no, we have not even that much breathing space. The imperial carriages travel at four times the speed of any other conveyance. He will return this afternoon. When he does, he is going to be in an ugly temper."

13

A SLICE OF FESTIVAL CAKE

The intendant sent his people to make ready, then beckoned Elen to follow him into his private sanctum. Once there, he spoke in the casual way the two of them had developed over the years, more uncle to niece than lord to menial.

"Elen. What is your urgent news?"

"I killed Spore in the bone pile on Lancer's Ridge. A fresh cap. It caught a mouse while I was there—"

The old, stark grief flashed across his face, and she knew to keep talking.

"—I killed the poor creature at once and destroyed it. The irruption was confined to a single sedge plant. No sign of spreading."

He absorbed the words as stoically as ever, a resigned sigh rather than a shocked gasp. "Ah! The Heavens challenge us! Not the news I wanted with everything else piled atop this day, and the Halt already shorthanded. When I asked for this posting I had hoped for a safe place to raise my children, away from the capital. Yet here we are."

He studied the family portraits hung in a row along one wall. They were half-sized copies of the portraits of parents, grandparents, and great-grandparents, whose originals hung in Karis Manor's ancestry hall in the capital city. His portrait was displayed alongside that of his deceased wife, her round, good-natured face wreathed with mourning white. His eldest daughter was likewise wreathed in white, the spirited young woman he had lost in the terrible Wormwood Irruption. Uliana had been painted in her even shyer youth, her hair crowned with a wreath of lilies for obedience. The last forlorn portrait was of the youngest child, a son required to live in the intendant's ancestral Manor in the capital. It was a form of hostage-taking, to make sure the intendant was at all times obedient to the Manor's political goals, whatever he may personally have thought of them.

Elen bowed her head in respect. The intendant was a good man, the best she had ever known. Although that wasn't much of a scale to be weighed on.

He straightened his shoulders. "The sun rises and sets without concern for our lagging steps. Cariol, track down the captain. Have her meet us in Map Hall. Bring refreshments for the deputy courier, if you will, and a cup of hoji juice for me, and tea for the rest of you."

They walked to Map Hall, where Surveyor Captain Jinyan was already waiting, having heard the news from Ujin. The captain had unrolled the second section of the most detailed of the Lancer's Ridge maps, which included the bone pile and the abandoned village. Elen indicated the exact spot where she'd found Spore, so it could be permanently marked for the record. After she was sure the captain had fixed its location properly, she went to the intendancy logbook and entered her latest transmission log, a record of all the contacts and deliveries and receipts she had made at each village and hamlet along her most recent circuit.

That accomplished, her part of the work was done for this month. The surveyors were responsible for sending amended copies and official reports onward to the provincial government and the palace administration, and for answering the flood of queries from investigative surveyors that would ensue once the news was sent. While the intendant and the captain talked, she went over to the side table where Cariol had set a tray of stuffed rolls and poultry skewers, hot from the kitchen.

The intendant studied the map and its freshly inked white circle, so close to the Halt and within about fifty paces of a regularly traveled upland route. "This is a grave emergency. We must step up patrols."

"We're stretched thin as it is, my lord," said the captain. "I'd like to request a levy to add another ten deputy sentinels to our unit. They can take on gate duty and free up the best of our veteran sentinels, who I'd like to promote to deputy surveyor. They'll have to undergo intensive training in a short time, which will add to the expense. I don't see we have any choice."

The intendant tapped a cluster of faded circles a few miles outside the Halt, marked on the map fourteen years ago. The Wormwood Irruption had killed eighty-one people, including his daughter, who had ridden out to investigate when the first report had come in.

He said, "This year's treasury allowance is depleted. But as you say, Captain, we have no choice. Under the circumstances, I can unearth emergency funds."

Elen was pretty sure that he meant selling some of his deceased wife's jewelry.

"For now, until you have your new personnel, you may also make use of any deputy couriers who are between routes. That includes you, Elen. Go home, get whatever you need for a patrol run. Captain Jinyan will plot routes for the first patrol cycle, starting immediately."

"What about my nephew? If I'm out on patrol, there's no one to stand with him at the shrine or speak as his guardian before the justiciar's bench for Declaration."

"Ah, yes, Midwife Aoving's child. Has the youth made a decision known to you?"

The captain looked up with interest. Declaration Week was everyone's business in any community, a source of speculation and talk throughout the year. On the final Day of Declaration, apprenticeships, betrothals, and other life changes were publicly announced and sealed by the grace of the emperor's benevolent hand and beneath the auspices of the High Heavens. Two years ago, in the wake of his mother's death, Kem had made a public Declaration of his new name and status, as was his right under imperial law, even if it couldn't be legally sealed until his seventeenth birthday, which happened to coincide with Declaration Day this year. People were naturally curious if he intended something equally dramatic now that he had reached the age when imperial law required youths to choose a profession.

For most young people, a Declaration of profession was a formality. Their families and backgrounds dictated their choices. Because his mother's and aunt's status in the Halt had always been anomalous, given that they were outsiders with no permanent ties except those they created themselves, the boy was a bit of a curiosity. In a way, he'd been cosseted, like an exotic pet the locals cared for in common because his mother, the midwife, and his aunt, the deputy courier, often had to travel and be away from home, in service of the needs of the intendancy.

"He hasn't decided yet, or so he's said to me," Elen replied.

"He was certain the other time," remarked the captain with a lifted eyebrow.

"That's a different sort of declaration, isn't it?" said the intendant. "All the more likely to be certain because of it. Because it has nothing to do with who your people are and what they expect of you on behalf of your Manor." Bitterness soured his tone.

"It might, for some," said Elen, thinking of Kem's complicated and not always easy relationship with his mother.

"True enough." He cleared his throat hastily. "Elen, you've refused surveyor training before because of your responsibilities to Midwife Aoving and young Kem. But with his Declaration Day upon him, he'll be busy with an apprenticeship even if he stays here and still lives with you. This might be the time for you to think on it."

It was true she'd refused the intendant's previous offer of an elevation into the Imperial Order of Surveyors because surveyors were often out for months at a time. That had been too long to be away from fragile Aoving and a growing child.

"I'd welcome it," said the captain. "You've a nose for Spore that's unrivaled. If you've any hesitation, be sure I will support you from inside the order. I know surveyors are generally chosen from the Manor-born. Our order can be insular and possessive of its privileges. But the best surveyor I worked with came from outside the Manors. I'm not one to lean on ancestry and protocol in this matter."

"I thank you with all my heart, Intendant. Captain, your words do me honor. It's tempting. I've long wanted . . ." She hesitated. *I've long wanted to know their secrets* was not the right thing to say. "I admire the surveyors. Such an honor and responsibility seemed out of reach because I'm not Manor-born. Let me see Kem settled."

"Of course the lad's situation must come first," said the intendant graciously since, at any time in the last fourteen years, he could have ordered her to do what he wanted and she'd have had to do it or else flee from Orledder as a fugitive. "But the patrol cannot wait. Fetch what you need from your home. I'll send word to the chatelaine at the caravanserai to have a bath and provisions readied for you. The captain will have a sentinel assemble a local map, as well as a stock of salt spirits, tinder, and obsidian chips. Six days will be sufficient for you to track the length of Lancer's Ridge in either direction. You can be back in time for Declaration Day. While you are out on patrol, I'll give permission for Kem to stay with Archivist Heyadi and her nephew, so you can be sure he's safe."

"A generous gesture, Intendant. With your permission, I'll ask Kem which he prefers, to stay in the Residence with Archivist Heyadi or in the cottage as he usually does when I'm on courier duty. He's a responsible youth. He's never given me any reason not to trust him."

"It's true, he's not one to get into much mischief, although I can't say the same for young Joef."

They shared a smile.

The captain said, "I hear Joef will Declare for the Archivists' Guild, but I think a restless, strong, cheerful fellow like him is better suited to a sentinel's life. Good officer material. I'd take him in a heartbeat. But it's not up to me, is it? Though, it could be up to you." Jinyan gave a cutting look toward the intendant. They'd had this argument before.

Elen knew when to slide out of the way. She crossed arms on chest and bowed. "My thanks."

After the intendant raised a hand in dismissal, she grabbed the last roll and left.

The Residence's archives lay within the administrative wing on the southeast side of the square, aligned toward the heartland of the empire. The archives had no door opening directly onto the square, but their attic storage stretched all the way to the exterior wall that overlooked the plaza. A lattice screen built up under the eaves offered ventilation to keep air circulating through the shelves and cupboards of scrolls, memorials, and official correspondence that were too old to be frequently referenced but could not be disposed of.

The plaza had emptied out. Residence menials were sweeping and polishing with renewed vigor in expectation of the prince's imminent return and bad temper. Her courier's token got her past the sentinels standing at the doors to the administration wing. They knew her, but the token remained a necessary formality.

She walked past the waiting hall, normally full at this hour but emptied by the imperial visit, and turned toward the main corridor. Typically, if the boys weren't at school or engaged in chores or sports, she would find them in a back corner of Archives Hall, rifling through collections of architectural treatises or snort-giggling over illustrated sex manuals. Instead, they jumped up from a bench in the waiting hall and rushed over to her.

"We saw the prince!" Kem announced with the greatest excitement. "Did you see him?"

Elen grinned. "I did see quite a bit more of him than I expected, since I was with the intendant."

"Did he speak?" asked Joef, all breathy amazement. "What sort of voice does he have?"

"One accustomed to commanding people to do his bidding."

Kem snorted, used to her dry sarcasm.

Joef paid no attention as he loomed over her excitedly. "He wore the indigo of the wardens. He is really the prince-warden, the all-seeing eye?"

"So it seems, although he did not confirm the matter with me."

Both boys gasped, deliciously scandalized by her disrespect toward an imperial scion. She tore the roll into halves and gave one to each lad. It was amazing how fast youths could inhale food.

"I'm being sent back out because of the Spore." She easily identified Kem's eye-flare of alarm. "But I'll be back by Declaration Day. Kem, do you want to stay with Joef here, or at the cottage?"

"I'll stay at the cottage," he said stoutly. "Someone needs to harvest the quince and the last of the apples and greens. I'd rather have some time to myself."

"Without me?" Joef demanded, face falling.

"You know where I live. I heard your aunt say you'll be busy with your final archivist tests. All that writing, Joef. Nothing but writing. I know how you love sitting at the writing desk writing all afternoon while I'm out in the sunshine and air. You'll never see sunshine and air again, I don't suppose. Just ink and your hands getting white as maggots with each passing year from lack of sun."

Joef gave a mock roar and took a swipe at Kem, and they crouched into a faked fistfight, like a battle on a stage. She recognized the pattern of moves from the popular play *The Five Cunning Brigands Without Compare*. Every traveling troupe of entertainers put it on at least once when they stopped over at a Halt. She and Aoving and toddler Kem had sneaked into Orledder during such a performance, with all attention rapt elsewhere, right before the messenger had come running in from Wormwood Moat, shouting about an irruption. People's agonizing deaths had given her and Aoving a chance for a new life, and she hated that a part of her was horribly grateful for the chance. The viper stirred where it wrapped around her heart.

"Kem!" She spoke more sharply than she'd intended. He looked at her, startled at her tone, but she found a cheerful expression from her inexhaustible store of presenting the face she needed the world to see. "I have to go. Are you coming?"

He and Joef let up the fake fight at once.

"I do have to go finish my testing trials," admitted Joef sheepishly. The lads slapped each other on the back, Elen nodded to Joef, and they parted.

She and Kem walked out of the Residence compound and through the intendant's quarter toward East Ramp, the one she'd entered by. Culverts on either side of the ramp separated the Sul River into two canals. These flowed west through the Halt and out, through another pair of culverts, beneath the western half of the split road. Eleven cottages were built into the wedge formed where the ramp met the high wall of the raised road, with the canal between them and the ramp. Surrounded by a fence on the interior side, the cottages housed Orledder's deputy couriers.

Kem whistled merrily as they hurried through the fruit trees and small garden strips. Theirs was the smallest cottage, set up against the high wall-like bank on which the road was built. Before the avalanche, merchant and military traffic had rumbled through constantly, north and south. But she'd not minded the backdrop of noise. In her early childhood, spent living outside the empire, silence had been the real threat. Silence meant a Pall was rising, smothering life, turning fresh-hearted songbirds into voiceless monsters, devouring the unprotected alongside the unwary.

"You all right?" Kem asked as they entered their enclosed entry porch. "You must be tired. You didn't get much sleep last night. I bet you were watching over me, weren't you?"

The haunt's slyly sardonic smile rose in her memory. He'd have had a few choice words to say about the habits of princes, she was sure. If she set off this afternoon, she might overnight at Three Spires again tonight, at the full moon, one of the three bright nights when there was enough moonlight to allow a haunt to walk. She could talk to him again.

"No, no, what can you be thinking?" she muttered, then laughed. Imagine harboring such a fancy! Worse, she'd asked the haunt if he was a sorcerer, and he hadn't answered. Charm was a dangerous snare, as potent as rose-oil scent in luring in an unwilling victim.

Noticing Kem's puzzled expression, she tweaked his cheek between her fingers the way she'd done when he was little. "Yes, of course I was awake all night watching over you, my precious little sprout, while you snored."

"Ouch! You *are* tired!" He rolled his eyes as she released him. They set down their packs and took off their boots. He added, "I can pack for you while you take a nap."

A nap was tempting. The least prudent thing she could do was push herself into a state of exhaustion before starting a patrol to look for Spore.

"Do that, and my thanks. The intendant has granted me a token for a bath and provisions from the caravanserai."

"Why not the Residence baths and kitchen?" An edge in his tone caught her attention.

"What's wrong?"

"Is the intendant snubbing you?"

"Oh! No, no, not at all. The prince went north, thinking the road is open. They need every pair of hands to make ready for when he returns, probably late this afternoon, at the speed those carriages go."

"I see what you mean. Do you think the prince will be mad?"

"I think the prince will be furious. And I think the prince will blame the intendant instead of the rival prince who probably sent him this way on purpose to make trouble. That's the intendant's theory, anyway. The thing is, the intendant is an easier target, less powerful, and right in front of the prince's handsome nose. But I might be wrong. We can hope. Anyway, I'll go over to the baths. You can sort everything here and bring it to me. I'll take a nap there. I promise."

"I'll give you four hours." He indicated the cabinet clock set on the mantelpiece. "Will that be enough?"

"Make it two."

"Three," he bargained. "What if there's more Spore and you're too tired to notice?"

"All right. Three."

"I'll brush your jacket clean, and wipe and polish your boots."

"And I'll let you!" She swatted his shoulder affectionately and left him to it. He knew exactly what went in her courier pack, as well as what had gone into his mother's midwifery chest. From the earliest age, he had wanted to help them make ready to go on their rounds. It gave him a sense he was doing his part.

Outside, she waved at Deputy Courier Gage's voluptuous spouse, Baima, who blew Elen a kiss from her doorway. Not that they'd ever done it a second time, after that one stormy, lonely night, but it was their little secret and they remained good friends. Like pilfering a slice of festival cake from an imperial shrine, something you could never admit you'd taken but whose sweet taste you would never forget. She grinned, enjoying both memories. Not that she'd ever filched a festival cake a second time either, but the chance she'd taken had been worth every mouthful. She refused to regret moments of sweetness stolen from a harsh world that would as soon kill her as cradle her.

14

ORDER CREATES TRANQUILITY

ORDER CREATES TRANQUILITY.

Therefore, the Tranquil Empire is built on order so all may know and act within their declared place in the empire and there shall be no confusion.

Thus, the emperor stands in the First Estate, shielding the land and its people from all that may attempt to harm its tranquil harmony.

The crown prince stands in the Second Estate, making ready to take up the shield when a blessed emperor returns to the heart of the High Heavens by departing the mortal world.

The princes of the Third Estate are those deemed worthy and capable enough to ascend to the Second Estate, should that become necessary.

The princes of the Fourth Estate are those born into the Flower Court to a prince or a prince's consort.

A child born to a prince of the Fourth or Third Estate, or to such a prince's concubine or bed partner, and who by happenstance or design is born outside the environs of the Flower Court, stands as a prince of the Fifth Estate.

When a prince marries outside the palace and its extended clan lines, any child they sire or birth stands as a prince of the Sixth Estate, and any child that child sires or births, outside the Flower Court, will not receive the title of prince.

Princes of the Fifth and Sixth Estate are the most numerous and of the least account.

Beneath the princely Estates stand the Manors, sometimes called the bedrock upon which the palace rests.

Beneath the Manors stand the empire's subjects, each to their appointed place and profession, according to their own Declaration and its approval by a local justiciar and the imperial administration.

The complete *Grand Ladder of One Hundred Steps* codifies the descending rungs of rank, position, and status for all who live beneath the imperial shield. While copies of this volume can be found in each of the provincial governors' palaces, the original resides in the

Diamond Archives of the Pavilion of Orderly Benevolence in the southeast quarter of the imperial palace.

In the words of the Lotus General, "To act outside order is to upend the world."

Nevertheless, a few of the bolder poets, in the early days of the empire, noted that the Lotus General himself upended the world of the Seven Golden Kingdoms so he could establish an orderly and tranquil empire. However, their work fell under the ban of the imperial censors and was gathered and burned. Its traces can now only be found in fragments left forgotten on overcrowded and unsorted shelves in provincial archives, or buried in sealed pots in Heart Temple gardens, if one knows where to dig.

From *The Official's Handbook of the Empire* as compiled by
Luviara, theurgist, working at the behest of the
Inner Chamber of the Heart Temple

15

THE THIRD ATONER

Elen crossed the south canal, the cross-Halt road, and the north canal by means of a long, low bridge that led into the merchant quarter. The official caravanserai was under the control of the intendant. Its enclosed courtyard was currently empty of wagons and visitors, but employees were bustling around because they'd gotten word a caravan was coming, the one the prince had overtaken and left behind.

A token awaited Elen in the chatelaine's office. A private bathing room had been set aside for her use. It was one of the expensive ones, with a tiled washing floor, and was furnished with bamboo pipes connected to the cistern on the roof, brass rinse buckets, clean brushes, a grooming kit, and soap. The wooden soaking tub in the corner was already filled with hot water.

She stripped and set her grubby clothes onto a bench. Standing on the tile floor, she washed herself, top to toe. It was impossible not to remember the naked prince. Had he been preening? She thought not. He'd seemed oblivious to the other people in the room, only able to perceive himself.

Bathing was splendid, a luxury she would never take for granted. Clean, scented skin was splendid. Clean, trimmed fingernails were splendid. Clean, lice-free hair was splendid.

With a grateful sigh, she sank into the hot soaking tub. Head resting on the tub's rim, she shut her eyes. The water's heat permeated her flesh. She let go of the journey's unexpected developments: the provocative and potentially perilous haunt, the maggot-pale bud of Spore hidden in the dirt, the haughty prince. Her viper, quiescent as it slumbered. Her eyelids fluttered. She slid into a hazy doze that dissolved into a misty recollection of one of her earliest memories, in a place whose name she does not recall and may never have known.

She stands alongside another girl. They are both very young, likely not more than five or six years of age, although she has no way of knowing. The other girl is a stranger, newly brought into the master's keeping. Both girls are raggedly dressed in clothing too big for them, scraps taken off the last atoner who died. Clothes aren't alive, and thus safe to pass on to the next atoner, because Spore can't lodge in them. It is twilight. Wagons and nervous retainers wait behind her. A soldier prods the other girl with the butt of his spear. As the newest atoner, this stranger is required to be first to walk down the lane that cuts through a hollow thick with trees. There is a light barely visible in the distance where the ground rises beyond the hollow. This lantern marks their destination, a ramp that leads up an embankment and onto a road forbidden to atoners, although it will become the master's safe haven for the night, if they can reach it. But they have all heard the Pall's whispery scrape, rising hidden amid the trees. She smells the rose-oil scent that means Spore is irrupting nearby.

The spear pushes the other girl forward. Small as she is, the little girl cannot resist; she starts to cry with fear. A whip rises among the guards. In an instant it will snap. So it is up to El to protect the newcomer, if not from the threat of Spore and Pall—that's not possible—then at least from the strike of the whip. She grasps the other girl's hand to show she will go with her; they'll go together, not alone. It is the first time she holds the hand of the girl who will become her sister, but not the last. They make it through the wooded hollow and all the way to the ramp before the third atoner, the one walking at the end of the procession, screams.

Elen jolted up, eyes flying open, water splashing out of the tub. The sound came again, but it was a shriek of laughter from the caravanserai's parlor where drinks and food were served. Not a scream of terror followed by the wet impacts of flesh being hacked to the bone as the soldiers killed and then burned the atoner so the Spore that had latched onto him could not spread to anyone else. It had all happened long ago. She wasn't there anymore.

Trembling, she rubbed her eyes. Mostly, she had been able to leave behind memories of her childhood. But whenever the viper fed on Spore it left her vulnerable to flashbacks of other Spore encounters. Over the years, the dreams had mostly faded. These days she slept soundly, a trick she'd learned after she and Aoving had miraculously escaped from the place they had no name for, the home of their earliest memories. They had made their innocent, desperate way through supposedly impassable Pall and into what they had eventually learned was the Tranquil Empire, to a northern province called Woodfall.

Not that their lives in Woodfall Province had been better for Aoving, once her budding adolescent beauty attracted the eye of a lord. But at least they hadn't been hungry all the time. Elen had earned a place

in the lord's militia as a trainee, where she'd learned to scout, to use a
bow, knife, and spear, to ride a horse, to read and write, and to draw
and interpret maps.

After Aoving's baby was born, they had experienced some months
of a more-or-less peaceful existence in the Manor. But when that
peace was shattered in a most horrible way, they had run again. Accident, or fate, had brought them to Ilvewind Province and eventually
to Orledder Halt. Here they had stayed.

Elen had taken the risk of hoping this home would be a safe
haven. In a way, for her sister, it had been. Aoving had found peace
in midwifery, working among villagers and the poorest hamlets. It
was enough.

People like her and Aoving were but fragile sticks at the mercy of
a roaring river. To survive as long as they had, to grasp even a sliver
of autonomy, was a triumph beyond anything Elen had ever dreamed
of when she had been a frightened little girl reaching out to hold the
hand of an even more frightened little girl.

The light through the lattice had shifted, drawn into long afternoon
shadows. She had slept longer than she'd realized. The pile of clothing
she'd left on the bench was gone, replaced by a neat stack of clean
garments and her polished boots. That Kem! He'd sneaked in and out
without waking her. Of course he had, and taken her dirty clothes
with him.

The water was cooling fast, making her shiver. She heaved herself
out of the deep tub, water dripping onto the plank floor. After tow-
eling off, she dressed.

Kem was waiting in the parlor, leaning on the counter as he chatted with the manager's daughter, Relia, whenever she could take a
moment from her duties to spare a few words. Kem had had a crush
on Relia for as long as Elen could remember, but she was a clever, ambitious girl who had her gaze set on becoming an imperial chatelaine,
with a chance to work in an administrative wing of the palace and the
family connections to make it happen. Kem had barely enough status
to be friendly with her. Certainly, he was far out of the running as a
romantic prospect. But by the goofy smile on his face as he watched
Relia pouring drinks, hope died hard.

Coming up beside him, Elen tapped his arm. "You coming with
me to the Residence or want to stay here?"

He glanced toward Relia, but she had turned her back to peruse
an accounts book. "I'll come. I put the provisions into the pack.

Everything is sorted. You can thank me by getting back in time for Declaration Day."

As she shouldered the pack, she almost asked him if he had finally decided, but the tight look about his eyes kept her quiet. They wound their way past empty tables toward the door. Midafternoon, there weren't many customers unless a caravan was passing through, and caravans usually arrived late in the day, since Halts were located a day's march apart.

In an undertone, Kem said, "I know nothing can come of it, but I like her, even if you don't."

"I never said that."

"You looked it just now."

"Did I?"

He smiled sadly. "It wasn't you. You never do that. It was Mama. She never approved of Relia wanting to go to the heartland and become a chatelaine in the palace. She said people who crave power have rotting hands, even if on the outside they look clean and whole."

"That sounds like the kind of thing your mother would say."

As they reached the door, it was flung open from the outside. Relia's younger brother rushed in, shoving past them.

"They're here!" the boy cried excitedly. "The lord spoke to me! I'm to bring him a mug of our best ale! Papa! Relia! Did you hear? He looked at me and spoke to me himself, not through his interlocutor! Hurry!"

Elen and Kem stepped outside into the entry courtyard, alive with the noise of arrival. Wagons, animals, and a crowd of people surged into the wide yard.

The old doorman nodded at her. "Look at those banners. These must be the supplies for the imperial engineers the intendant's been promised for months. Now they can finally get back to work."

"Look at the bull elks!" Kem tugged excitedly on Elen's arm. "They're not wearing imperial harness so they can't be from the imperial army. Do you think they're part of the levy to assist the engineers? They must be, because it doesn't make sense for elk riders from Woodfall to come this way since the road is blocked."

The elks were being held by grooms as their riders dismounted. Seeing them up close was a kick in the gut. Elen stopped, gulped, fought for a breath.

"Aunt?" Kem's voice reached her as if from a great distance down the drifts of years.

A cold shock like plunging into an icy lake spilled down her body. Her gaze stuck on the tallest of the riders, a man with brawny shoulders and hair gone gray beneath a lord's golden circlet. It couldn't possibly be him, not after all this time.

Relia's brother came up beside Elen, best brass mug in hand. "Lord Duenn! Your ale!"

The man turned toward the sound of the lad's voice. Before Elen could duck aside, could conceal herself behind the doorman, he saw her. He pointed with his lord's whip. His shout bellowed above the commotion in the yard.

"Thief! Murderer! Arrest her at once!"

16

A False and Rotten Heart

Kem," she said in a strangled voice. "Run."

All that came out was an unintelligible croak. Kem stared at her in confusion. By then, it was too late. Lord Duenn strode over with his personal escort crowding around him. None drew swords, not in a Halt and not without the intendant's permission, but the speed with which they surrounded her was all the weapon they needed. She could not move.

Lord Duenn loomed before her, eyes crackling with fury. He drew his whip, raised it to strike her. She braced for the impact.

Before the whip could fall, Kem stepped in front of Elen. He set hands on hips and stuck his chin forward, a tall youth with a big-boned frame very like that of the lord he now faced.

The lord aggressively prodded Kem in the shoulder with the thong of the whip, and when Kem shifted only a tiny bit, the man drew his arm back to strike. But then he paused, examining the boy.

With a dumbstruck expression, he lowered the whip. "Holy Heavens! This must be Kema! You look very like your mother. Same hair. Not as pretty as her, but put you in a decent gown and do up your hair properly with jewels, and I can negotiate a lucrative marriage for you."

"My name is Kem, so Declared at the imperial shrine," said the boy with the patience he'd practiced for the first year after his Declaration.

Lord Duenn slapped him.

The sound snapped in the now-silent stable yard, followed by gasps of alarm. Everyone was staring. Kem rocked back from the force of the blow, but he did not flinch. He stared with bewildered shock.

"Your name is Kema. It's the name I gave my daughter the day she was born to my concubine Owlet." He addressed his interlocutor, a younger, surlier-looking man than the mild old interlocutor Elen remembered from their five years at Duenn Manor. "I call her Owlet, for her big eyes, always staring."

"In fear," murmured Elen in a hoarse whisper.

Lord Duenn did not hear because he was still talking. "She was my favorite."

"She was not," spat Elen, forgetting prudence. "You were done with her. You handed her over to the barracks. You said your soldiers needed their *fun*."

He slammed her in the belly with the butt of his whip. The blow doubled her over, pain radiating deep into her core. Through the agony, she heard him launch into one of his beloved speeches, his voice carrying across the stable yard. His Woodfall accent was pronounced, although he spoke with formal imperial diction.

"*Ellet*. That is the name they called this one, a sneaky, sly weasel. A quick learner, who would volunteer for any task if it got her an extra slice of bread or a look into a chamber where she didn't belong. You were not at the Manor in those days, so you never met Captain Roel." This comment was addressed to the interlocutor but meant for all. "The poor captain was entirely taken in by her, treated her like a son, though she's got no cock to make her a man even if she dresses and walks like one. I know you folk in the heartland of the empire don't care about such things, mixing folk up as if people are stew, more's the pity for you. But we in the north do care. The emperor leaves us be to live and act as we wish in our own territories because we are loyal to the empire and pay a generous tithe to the temple and the palace. *She* was never loyal, though she lived safely inside the Manor walls for five years. She ate at the Manor table and took the place of a youth who could have become an honorable militiaman. She never walked with honor. She was a thief looking to steal my bread and my woman and my child. Now I've caught up with her. Find Owlet. Bring her to me."

Elen was finally able to straighten, teeth set against the throb in her abdomen. There would be a bruise. But as much as it ached to think of Aoving dead, at least her sister would be spared this reunion. "She is dead. Out of your reach."

"We will soon learn the truth of that claim." Lord Duenn grabbed the mug of ale from the chatelaine's son and drained it in one slug. "Take me to the intendant. Not you!"

Again he jabbed at Elen, who this time had enough warning to tighten her muscles, although she gave an exaggerated yelp and made sure to pretend the blow hurt more than it did.

"Are you all right?" Kem grabbed her elbow. His eyes brimmed with tears that he fought to hold back. The instant she straightened, his expression tightened. He let go of her and whispered in a trembling voice, "Is it true?"

Lord Duenn grabbed the boy's arm. "You'll walk beside me, Kema, as befits my daughter. We'll get you decent clothing. You look like a dirty magpie who pecked through a rag pile."

Kem set his jaw and said nothing. He had gotten his stubborn look fixed onto his face, the one she recognized from his arguments with his mother. Aoving had loved him, but she'd been fighting her own deadly spore of destruction all those years. As he'd reached adolescence, Kem's lofty proclamations about life and his insistence that there was an absolute difference between right and wrong would set Aoving off. He wasn't able to understand that it was because his mother was scared for him, for what would become of a child who was confident enough to know himself, and yet who didn't comprehend how pitiless the world was. Not the way El and Ao, two tiny girls clasping hands in shared terror, had lived it from their earliest years.

"Move! Move!" shouted Duenn, never one to wait for his interlocutor to speak when he could hear the sound of his own voice instead.

Elen stumbled along, surrounded by Duenn militiamen, some of whom she recognized from her days among them. They did not speak to her, although she heard mutters of "Ellet, the cheat" and "Ellet, that thief of a crow" and once, "Sure, but do you remember the time she got through the labyrinth up at Fire Rocks faster than anyone else? And without a scratch on her?"

There was no opening to run. Worse, she was cut off from Kem, who was forced to walk next to Lord Duenn at the head of the procession.

That was the first difference between their nameless homeland and the Tranquil Empire, which child El had noticed those many years ago. In the Nameless Land, the masters walked in the center, with their retainers around them and the atoners at the edges where folk were most vulnerable to Spore. In the empire, the lords and princes and emperors led the way, and none were allowed to walk ahead of them.

For a long time, El had marveled that these imperial lords possessed such power that they were not afraid of Spore. She had come to learn it was because the empire used its resources to seek out, burn, manage, and map the Pall and its irruptions. That, more than anything, was the knowledge she had set herself to learn. She'd always known the past might . . . *would* . . . catch up to them someday. When it did, she'd meant to be ready to run again.

Now this, taken utterly by surprise.

The viper shifted against her heart. *Not yet,* she whispered, quieting it. *Not yet.*

There was no point in being angry. She could kill Duenn but at the cost of her own life, and then who would protect Kem? She needed to wait for an opening, or make one.

They reached the Residence gates. The ringing of a bell was followed by the interlocutor's huzzah and proclamation, announcing the arrival of the lord of Duenn Manor. By the time they crossed the entry plaza and entered the audience hall, the intendant was seated in his chair of office, looking composed.

He rose as a courtesy. Intendants were third-rank officials in the palace hierarchy and normally held lesser status than a lord of a Manor. But this intendant was born to a heartland Manor whose prestige must always outrank that of a provincial Manor, no matter how wealthy the latter might be.

"Lord Duenn. You are welcome in Orledder Halt." The intendant's gaze took in the order of march, eyes creasing with puzzlement as he noted Kem at the side of the lord, and Elen surrounded by Duenn Manor militiamen.

"Respected Intendant, please accept my courtesies." Duenn gestured.

Two menials hurried forward with two boxes. The smaller, when opened, revealed itself to be a gift of precious oils in stoppered vials. The larger contained a cradle carved entirely out of hallow-wood, a precious gift, indeed.

The two interlocutors exchanged formal greetings. The Duenn Manor interlocutor presented the intendant with the caravan's manifest and explained that the cargo was the promised supplies for the engineers.

The intendant examined the manifest, eyebrows lifting twice as he read something that intrigued or surprised him. After he had finished, he addressed the lord directly. "I will be relieved to see the road cleared at last. We have waited quite some time. The delay has affected all of our fortunes."

"Yes, yes," agreed Lord Duenn. "Indeed, Duenn Manor's caravans do not normally use this route, as we reside in the western region of Woodfall Province. But that is not why I asked to accompany this caravan. For many years, we all assumed the fugitives had died in the Pall."

"Which fugitives do you speak of?" the intendant inquired politely.

"I thought they were dead, and thus did not pursue the matter. Then my agents chanced upon a possible lead in the Ilvewind Cross census, a mention of my daughter's name, which comes from the old language used in Woodfall, before the empire. I set a search in motion, and here she is."

The intendant looked at Elen, as if thinking Elen was the daughter in question. Duenn was old enough that he could have fathered her.

"Kema Duennar is my daughter," said Duenn with a smug grimace of satisfaction. "Her mother was my concubine, whom I called Owlet. Is it true she is dead?"

"I know no one named Owlet," said the intendant. "However, the lad's mother, Aoving, has ascended to High Heaven. One of many who died in the avalanche that blocked the road."

"Call her what you wish. She had no legal name because she came from outside Duenn Manor and was never registered in any imperial census. She was fortunate that my chatelaine generously took her onto the household staff and gave her the valuable token of Manor residence. I have the census papers to prove Kema's birth status, if you need papers. My personal oath and the witness of my chatelaine and militiamen ought to be sufficient."

"I'm not sure what is being claimed here," said the intendant.

Elen snuck a glance at Kem, but he was staring at the floor, shoulders tight as he listened.

The lord scoffed. "Is that not obvious? The mother, with the connivance of this thief, stole my daughter from me."

"Elen is his aunt," said the intendant, hand straying to stroke his beard.

"Is that what she claimed? She's not his aunt. She and the mother are not sisters by blood, whatever they called themselves. She cannot prove a legal blood-tie to my child. Nor is *Elen* the name she used when she ate Duenn Manor's bread and slept peacefully inside Duenn Manor's walls. Once the census papers are cleared through you, in your capacity as justiciar of Orledder, I will take my daughter home with me."

"I have to pee," said Kem suddenly, hoarsely.

Elen didn't like Kem's odds if he tried to run, so she gave a little dip of her chin, a delicate *No* that others might not recognize as a signal. But he wasn't looking at her.

Lord Duenn laughed coarsely. "That old trick. We'll get a bucket and a curtain, and you can do your business in the same room as my people. You won't be alone until we're back at Duenn Manor and you are secure in the treasure wing." He paused, then added in a curt tone, "Take the girl outside."

His guards hustled an unresisting Kem out the door.

In the uncomfortable silence that followed, the intendant looked through the papers.

His stern expression soured into a frown. "These appear to be in order. According to procedure, I will send them to my archivist for her seal."

"As you must," agreed Lord Duenn. "As for this thief, she is also a murderer. When she was a sentinel in Duenn Manor, she killed her own captain, Roel Duennol."

The accusation brought silence and many shocked stares.

The intendant rubbed his forehead, looking exhausted. "This is a grave charge. Deputy Courier, do you have anything to say?"

Lord Duenn spoke before Elen could. "This person is still a member of the Duenn Manor militia. She was never formally released from my service. Therefore, Intendant, I need not ask your permission. I can invoke my right as lord of Duenn Manor to have this menial executed immediately for her offenses against the Manor."

He signaled, and the militiamen on either side of her wrenched her down to her knees. One pushed her head down, as if putting her in place for the lop of an axe against her exposed neck. Her body tingled with old, remembered terror. Did Duenn intend to draw his sword and kill her on the spot?

Yet, at the same time, the threat of imminent death stirred the viper at her heart, and sharpened her mind. She noted the intendant glance toward his sentinel captain and give a nod; noted sentinels shifting position, in case they needed to fight the newcomers.

In a slow, cold voice, the intendant said, "This is highly irregular."

Duenn cleared his throat. "Very well. As a courtesy to your authority, I call for an investigation. Let no one say I have used this matter to carry out a personal vendetta. It would be best if the trial were held in Duenn Manor, where folk recall the unpleasant incident and can give testimony. To that end, now that I have found my daughter, I will turn over the manifest of caravan goods into your keeping."

"And then?" the intendant asked, still in that chilly tone.

"My intention is to return with my party to Ilvewind Cross, record my claim for the child with the provincial governor, and afterward make my way home into the western territory of Woodfall via the Northwest Road. I will certainly be glad to never again set foot in this Heavens-forsaken intendancy."

Silence followed this insulting statement. No one dared speak aloud, but one of the militiamen next to Elen whispered, "Maybe you don't remember me, but I remember how you cheated and won that card game, and took my gloves as your prize. I'll get you back for it, you'll see." He nudged her with a boot, not hard enough to knock her over, but firm enough to promise a beating to come.

Breathe, she told herself, looking up toward the front of the hall as the hand of the other militiaman kept her pressed to her knees.

The intendant spoke in a low voice to his valet, who hurried out. After Cariol was out of the chamber, the intendant turned back to Lord Duenn. Except for that one startled glance at the word "murderer," he had not looked at Elen.

"As I said, Lord Duenn, this is a grave accusation made against one of my most valued couriers. A person who just this morning discovered and rooted out Spore atop the ridge that rises to the east of us. You must understand, we are in a constant battle against the Pall and its Spore."

"Do you think I do not know that, living in Woodfall Province? Duenn Manor is proud to be foremost among those who supply hallow-wood for the empire."

"Therefore, you'll understand why I will need more than your public statement before I am willing to so lightly give up a deputy courier who has proven her worth more than once in our ongoing war against the Pall. I have a duty to the empire and the emperor."

"That may be, but I have my right and honor as lord of Duenn Manor. If you must delay me, then I lay my case before you, Intendant, in your capacity as justiciar. Whenever it is convenient for you. Now, if you wish. This evening, if you will. Tomorrow, if I must. Next month, if that is what is required of me. I will not stir from this Halt until I am assured justice will be served, according to the oversight of the High Heavens and the law of the empire."

"I see." The intendant handed the census papers to Captain Jinyan, who kept glancing at Elen with an unfathomable expression: Pity? Disgust? Anger? Sympathy? "Convey these papers to the imperial archivist for her thorough analysis."

"I'll send my captain to witness the archivist's inspection," said Duenn, looking offended.

"Do you not trust me?" asked the intendant, with a raised eyebrow.

"I do not trust this thief not to have stolen your trust. That is how she abused her position in Duenn Manor. She stole a sinecure of service to the Manor that could have gone to a more deserving person. People liked her. They confided in her. They gave her chances they'd not have given others, because they trusted her glib chatter and friendly smile. Only when it was too late did they realize that not a word that comes out of her mouth is ever true. Only when it was too late did they realize how her easy smiles conceal a false and rotten heart."

17

BAIT

Lord Duenn's long-winded prattling allowed Elen's shock to ease. Few were watching her, their attention on the lord's booming voice and choppy gestures. She knew better than to protest, to argue, to push back. Duenn had all the power in this exchange. She had none. Her mind turned through what options might be left. The census papers were accurate. Archivist Heyadi would find them legitimate.

So, Kem first. Duenn would take the boy home and force him to wear a woman's name, force him to marry to benefit the Manor, even imprison him for the rest of his life for fear he might run away, as his mother had done. Elen had taken Kem on longer and longer hikes as he grew older, so he would learn the ropes of overland travel. Aoving had taught him plant lore so he would know what he could eat in the wild and what plants could heal and which would poison. They had prepared, should this day come.

Now, the day was upon them, and she didn't like the odds.

The intendant cleared his throat. When she looked at him, his right hand casually made the open-hand-to-closed-fist gesture that his sentinels used to mean "We need to talk privately."

"Lord Duenn," he said. "It will take the archivist some time to process the documents. Please allow me to offer you refreshments in my parlor. I can arrange for a suite of rooms if you prefer to rest. You have been traveling for some time, I conclude."

"For some months, yes," Duenn huffed, as if his impassioned speech had tired him. Maybe it had. He looked worn about the edges in a way he hadn't fourteen years ago. "It would suit my bones to sit for a while and take refreshment. This has all come as a shock."

"I can well imagine," agreed the intendant. "My chatelaine will show you to a suite, and send food and drink."

Duenn pushed past the militiamen, grabbed Elen's arm so tightly she winced, and roughly hauled her to her feet. "The criminal comes with me."

The intendant smiled in the pleasant way he had that seemed like an apology but was really a tactical maneuver. "Lord Duenn, this is an imperial Residence. I do not allow my outdoor staff and menials like deputy couriers to set foot in the wing set aside for the use of Manor visitors. We keep palace-trained menials in service here to attend to the Manor-born. If you are concerned about security in my Residence . . ." He paused to allow the accusation to sink in.

The lord said nothing, his refusal to answer a deliberate insult.

The intendant's smile had a threatening softness and an iron gentility. "Lord Duenn, I will remind you that I am intendant and justiciar here. This is my jurisdiction, not yours. Any deputy courier assigned to my intendancy is thereby my responsibility. I will lock the accused into a holding cell in the sentinel wing until after—"

"I want the case heard right now. This instant!"

"It will have to be later," said the intendant, not mentioning the prince or his imminent return.

Strange, Elen thought, that Lord Duenn did not ask about the imperial carriages that had passed him by earlier, on the road. On the other hand, he was a man much taken up with his mirror, seeing the world only in the ways it reflected his own concerns and importance. If a prince had passed through, then what did it matter to him? He was an incurious man, which gave Elen hope.

Duenn puffed and grunted, but the intendant's argument was unassailable. "I see no way around your objections, although I agree under protest. But I'll delegate a pair of my militiamen to stand guard over the prisoner."

"You may accompany us to the cellblock, if you wish," said the intendant graciously. Not by a hair did he reveal he had gotten his way, but Elen knew him. He was grim, certainly, but he was also withholding judgment about the accusation. It was all she could ask for.

The intendant gave orders to his sentinels to escort Elen to the cellblock. Lord Duenn insisted on going as well, with two of his militiamen in attendance, one wearing a captain's badge and the other the man who had lost his gloves to Elen in a long-ago card game. She didn't recall the game or the gloves. Probably she had traded them for something she needed more.

A large party therefore accompanied her to the rear of the Residence and past the stables to a windowless blockhouse. Its heavy door let into a gated entry where the guards stood watch. Beyond an inner gate ran a single, dead-end corridor with five barred cells on each side. The interior stank of mildew and urine. The cells closest to the door usually held drunks and petty thieves, but it was traditional for the intendant to grant an amnesty on the eve of Declaration Week, so the place was empty.

Surrounded by intendancy sentinels, all people she knew, Elen was marched to the last cell. Lord Duenn pushed rudely forward. By lamplight, the man insisted on personally investigating the walls, as well as the lack of windows save for slits for ventilation too narrow for a body to squeeze through, before loudly declaring himself satisfied that the cell was secure enough for his liking. He himself shoved her inside, waited until the bars were locked into place, and tromped out. His militiamen followed; the one who had mentioned the gloves cast a nasty glance back at her, promising violence. The gate into the guardroom slammed shut.

Voices drifted away as Duenn departed from the blockhouse, pontificating in his loud voice all the while. Throughout this entire wretched procession she had not even gotten a last glimpse of Kem; he was already sickeningly out of her reach. She didn't care about herself, not compared to what Kem would endure if Duenn was allowed to take him. Yet what could she do? What options did she have?

After setting her pack on the floor, she stood alone in dimness, gripping the bars, cold with foreboding. The gate at the end of the central corridor was a heavy door, banded with iron, with a barred grille set into it through which the guards could peer down the corridor and see all the cells.

The latch of the guardroom gate shifted, a mere scrape. The heavy wood door creaked open a crack. A shape pressed into the gap. The glint of a knife blade caught on a beam of light.

"Here, now!" called Ujin's familiar voice from the guardroom beyond. Ujin didn't normally have blockhouse duty, but the intendant trusted him. "We keep that door closed, friend, so we don't have to smell the stink! Come sit down! Let's have a game of dice, eh!"

The glint vanished as the knife was withdrawn and the door closed. Through the grille's opening, she heard the Orledder sentinels joking loudly with their new companions about whether horseshit or elkshit smelled worse. Ujin began singing a popular song, which had a foot-stomping chorus the rest could join in on and about one hundred increasingly lewd verses. As they sang the first refrain of "Just one more time, dear," a shadow stirred at the back wall of the corridor.

"I need an explanation," said the intendant in a low voice.

18

ALL WE HAD TO LOSE WAS OUR LIVES

"I appreciate the trust you show me," Elen said as quietly as possible, grateful for the noisy singing. Obviously, the intendant had arranged it.

"I am disappointed," he said in a cool tone. "I thought you trusted me in return."

She had to rest her head against the bars as emotion hit her hard. People did not help the likes of her. What if she didn't deserve his trust? She was everything Lord Duenn claimed: a thief, a murderer, a liar. Yet that was only one way of looking at the story. She was a survivor. Aoving's beloved sister and Kem's aunt, even if they weren't blood kin. But what are blood kin, after all? They might be your staunchest allies or your most vicious betrayers.

"If I am to help you, I need trust from you in return, Elen."

She raised her head. "I have served you loyally, without fail. I have never betrayed your generosity."

He shook his head, as a teacher might at receiving the wrong answer from a student who was capable of more. "Elen, I know you well, and yet do not know you at all. That is not what I am asking. When you and Midwife Aoving asked for permission to reside here, you told me you are not Manor-born."

"We are not."

"So." His frown cut her to the heart. "You were precise in your choice of words, in a way meant to mislead me. You were speaking only of yourself and your sister."

She said nothing because he was correct. They'd been so careful.

Shifting from one foot to the other, he went on. "I am sorry to say, I must now believe you deliberately hid from me that Kem is the child of a Manor's lord."

"Aoving did not become Lord Duenn's concubine because she wanted to be. He abused her."

"Having met him, I don't doubt it. But the law is the law."

How she hated that tiresome phrase! "After Kem was weaned, his second winter, Lord Duenn got tired of Owlet, as he called her.

He took Kem from her to be raised by his wife, and handed Aoving over to the barracks. He knew what would happen to her there. I think it gave him pleasure to know he could allow his people to get away with cruel and brutal things that would have been criminal if committed outside a Manor. But the *law* allows him full command over the lives of the people in his household. She would have died if we hadn't run."

"I am not unsympathetic to her plight. I assume that the lord's castoff went first to the captain of the barracks militia, this Roel."

Her hands spasmed around the bars. "Yes," she choked out. "I had thought he was a decent man, who would never—" But she could say no more. Memory was a venom burning through her mind.

He sighed. "I allow no such abuses in the territory I administer, in so far as I hear of them. But as justiciar over Orledder Intendancy, I cannot rule otherwise than to return the youth to his legally recognized sire. Kem is Manor-born. The Manors do not release control over those born into their halls. Especially not those born into a ruling kin-line."

She closed the curtains on that terrible night, shut it away again, and steadied her breathing. "What if I had told you the truth about Kem when we first came here?"

The intendant's body tensed as he considered her words. As he remembered how they'd met in the midst of a Spore outbreak.

How he'd seen his daughter on the other side of a moat as Spore irrupted through the village. How he'd splashed across, so desperate to save his beloved girl that he didn't stop to think that it was already too late. How no one in his retinue had dashed after him to pull him back because they were all too terrified by a horrific twisting growth of Spore that had somehow been carried inside the protection of the moat. Before their shocked eyes, Spore had devoured people and animals and plants alike into a towering, whistling, dome-like web that throbbed as it leaned toward them—yet was unable to reach them across the barrier of water.

Then, a stranger, a girl no older than his eldest child who was about to die, had gone into the moat after him. Elen had caught up to the intendant and dragged him back just as he'd been scrambling up the moat's interior wall. She had spotted Spore crawling along his sleeve and readying to bury itself in the flesh of his hand. At that moment, she'd had a choice: to shove him forward to die with his daughter and the villagers—because it was far too late to rescue them—or risk discovery to save him.

Shoving him forward, in the sight of all, would only make her look like a murderer. So partly, the choice she made was self-preservation. But mostly, it was because he had spoken so kindly to her and Aoving when they had been brought to his desk the day before, to receive a three-day pass to stay in the local Heart Hostel, according to the law of the empire. That kindness fell like rain onto parched ground.

So, acting on gut instinct, she had released the viper as she pulled him back, and it had twined down his arm to eat the Spore. He alone had seen it. By the time they'd gotten safely back to the outer shore, the viper had crawled back into her body.

Still, he could have condemned her to death as a Pall-ridden monstrosity. He could have had her immolated on the burning ground, had he wished. But he was an honorable man, and he had pledged to tell no one because he owed her his life. Afterward, he had given her and Aoving permission to remain at the Halt and to take up officially licensed work, as long as Elen agreed to train as a courier. A strategic man, he'd instantly understood that the viper would make her invaluable on the high paths and isolated trails of the hill country.

All this she had time to recall, and yet he did not speak. His silence frightened her, so she went on, as if she could delay a catastrophe with a flood of words.

"The viper was enough of a shock," she said in a low voice. "But you understood that it offers me enhanced warning of the presence of Spore that it keeps the intendancy safer than it would be otherwise. That was a choice your authority allowed you to make, to allow me to stay and train as a courier. But what would the law have required for Kem? You are an honest man, Intendant, as well as an honored justiciar. You'd have felt obliged to return us all to Duenn Manor, wouldn't you?"

He sighed grievously, a man made weary by multiple sorrows in his long life. "You were wrong to withhold this information from me, but I can see why you held it back. You never thought of leaving the child behind when you fled?"

Her hands convulsed on the bars. "Of course not! Would you?" Then she thought of his son, forced to live far away, in the heartland. "My apologies, Intendant."

"You need not apologize for speaking the truth. I have not your courage."

"I am not here to judge the courage of others whose situation is nothing like mine. Ao and I had nothing to lose. That made the choice easy for us. Easier than for you, because you have other children, other kin, other responsibilities. Your office of intendant and justiciar to fulfill. These are all things you can lose. All we had to lose was our lives."

He gave a little grunt which, she knew, meant he was ironically amused. "Spoken with your usual generosity of spirit."

"I am not generous."

"So you say, but I see it differently. That's neither here nor there. Did you never think to disguise or change the child's name? That seems unlike you."

"We didn't know it was unusual. There were others who had similar names."

"You didn't realize a Woodfall Province name might seem unusual elsewhere?"

"No." She regretted it now, but it had simply never occurred to either of them.

"It's funny," he said, in a tone that meant it wasn't funny. "You speak like an Orledder local now. From your way of talking, no one would ever know you didn't grow up here. But Midwife Aoving never lost her northern accent. I also remember Archivist Heyadi once remarking it wasn't quite a Woodfall accent. She has an ear for such nuances. At the time, you said you came originally from sparsely settled hill country. A region with no Manor."

"That's right." She'd rehearsed the telling of this version of her childhood so many times that it rose to her lips as if it were the truth. "It was so isolated, I don't remember ever hearing news of the empire. Children like us knew nothing of what lay beyond the next hill."

"A careful way of not telling me anything useful about where you came from originally, is it not? Vague generalities are like spring water, easy to drink but cold."

She couldn't bear for him to think ill of her. Most of the people in her life she liked, or disliked, against a backdrop of indifference. Ties must be severable at a moment's notice. Sentiment shackled you, so it was better never to bind oneself. Yet people sought affection because it was like air and water: necessary for life. She knew better than to trust, yet sometimes her heart pulled her into those chains.

"Intendant . . . Uncle, if I may call you so . . . I do not know the name of the place where she and I lived as children. We left there very young to escape being killed by Spore." This, at least, was partially true. "We were grateful to find a place in Duenn Manor, where we could live behind a moat and walls. Eat every day. Gain skills that would make us useful and help us survive."

"Manors rarely take in outsiders."

"So we learned later on. There'd been a terrible sickness in the province. A pale crust, like the rime of salt ponds, would form on people's tongues and close up their throats. No one knew if it was a new disease or a new form of Spore. They had lost so many people that the Manor was eager to take in outsiders to fill out their work force."

"Ah. Yes. The White Tongue Plague hit Woodfall and Manywaters Provinces particularly hard. That was the last reign year of the Lily Emperor. The plague was said to herald his death, a sign from the High Heavens that he, too, would waste away, that his time was closing like a gate. It was the same year I came to Orledder Intendancy."

"I'm sorry," she said, impelled by a rush of shame and fear. She felt shame that she had concealed so much of their past from a good man who had helped them. But fear overwhelmed shame. What if the intendant decided he could no longer trust her? She had to keep him on her side if she wanted to get Kem out of this. "We were so afraid. And we loved it here. Orledder is the first safe haven we ever found."

The pressure of the intendant's regard had its own intimidating weight. He was an intelligent and fair-minded man experienced in the ways of people trying to wriggle off a hook they'd caught themselves on. She thought he was going to ask her about the murder charge, but instead he gestured toward his own forearm. "You never told me how you came to carry such a deadly thing inside you. Out of courtesy, I never asked. Perhaps it is time for me to hear the truth."

Elen had a story made up about that, too, but her throat closed up on the words. She could not bear to lie to him about it, so she didn't know what to say.

A shrill horn blast pierced the thick walls of the blockhouse.

There came a stampede of footsteps and a clamor of voices outside. The interior gate opened. Captain Jinyan's familiar broad-shouldered form stood framed in the light.

"Intendant, the prince has returned."

19

The Opening

There it was. The opening. Bold and outrageous, impossible and desperate. But a path, where she'd seen none before.

Elen whispered, "Intendant, how likely is it the prince's messages went astray by accident? Isn't it more likely—as you suggested—that the messages were never sent, on purpose, but the prince was told they were sent?"

"Do you mean how likely is it that Prince Astaylin is trying to undercut Prince Gevulin's status in the palace by preventing him from completing his mission and making him look like an incompetent fool? It could be. It's also possible Prince Gevulin is incompetent and a fool. But he did send a griffin scout, who, according to the prince, delivered a message at Ilvewind Cross but never arrived here. Usually such matters can be explained by incompetence, but malice remains a possibility."

"I beg you, Intendant, take me with you to greet the prince."

"What is it you hope to accomplish? When Lord Duenn sees you, I'll be taken to task for releasing you from the cellblock. He'll have another chance to execute you outright. At the least, he will pressure me again to hand you over to him by saying I broke my side of the bargain about keeping you locked up. And he won't be wrong."

"I alerted you to the secret, temporary crossing over Grinder's Cut I discovered months ago."

"The smugglers' route?"

"Yes, the one you haven't acted on yet because you want to figure out who's behind it. Do you think the prince will wish to try his luck going the overland route through the Moonrise Hills rather than crawling back to the palace with his tail between his legs?" She grew breathless with the urgent hope that she might save Kem. It was hard to speak calmly.

"Ah. I see. You think you can get the prince across the Cut."

"He looks able to manage a hike through the hills. Once past the Cut—"

"If you don't die in the attempt."

"Yes, if we don't die, then I can guide his party to the imperial road north of the Cut."

"That's your gamble? That the prince, realizing he has been treacherously misled, will do anything to reach Far Boundary Vigil? Even risk his life?"

"You understand the inner workings of the palace in a way I cannot. Isn't this a lethal game a prince can't afford to lose?"

He chuckled drily. "You are the quickest-witted person I know, except for my dear dead girl. But you are correct. Prince Gevulin can't risk losing a power struggle in the palace. As we both know, he is the only person who can override Lord Duenn. Or at least, the only person in the Halt today."

"Tomorrow will be too late."

"Yes, if you mean too late for Kem. But I don't see how this helps the boy."

"I'll say I need Kem to act as my assistant on the journey. First of all, a guide has to know where the crossing is. Then it takes two people to rig a bridge, and to rig it you have to have no fear of heights. Kem's agile and strong, and he's not afraid of heights."

"Yes. He and Joef have entertained us more than once with their rope-balancing acrobatics. And it was Joef who broke his ankle, not Kem, as I recall."

"That's right. It's worth a try, isn't it?"

The horn blatted again, closer.

"Intendant, I must recommend we go," said Jinyan from the threshold. "To keep a prince waiting, and especially when he will be looking for someone to blame, may be fatal."

The intendant began to walk toward the gate, then halted, stroking his beard. Light from the door illuminated his face. She knew that expression. He'd once told her a person who could think several moves ahead could plot their way out of a corner. "Captain, go at once to Lord Duenn and tell him he must not trouble the prince in any way, but shall remain in his guest suite until summoned."

"Intendant." The captain clipped her heels together and departed, leaving the gate open and the guardroom empty.

The two stood for several breaths in silence and darkness. Even as kindly as he treated her, even now that the air of secrecy was partially broken, Elen hesitated to initiate speech without the intendant's permission while lacking the presence of an interlocutor. So she waited.

He returned to the cell, gripping one of the bars. She braced herself, expecting him to ask again about the viper, but he was a man of action who knew to face the most pressing problem first.

"Neither of us know the prince. I cannot judge from our brief acquaintance whether he is the sort of person who is likely to welcome a freely given offer of help as his due, or one who will be more likely to act if he thinks people are trying to keep something from him. He may well wish to blame me, since he can't get his hands on his rival. But we must hope he has realized he was sent on an errand meant to make him look like the fool. If he sees the overland route as a way to thwart his rival, that should attract his interest."

"Why bring Lord Duenn into contact with the prince? You telling his lordship to stay away will surely spur him to barge in."

His hand tightened on the bar. "Yes, I'm counting on it. I have a hunch. I don't know the factions inside the palace. But Lord Duenn was escorting supplies for the engineers."

"I see. Prince Astaylin is the Exalted General of the Corps of Imperial Engineers."

"We must ask ourselves why the lord of Duenn Manor is escorting crucial supplies for the imperial engineers. Why involve a Manor at all, much less its lord? The obvious answer is that Woodfall Province benefits from this road being reopened. But what if there is another reason? What if Prince Astaylin saw an opportunity to spy on her brother, or impede him somehow, with the aid of Duenn Manor? We have to consider the possibility of palace intrigue being part of this entire venture."

He turned at the sound of rapid footfalls, multiple people approaching in a hurry. Elen grabbed her pack. Swinging open the door, the intendant ushered her out. They hastened through the guardroom and got out the door, into the blockhouse's forecourt, just as the prince and his retinue arrived, on foot.

The prince wore a blistering scowl. "Are you in on the conspiracy?"

He charged up to the intendant, and with a riding whip, struck the old man so hard across the face that the sound reverberated amid the forecourt's high walls.

Elen jumped, startled by the speed and the sound and the suddenness. Captain Jinyan's hand darted to her sword, before she caught herself as two imperial wardens shifted to glare at her. To draw a weapon on a prince was to invite immediate death. To display a naked blade in the imperial presence was treason.

No one in the prince's entourage seemed surprised by the whip's blow, as if they'd experienced his temper many times. As for the intendant, he recovered with a single breath, even as the mark of the whip brought a red welt to his cheek.

"What have you to say for yourself, Intendant?" the prince demanded. "Were you ordered to conceal the messages? Ignore them?"

"Your Highness, I will not pretend injured ignorance of your accusation." The intendant spoke in a mild tone, although Elen heard the steel woven beneath it. "Why the messages about your expedition did not arrive here, I do not know. I have not even received reports of a griffin scout passing overhead. I swear to you on the honor of the High Heavens that no such scout landed here. Why you were told at the palace that the road was passable, I cannot know. The imperial engineers have been working to reopen it for almost two years, so they know it remains closed. With respect and humility, please allow me to remind you that I twice asked you about the messages. I warned you the road is blocked." He then paused.

The prince's expression swept from rage to puzzled suspicion. "What do you intend by this impertinent speech?"

"Why, only to suggest there is another possible route, Your Highness."

"So, to mock me! As prince-warden, I know perfectly well the only other route to reach Far Boundary Vigil is to return to Ilvewind Cross and go weeks out of my way by the Northwest Road and then north on the Feldspar Road into western Woodfall, and thence northeast to Far Boundary Pall."

"That is a sure route," agreed the intendant.

"Have I not made myself clear? This is warden business of the greatest urgency. I don't have weeks and months to spare."

"Your Highness, I have a solution, if you will hear me."

The prince paced away, halted with hands made into fists, then returned with shorter and even more agitated steps. He planted himself belligerently in front of the intendant, hands twitching as if he wanted to whip the old man again. But he had enough self-control not to do it. Watching the flicker of his eyes and the press of his mouth, Elen guessed he was desperate.

"How can I trust you? Because it is clear I was deliberately sent by this route to slow me down. Deliberately undermined by someone who desires both my failure and my disgrace."

"Your Highness!" whispered the prince's warden captain in a

scandalized tone. "Such public airing of rumor and dirty laundry will rebound upon you when it gets back to the ears of the palace, as it surely will."

The prince rounded on the warden captain angrily. "The damage has already been done, and accomplished in silence, and with cunning and malicious intent. I am repaid for my trust in my sister with this stab in the back, am I not? I believed in her friendly overtures. I fed innocently on her lies. Now they choke me, as she must have always intended."

20

THERE IS ANOTHER WAY

An uncomfortable silence froze everyone's tongues. Prince Gevulin looked around the forecourt as if at a mass of simpletons who could not understand the most basic instructions.

"Who else but the Exalted Prince General of the Imperial Order of Engineers could have halted the messages? Who else could have convinced me the information they gave about the state of the roads was correct? That I need not check by sending any of my wardens to the surveyors' office or to inquire of any engineers? Simo, have you some other explanation in mind?" He glared at his warden captain, a wiry, weathered man who looked as if he had spent all of his life outdoors tirelessly walking the roads.

Simo bowed his head. "As you say, Your Highness."

"Ipis?" This to the youngest warden, a stocky, muscular woman with the most stolidly inexpressive face Elen had ever seen.

"Your Highness." Ipis nodded, wise enough not to argue with a prince, and especially not when he was in this sort of mood.

The prince skipped his gaze over the other wardens and glared at the oldest of the menials, an elderly man with an assured demeanor. Elen recognized him as the menial who had struck her—twice!—with the fly whisk.

The prince's upper lip quivered. For an odd and almost illusory instant, she caught in his face a glimpse of a frustrated young boy seeking comfort from a trusted adult. "What do you say, Hemerlin?"

The menial bowed with neat precision. He had work-worn hands but a carefully tended face, as if he used the same unguents and remedies as concubines to tend to his complexion. "Your Highness, it lies beyond my purview to comment on the behavior of princes."

"You, Hemerlin? You know better than I that menials see into every crevice and corner, that you listen past every curtain, that you enter and leave every chamber in the palace as softly as a feather. That it is your duty to be always within reach should we need our hair combed or our tea replenished. Nothing happens that you don't observe."

Hemerlin bowed again, arms crossed on his chest. "Your Highness."

Was his tone ironic? Something passed between the prince and menial that went above Elen's head, a secret message or a veiled threat.

The theurgist and interlocutor Luviara observed these exchanges with fearless interest, like a raven watching to see if treasure would be revealed by the spades of enthusiastic ditchdiggers. At last, having not spoken before this, she raised her hands in the manner of a beggar pleading for lordly generosity. "Your Highness, with your permission, I would venture an observation. A question, really."

The prince glanced at her, surprised to hear her speak. He did not seem to have the same intimacy with her as he had with his wardens, his concubines, and his menials. After a pause, and with a graciously haughty inclination of his head, he indicated she could proceed.

"If the road is blocked, how can the wardens not know? Would a blocked road not also block the means by which the Vigil wardens communicate rapidly, across great distances, with the central Warden Hall? It is said that witchery is bound into the bones of the roads, and that only wardens ken this secret."

"Even if a road has been buried under an avalanche, that doesn't mean its bones have been severed," he said testily. "We wardens can communicate with our Vigils as long as the bones of the roads remain intact. That's true whether the pavement lies atop the ground or becomes buried beneath a fall of rock. And that, Luviara, is the most any warden will ever tell you."

"I wished merely to confirm how it seemed, to me, that as far as the wardens knew, the road remained intact."

"Must I state it again?" he snapped. "I was misled into believing there was no obstacle to my travel."

"So once the road is cleared, it will be usable again, just as it was before, with no loss of protection against the Pall."

"If the engineers can clear it. I begin to doubt their capacity, since it seems almost two years have passed, and they have found no solution to clearing the road. No wonder my sister seeks to hamper me. She fears any success on my part will enhance my status at court, while hers has suffered because her engineers have failed to clear a crucial imperial road."

Everyone but the prince—and Elen—looked to the ground, as if fearing to be struck by lightning. The inner struggles of the palace were meant to take place far away from the doings of ordinary life, both exalted and concealed by the favor of the High Heavens upon the imperial lineage. Anyway, it was always perilous to hear the whispers of the powerful, since they would as soon kill you as let you walk away if they thought you knew a single one of their secrets. But she had to stay vigilant, to figure out how to free Kem.

"And yet," the prince added with an expression of sour contemplation, "who is to say my sister is wrong? For I am stymied. I have no choice but to retrace my steps to Ilvewind Cross and take the longer route around to the west." He shook his head with disgust, braids swishing at the movement. "And on top of all that, such a detour will cause me to miss the emperor's naming anniversary. My blessed mother will understand, even if everyone else censures me for disrespect. My blessed mother's good opinion must content me once my fall from imperial grace condemns me to a life of exile or imprisonment."

After an anxious pause, the intendant cleared his throat. He cast a meaningful look at Luviara, to whom he addressed his remark. "There is another way, if His Highness will allow me to explain."

"I need an explanation of how I have been hung out to dry by these false reports!" cried the prince, pacing again, as restless as a caged beast walking round and round in an angry, infinite circle. "Why did no one warn me? How did my wardens not know, Simo?"

Simo cleared his throat, as if struggling to find appropriate words.

The prince sallied on. "Has the Imperial Order of Wardens become so toothless that we are toys for the other prince generals to play with? What say you, Intendant?"

"Your Highness, I am intendant and justiciar of Orledder Intendancy. I am not an official in the palace. However, there is a route through the Moonrise Hills, a footpath that can bring you to a smugglers' bridge across Grinder's Cut. It's the only crossing point, except for the imperial road. You would honor me if you allowed me to lend you a deputy courier and her assistant. She knows the route well and can guide you. It will take ten or more days to get across the Cut, instead of the usual three, because you must go on foot through rugged hills. But compared to taking the detour to the west, it will save weeks of travel time."

"Is this possible?" the prince demanded of his wardens. "Why have you not informed me of this route?"

Simo said, "Your Highness, we are not couriers or surveyors to know the countryside beyond the roads. The intendant surely has surveyors who can accompany you."

"Intendant?"

"All my surveyors are out on patrol. However, the deputy courier I speak of happens to be available." He indicated Elen.

The prince did not even glance at her. She was too lowly a person for an exalted imperial scion to acknowledge. "You could guide me yourself, Intendant."

"The path is too strenuous for me, I fear, Your Highness. I am plagued with weak lungs from a bout of pneumonia, the same that took my wife to the Halcyon Court Beyond the Last Star three years ago. This deputy courier knows the route better than anyone in Orledder Intendancy. It has been her route for ten years. I highly recommend her to you, as you wish to reach the Vigil as soon as possible, not to mention as you also seek to return to the capital in time for the emperor's naming anniversary—"

The intendant broke off, hearing a clatter of footsteps. A smile flickered as he glanced first toward Elen with a barely noticeable dip of the chin to warn her, then toward the arch.

Lord Duenn marched into the forecourt, looking puffed up with consequence and bloated with impatient fury. He was accompanied by his captain, his interlocutor, a chatelaine, and Kem, who was bracketed by two militiamen, including surly-mouthed Gloves.

Kem wore a mulish expression. A feverishly bright smile tilted his mouth, as if he had thought of something very, very clever, like the Residence cats when they deigned to bring you the gift of a dead rat. Oh dear. This would bear watching. She had to stay on her toes. The speed of events raced like a galloping horse ahead of a blistering storm.

Lord Duenn was on his high horse, already blustering. "What means this? Why have I not been informed that travelers from the palace have arrived? Why have the visitors not called upon me, as would be their duty toward me and my consequence?" He saw the prince and stopped dead, going ashen as the blood bled from his cheeks. Belatedly, he bowed. "Your Highness, Prince Gevulin."

"I have never seen you before," said the prince, with a contemptuous twitch to his lips. "Who are you, to claim to know me and to speak so boldly in my presence? Do you not even know the proper protocol? Announce yourself to my interlocutor."

The Duenn interlocutor said, "Lord Duenn, of Duenn Manor, Woodfall Province."

The prince's eyes narrowed. "Duenn Manor. Where have I heard of you before? Ah, I have it! Duenn Manor was among the Manor-born escort who marched in the entourage of Prince Astaylin, Prince of the Third Estate and Exalted General of the Imperial Engineers. That was at the Feast of Lost Couplets, was it not?"

"We were so honored, Your Highness. Prince Astaylin's favor has been a light in our dark times."

"I see," said the prince.

Even Lord Duenn was intelligent enough, past his bluster, to hear the menace in those two words. He hesitated as he tried to figure out what he had said to cause the prince to respond with such a grim expression.

As every gaze settled on the thread of conflict now stretching between lord and prince, Kem took his chance. He bolted forward, breaking free from the militiamen, and shoved past the chatelaine. Swiftly, he danced sideways to avoid Lord Duenn's angry grab for his arm. With a final lunge, the boy flung himself down to his knees before the prince.

"Worthy Interlocutor, pray allow me to speak before His Highness, the Exalted Prince-Warden. I am the Manor-born child of Lord Duenn. According to the law of the empire, I am of age to make my Declaration. As is my right, and as I am qualified to do as one of the Manor-born, I Declare for the service of the wardens."

21

AN EFFUSION OF UGLY SATISFACTION

Elen gasped at the brilliant effrontery of the Declaration. That was her boy! What a gamble!

"Impossible!" cried Lord Duenn. "I won't allow it!"

The angry words dropped into a heavy silence. Elen held her breath as Prince Gevulin studied the kneeling Kem, then examined Lord Duenn. Coming to some conclusion, the prince smiled.

Although he was a handsome man, it was not a handsome smile. His expression turned sly, even cruel, as his lips curved with an effusion of ugly satisfaction. His gaze lifted to take in the assembly. He wore the look of a man perfectly willing to whip his way through an inoffensive gathering, as long as it gets him to the other side, where his desired reward awaits. He spoke with the expectation of being heard.

"As Exalted Prince-Warden, as All-Seeing Eye of the Wardens, I accept the Declaration of this young person."

Yes! Elen could breathe again.

"No!" shouted Duenn. "This is my child, who must obey me, according to the precepts of the High Heavens, which rule us all!"

Elen flinched, an old instinct from the years when outbursts by Lord Duenn ruled their lives.

The prince ignored the words as if they were nothing more than the buzzing of a cicada. He turned his gaze to Kem. "As you accept the obligation, you may arise into your new rank and profession as a novice warden. They who enter the imperial service belong to the emperor forever after, forsaking their Manor and binding their lives to the palace."

Duenn barged forward as his sentinels dithered, wanting to grab him but afraid to touch him against his will.

"I just got her back, and I won't let you have her! You can't take her!"

With rushed steps, Duenn closed the distance between himself and the prince, expecting his greater height, brawn, and age to intimidate the younger, slighter man. Elen braced herself. She'd never seen Duenn lose a fight.

Gevulin did not move or flinch but rather stood straighter and taller. He casually extended an arm, and Simo placed a short sword there with such speed it seemed it had sprouted in his hand by magic.

The Duenn Manor interlocutor gulped an incomprehensible word of warning, too afraid to speak aloud and too appalled not to speak. Nevertheless, the garbled croak—or the blade—had its desired effect. Lord Duenn jerked to a halt just beyond the sword's reach. Elen exulted to see him forced to stop.

The prince spoke in a cold voice, sword edge gleaming. "Do you mean to assault my exalted person, Lord Duenn?"

Duenn choked, gasped, growled beneath his breath. His hands gripped into fists, and his shoulders heaved. "You cannot just steal my child from me!"

"Are you calling me a thief, Lord Duenn?" said the prince with a dangerous widening of his smile, almost a dare. It was magnificent.

"I . . . I . . ." Duenn sputtered, red-faced.

Even Manor lords did not shout at princes. It was treason against the High Heavens, unless, of course, the prince in question was disgraced and about to be severed from all the honors of the palace and their connection to the Flower Court. Elen wondered what Prince Astaylin had told Duenn about her younger brother Gevulin. Why had she chosen Duenn Manor's lord to escort the cargo belonging to the imperial engineers?

Gevulin went on in a tone all the more threatening because it was so conversational and calm. "Do you challenge the Law of Declaration? The authority of the emperor? Are you challenging *me*? My right as all-seeing eye to accept a legal Declaration made by an eligible youth to join the respected ranks of the imperial wardens? Did someone put you up to this? Perhaps promised a payment in cash? Perhaps your coffers are full enough, but influence would be tempting, would it not? The palace beckons like a fevered dream to ambitious provincial lords of the merely meritorious Manors who live far from the heartland and envy the stature of the Six Noble Manors and the Eight August Manors."

The prince was enjoying himself. Elen had a sudden instinct that his rapid rise to become prince-warden and all-seeing eye had everything to do with his own ambitions and ruthlessness. He wanted someone to punish for the nasty trick his sister prince had played on him. Duenn was standing right there.

"Yet, Lord Duenn, that is all it is for the likes of you. A dream. You may leave my presence."

Duenn could not disobey a direct command. He began to turn away, then paused. In a furious whisper, he addressed Kem. "Rescind this selfish Declaration, or you will regret the consequences!"

Without lifting his bowed head, Kem flicked a glance up at Elen. She dipped her chin to signal that he'd made the best play open to him, one she hadn't even thought of. What a quick thinker! He'd saved himself.

Yet Kem did not nod back or acknowledge her. Instead, he looked abruptly away, mouth tightening.

Still on his knees, he crossed his arms on his chest and bowed toward the prince while repeating the ritual words of Declaration.

"Your Highness, the obligation of service is mine, as it belongs to each of us. With our service, we become the pillars holding up the emperor, who rules the Tranquil Empire with a merciful and just hand, as it is ordained under the High Heavens. With honor and honesty, with duty and gratitude, I, Kem Aovingson, Manor-born by the seed of Lord Duenn of Duenn Manor, pledge my labor and my life to the imperial wardens. Let it be recorded that my Declaration has been spoken and accepted at the hand of His Highness Gevulin, Prince-Warden of the Imperial Order of Wardens, Exalted General of the All-Seeing Eye, Captain of a Thousand, Adept of—" He recited, word for word, the interlocutor's entire lengthy introduction for the prince, having a capacious memory for things that interested him. "May the Heart of the Tranquil Empire and the Strength of its Emperor shine unto All Eternity beneath the Implacable Mercy and Gracious Justice of the Heavens."

It was so hard not to let her face show the gloating triumph she felt in every fiber of her flesh. Watching Duenn stalk out of the courtyard, Elen hoped his sweating and seething presaged an apoplectic fit that would fell him frothing to the ground in a spasm of fury, but alas, it was not to be. Lord Duenn was exactly the kind of evil-minded and power-drunk man who escaped unscathed from every encounter. He and his retinue vanished beyond the arch. All that was left was the sound of his voice, raging at his own people, since he had no one else to yell at. Even those shouts faded as they retreated to their assigned rooms in the Residence.

A peaceful hush descended.

The prince gave the sword back to Simo. He spoke to his people.

"I don't have time to deal with Duenn Manor now. We need to move quickly. Ipis, you'll be in charge of the novice. Hemerlin, find the young man an appropriate duty uniform in our baggage. But do it once we've camped for the night, as I intend to accept the intendant's offer of a guide. We will take the route over the Moonrise Hills."

"The imperial suite awaits you, Your Highness," said the intendant so smoothly and expressionlessly that only those who knew him best could see a crimp of expectation on his lips. He was angling for a reaction.

"It does not, for we leave at once."

The intendant's feigned shock did not fool Elen. "At once? But it is late in the afternoon, Your Highness."

"There is still light for our journey. I intend to push forward."

"I cannot recommend—"

"I did not ask for your recommendation."

"Your Highness, it will be dark in three hours. Spore was discovered this morning within fifty paces of the path you'll take."

"You claim your deputy courier is competent to lead us, and knows the route well, including signs of Spore."

"I do so claim."

The prince flicked a hand as if with his whip. "Wardens train to handle Spore that erupts in combs, the worst of infestations. Orledder Intendancy has no such underground cave systems, does it?"

"It does not, Your Highness."

"Exactly. Your competent deputy courier cannot have as much experience at Spore eradication as young Ipis, who is on her first expedition outside the capital but already an experienced and versatile Spore-killer. My wardens and I can easily handle upland Spore. I don't have time to rest. We go at once."

The intendant had gauged the prince's response perfectly as one who would overrule the intendant's reasonable objections in favor of his own angry impatience. The old man looked at Elen, one eyebrow raised. She answered with the sentinel hand sign of agreement.

"Of course, Your Highness," said the intendant with a bow. "It shall be as you require."

The theurgist frowned at this byplay. For an official to ask the opinion of a deputy courier in the face of a prince's command was unheard of, but the old woman said nothing. The prince hadn't caught the exchange or, more likely, the actions and words of a deputy courier were beneath his notice.

Hoping that was so, Elen edged over next to Cariol. In a whisper, she said, "I beg a favor. Quickly find Joef. Ask him to go to my cottage and fetch the full pack in the chest beside Kem's bed."

The intendant had also heard and waved at Cariol to go. The valet went one direction as the intendant and Elen accompanied the prince in another. Gevulin had a ground-eating stride the intendant could not keep up with.

"May the High Heavens watch over you all," said the intendant as he fell behind, wheezing.

Elen tipped a hand to her head in respect. He nodded in reply, and she hurried outside to catch up. From the portico she could see the entry to the guest wing. The Duenn captain and Gloves stood in the open doorway. They fulminated with such blistering anger that, when they saw her, she felt their hatred as if it were a blast of stinging ash flung into her face. *This isn't over,* their expressions seemed to say.

Suddenly anxious, Elen looked for Kem. The boy had clambered up to sit atop the second carriage with Ipis. The young warden said something to Kem with a smile, and he grinned in his merry way, looking more excited than she'd seen him in all the months since his mother's death.

The old menial, Hemerlin, impatiently waved his fly whisk, indicating Elen should climb up onto the driver's seat of the first carriage, beside him. The panthers stood so still she wondered if whatever magic drove them had wound down, although lines of glimmering force swept in visible patterns across their silky black coats. As she settled onto the seat, their ears twitched as if they'd heard her. One growled softly as another's tail lashed. Almost as if they'd sensed the presence of the viper, she thought uneasily. Hemerlin gave a curt whistle, and the beasts settled back to stiffness.

The carriage door clicked shut below, followed by a triple rap onto the carriage roof from inside. Hemerlin whistled in a different cadence, answered by whistles from the drivers of the other carriages.

Elen said, "We can't take the carriages into the Moonrise Hills. The path is only passable on foot, with pack animals if you need to haul goods beyond what a person can carry."

Hemerlin gave her a long look meant to wither her spirit. "No one has spoken to you, Deputy Courier. You'll be informed when your opinion is requested."

She stifled a laugh. They'd find out soon enough. It was no skin off her nose. Kem was safe, or as safe as he could be for now. As she braced her pack between her legs, she saw Lord Duenn glaring from a balcony. His grimacing features reminded her of the clownish villain in *The Five Cunning Brigands Without Compare*. Naturally, the brigands bested the evil lord in the end. How she wanted to wave merrily at Duenn in a final taunt, but she refrained.

Hemerlin collected the reins. "Hyah!"

The panthers surged forward, onlookers scattering as the carriages began to roll.

They were on their way.

22

BEST ADMIRED FROM A DISTANCE

As the cavalcade swept out of the Residence, Elen had to decide whether to speak first and be punished, or to let Hemerlin turn south when he needed to turn north and only belatedly figure out he had gone wrong by not consulting her. The latter was an entertaining scenario that, in other circumstances, she would have allowed to spool out just to see what would happen. But she would be blamed no matter which choice she made. Meanwhile, Lord Duenn brooded in the Residence, eager to find any possible way to yank Kem back into his cruel clutches.

So she spoke. "North, not south."

"There is a lane that branches off the road to the south of the Halt," he objected with the haughty confidence of a man who knows the map but not the land.

"Yes, that is Sul River Street. It swings around south through orchards, fields, and past the brickworks and the furnace. Eventually a side lane turns back north to the Upper Sul Bridge. It is a lovely drive, to be sure, but I would not wish to delay the prince on even the most scenic of detours. If we go that route, we will still be in the lowlands when the sun sets instead of up the ridge and into the hills."

He did not reply. However, he turned the carriage north. Bystanders crossed arms on chests and bowed as the carriages passed. Faces peered out of windows, and elders and children crowded onto balconies to stare with awestruck expressions at the passing beasts. The silence along Orledder's normally cheerful and noisy streets fell strange on Elen's ears, only the scraping rhythm of wheels on stone. It reminded her of her earlier dream. In her childhood, silence was the herald of death. She shuddered, hoping the memory was not an ill omen for the journey.

They reached the central square of the Halt, emptying as people scrambled to get out of the way. No one really wanted to be too close to the palace. As it said in the old poem, "its splendid towers and ramparts best admired from a distance."

Elen said to Hemerlin, "Take East Ramp. Yes. There! Pray forgive my speaking out of turn, but if you wish for my services as a guide, then I must be allowed to speak without waiting for others to ask me about a route they do not know."

"You are coarse and arrogant."

She pressed a hand to her heart in a gesture of heartfelt apology made famous in the play *The Wicked Menial's Revenge*. In her soapiest tone, she said, "I am grateful to be honored with this opportunity to serve an exalted prince."

His hands tightened on the reins as he nudged the panthers to turn onto the ramp. "Do not think there is a place for you in the prince's retinue, if that is what you are angling for."

What she was angling for was Kem's safety. Being a warden wasn't safe, and it wasn't at all what she would have chosen for him. He'd have a tough time among Manor-raised people, where his provincial manners and rustic accent would stick out like a sore thumb. But he had to Declare for something. Yesterday, she'd had different hopes for him. Today, keeping him out of Lord Duenn's hands was all that mattered.

The carriage lumbered up the ramp. Seated up on the carriage, Elen felt no discomfort as they crossed the road, only a slight uneasiness that might have been the viper stirring restlessly or might have been her own anxious anticipation. About two hundred paces ahead, on the lane through the outer district, she spotted a youth wearing the yellow headband of an imperial messenger.

As the carriage reached the bottom of the outer ramp, she raised a hand in greeting to Emmar and Hilsit. The sentinels stared in round-mouthed shock to see her seated on the driver's bench of a royal carriage. Belatedly, they bobbed awkward bows.

She called down, "Who is that runner who just passed? Do you know who sent them?"

The sentinels didn't hear because they got distracted by Joef charging up, flushed and out of breath as he tried to shout a farewell. He tossed the pack up to Kem, on the second carriage. The lad caught it deftly. Joef grimaced, first looking ready to burst into tears and then waving wildly, bouncing on his toes, as they rolled on to leave him behind.

The laborers in the fields halted at their work and bent like grain beneath a strong wind to honor the passing royal. The cavalcade rushed onward through the moated outer ward of the Halt. When they reached the earthworks, they crossed the moat and followed the cart track along the river, back the way Elen had come just this morning. It felt as if she and Kem had returned weeks ago. She was as wrung out as if she'd run all day, and maybe, in a way, she had, if being hit over and over with fresh shocks was a race against how much surprise a person could take before they broke down. But she'd never had the luxury of breaking down. All her life she'd had to be strong for Aoving and then for Kem.

The carriage absorbed the grassy lane's bumps with ease. Instead of turning on the footpath that would cut across the Boulders, she gestured for Hemerlin to continue along the river track.

"Is there not a shorter route through here?" he asked curtly, indicating the footpath.

"If these carriages can climb steps carved into huge rocks, then we may take this turning. Otherwise, we must take a longer way around the Boulders into the woodland. I defer to your wisdom on this matter."

His eyebrows quirked with anger, recognizing the irony in her tone. "Do not challenge me, Deputy Courier."

"I pray for pardon. I do not know the proper address for a palace menial. In the intendant's Residence, the menials are addressed by name."

"You may address me as Chief Menial Hemerlin."

"You honor me, Chief Menial Hemerlin."

"That I do," he muttered under his breath.

They drove along the river. The setting sun cast its grieving light along the waters, as it was said in the elegy composed by one of the many poets exiled from court in past reigns.

"Turn here." She indicated a wide lane that cut into the upper woodland, with trees carefully coppiced under the eye of the intendant's agricultural officials.

The lane grew bumpier as they approached the ridge, as the land began to slope and rumple. So far, the lane had two well-worn ruts and continued north along the base of the ridge past a string of lowland villages. A hallow-wood guidepost marked the turnoff where the main path into the Moonrise Hills began to climb the ridge. There was a ditch-ringed, stone-walled trading post just out of sight behind a thick stand of cypress. Merchants stopped there to exchange wagons for mules, donkeys, and mouflon, or to transfer their goods into the hands of an experienced upland, or lowland, trader, depending on which direction they were coming from.

"You can leave the carriages at Lancer's Post, past the cypresses,"

THE WITCH ROADS   117

she said. "The official will delegate pack animals to your party for the rest of the journey."

Hemerlin did not even look her way. He turned the carriage onto the path. The panthers surged forward as they strained up the steepening ascent.

Elen was so shocked she couldn't speak but she finally found her voice. "Chief Menial Hemerlin, no one takes wagons this way."

"The prince is not *no one*, Deputy Courier."

"I mean to say, the path grows narrower. It's for foot traffic and pack animals. It's not meant for wheeled vehicles pulled by beasts. There's no room. We'll crash over the side."

He did not reply, did not even acknowledge her warning. Up they rolled, the panthers straining as the ascent steepened. She eyed the path above as it became a switchback toward the top of the ridge, measuring where they would reach the limit of their wheel span. At what point would she have to leap? When would the wheels slip over the edge of the leveled path and the carriage plunge and crack down the steep slope? Could she signal to Kem? She glanced back, but he was grinning as he and Ipis chattered, unaware of the danger. Her body coiled with tension. The viper flickered awake with a pulse of adrenaline.

Yet somehow, the carriages kept climbing. Somehow, the path remained wide enough. Was her view of the path an illusion? Was it really wider than she thought? Had she misjudged?

Yet it seemed to her that the wheels rolled across empty air, as if held up on an invisible surface. Was the theurgist using magic? A humble deputy courier was not privy to such arcane knowledge. People like her could never gain access to the intensive study regime necessary to master it. Even if she could have, she'd never be able to risk imperial officials discovering the viper.

Still, knowing if it was magic might have made the ascent easier on her nerves, even for a person like her, who didn't rattle easily. It was impossible to shake a vision of them tumbling over and over as the carriage shattered around her broken body. Her hands gripped the driver's rail. If Hemerlin noticed, he was kind enough not to mock her. More likely, the palace menial simply did not care about her distress.

With a jolt created by a sudden release of pressure, they reached the top of the ridge. Elen forcibly relaxed her hands. Up here, the path widened, running both north and south along the gentle back slope of the ridge. This long saddle of land dropped, to the south, into the valley where the hamlet lay, and to the north and east wound up into the rugged hills.

Behind them, the other two carriages rolled into view as they topped the ridge. Wisps like steam rose from the stallions and the beasts, reminding Elen of threads of Spore, but when she inhaled, she smelled nothing of rose oil, only a metallic scent that reminded her of a forge. Captain Simo strode at the rear of the procession, accompanied by two wardens, each holding a bow.

"North," she said.

Hemerlin directed the panthers. "Where was the Spore?" he asked.

"There, among the bones."

Dusk had flowered across the land. A fading patch of light illuminated the bone pile and, beyond it, the ruins of the abandoned village.

She added, "It will be dark soon. We should head down to the base of the promontory. There's a hamlet there where we can shelter for the night." Poor Urnesso. What would he make of her new "consequence" in the retinue of a prince? "Their ditch is properly watered and salted according to the imperial precepts."

"The moon is full tonight. We can travel by its light. It is wardens' work to move swiftly on the emperor's business. We'll continue on." His tone did not encourage disagreement. Abruptly, he stiffened as he gazed at the promontory. "What manner of buildings are those? There, in the distance."

Two raps signaled from inside the carriage. Hemerlin slowed the panthers to a stop. The other carriages halted behind. A menial leaped off the board at the back of the carriage and hurried forward to open the door. The prince stepped out. He pointed with his whip.

"Are those Spires?" he demanded.

Luviara got down from the second carriage, dabbing her forehead with a handkerchief. She looked as sweaty and tired as if she'd just finished a hard run. "Your Highness?"

"I asked, are those Spires?"

Luviara spotted Elen on the driver's bench. "Deputy Courier, are those Spires?"

"Yes, Worthy Interlocutor. There is an intact Spires triangle on the promontory. As the poet said, 'best admired from a distance.'"

Luviara repeated Elen's words to the prince.

"Intact!" he exclaimed.

The Spires gleamed in the last golden light of the setting sun. If she were a haunt wanting to attract prey, Elen thought, she could not have conjured up a more alluring vision. The prince stared like a man who thirsts and has at long last seen water.

After a protracted pause, he addressed Captain Simo. "I've read that a person can observe marvels if they ascend an intact Spires compound on the night of a full moon. We must go there at once."

Elen said, to Luviara, "Your Worthiness, I advise against such an expedition, because—"

The prince climbed back into the carriage as she was speaking. He had taken no more notice of Elen than he would a rock. As the door thunked shut, she broke off. No use beating her head against a barrier she could not open.

Simo appeared below, looking up at her. "Deputy Courier, you will accompany me to show me where you discovered the Spore."

Her lips pressed together, and she squelched the warning. She had no authority here. After shouldering her pack, she climbed down.

The carriages rolled on. Kem did not look back as she was left behind with Simo and two other wardens.

23

Elen had worked with surveyors and sentinels but never with wardens. Choosing caution, she touched clasped hands to her chest to signal her respect.

"Go on," said Simo. He unsheathed a slim sword forged of shrive-steel, with its characteristic blue-black gleam. One of the wardens kept out his bow—long-black-hair-in-a-bun Jirvy—while the other—short-haired Xilsi—slung her bow at her back, swapping it out for a spear tipped with a shrive-steel point.

Dagger in hand, Elen began to walk, indicating with words and by pointing where she routinely set her feet. They followed her with the taciturn determination of hunters. The wind rustled the grass and made the thorny black-claw brush click and clack. The swish of a mouse tail vanishing beneath a flowering bush caught Simo's attention. Elen tensed. Simo extended a hand and, rubbing his fingers together as if wiping dust from them, whistled a strange melody. As if under a spell, the mouse crept out from the bush. It had a healthy brown coat and bright black eyes. Simo snapped his fingers, and it scurried away.

"Active mice are a sign of a healthy environment," he said, with a nod. "And birdsong. I hear rock pigeons, robins, and scatter-wings."

Unlike the prince, the wardens did not ignore Elen, as if she did not exist. Nor did they question her every move, as Hemerlin had. She guided them to the bone pile, succinctly described its local history and looping track, and knelt to show them the ashy scar where she'd killed the Spore. Xilsi probed the scar with her spear's tip. Simo sprinkled some kind of powder all around and over the withered skeleton of the bush whose essence—life energy—the Spore had consumed. He spoke words in a singsong language Elen did not recognize. The powder twinkled. Something moved that was neither shadow nor light, and she thought it might be a salt spirit, but she didn't ask. It felt different from the salt spirits she had access to. Maybe someday Kem would know.

The glittering dust twisted, rising heavenward, but then spun back—as if deliberately—and *puffed* aggressively at Elen. A sharp hiss chased past her face, blowing into her eyes. The pressure dissipated, and the spirit was gone.

"Odd," said Simo, looking at her, but instead of saying more, he shrugged and stood. "I am satisfied that nothing remains of this irruption."

She inclined her head to acknowledge the statement. They did not wait for her but spread out to return to the main path by sweeping around the bone pile and covering a great deal more ground than before, gazes turned to the earth as they searched for other signs of fresh Spore. By now, the dusk had deepened. The moon appeared above the hills to the east. Elen looked that way nervously, but it was not yet high enough to top the wall of the Spires compound. Their tall, peaked tower roofs caught the last gleam of the setting sun and melded it with the first silvery beams of the rising moon.

She kept thinking of the way the prince had stared at the Spires. Though she knew she ought not to speak without being spoken to, she nevertheless said, "Should we not rejoin the others quickly? Before it is full dark?"

Simo looked her up and down. His eyes had a strange glimmer, as if lit from within or aided by yet another spirit. Which might explain why wardens were willing to travel at night, if they were aided by magic as well as shrive-steel.

"Is there something you fear, Deputy Courier? Something of the night, or something else you have not informed us of?"

"Chief Menial Hemerlin gave me little enough chance to inform him of anything," she remarked, forgetting herself.

Xilsi snickered. "Ha! A wickedly true assessment!"

Jirvy frowned, but Elen had the curious instinct it was Xilsi's comment, and not Elen's, that had annoyed him.

Simo said, "Deputy Courier, do not overstep your station in life by speaking disrespectfully of those who stand above you. This is the only warning I will give, and that as a courtesy due to the intendant's connection to Karis Manor."

He started walking. She hastened to fall in behind him. Xilsi and Jirvy brought up the rear. They took a brisk, ground-eating stride, faster than her normal circuit stride but nothing she couldn't keep up with for the distance from here to the Spires. Yet what if they did not get there soon enough? What could she even say to convince the prince not to go into the Spires on a moon-bright night?

Maybe she should just let him enter unaware of the danger. What would the haunt do? And would she want the haunt to do it? Yet wouldn't that make her exactly the same as the masters who had sent out children like her and Aoving ahead of their traveling parties, in order to attract Spore? Years and years ago, Ao had made her promise to never be the kind of person who would use and discard others. Because she refused to lose faith with Aoving, Elen sighed and spoke.

"Captain Simo, it would be both dangerous and foolhardy for the imperial party to enter the Spires once the moon rises. There is an old legend—"

"Silence. It is not your place to advise an exalted prince on matters he has himself studied in the imperial archives."

She shut her mouth.

After passing the split in the path, they toiled up to the promontory. It was night now, gauzy with moonlight, but the sun was gone and the breeze made her nervous, though it smelled only of late-season flowers and a whiff of hearth-smoke from the hamlet below. The carriages had been forced to halt where the point of land narrowed. About one hundred paces beyond the carriages, the double column of statues lined the ominous causeway.

The beasts had been unhitched and set head-to-tail in a protective fence around the three carriages. The vehicles had been arranged in a triangle, creating a central space within for the party's encampment. The camp was lit by glass spheres encasing fire spirits, strange and wondrous lights Elen had only ever seen in the company of theurgists.

A menial was examining the beasts one by one, as a groom would care for living animals, making sure they'd taken no harm from the day's effort. Another menial had crawled under the second carriage, checking its axle. Looking almost like a haunt in the night, a warden paced a circuit beyond the beasts.

No one took any notice of Elen as she slipped between the third and second carriages to get a better look into the camp.

An awning covered half the area. Under its shelter, a young menial was setting up cots, while an older menial knelt on a thick mat, polishing gear. Luviara sat in a folding chair, writing in a journal. The other half of the area was open to the sky so smoke could freely rise from a fire burning in a portable hearth. At a camp table crammed with utensils and pots, a scowling cook supervised two assistants as they brewed tea and prepared a meal.

The prince's carriage had its doors open on both sides. The interior was unexpectedly simple: a padded seat and a stand where a book or scroll could be fixed. However, a cunningly constructed deck had been unfolded to give extra room, a means by which His Exalted Highness could sit well off the ground and take his ease. The concubines were busy hanging curtains, draping the table with silk, and setting out porcelain from a padded traveling chest. They spoke to each other in an undertone, casting nervous glances toward the silent Spires and the beast-headed statues that stood about thirty paces away. Another menial sat cross-legged inside the second carriage, mending a torn sleeve on a robe whose gold-and-silver-threaded embroidery shimmered where moonlight caught at it.

Where was Kem? Elen looked for Ipis, too, but saw neither.

Simo had approached Hemerlin, interrupting him just as the chief menial was berating a young menial haplessly struggling to prepare a suitable bath for the prince when there were no sources of free-running water at hand. Jirvy and Xilsi had lagged behind, quartering the ground for signs of Spore, although Elen could have told them she'd never found Spore this close to the Spires. Surely the wardens knew that, didn't they? Maybe they were avoiding Hemerlin. Or, if she judged by their choppy movements and clipped steps, they were arguing. None of her business!

Where was the prince?

At the Residence, she'd tallied up the numbers: the prince, seven wardens, two concubines, eleven menials, and the interlocutor. She walked all the way around the encampment, following the trail of a warden whose name she did not know. In other circumstances, she would have been amazed and amused by this hive of luxury buzzing in the midst of rough hills, all to cater to one person's sensibilities and demands. The draft animals stood stone-still, with threads of mist rising off their bodies. Elen's stomach rumbled, and she licked dry lips, thirsty, but she kept searching. She did not see Kem. Where was Kem? There was one menial missing, too, and one warden unaccounted for.

Dread pooled in the pit of her belly. There was only one place left to look.

She left the carriages and the lamplight behind and walked toward the towers, out onto the causeway with the statues. At such a height, the wind usually tugged and moaned at all hours but there was no wind at all, only stillness, as if a hand had settled down over the world before it crushed all life. The sheer cliffs on either side seemed even more terrifying than they had yesterday, hungrier, waiting for someone to stumble off and fall to their death. She nodded to each statue as she passed—the winged eagle captain, the rat soldier, the tiger woman, the ram-headed man—as if by this courtesy they would pardon her transgression, spare her from the torque of whatever sorcery lingered in these towers. Not wake suddenly to attack her.

The statue of the handsome man holding the dragon's head was gone.

Gone.

Stone could not walk. But haunts could walk here, at the Spires, on a moon-bright night.

Let me borrow the youth who sleeps beside you.

Sick fear shook through her. What if the prince had commanded Kem to escort him into the Spires? She swayed on legs suddenly too weak to hold her up. Sweat broke on her body. A cloud of darkness smeared her vision. She should have told Kem the truth. Now she would lose him because she hadn't trusted him. It was all her fault. Her fault. Her fault. Her whole life pitched and rolled, torn off its axis. In the distance, a bell's heavy tone reverberated in the air, setting her pulse racing. Its resonant call rippled across the promontory until, dizzied, she staggered a step sideways, closer to the edge.

Digging her knuckles into her eyes, she fought back. She breathed. She steadied herself. She knew how to do this. She had to do this, to hold fast, to face the fear, to keep walking forward because she had no choice.

A shout carried from behind the dark arch that led through the wall and into the ancient compound. Was that Kem's cry from inside the courtyard? Was it too late? Had he been taken? She froze, as if the surrounding statues had grasped her with invisible bands and held her tight.

People appeared, stumbling down the stone staircase. There were four. One was a grotesque, multi-limbed figure, a person in the throes of transforming into a Spore-ridden monster. Where was Kem?

They came clear of the wall's shadow and into the light of the full moon to reveal five people, not four. The big, strapping menial was carrying the prince in his arms as easily as one carried a sleeping child.

Kem walked in the lead alongside Ipis, showing no sign of injury.

But why would he show any sign of injury if he had already been taken by the haunt?

"Kem, are you all right? What happened?"

"Move aside for the prince," Kem snapped. He flinched, hearing how surly and rude he sounded, and added in an undertone, as if to himself, "She's not my aunt."

He strode past with such seething anger that Elen stumbled aside to get out of his way. Her back bumped up against a statue, thanks be to the High Heavens, because otherwise she was so rattled she would literally have stepped backward off the cliff.

She thought about taking that step deliberately and just falling. She already felt as if she were falling. *She's not my aunt.*

Footsteps pounded up from the camp.

"Out of my way!" Simo burst past Kem and Ipis, racing toward the Spires with Jirvy and Xilsi at his heels. He flung more words over his shoulder as he ran. "Ipis! Wait there!"

He reached the big man, gesticulating wildly as he spoke to the warden who had accompanied the prince. Jirvy and Xilsi started up the stone staircase, but the other warden shouted at them, and they reversed course and followed the others as they hurried back toward the carriages.

Simo came first, leading the way past Elen, who hadn't moved from among the statues. Behind him, the big man lumbered, the prince slack in his arms. Just as the menial passed Elen, the prince's eyes fluttered open. He looked straight onto her face where the moonlight poured over it. His gaze widened as if in surprised recognition. A smile flickered on his lips. Then he gasped and shut his eyes, retching as if something had caught in his throat that he couldn't expel.

"Hurry! Hurry!" cried Simo. "Take him to Hemerlin."

Kem and Ipis moved back to let the big menial through with the prince.

Simo halted in front of Ipis. "Was he struck? Was there Spore? What happened?"

Ipis said, "No, Captain. The ruins are uncontaminated. They're empty of all life. It was so strange. We stood on the central pavement, as Novice Kem suggested we do. His Highness wanted to explore, and he walked around the courtyard, gesturing and speaking words none of us could make out, as if he were in conversation with himself. Then he collapsed in a faint."

Elen said urgently, "Kem, what happened?"

Kem halted as if her voice hit him like a blow. His lip curled with anger, but for whom, she wasn't sure. He said, in a low voice, "I told everyone to stay on the holystone pavement, since you don't trust me to have thought of that. But the prince didn't listen."

Simo glanced back. "Kem! Move along! Hurry!"

He and the others hurried on in the wake of the prince. Xilsi and Jirvy brought up the rear, jogging past Elen as if they had not seen her. Menials raced out from the camp, holding globe-lamps to light their way. Not one looked back to see if she was coming. The people hurried inside the wall of carriages. The camp came alive like disturbed wasps, voices a frantic hum in the night as everyone scrambled to care for their afflicted prince.

She's not my aunt.

Since you don't trust me.

What did these comments mean?

At length, she could breathe normally again. For now, Kem was safe, and that was enough.

The wind picked up as the moon rose higher. She lifted her gaze to the towers, thinking that, from out here, she might see the high scaffolding shine beneath the moon. But all she saw was darkness, as if there was nothing inside the walls, as if the Spires weren't a haven or a lookout but rather a door that led out of this world and into a place no human was meant to go.

After taking a breath to steady herself, she set a hand behind her, resting it against the statue whose solidity had saved her. She'd give herself one more calming breath before heading back to camp. Only then did she realize she was facing the statue of the woman who was holding the head of a young man in her arms. That couldn't be right.

Turning, she faced the statue she was so sure had been missing before. Had she hallucinated that it was gone because she'd been so frightened for Kem?

The statue was the same as it had always been, all these years she'd walked the circuit of the Moonrise Hills. It wore the face of the haunt she'd spoken to last night, with his intriguing smile, lips half-parted as if he were about to speak an ironically sly comment. In his hands, he held not the carved dragon's head she'd seen before. He held a stone head carved with the features of Prince Gevulin.

24

When the Pall first rose in the reign of the sentimental Azalea Emperor, a Prince of the Fourth Estate was sent to investigate.

When he did not return, a Prince of the Third Estate was sent to investigate.

When she did not return, the beloved Crown Prince went to the emperor and said, "Let this be my responsibility."

The emperor had only recently elevated the Crown Prince to the Second Estate. This Crown Prince was the child of the emperor's favorite consort, a child of grace and beauty, obedient and charming, intelligent and in all ways honorable, dutiful, and competent to become emperor in time. The emperor refused to send the beloved Crown Prince into the fray and instead rode out himself.

When he did not return, the Crown Prince became the ill-advised Mallow Emperor, for she did not do her duty to the empire by ruling and sending out others in her stead. Instead, she went in search of her father, and she never returned.

Thus, her unfavored uncle crowned himself the Oak Emperor, said to be strong but seen to be rigid. For two years the empire suffered as the Pall spread and people died.

Just when all was believed to be lost and the empire doomed, the prince of the Fourth Estate, who had been the first to go out to investigate, returned home, against all expectation. He had explored the shore of the Pall and had, he claimed, even sailed down a river beneath the Pall. He brought a sheaf of ideas to the council, listing measures that could be taken to safeguard the empire and its population. These the Oak Emperor rejected.

Within a month, the Oak Emperor was dead, and the returned prince took the throne as the Willow Emperor. He implemented his new bureaucracy, upon which the empire has survived to this day.

From *The Official's Handbook of the Empire* as compiled by
Luviara, theurgist, working at the behest of the
Inner Chamber of the Heart Temple

25

THE THIEF

Elen woke at dawn, as she always did, and was surprised to find herself stretched out on one of the cots. The events of yesterday evening broke onto the surface of her memory as she oriented herself to her new circumstances.

Kem was safe.

She'd followed the frantic group back to the carriages. No one was using the cots because the prince's retinue were all flapping and squawking in fear for him, so she had decided to rest while she had the chance. She had lain down on one of the cots, fully clothed except for her boots, expecting to be rousted at any moment. Yet here she still was, after a sound sleep.

"You're awake. Good. I have questions for you." Luviara perched on the edge of a camp stool, hands gripping her journal as she peered at Elen in the dawn's twilight.

The theurgist's gaze made her nervous. Luviara wanted something. Elen did her best to avoid people when they were in this sort of mood, but there was no avoiding the prince's interlocutor. She sat up, hating to meet questions lying down, and swung her feet over to lace on her boots. Rule One in her ledger was *Securely Fasten Your Boots Before Wading into Trouble.*

"A gracious morning, Your Worthiness. May I ask if the prince has recovered from his faint?"

The theurgist's gaze darted toward the prince's carriage. The curtains into the interior had been opened. The bench inside, unfolded into a bed, lay empty, with rumpled blankets all that remained of the prince's presence. The two concubines knelt on the deck extension, whispering to each other as they held hands.

"He woke not long ago, Deputy Courier."

"I hope the morning found him well," Elen added carefully.

Luviara's mouth twitched. She cleared her throat, as if she had just changed her mind about what she wanted to say. "Perhaps it was something he ate at the Halt. When he woke, he refused food and has been unusually quiet."

"I see. And where is he now? If I may ask."

"You are a clever woman," said the theurgist, in a tone that made the words sound sinister, "so I will warn you that questions from a deputy courier inquiring about the prince will not be welcome."

"Of course, Your Worthiness. My only hope is to be of service to the palace, in whose magnificence I am scarcely more significant than a flea."

Luviara's eyebrows cocked upward skeptically.

Elen decided she had laid it on too thickly, so she bent her head, meaning to appear humble. "Before you ask your questions, may I first relieve myself and wash my hands and face?"

Luviara beckoned. The youngest menial, the one Elen had seen setting up the cots last night, trotted over. Unlike the other menials, he had short hair that was not long enough to pull back into an adult's bun or topknot. "Snip, show the deputy courier to the menials' privy."

The youth gave a bow of obedience before turning and walking away, not looking back as Elen hurried after. The prince no doubt conducted his business in a golden bucket, with his concubines to hold and aim his penis so he wouldn't have to sully his hands, and to clean his handsome buttocks afterward, gently, with moist silk handkerchiefs. The thought made her give a snort of amusement, though nothing too loud. Naturally she was delighted to find two small, curtained shelters set up on the strip of ground between the carriages and the ring of beasts. Snip led her to the one with curtains dyed the same pale lichen-purple as the menial uniforms. The other curtains were warden blue.

"Is the other shelter reserved for the wardens?" she asked.

Snip gave her a look of alarm that merely acted to draw attention to the youth's lustrous brown eyes and smooth cheeks and jawline, no trace of a beard. He wore a boy's earring and was perhaps a year or two older than Kem. Although, like Kem, he might have Declared, Elen wondered if the nickname meant he had been castrated as a child, a pre-empire custom said to still be observed in the palace. Hardly a question she was about to ask! It would be cruel, whatever the answer, and yet she couldn't help but puzzle over the menial's unusual name.

When Snip gave no answer, she went into the menials' latrine. Inside, the shelter was divided into two tiny compartments. In one, a stand held a basin, a pitcher, and soap. In the other, a short bench with a hole sat over a bucket, fragrant with use. After relieving herself, she washed her hands and then her face, and came out into the cold early-morning air with water glistening on her skin. Snip gave her dripping hands a sharp look. Like the other menials, Snip had a kerchief-sized linen towel clipped to his belt. Elen's lack certainly marked her as a person who did not come from the palace. With a curt gesture of dismissal, Snip hurried back into the camp, leaving Elen to her own devices. Perhaps Snip was refusing to speak to her because, in Snip's world, a provincial deputy courier ranked far below a palace servant and thus required an interlocutor's services in order to speak to anyone who lived or served within the palace.

Elen walked beyond the ring of beasts to survey the promontory as the sun rose behind it. The towers looked unchanged, the statues unmoving, all six present although she was too far to see their features. But she was surprised to see every warden, including Kem, standing on the path and staring back the way they'd come from Lancer's Ridge. Then she saw why.

The prince came walking up the path at a measured pace, as if he had gone down to the holystone post that marked the turnoff to Three Spires and was now returning to camp. No one was with him, even though it was a significant walk down and back for an exalted scion of the palace to take all alone.

The wardens stared tensely, as if they'd been ordered to keep their distance and were expecting him to explode into a shower of sparks at any moment. Hemerlin stood a few steps behind the wardens, hands clenched and gaze fixed on the approaching prince. Elen couldn't tell if the old menial was staring with apprehension or with suspicion that something wasn't as it ought to be.

The prince's face and body looked the same, but Elen couldn't shake a nagging sense that his gait and posture were different, more relaxed, and with less self-important swagger. Probably she was only seeing what she wanted to see.

Merciful Heavens! Was that what she wanted? To speak to the haunt again, even if he had stolen the prince's body? Yet hadn't the haunt said he had to be invited in? No, that wasn't what he had said. He'd told her that he would ask, but he hadn't said he *had* to ask in order to possess a body. Only that he promised to return Kem's body "unharmed," as if a haunt could be believed. What was a haunt, after all, if not a soul caught between this world and the judgment of the High Heavens, where it had refused to go? To walk in this world, he had to inhabit someone else's body. That was theft.

Even beyond all that, he hadn't answered her question when she'd asked if he was a sorcerer.

Luviara appeared at her side. "Deputy Courier, as you are finished with your morning ablutions, I require your answers to my questions. Attend me, if you please. We will depart as soon as the prince returns from his dawn perambulation."

Elen looked into the camp. Snip was folding up the cot she had slept on, and the concubines were unrigging the deck's curtains. The cook was sealing up a traveling pot of hot tea for the road, while his assistants stowed the traveling kitchen. "They're moving fast."

"Palace menials perform their duties well, or they wouldn't still be in the palace. This way."

Luviara led Elen across the path, keeping clear of the cluster of wardens, and led her toward the statues. She halted before they reached the causeway, thank goodness. From this distance, the head that so uncannily resembled Prince Gevulin's couldn't be clearly seen.

"The prince has told us to make ready to depart and to not stray toward the Spires because there is no time to fetch us back. I was not invited to go with the party that entered the ruins last night. I confess to the sharpest curiosity. You have been inside?"

"I have. I walk this circuit every month, the same route, as I have for ten years. I scout the ruins for Spore each season, as part of my regular rounds."

"You know this place well."

"I do know it well. Better than anyone alive, I daresay."

"No false modesty for you, Deputy Courier."

As if competence were something to apologize for! Jaw tight, Elen said, "I don't have time for false modesty, Worthy Interlocutor. Pray, pardon my blunt speaking."

"No, indeed, I welcome it. Tell me what you know of this place."

Elen knew how to play this game. Give the minimum and make them ask for more. "The locals call it Three Spires. Inside, you will find a holystone pavement, a trough, and a pure-water spring."

"An odd place to find a spring, I should think."

"There's another spring—not pure-water—at the base of the promontory. That is why the hamlet was built there. As far as I've been told, there has always been a spring up here, however odd it may seem."

Luviara glanced at her, as if she suspected Elen of mocking her. "Has anyone from the Halt ever tried to discover the spring's source? How it rises so far through the rock?"

"I doubt it. The locals fear this place. They would never trouble the area with digging or poking around."

"I see. There are a number of ancient towers and compounds of this type across the empire. More can be found in the borderlands of the Desolation, and even along the eastern frontier. These towers, or *spires* as they're called, were raised long before the founding of the Tranquil Empire."

"The archivists write that the first emperor built them."

Luviara tipped her head with a flash of irritation. "The early gazettes do claim that. Those were written by flattering officials who hoped to gain a higher rank in the new empire."

"I see," said Elen, careful to hide her amazement. Even Joef's aunt, who always had an opinion about archives and archivists, never spoke so critically.

Luviara went on. "Chronicles written by actual scholars agree the Spires come from a much earlier age. Although it's true these accounts are kept inside the Diamond Chamber, accessible only to a few."

"Do they say the Spires come from the wicked age of the evil sorcerer-kings? That's what the locals say."

"Sorcerer-kings are an appealingly dramatic legend, but we have no records to prove they actually existed."

"Isn't sorcery forbidden on pain of burning? Wouldn't the presence of such a ban suggest sorcerers once existed?"

"A ban is not proof. There's been no trace of sorcery ever found in the empire. Just vague warnings about its evil, in old chronicles and lurid theater. Legends may spring from any kind of misunderstood source or fanciful storytelling. To investigate the truth of the past is the task my superiors set me when I was young. Among other things, I have a particular interest in these tower compounds."

Elen nodded encouragingly, hoping the theurgist would go on and maybe even reveal secrets that a humble deputy courier could not otherwise access.

And Luviara did go on. "So far, I have explored seventeen such ruins, none as intact as these Spires are. According to *Wisdom of the Four Sages*, the Spires were built by an ancient people, for their own purposes, after which they vanished forever from the world."

Was the vision seen from the scaffolding a magical illusion that had somehow remained stable for untold generations, or was it something else? And if so, then what was it? A vision of the High Heavens? Or of the builders themselves?

Luviara's hand tightened on her journal. "Have you some information you can share with me? Local stories, perhaps? I welcome such accounts to add to my storehouse."

Elen smiled in her most pleasant manner, what Kem called her "putting folks off" expression. "My . . . ah . . ." She carefully did not glance toward Kem. ". . . my colleague and I recently read *Cantilever of the Wits.*"

"You're well-read for a deputy courier."

"The intendant encourages study and reflection for his officials. His archivist brings in all the latest work from the heartland. The author of the *Cantilever* suggests the wicked sorcerer-kings of old built the Spires for evil reasons. As it says, 'Not through the manipulation of benign spirits but by the corruption of poisonous sorcery did the wicked sorcerer-kings wield a withering power that, instead of elevating them to the High Heavens as they had in their arrogance desired, instead raked them entirely from the land like waste raked from a garden to clear it of toxins and pests.'"

The theurgist sighed. "I see you are determined to champion the more lurid tales of the poets and playwrights."

"*Cantilever of the Wits* was written by a noted philosopher, was it not?"

"In the heartland, we would say a 'wineshop philosopher,' but you are correct that his writings are popular these days."

"What have your investigations revealed to you, Interlocutor?" Elen guessed it would be hard for a person like Luviara to resist a chance to expound on her pet ideas. So it proved.

"It's true that *Wisdom of the Four Sages* is too cautious in the conclusions it draws. In this regard, I prefer *Catechism of the Lost Days.* Its authors identify the 'old ones' who built the towers as the forebears of the aivur."

"The aivur didn't vanish, though."

"No, but they are barbarians who live to fight and raid along our borders. Therefore, it's difficult for people to imagine they might have built such impressive structures, especially since none of the nations of the Wolves—not Sea, not Blood, not Forest—live in magnificent cities built out of stone with skilled masonry and masterful craftsmanship. But I would argue the proof lies in the statues. These seem

to represent people strengthened by the attributes of powerful animals. Thus, they are more dangerous than any human enemy."

"Is that what you believe?"

"The authors of *Catechism of the Lost Days* had self-interested reasons for writing about the aivur in a hostile way, as the *Catechism*
was distributed at the same time as the Magnolia Emperor's exile
decree. It's likely they were writing at her command, in order to turn
popular opinion against the aivur. That's why I take the *Catechism of
the Lost Days* with a grain of salt."

Elen had a hard time keeping a bland expression. Such words bordered on treasonous speech against the throne, to suggest the emperor had manufactured outrage in order to hurry along her demand
that all aivur then living within the borders of the empire depart to
the frontier.

Luviara went on without pausing, wrapped up in her enthusiasm
for the topic. "A link between the mysterious builders and the living
aivur of today is not one I have been able to confirm, one way or
the other. That's why this set of statues interests me particularly. At
other walkways leading to other Spires I have seen wrecked plinths,
broken legs, those with no head or torso, and an occasional damaged but mostly complete statue, some of which wear the heads of
animals. Usually with the features partly smashed. But never have
I seen six intact, untouched statues as we see here. I did not even
know this group existed, which is a complaint I intend to file with
the surveyors when we return."

"Return from where?" Elen asked.

Luviara shook a hand in a scolding gesture. "When we return
from the prince's mission, which is no business of yours, Deputy
Courier."

Elen dipped her chin, ready to be done with this troubling conversation, which skated far too close to dangerous waters for her
liking. Maybe a theurgist had some kind of protection that allowed
her to speculate so freely in a public space. A deputy courier did not.
"As you say, I am merely a guide. To that end, I should fetch my
pack, so I do not delay our departure."

"I have not finished my questions. According to *Wisdom of the
Four Sages,* the statues are intended as representations of the builders. But in *Catechism of the Lost Days,* it is suggested the statues
might actually *be* the builders."

"Are you saying the theurgists believe magic can turn a person into stone?" Elen thought of how the statue had vanished and re-appeared.

"Theurgy cannot do so, but perhaps sorcery could. How can we know what the ancients could accomplish?" Luviara flicked a gesture heavenward, as if in appeal to the High Heavens. "No theurgist kens the root of sorcery."

"You said you don't believe that the wicked sorcerer-kings of old ever existed."

"I did not say that. I said I don't have proof, only conjecture. However, it is fair to say that lack of proof also doesn't mean a thing didn't happen. Many sages claim such powerful sorcery never existed, that it is a fable. The powers sorcerers are said to have seem impossible. Others say that, even if sorcery did exist once, the knowledge of true sorcery was lost long ago and the febrile attempts of the occasional desperate criminal to practice its cruel arts are just play-acting, not real. Yet when she promulgated her exile decree, the Magnolia Emperor quoted scholars who claim the Sea Wolves and Blood Wolves and Forest Wolves still practice a debased form of sorcery. That they carry poison inside them in the form of ingested Spore that has twisted their hearts into those of beasts. That is why they think only of their earthly appetites, and not of the exalted decrees of the High Heavens."

Elen rubbed her forearm, caught herself doing it, and squeezed her hand into a fist as she lowered it to her side. "What is your question, Your Worthiness?"

Luviara gave her a long look. "You know something you're not telling."

"How many delightful people I've had sexual congress with?" said Elen lightly. She expected the theurgist to berate her. Instead, the woman laughed.

"I like you, Deputy Courier. But there is something about you I cannot explain." She held up her journal. "I've spent my life recording the unusual, the hidden, the puzzles and labyrinths to which we, as yet, have no answers, or perhaps have lost an answer our forebears once knew. Are you one of those puzzles?"

"I do not see what is puzzling about my loyal work. Deputy couriers are found in every intendancy in the empire. I am one of eleven such deputies based in Orledder Halt. We serve at the behest of the intendant."

"Yet a Manor lord calls you a thief and murderer. Meanwhile, in the Halt, I heard people refer to you as the boy's aunt. That made me wonder why he speaks in the Orledder manner and not with the Woodfall lilt, as Lord Duenn and his followers? Was he not raised in Duenn Manor? I call it a puzzle. What would you call it, Deputy Courier?"

"I would call it time to depart," said a new voice, an amiable voice, speaking behind Elen.

She didn't recognize the man's voice, not until she saw Luviara's face tighten with surprise and dismay.

The woman slapped a hand to her chest as if she were reflexively protecting herself. "Your Highness!"

"So it seems."

A stunned Elen turned to find Prince Gevulin standing an arm's length behind her, studying her with what looked remarkably like jubilation, as if he'd finally understood a convoluted joke.

26

A PRAGMATIC SUGGESTION

The deputy courier, in the flesh," he added, with the haunt's sardonic smile.

Elen pressed a hand to her heart, the only reaction she could manage. The intensity of his gaze staggered her. Her legs felt numb.

She licked her lips once, twice, a third time, and finally choked out, "Your Exalted Highness."

"So I am repeatedly reminded. Yet what does it all mean, I wonder." He cast his gaze around the promontory, along the slopes, and up at the ridge, as if scouting his position. "I thought there would be more trees."

How does this work? she wondered as her thoughts bolted into a wild gallop. Was the prince playing a deep game, or was this truly the haunt alight and alive behind the prince's eyes? If it was the haunt, did he have access to the prince's memories or was he walking as in dark night, trying to negotiate without being able to see a single landmark? What would happen if his retinue became suspicious? Yet had any of them, even Luviara, ever heard a tale of a Spire-haunt who steals bodies? Elen hadn't, not until yesterday, because she'd never thought to ask and her predecessor had never mentioned it, if he'd even known. Therefore, why would such a possibility occur to these city-bred outsiders from the heartland? Furthermore, Luviara had admitted she'd never seen an intact Spire, so maybe she'd had no chance to stumble across any stories about haunts related to a full set of towers.

The wardens clustered behind the prince. They all wore similar expressions of bafflement and alarm. It confirmed Elen's guess that this behavior was out of character for the man they served. Their confused hesitation gave her an opening to warn him, if indeed it was the haunt. If indeed it was not just the prince showing a more relaxed side of himself. But she found it difficult to imagine the Master of the Lyre and Preeminent Bard of the Twelve Cycles and the Three Hundred and Sixty Poems of the Glorious Founder ever relaxing so far as to address a provincial deputy courier.

She had to take this chance to confirm what she alone suspected. Only then could she decide how to proceed.

To speak to him directly would unleash all manner of trouble, so she turned to Luviara. Like the wardens, the theurgist was trying not to gape at the exalted prince.

Elen said, "Worthy Interlocutor, I speak to you as I am commanded to do. As a mere deputy courier, I am scarcely fit to address any imperial warden, much less the All-Seeing Eye of the Imperial Order of Wardens, an exalted Prince of the Third Estate who serves the Magnolia Emperor, His Blessed Elder Sister, as do all those fortunate enough to live in the Tranquil Empire which she rules. But I request, with humility, that you relay my words to the exalted prince, for his consideration."

Worried someone would interrupt her, she raced on in a voice too loud and with words tumbling too fast for people to easily break in.

"In Orledder Halt, from which we so recently departed, just yesterday afternoon, the intendant established that this detour through the Moonrise Hills is necessary. That's because of the avalanche that blocks the imperial road through Grinder's Cut. Of course, I hope His Exalted Highness will discover the new route to be pleasing, since I am tasked with guiding him to the only other place where we can cross the deep canyon we call the Cut. I understand the exalted prince requires our journey to be as swift as possible, because his schedule requires urgency. To that end, I ask you, I implore you, to suggest to the exalted prince that he send the carriages and beasts back to Orledder Halt. They will only slow us down in the hills. They cannot cross the Cut, not by any means nor magic, except on the imperial road via Five Bridges. Also, as one who knows this route through the Moonrise Hills, I would suggest the exalted prince reduce the numbers of his retinue."

Captain Simo stepped forward as if to object. Elen rushed on before he could break in.

"First of all, we will move faster by taking only the strongest who can maintain a steady pace. Second, we will pass through hill country villages and hamlets. Such communities will be honored to provide shelter and food for such an exalted visitor. However, these are small communities who struggle to have enough to eat from season to season. I must humbly suggest that a smaller party will place less of a burden on the locals. There is no need to use up food the locals will desperately need come early spring. The palace does not wish its subjects to starve. As it is said, the emperor stands as the Shield of Peace and Prosperity. Let the exalted prince tread lightly on his journey into the north."

The words had rushed out with such force and at such speed that, when she paused, there was a gap of silence as if no one was sure if she had finished, or were shocked she had the temerity to say so much. Simo appeared confounded, while Luviara blinked. Elen wasn't sure if it was a signal meant for her or merely the theurgist gathering her thoughts.

No need to wonder what Chief Menial Hemerlin thought of her speech. Anger reddened his face. "How dare you! A mere deputy courier, to speak with such insolence—"

"I say," said the prince, raising a hand. The gesture halted Hemerlin in his tracks. "I say, this sounds like a pragmatic suggestion that will allow my urgent mission to succeed. Unless there is some unspoken desire among some of you for my mission not to succeed? Would it not be best to tell me now, if that were true?"

He examined Hemerlin with a quizzical frown, and then the gathered wardens, and the menials and concubines who had emerged from the encampment to watch the exchange. Elen did not know these people at all, but in any other company, she would have thought them to be as mystified as if they had never heard the like before and didn't know what to make of it.

"Is there anyone here who believes the mission should not succeed?" The prince's brow clouded with intimidating disapproval.

Every person, menial and warden alike, dropped to their knees. Elen realized she alone still stood. She knelt as well, hoping no one had noticed her lapse. Fortunately, they had all covered their faces with their hands as a mark of shame.

"The fault is ours, Exalted Highness," cried Hemerlin into his palms. "I pray to the High Heavens that you will punish us as we deserve, according to your accustomed practice."

The prince caught Elen's eye. She had neglected to cover her face in abject humility, mainly because she hadn't known she was supposed to.

She gave a slight shake to her head, hoping he would interpret it as a warning against any attempt to guess at the prince's accustomed practice. Was Hemerlin setting a trap? Or was this palace protocol?

The prince shrugged in answer, lifting his hands as if to ask how he should therefore proceed.

She rolled a hand in a circular motion as encouragement for him to go on as he had begun.

He gave a little cough, then continued speaking. "Alas, matters of discipline must wait. We will proceed into the north with all haste. Therefore, send the carriages and beasts back to Orledder Halt."

Again he paused, tilting a glance at her in query. Again, she nodded, grateful the retinue were still cowering behind their hands, fearful of his displeasure. Was Hemerlin peeking? She hoped not.

"We will proceed with the smallest party that is feasible for the journey." He considered the Spires. A complicated expression played across his face, one she could not interpret. He gave a curt sigh, as of someone making ready for an unpleasant task. "I am thirsty. While I drink, you will sort things out. Then we will go."

Again, he quirked an inquiring eyebrow at her, and she dipped her chin in the hope he would understand that being very general in his commands was his best means for going forward.

"Very good!" he finished cheerfully. No one moved. He added, with a puzzled frown, "Is there some reason you are all waiting?"

She thought he meant it as a genuine question, but the wardens and menials heard it as displeasure and sprang into action. For herself, she fetched her pack and settled into a comfortable squat on the path to wait out of their way.

The camp was stowed and secured in chests and bags. The prince stood watching while activity swirled around him, with him at its center. By the door to the prince's carriage, the concubines had a heated discussion, which ended with multiple bows before the prince, after which he was offered different footgear. Obedient to their wishes and clearly intrigued by the new boots, he sat on a footstool brought for him and allowed them to take off the carriage shoes he was wearing and replace them with walking boots.

The byplay distracted Elen for too long. The carriages were closed up and pulled into a column, and the beasts woken and harnessed. It was time to go. What of Kem? She'd lost track of Kem!

She jumped to her feet, craning her neck. At first, she didn't see him among the people making ready to leave with the carriages, nor with the smaller group gathered around the prince. Then she realized Kem had already headed out. He was walking with Ipis down toward the holystone post, as scouts sent ahead. She hadn't noticed him pass because he was wearing a warden's uniform instead of the long jacket she'd patched so many times that she could have identified it with her eyes closed, simply by feeling out the pattern of mending.

Ipis halted every few paces and drew patterns onto the ground with the tip of her shrive-steel saber, a glow burning brightly where the tip touched the ground before fading to nothing. Besides the uniform, Kem had also been given a shrive-steel saber, as if the wardens kept extra of these most precious implements. Probably they did. They used them to kill Spore.

As Ipis made comments to Kem, too distant for Elen to hear, Kem copied the pattern the warden had drawn, although his sword tip did not spark as hers had. He was careful and precise, as he always was. When he finished, the young woman patted him on the shoulder with a big grin. They spoke together with easy camaraderie. He laughed. Ipis waved toward the sky as if that explained something she was telling him.

The two young people had hit it off, Elen thought. To the other wardens, Kem was Manor-born and thus worthy of being in their company. He wouldn't be treated with contempt.

Yet she was aware of a sour bite to her relief, the fear that Kem might find a warden's life appealing. That he was walking away from his life with her. Had her hope that he would find a way to stay in Orledder Halt been concern for his safety in a harsh world, or just her own desire to keep him close?

She had no memory of ever being truly alone in her life, even as difficult as that life had been. Her muddiest early memories were of arms holding her gently and faces smiling, their features forgotten, but a sense of care and concern knitted into her bones. She had lost these others somehow, although she had no clear memory of who they had been or how tiny El had become separated from them. By accident? By force? Had she been lost? Or cast away?

The snap of leather cords painfully stung her arm, out of nowhere. She swung around, ready to defend herself. While she'd been staring at Kem, Hemerlin had approached. He raised the fly whisk, making ready to strike a second time. The viper flared to life, as sharp as a prickling of needles. Everything slowed, the air, the flick of the cords, the contempt in the man's glare like a cloud of ash boiling toward her. Elen shifted sideways so the second flick of the cords missed her.

"Deputy Courier, your attention!" Hemerlin was clearly angry at her refusal to be struck. But he didn't try again. "We did not bring you to stand scatter-witted and dumbfounded among us. We depart at once. Hop! Hop! No time to daydream."

"Chief Menial, I am ready to go whenever the party is assembled."

"Don't think I don't understand what you did."

"What I did?" she asked foolishly. Had he realized the truth?

"You spoke out of turn. You wish for a reward for your services beyond what is due to the likes of you, by pretending you are crucial to the success of the prince's mission. You'll no doubt cheat to obtain it. Don't think I don't see through you and your scheme."

She had to school her expression to hide her relief. He just thought she was greedy and ambitious. "I serve the empire, Chief Menial. If you consult my service record at the Halt, you will find it exemplary. My current responsibility is to guide His Exalted Highness across the Cut."

Hemerlin's lips curled back angrily. "You are insolent and disrespectful. Your sort may get away with that kind of behavior among officials like the Orledder intendant, who have been exiled to the provinces, but you will not be able to get away with it under my supervision. Do I make myself understood to you?"

She opened her eyes wide to give herself an expression of innocence, as difficult as it was for her to manage the look. "Are you to be one of the party accompanying His Exalted Highness?"

He quivered, chin trembling. "You may believe me to be too old for a grueling journey, but I assure you, Deputy Courier, I will not be the one to fall behind."

"I said nothing about your age or fitness, Chief Menial. I was only asking the question so I could know how many people to expect."

"No one merely asks a question. There is always an ulterior motive."

She was growing tired of his antagonism but, however angry he made her, she knew enough to pretend to misunderstand the thrust of his remark. "Perhaps that is true in the sophisticated palace, Chief Menial. But out here in the provinces, we are a simple people. Such layers of meaning lie far beyond our humble experience."

"You are an accused thief and murderer. I will be keeping an eye on you."

"As you wish, Chief Menial. I have nothing to hide." She delivered the lie straight to his face. Her exchange with the-prince-who-might-be-the-haunt had given her firmer ground to stand on. The haunt needed to go north, and the prince's party needed to go north, and she truly was the only one who could get them there. For now, that gave her a measure of protection.

27

DESTINED TO BE A CHARMING ADVENTURE
AND NOT A TEDIOUS SLOG

The carriages departed with sparks of magic shimmering off the beasts. The concubines leaned out of their carriage window to wave silk handkerchiefs in sobbing farewells. Elen couldn't tell if their emotion was real, or feigned according to palace protocol. One of the wardens was assigned to return with the carriages to Orledder Halt, where Lord Duenn was certainly brooding on revenge. To her relief, the warden sent back was not Kem. Although he was now wearing a warden's uniform, it was only the prince's authority that truly protected him.

She had to take charge of the next stage of the journey. Even stripped down to a "small" party, they were eleven, a bigger group than she had hoped for, but she'd work with what she had.

In her experience, it was best to simply start as she meant to go on. She set out walking and left the rest to follow in whatever formation they chose. First, she descended from the promontory to the holystone post where the path split. The carriages had taken the path back to Lancer's Ridge, while she turned north onto the route that led into the Moonrise Hills. She walked alone at the front, which suited her just fine. The first stage of the journey was a four-or-five-hour hike through what the locals called High Horse Valley, an upland saddle of ground whose slope ran steadily upward toward the true beginning of the Moonrise Hills.

About ten paces behind her walked Xilsi, alert, on guard. Behind Xilsi walked a warden Elen didn't recognize at first because the man was wearing an indigo scarf that concealed his hair. It took her a moment to recognize long-black-hair-in-a-bun Jirvy. In the empire, scarves were worn by women, not by men, yet the fantastically elaborate knotwork fastening the scarf gave the warden a swaggering air. No one else gave him a second glance, which made her think they had seen him wearing scarves before. He had a southern lilt to his speech; maybe folks wore things differently in the southern provinces. It was none of Elen's business, and, honestly, she admired how striking the style looked on him. Once, Xilsi glanced back as if annoyed, or checking Jirvy out, but Xilsi was a warden who knew her business and otherwise kept her attention on the landscape.

Simo ranged on and off the path, seeking signs of Spore. The big menial, Fulmo, came next. All the wardens carried extra gear to make up for the loss of the carriages. Fulmo carried a pack three times the size of everyone else's, but its weight did not seem to bother him.

By now Elen was sure that Fulmo was not an extremely large human but a gagast. The gagast homeland was rumored to be far to the east, or maybe beyond the trackless southern forests. They were rarely mentioned in early chronicles of the empire. A generation ago, small groups of them had appeared out of the Desolation, calling themselves exiles. The Hibiscus Emperor had magnanimously allowed them to serve in the palace.

Gevulin walked directly behind Fulmo. The prince was burdened only by a sheathed shrive-steel sword, a bow quiver with arrows slung across his back, his riding whip, and a small leather pouch like the one every deputy courier carried that held the tools for killing Spore. He was looking around with delighted interest. When he caught Elen's eye on him, he grinned. It wasn't so much that he was close enough for her to see his expression; it was the sudden lift to his walk and the amused tilt of his chin.

High Heavens! Was she glad of a prince's attention? Or, perhaps worse, that of a mysterious and perilous haunt?

This would not do. Yet she felt lightened, as if this expedition was destined to be a charming adventure and not a tedious slog. A hawk in the distance distracted the prince. He looked away to follow its flight as it stooped, diving after prey.

The sixth warden, Qari, was a stolid, silent man who had yet to speak in Elen's hearing. He walked behind the prince, alongside Luviara. The theurgist seemed to be having no trouble keeping up, despite her age. It was Hemerlin who was already lagging as they climbed. Kem and Ipis had been assigned as the rearguard. Kem was pointing out a pair of twin peaks now coming into view to the east, likely instructing Ipis in the local landmarks, as Elen had for him.

It was a good day to be outdoors. The sky was dappled with clouds like clumps of uncombed wool. The wind was cool but not cold, brisk but not strong. Late-blooming winter-beacon bushes dotted the hillside with purple flowers that only bloomed in autumn. Rock pigeons settled on a stony patch of ground to preen in the morning sun. No sweet rose-oil scent tainted the air. Maybe it would be an uneventful journey. A person could hope.

Captain Simo fell into step beside her with the ease of a man who has walked long distances. "What make you of the weather, Deputy Courier?"

They had come up high enough to get a dazzling view beyond Lancer's Ridge and onto the lowlands, the winding silver ribbon of the Sul River, the patches of woodland and the stripes of fields. Even from this great distance, the imperial road was visible like a brushstroke drawn across the land, one of the sinews that knit the empire into its whole.

She gestured toward the southwest. "We may get rain later in the afternoon. You can see a front shifting in as haze."

He squinted, shaded his eyes, and said, "You have sharp vision."

"I know what to look for."

He grunted softly.

She added, "By then, we should be in the forest. The trees will grant us some protection."

"Why are there no trees here?" he asked. The great saddle of land swept down below them with its thick grass and low-growing bushes.

"According to the records, one of the earliest irruptions of Spore happened here, during the reign of the Azalea Emperor. That's when the ruined village we passed had to be abandoned."

"The bone pile is from that irruption?"

"As far as I know. It was what surveyors call a fast-blowing irruption. Every living thing in this contained watershed was corrupted. A firebreak had to be dug to stop the spread, and everything inside it got burned. Plants, animals, people, everything. Nothing grew afterward for many years but eventually ground cover, grass, and shrubs came up, as we see now."

"Does Spore rise here often?"

"I'm told that, after the main irruption, for quite a while there were small outbreaks every year. The area had to be patrolled constantly, but it's been quiet for the ten years I've walked this route. I hope it is not rising again."

"Normally Spore avoids higher elevations."

"With your permission, Captain, I will note that Spore rises everywhere. It is Palls that cannot get a grip in high country. As a surveyor once said to me, 'The Pall hates salt, and yet sinks toward the level of the sea.'"

He frowned and did not reply. She wasn't sure if she had offended him by correcting him, or if he was thinking over what she'd said. Yet he was a man at least fifteen years older than she was, perhaps as old as fifty, experienced and competent enough to be accompanying a prince as his captain, a position of great honor and responsibility. He must know such a basic fact about Spore and the Pall. Was he testing her?

She could test, too. "I thought that for a journey of such length, an exalted highness would be accompanied by an imperial surveyor, who would know about the land beyond the roads."

"We did not expect to leave the road," he said curtly.

Simo left her and began ranging again, up and down and back and forth along the path, gaze scanning the ground and then the horizon and then the sky, as restless as a man must be who seeks to protect his precious charge. It must gall him to know that he, like his prince, had been so easily misled by a rival hoping to harm the prince. Fortunately, the convoluted inner workings of the palace were none of Elen's business.

She proceeded in silence through the morning, enjoying the solitude even as she crept glances back to check on Kem. And to study the prince. If he was the prince.

As the sun reached zenith, they topped the long northern side of the upland valley. From here they would enter the Moonrise Hills with its ragged landscape rising and falling and rising toward a high plateau to the north. Trees began to grow on the northern side of the watershed, straggling at first, and then filling the land beyond with the rich scent of life. She could see birds on the wing, hear the creep and buzz of insects. In the far distance, at the edge of her hearing, she heard the chop of an axe against wood. Lazy drifts of smoke marked Sfendia Moat, her goal for the first day's march. They could reach there by nightfall if they pushed. Otherwise, they would have to overnight at Thistle Spring, and she didn't fancy its lack of defenses, in case there were bandits.

Xilsi and Jirvy halted to look back.

Xilsi said aloud, "Quite a view." The woman pointed at the distant Spires, so far away they might have been bony fingers trying to claw out of the rock.

Jirvy crossed his arms and ignored her.

The prince walked about one hundred paces behind, accompanied by Fulmo, Qari, and Luviara. The theurgist still had no trouble keeping pace with the younger folk. Her stride was long and easy, her body relaxed as she walked in the manner of a person who has journeyed on foot a great deal and enjoys it.

A long way back, the small figure that was Hemerlin toiled alone, clearly winded as he struggled up the long slope. Because they'd been assigned as rearguard, Kem and Ipis had no choice but to hang back behind the chief menial. As she watched, Kem came forward and seemed to be offering assistance to the man. She couldn't hear what was said, but Kem retreated, shoulders hunched defensively. Ipis set a hand on his shoulder and leaned close to speak in a supportive way. After a moment, he lifted his chin and nodded. A twinge of regret pinched Elen's heart. She'd always been the one to comfort him. Yet wasn't it heartening that he was getting along well with the person assigned to supervise his training? Camaraderie had to be good news. He'd taken the escape route open to him. There was no going back, since going back meant either Duenn Manor or life as a hunted fugitive. She knew better than to wish either of those fates upon her beloved boy.

"Deputy Courier!" Simo came up. "Is there a secure place the prince can rest for a short break?"

"Yes, Warden. That ring of cypresses—do you see it?"

"About two hundred paces down the trail?"

"It's a travelers' campsite."

Simo sent Xilsi and Jirvy to investigate, then waited alongside Elen. The prince strode vigorously up, not at all out of breath. She began to think His Exalted Highness had indeed climbed ten peaks, or even danced them, but as much as she wanted to make a jesting comment, she knew better than to do so. He clasped his hands behind his back and scanned the view with keen interest, but said nothing.

Luviara was puffing but also smiling. "Deputy Courier! I believe I have at last put it together. This must be the site of the great burning, what some chronicles call the Root and Branch Irruption, and others call the High Horse Valley Irruption."

"Yes, Your Worthiness. The ruined village we passed was known for its extensive herds. They supplied the needs of the Orledder Residency and provided pack horses for trade in the hills. But that was a long time ago. It's all gone now."

Down by the cypress circle, Xilsi gestured an all clear.

"Your Highness," said Simo, "there is a campsite where we can break for a short rest and refreshment. If you will."

The prince looked toward Xilsi, then back toward Hemerlin,

still a significant distance away. His gaze slid toward Elen, and he arched an eyebrow, as if to ask what the correct decision would be.

Simo followed the wordless exchange with a frown. "Your Highness, I will escort you to the campsite. Qari will wait here for the others."

"I can wait," said Elen, hoping for a chance to speak to Kem.

"Qari will wait for the others," said Simo. "As for you, Deputy Courier, this break will be a good time for you to show us your map."

"My apologies, Warden. I'm not a surveyor, to carry a map. The route is all in my head."

"I see." He bowed to the prince. "Your Highness, if you will allow me to accompany you."

The prince cast one look back toward the stragglers, then descended to Xilsi. The cypress grew where the ground leveled out in a kind of terrace. Twelve slender cypresses surrounded a travelers' campsite with a brick hearth, stone blocks laid as benches, and a lean-to set to give shelter from wind, rain, or snow. Elen had wondered who would serve the prince in the absence of any menials besides the hulking Fulmo, but the big gagast had a deft and delicate hand, despite his size. He unpacked a sealed pot of hot tea, beautifully carved ebony-wood cups, and lacquered food boxes decoratively packed with halved cooked eggs, cold fried chicken, burdock root, bean curd, pickled vegetables, and cold noodles.

Elen sat off to one side with a round of flatbread and a wedge of salty cheese. The group ate in silence, with first Xilsi and then Jirvy standing watch. After the prince had finished, and Fulmo had wiped clean His Exalted Highness's hands, Simo called Elen over. She pressed her hands to her chest respectfully as the prince, seated on a stone slab, regarded her almost slyly, as if wondering how she would handle whatever came next.

"What can you tell us about the route ahead?" Luviara asked.

"Worthy Interlocutor, my thanks. May I ask if the wardens carry any surveyors' maps of this region?"

"We do not," said Simo curtly. "Our business is the roads, not the countryside."

"So be it. Fortunately, I know these hills well. It will be possible to reach Grinder's Cut in six days, if we can keep to the pace I have set so far."

She had been thinking about Hemerlin's suspicious nature all morning. This was her chance to get rid of him.

She went on, "However, I regret to inform you that the path ahead will challenge the chief menial. This slope has already set him back. It is by no means the worst of what we'll face today, much less tomorrow. For example, today we can reach Sfendia Moat by sunset, but not if we have to travel at his pace. I mean no disrespect to an imperial servant. If this party wishes to make good time, then I am not sure what to tell you." She looked through a gap between the trees, toward the top of the slope, but there was still no sign of Hemerlin. Qari had vanished, and Elen had no idea why.

"Leave Hemerlin behind if he cannot keep up," said the prince.

Simo grimaced. "Your Highness! Chief Menial Hemerlin has served you since you were a child. He knows you better than anyone. Indeed, you have never traveled anywhere without him in attendance. You cannot simply abandon him."

"Abandon? I did not say to abandon the man. He may follow the carriages back to the Halt, may he not? Is that impractical or impossible? What does the deputy courier say?"

"He could do so, it's true," Elen said encouragingly. "With help he can return to Orledder Halt safely by sunset, although he would need to turn around now to manage it."

The prince raised a hand imperiously. "Simo, make it happen. We have rested for long enough. We must move on."

"What about Kem?" Elen said, then caught herself and added, "Worthy Interlocutor, I beg your pardon for speaking out of turn. What of Novice Warden Kem? He and Warden Ipis aren't here yet."

"A trainee is of little use to us on this sort of journey," said Simo. "We can easily detach him to escort the chief menial back."

The prince rose, and she felt him studying her face. He said, "No, no, send someone else. The best training for a fledgling is to fly, not to be stuck in the nest."

Xilsi looked up from the food she was eating. "Simo, you know why I volunteered for this mission. Don't send me back."

The captain sighed. "Qari, then, although I hate to lose him. He's a good fighter, are we to meet any brigands in these hills."

The prince smiled, and there was something eager, almost cruel, in his eyes. "Brigands will certainly regret meeting us. That's settled, then. Let us go. The others can catch up, can they not?"

28

The prince headed back to the path, Xilsi and Jirvy hurrying to keep pace. Elen grabbed her pack and hastened after. By the hearth, Fulmo was repacking. She paused beside him and said, "Are you all right, Menial Fulmo? Do you need help?"

A low sound rumbled in his chest, and he flicked a hand—a hand big enough to wrench her head from her shoulders, she did not doubt—to show she could go on about her business.

Luviara chuckled. "Fear not. We won't lose the doughty Fulmo."

Simo had gone back to find Qari and the others. Elen still could not see them. Suddenly, the sound of Hemerlin's voice pierced the midday calm with the start of a fierce argument. Best to get as far away from that tumult as possible! Elen headed after the prince, who stood aside to allow her to take the lead. They descended into a drowsy woodland striped with shadows and light. After some time, the number of footfalls behind her doubled, and she looked back to see Simo, Kem, and Ipis catching up at a jog. Behind them came Fulmo, his big strides devouring twice as much ground, and she realized he had to hold back to not outpace the others.

She settled in for a long afternoon of ascents and descents. There was one rough scramble up a rocky escarpment hewn with primitive stairs. She called a halt at the exposed landmark known as Thistle Spring. Pure-water springs were commonly found in difficult-to-reach places, like this windswept terrace too small to house a settlement and the fields or grazing needed to support it. A small Heart Temple had been built, with a crude wall to create a courtyard. A bamboo pipe stuck into a large black stub of rock filtered the spring's water into a holystone basin that someone long ago had hauled up here. The basin's overflow trickled into a trough carved from the local rock. There was also an emergency shelter tucked into a shallow cave. A custodian came out at intervals to clean and repair the temple, but no one was here now.

As the wardens waited their turn to drink from the basin, Elen slid over to where Kem stood at the temple gate. Resting her fingers on his arm, she murmured, "How are you doing? Is all well?"

His mouth pinched. "I'm fine. Can't you see I'm busy?" He jerked his arm away and stalked down to where Ipis was standing guard at the hewn stairs that led up to the terrace and its blessed spring.

Elen winced. The encounter with Lord Duenn and the past he represented had all happened so fast, and in the worst way. The prince was watching her, and she thought he was about to ask a question. She dipped her chin in warning, hoping he would say nothing.

Simo finished filling his leather bottle and called out, "Let's move!"

The prince said, "Have all in the party had a drink from the spring?"

"Yes, yes," said Simo impatiently, looking at the sky. It would be dark soon.

"I believe the deputy courier has not yet drunk. Let her do so."

"Pray give my thanks to His Highness," Elen said to Luviara, torn between wishing the prince had said nothing and being grateful that he had. On her circuit, she always filled her bottle with Thistle Spring's pure-water. Such water was said to grant vigor and health. Maybe so, but regardless, pure-water would slow down Spore if a person had nothing else.

"Make haste!" snapped Simo.

She filled her leather bottle, took a draught of the refreshingly cold water, filled the bottle again, and wiped her face and washed her hands with water that had collected in the trough. Then she led the way onward.

They reached Sfendia Moat in the last hour before sunset. Children brought in the goats with ringing bells and herded sheep into a stockade ringed by a water-filled ditch. Folk were still out in the gardens, preparing fields for the coming winter.

One of the tillers spotted her and came running. "Deputy Courier, do you bring a reply from my sister?"

"Not now," said Elen kindly.

The woman took in the presence of the wardens and stopped in her tracks, staring. Wardens didn't come to hill country villages, not even ones like Sfendia, which boasted a true moat lined with holy-stone.

Curious people gathered up their tools and hurried after the party, eager to find out who had come. At the bridge, the sentinel on duty said, "What's this, Elen? How are you come back so soon? Are these wardens?"

Luviara took charge, raising her voice with a piercing announcement. A prince of the imperial line! Captain of a Thousand! Guardian of the Absinthe Grove!

Everything in the village came to a halt.

The village archon cleared out his own compound so the prince might spend the night in the best bed the village had to offer. Villagers came crowding to sit in the dirt plaza before the archon's house, hoping for a glimpse of the exalted highness. Nothing so exciting had ever happened here. The youngest child present would pass on the memory of this day to their grandchildren, should they live that long.

Since Elen did not belong in the retinue, she was happy to retire to her usual traveling quarters at the village's tiny Heart Temple. The temple served the village's ritual needs and, as required by imperial law, provided a hostelry for travelers who hadn't the means to pay for room and board, as well as minor officials like deputy couriers.

This temple lacked a pure-water spring like the one at Thistle Spring, so the local archon hadn't invested extra effort to expand it. A Declaration Week wreath hung at the modest entry porch. The arch let onto a walled courtyard. The altar was tucked into the eastern wall, which backed up against the archon's compound. The temple had only a single custodian, no theurgist or specialized healer. The custodian slept in a tiny room built into the south wall. The hostel itself was nothing more than a long stone room with shutters and a row of crude bunk beds, laced with rope to sleep on. Elen had slept in far worse places. The hostel was safe, dry, and heated by a brick oven in the winter that could double as a hearth for warming porridge. The temple had its own latrine connected to the more elaborate plumbing system in the archon's compound.

The temple's custodian was going out the gate as she came in. Ralt was a wizened, good-natured old fellow, who liked to play a game of draughts on the evenings she stayed at the temple. Today, he clapped his hands together nervously. "Forgive me! I'm on my way to attend the archon. Is it true?"

"Yes, the wardens are escorting a prince. Did an imperial messenger come through from Orledder Halt? It can't have been yesterday, so maybe earlier today?"

"No messenger stopped here at the temple."

"No? I saw a messenger leave the Halt, wearing a yellow headband."

Maybe the runner had gone elsewhere, unrelated to the prince. Yet it seemed unlikely.

"Apologies, Deputy Courier." His gaze darted past her toward the street. People were still hurrying past, headed for the plaza in front of the archon's compound.

"Go on. You'll not see His Exalted Highness's like again."

Ralt hurried out just as a stout, middle-aged woman appeared. Tevira had the strong forearms of a baker. Instead of her work-day apron, she'd pulled on her treasured festival tabard, and she'd scrubbed her face and hands, one knuckle bleeding slightly where she'd rubbed too anxiously. "Deputy Courier, you're back so soon. I've had no chance to collect more of the payment due to the lender."

"That's not why I'm here. The payment's not due yet. Be calm."

Yet Tevira dithered. "I had a whole batch of my sesame flatbread. I know how you like that specially, but the archon commandeered it all."

"Yes, I understand, Tevira. Did you see a messenger come through earlier today?"

"A messenger?" The question baffled the baker.

"Never mind. Go on. This shall be a festival night indeed for Sfendia Moat. You don't want to miss any of it. I'm sure the Exalted Highness will praise your excellent baking."

The woman fanned herself with a hand. "I think I would faint should such an exalted visitor taste my humble bread. My thanks! My thanks!" Then she, too, was gone.

Elen was happy to be left to herself. She set aside her curios-ity about the mysterious runner and busied herself cooking barley porridge for her supper, which she flavored with late-season berries and aromatic spine-seal she'd gleaned from alongside the path as she'd had the chance. Afterward, because she didn't expect anyone to come into the temple, she took the opportunity to strip naked and wash thoroughly. She went to bed wearing only her under-shift, grateful for this rare chance on the road to be this clean and comfortable. Sfendia Moat was an orderly and peaceful village. She hardly expected the prince's party to be ready to go at dawn, espe-cially if the archon was allowed to entertain them with feasting and drinking, as a local official would surely wish to do.

As always, in Sfendia, she rolled her blanket onto her preferred lower bunk, which had a view out through open shutters and onto the courtyard. From here, she could both hear and see the fountain.

Every Heart Temple had a fountain in its courtyard, a constant stream of potable water poured into a basin and trough. As it was said in the temple liturgy: *All may drink at the Heart, for it is the knowledge of the Heart which eases our thirst and gives sustenance to life.* Some of these fountains were simple, some elaborate; a few were pure-water, while most were spring water or water piped in from the nearest free-flowing stream or river. Each was unique, according to the principle that each heart is bound to its own unique destiny beneath the High Heavens. The fountain in this humble temple was Elen's favorite of all the temples she stopped at on her regular circuit.

Its shallow, circular basin was a perfect place to cool off in the heat of summer. Children often came here to play, splashing under the kindly gaze of Custodian Ralt. People with ailments they hoped he could cure would sit on the benches waiting their turn to see him. But what made this fountain so particularly wonderful wasn't Ralt's company, however much she enjoyed their games of draughts and their rambling discussions. It was the playful design of the fountain itself.

Rather than depicting an animal, as most did, it used the varied height and diameter of its many spouts to create a kind of endless music. Normally, at night, from the hostel, the water's melody amid the quiet village would soothe her to sleep. This evening, she was disturbed by the constant buzz of noise and occasional bursts of huzzahs or clamorous bouts of energetic song from the archon's compound.

She lay a while, too restless to sleep, although she was tired. Where was Kem sleeping? Was he on watch? That he was angry at her was clear. Had she made the wrong choice to keep the truth from him? But she had done what Aoving had demanded, and Kem was Ao's child, not hers, even if in every other way he was her child too.

She'd had to respect Ao's wishes. Hadn't she? What if Kem refused to forgive her?

Far earlier than she expected, the rousing celebration came to an end. A dull silence settled over Sfendia Moat. Her troubled thoughts calmed as the fountain's music eased her, and her eyes closed.

She startled awake. The rhythm of the fountain's falls of water had altered. A splash sounded, movement rippling the waters in the basin.

Elen raised herself onto an elbow so she could see out the window's shutters. The moon was only one day past full. Now at zenith, its light drenched the courtyard in a silvery glamor, as if the High Heavens had poured an irresistible enchantment directly onto the earth.

Maybe they had.

Because standing in the basin with the water spilling down around and over him, facing away from her, was a naked man.

29

Elen thought her heart was going to pound out of her throat. With an effort, she swallowed, trying to calm her racing pulse.

"Ah, you're awake," said the man in a soft voice, though she hadn't spoken.

She eased up from the bunk, tucking her knife into her left hand. After smoothing her shift down over her thighs, she padded barefoot out the door and into the courtyard. Because he was still facing away from her, she had a splendid view of his broad back, narrow hips, superb buttocks, and muscular legs. He extended his arms as Prince Gevulin had done at the Halt while his concubines had washed him. His posture was one of ease, not of tension.

"I'm finally getting a good look at this body," he remarked, sounding amused as he studied himself from tip to toe. "It seems quite . . . serviceable. What do you think, Deputy Courier? Is this body a healthy and creditable example of its type?"

He turned to face her, his arms still extended, everything on display and he with no apparent self-consciousness. The moonlight gilded him. Prince Gevulin was a handsome man in the way a masterfully crafted statue is handsome, burnished and painted so all may admire it, and its workmanship and polish more important than the core of its essence. The haunt—whoever or whatever he was—was dangerously beautiful not because of his features or proportions, but because he was smiling with a perilous delight, mischief in his eyes that could as easily turn to rapacity.

Well. Two could play this game.

She fixed her gaze resolutely on his face. Nothing about his stance threatened her, but she was sure it was a test. "I think you are in danger of waking the custodian, or the archon, and having to explain an action no imperial prince would ever take."

"Ah, but you see, they are all asleep."

"The entire village is asleep?" She sidestepped to get a look into the custodian's room. Ralt slept with the door open so folk seeking aid might easily rouse him. There was enough light that she could make out the old custodian stretched out on his humble cot. Ralt snorted in his sleep, sighed, and settled back.

"Are you truly unfamiliar with this simple enchantment?" the haunt asked.

"I've never heard of such a thing. It doesn't seem so simple to me. It seems powerful."

"Things can be both powerful and simple. You, for example."

"Me?" Again, she met his gaze, starting to feel annoyed.

He examined her face, lips curving up. "Am I distracting you?"

"From my sleep? Yes, you are."

"I crept out of the compound in order to speak to you," he admitted, "and also because I needed to see who I am now and what I have to work with. I rather enjoy this body. I apologize if I have in any way offended you or caused you distress. It was not intentional."

"Wasn't it?"

"A misunderstanding, perhaps, of the customs of this place. I beg you, Deputy Courier, to acquit me of ill intent."

He lowered his arms, which made his nakedness seem more approachable, less of a deliberate provocation and more of a random accident. Yet she remained powerfully aware that he attracted her and that, for her part, she was clad in only her undershift, whose hem barely reached the midpoint of her thighs. The brush of soft fabric against her skin made her more aware of the ridiculous sexuality of the situation. She didn't even know him, and she wasn't one to bed down with strangers for a single night's pleasure. More than that, she didn't think he was trying to seduce her, not physically anyway. Or perhaps he was measuring what other forms of influence and power he possessed in his new body, the way a young child is thrilled to discover they can stand on their own two feet.

What exactly did he want? In an odd way, he seemed both naïve and terribly dangerous.

"All right then, why am I awake if all the others are asleep?" she asked.

"We already had this discussion, did we not?"

"At the Spires?"

"When you refused me the loan of your young companion. In retrospect, this body serves my purpose better than the youth would have, so I thank you. But I have a lot of questions and the sleep enchantment won't last all night. You and I need to agree on a plan."

He waded out of the basin, sat on its edge, and patted the stone rim beside him in invitation.

"I see." She found his clothing in a rumpled heap on the ground and fished out undergarments and what appeared to be a tunic meant to be worn beneath a warden's tabard. The fabric was obscenely smooth, making a person want to keep caressing it. Enough! She extended an arm. After a moment, he took the garments, examined them, and dressed like someone who is figuring out how clothing works while in the act of putting them on. Once garbed, he sat on a bench, facing the fountain.

She sat at the opposite end of the bench, setting the knife on her other side, where he couldn't see it. "So, you are the haunt."

"Is that your word for me? The problem is that I am ignorant just when I need knowledge most. I inhabit the body but not the mind."

"That must be a relief for those individuals whose bodies are taken like this."

He sat up straighter, looking affronted. "Is that sarcasm?"

"You tell me."

"A passage spell is a temporary measure, a transference under-taken between two consenting parties."

"Did the prince consent?"

He frowned, tapping a finger against his chin. "The prince and I engaged in a complicated discussion. I explained the situation and politely made my request for his aid. He didn't say no. He said something on the order of 'I dare you to try,' or 'As if you think you can overwhelm a prince of the imperial palace,' or 'I don't believe it's possible so make your best effort.' I took it as invitation enough."

"Did he truly understand what he was getting into?"

The haunt leaned toward her. She held her ground. It wasn't that he scared her, precisely, but that she was certain he had the means to harm her and chose not to.

His tone was serious, all his blithe words vanished. "The situation is desperate. It appears both I and the prince are headed in the same direction. What harm is there that I am conveyed to my destination if I do not place any obstacle in his journey? He will get there safely, and so will I."

"I object to people being taken without their consent. If I mean the principle to apply to those I love, then it must also apply to those I dislike and to those I don't know."

"Yet here we are, and I am not you, nor have I your compunctions about this matter." He sat back, as if the matter were settled, and of course it was. He was in the prince's body now, and she doubted that anyone but him knew how to get him out. "But you seem skeptical, Deputy Courier. As I said, transference is a spell, devised to be carried out freely, without coercion, in times of need. Trust is needed because both parties are, shall we say, asleep to the other. That means I have no access to the thoughts or memories of my host, while my host falls into a state resembling slumber while I walk in his body."

"So the prince won't remember any of this?"

"He will not."

What a relief! "In that case, I see why trust is needed."

"Regardless, I can't leave this body. I mean that literally. There is nowhere for me to go, so I am fixed inside this flesh for now."

"When can you leave it?"

"Do you miss the prince? Do you have a relationship with him?"

"I do not know him at all, nor did I speak to him, nor would he ever have spoken to me. The prince's fate does not concern me, except insofar as he represents the empire and thus we are required to honor him. He did inadvertently do me a favor, though."

"Did he? How could he have done that if he never spoke to you?"

First, above all, she had to act to protect Kem. "He accepted Kem— the youth you saw with me—as a warden. This matters because Kem's sire is a cruel man and far more powerful than I am. He wants to take Kem away and force him to be something he's not, force him to do his bidding. So I am grateful to the prince for that. As long as Kem remains a warden, Lord Duenn can't take him away."

"You care about the boy."

"I care about him more than anyone else alive. But you didn't answer my question. When can you leave the body?"

"I'll keep that information to myself, if you please."

"I don't please, but I don't see I have a choice. What are your questions?"

"Ah. Yes. My many, many questions. I appreciated your quick thinking this morning. You gave me enough information to proceed."

"You really know nothing of who and what Prince Gevulin is, or where you are?"

"Nothing at all, except such scraps as I pick up as I go along. I need more. Who am I, really?"

"The haunt? You'll have to tell me."

He smiled. "You'll not catch me out so easily. I know who I am. I mean, what is the prince's status and his mission? How should I act so as not to betray my true nature? It was clever of you to rid us of that man, Hemerlin. He was already suspicious. He knew the prince too well not to see through my guise."

"What do you think will happen if the wardens become suspicious?"

"I don't know. Do you care to find out?"

"For Kem's sake, I prefer the prince not be killed or imprisoned. So yes, I'll help you. It's clear you need an ally, if you're as ignorant as you claim."

He grinned charmingly. "I assure you, I am exactly as ignorant as I claim."

She laughed, caught herself as she thought of how Aoving would have scolded her for laughing inappropriately. But then she thought, why not be amused? Life is too short. She was entertained by the haunt that walked in the prince's body. Probably that made her a bad person, but she was already a thief and murderer, so she would add it to her catalog of crimes. "Very well. But I have a price. Tell me your name and who you really are."

"Over the course of this day, I've come to see you humans are as profligate with your names as if they hold no power."

"Names don't hold power. They're just markers like signposts. Titles hold power. Laws hold power. Weapons hold power."

"I would not agree. For example, a signpost can be true or false and thus holds a great deal of power to set you on the right path or the wrong one. But that's a discussion for another time. I am one of the Shorn."

"The Shorn?"

"We who were shorn of our bodies so we could fight against the Shivering Tide and the Hollow Wind. For too many of us, our ends came brutally soon. But for others, like me, we still wait in our appointed places."

This was an astounding statement! "Are the statues really people from ancient days, turned to stone?"

"We are each of us a real individual, but we were not 'turned to stone,' as you so quaintly phrase it. The statues are more of an entry point, if you will. A gate through which we can pass."

In the distance, a dog barked.

The haunt looked up at the sky, listening, then turned to Elen with new urgency. "The sleep enchantment will wear off soon. I promise I will answer more of your questions when next we have a chance to speak in private. But for now, what must I know about Prince Gevulin, who he is and what he seeks?"

She wanted to question him further about himself, but there wasn't time right now. "I don't know what his mission is, except he said it is urgent warden business. I'm just a guide for this stage of the journey. Are there no written documents or dispatches you can consult?"

"There are documents being carried by Fulmo, but I can't read them. If you can read them aloud while I watch and listen, I should be able to learn the writing system."

"A deputy courier is not going to be invited to read palace documents, much less aloud to the prince. When we stop for the night, say you have a headache and instruct one of your wardens to read the documents to you so you can reacquaint yourself with the situation as you decide how to go forward, now you have been forced to travel by this detour. But don't ask. I don't know anything about the palace. This is just what I've observed in the past day. A prince never asks. A prince commands. A prince expects. A prince will act immediately if shown any form of disrespect."

He rested his chin on his hand, watching her. His gaze was unsettling, like a shadow, absorbing light, or maybe like light expanding to engulf shadow. "Go on."

"I suppose the safest thing is for you to speak as little as possible. The wardens are well trained. They know what they're doing, so let them do it. Luviara is not a warden. She's a theurgist—"

"A theurgist? Ah, that explains the spirits who lurk around her."

"Spirits?"

"That's what theurgy is, is it not? Or am I mistaken?"

"I don't know, as I am not a theurgist. Are you a theurgist?"

He gave a soft snort. "I am not. What does it mean to be a theurgist in this place?"

"All theurgists are assigned to the Heart Temple. However, Luviara has for some reason been attached to the prince as his interlocutor. That's the person who speaks for the prince to anyone outside of his retinue."

"So I noticed. I kept silent and let her speak to the archon and notables of this village."

"Good. But's she clever and curious, and she knows a lot. She will be alert for oddities. Be careful with her. I don't know if she reports to someone else."

"Reports?"

"Oh. Yes. The intendant—he is the official in charge of the Halt where I'm based—has told me a bit about how the empire works. The wardens guard the witch roads."

"Witch roads?"

"The imperial roads that are protected by magic against the Pall and Spore. The prince is headed toward a place called Far Boundary Vigil."

"What is a Vigil?"

"It's a warden tower built where a witch road meets a Pall. The Vigil tower functions as a kind of gate, or sentry post, if you will. I'm not a warden so I don't know how Vigils work exactly, just that they exist. I don't know why the prince is going there. Keeping the roads safe and clear is part of what the wardens do. Wardens are also said to be spies and intelligencers for the emperor."

"Ah. Travelers on the road who can report what they see."

"Yes. Who did they meet? Did they hear gossip about a local official's actions? Were they treated with proper protocol and respect?"

"Do wardens also report to the emperor about the prince's actions?"

"Spying on their commander? That's a good question. I don't know. I have listened to the intendant talk about court, read a few histories, and I watch all the plays. I suppose the plays aren't necessarily accurate. But they feel as if they ought to be. Oh. Here's another bit. Gevulin isn't the crown prince. That would be Crown Prince Minaylin, who is a prince of the Second Estate. However, Gevulin is a prince of the Third Estate, which means he could become the crown prince if the current crown prince were to die, be executed, or be disgraced and removed. In other words, Gevulin could become crown prince if he can outmaneuver the other princes of the Third Estate who probably also hope to become crown prince if they can manage it."

"What is a crown prince?"

"The crown prince becomes emperor when the current emperor dies. Obviously, an emperor keeps an eye on potential heirs, while the rival princes keep an eye on each other."

"Ah. Palace intrigue. How tedious. To think folk mire themselves in such swamps when the winds that dance across the land are free for those of us with wings."

It was a delightfully poetic statement, but Elen was caught by one phrase. "The winds that dance. I wonder if that has anything to do with the Wind Dance. Do you have any memory of the prince's many accomplishments? Eloquent Grace of the Wind Dance, Artist of the Brush and Virtuoso of the Pen, Master of the Lyre and Preeminent Bard of the Twelve Cycles and the Three Hundred and Sixty Poems of the Glorious Founder."

"That sounds exhausting. No, I don't know any of that."

She thought of how he had stood with open arms in the basin, in the exact same posture as the prince had used at the Halt. "Maybe the physical actions will come more naturally to you because the body remembers."

"It could be. I feigned unconsciousness last night in order to listen in and pick up the language. If I didn't learn quickly, I'd have been dead long ago."

"Isn't a haunt already dead?"

"'Haunt' is your term, Deputy Courier. You haven't told me your name."

"His Exalted Highness Prince Gevulin would never deign to know the name of a humble courier like me, so it would be odd of you to know it. It wouldn't even occur to him to take any notice of me at all—" A dog barked nearby, answered by a second. "—and that will cause problems if you and I need to speak again. Which we will."

He picked up the rest of his clothing. "Keep going."

As he pulled on his uniform, she gave him the swiftest rundown she could of what had transpired, a choppy mass of information that skipped around as new things occurred to her. The prince's unexpected arrival at Orledder Halt. An apparent feud with Prince Astaylin that had expanded to create a conflict with Lord Duenn. The names of his retinue. Fulmo being a gagast which, curiously, he already knew, though she couldn't tell him how the gagast had come to serve the prince. That the empire was divided into provinces, which the imperial roads stitched together and which the rising lakes and seas of Pall cut apart. The avalanche blocking the Northern Road, which everyone knew about, yet which had been concealed from the prince. The need for a detour.

"And our path ahead?"

"I'll speak of it as we go. Our route and the countryside are things I can talk about openly in the prince's hearing without suspicion. We'll be walking for many days. I'll keep the pace fast, which gives you an excuse to focus on the march, not on conversation. As much as you can, say nothing. Let your wardens do their jobs. I don't think they suspect because I don't think they know that haunts exist and can take possession of a body."

"If they did suspect?"

"Make sure they don't. The penalty for sorcery is the same as the action taken to destroy Spore."

"Fire. Death by burning."

"How do you know that?" Was he a lost sorcerer? She still did not think it safe to ask, but the sleeping village made her uneasy.

"I'm a good listener, especially when I enjoy the person doing the talking." He smiled and, as if reflexively, extended an arm. For an instant, she thought he was going to take her hand into his, but then he frowned and pulled his hand back. His lips moved in a soundless comment she could not decipher. He walked to the altar on the eastern wall and, quite sacrilegiously, jumped up onto the offering plinth, making ready to clamber over the top of the wall and drop down in the archon's compound beyond.

He paused and looked down from the height. The moon bathed his face in a pleasing light. He stood as if the altar's empty plinth had been built for him, from which to descend to the earth out of the High Heavens, but that was a blasphemous thought. Only the emperor and his clan could claim kinship to the High Heavens. The rest of those who lived upon the land were but commonplace souls, tarnished shards instead of gleaming jewels.

In a low and curiously intense tone he said, "I would know your name as a courtesy, if it was your pleasure to share it with me, Deputy Courier. As for me, my true name cannot be voiced by human tongue. If we are ever again alone, you may call me Gesavura'alalin. An intertwining of names, if you will, as a courtesy to the prince. It's the best I can do, and I offer it with respect and . . . with hope."

On the shoreline between uncorrupted earth and the ever-seething Pall, there was always a hazy line between safety and risk. Here she stood, and in her head she told herself not to answer, but in her heart she was already speaking.

"Folk here call me Elen." She bit her lower lip, knowing she ought to stop. Yet the impulse squeezed out of her, to have someone know, now that Aoving was gone, her last link to the nameless land they had both come from. "But really, it's just El. Just that. From my earliest childhood."

He pressed a hand to his heart and inclined his head. Then he grabbed the top of the wall and gracefully pulled himself up and over. A thump marked his drop to the ground on the other side.

She stood for a long while, breathing under the moonlight as the fountain resumed its sweet refrain. Her soul felt scoured as by a merciless storm, and yet she couldn't stop smiling.

30

THAT UNEASY TIME

Elen reliably woke before dawn, in that unsettled time that was neither night nor day. It was the time she felt the most herself, she who was by all appearances human, flesh and blood and bone, but maybe no longer quite fully human, because she carried a viper in her heart. This early the light barely caught color, and the world was still mostly shades of gray. Those who labored at the humblest work had to be up, hauling out refuse and night soil, carrying water, rekindling banked cook fires. She'd never known a time she wasn't awake at this hour. In a way, even with the extra work, it was the most serene time of day, before the masters woke with their expectations and demands.

She dressed by feel and crept out to find Custodian Ralt seated on the bench where she had had her conversation with the haunt.

He offered her a roll and a cold piece of roasted chicken. "I confess, I filched it off the table last night, when I saw the guests had taken their fill. I thought of you. Probably you ate your usual barley porridge without complaint."

"Ah, but it was sweetened with berries, so I was content." She smiled as she accepted the food. "My thanks. You are kind."

With a humorous waggle of his eyebrows he said, "I ate my fill from the archon's table last night so I can afford to be kind. Try the roll. It's sweet."

She took one bite, then ate the rest too quickly. The meltingly soft white bread had a honey-spun flavor, more like festival food than everyday supper food. Maybe the archon, like the intendant, ate this sort of bread every day. She'd never been invited to eat at an archon's table, not in her ten years walking this route. Then again, she'd never eaten at the intendant's table either, although she had tasted delicacies from his kitchen.

"This is delicious."

"Did I see your nephew in warden's garb, seated with the prince's retinue?"

She sighed. "You did. Maybe we'll have time to talk when I come back this way."

"I can see there's a story there, but I suppose you must be careful, since you know what a gossip I am."

She laughed. He was very much a gossip, a mouth running over even as kind as he was. Yet it was part of his existence as custodian, serving as a go-between for people in the village when such services were needed.

"Oh, a bit of news," he said. "I asked around last night. There was a messenger who came through, but the youth halted only long enough for a fresh sack of provisions. One of the palace runners, trained for long journeys, not like our local youths, who never run more than a half-day's distance."

"My thanks. Next time we meet, I'll owe you gossip in exchange." She offered a courteous hand to heart in farewell.

After settling her pack on her back, she made her way to the moat. Just as she reached the bridge, the sentries on duty opened the inner gate to allow a young runner out, one of the local youths. The runner jogged across the bridge and onto the main path as the eastern sky lightened. The sentries, Adlin and Ferso, greeted her. Elen took care to become acquainted with all the local sentinels and custodians along her accustomed route. Anyway, she liked most of them.

She gestured as the youth vanished beyond the outer ring of fields, moving at the relaxed lope that local message-runners could keep up for half a morning. "What news is going out with the runner?"

Adlin had the white hair of an elder but he was as spry and excitable as a youth. He grinned. "The archon is eager to let his cousin know an exalted highness is coming, so she won't be taken by surprise as he was! Why did the intendant not send us a message?"

"It all happened suddenly. I hear a palace runner came through yesterday. You know anything about that?"

Adlin shook his head. "Wasn't on duty. I just heard the fellow was close-mouthed and proud, a real heartlander, if you take my meaning. Wore the yellow of a palace runner, so there you go."

"What is an exalted highness like to travel with?" asked Ferso in a low voice, no doubt worried that such a question was forbidden, but too curious not to ask.

She wanted to say, *He walks the same way the rest of us do, one stride at a time propelled by his very muscular buttocks,* but knew better. "He is a trained warrior. I thought an exalted prince might be unable to keep up with the hardship of a brisk journey, but he is a warden, of course."

"Yes, wardens are said to be as tough as nails, fighting Spore and brigands and traitors like they do," said Ferso in his serious way.

Adlin grinned. "I always fancied being a warden, but the likes of me is too lowly to be admitted to their ranks. Say, I got a close look last night at the kit of one of the wardens. Do you know what kind of horn they use on the belly of their bows? It was dark in the archon's hall by then, and I could swear it was gleaming, like it was magic."

"I don't know. We walked all day at a fast pace in order to reach here by nightfall. To be honest, palace wardens don't have much to say to a provincial deputy courier like me. I didn't get a good look at their equipment. But they do carry shrive-steel swords."

They whistled, impressed. One of the reasons they liked Elen was that she treated the upland people as no different from herself. Many people from the prosperous lowlands felt obliged to condescend to those who lived upland. She'd seen it herself: merchants trying to cheat them because they thought uplanders were stupid; guards trying to finagle a sexual encounter with a lad or lass by offering a coin, not understanding that sex wasn't commerce in these parts, it was either part of an alliance contracted between families or a night's passing pleasure that was no one's business once the sun rose.

Ferso looked around. They all heard the buzz of sound coming from the archon's compound. "Why's an exalted highness up here, anyway? My granny says no prince has ever walked the Moonrise Hills, and she knows everything."

"She does indeed, as she has informed me more than once, at length, when I brought her a letter." Elen raised her hands with a rueful smile as the two men chuckled. "I'm just their guide."

They nodded in understanding. It wasn't the business of the low to understand the high.

The prince and his wardens strode into view, headed toward the gate with the archon and his family in attendance. Folk had already emerged from their homes to line the street, to bow, to catch a last glimpse of this marvel. The haunt's expression was very serious. So very, very serious that Elen had to exhale sharply to stop herself from laughing. He was trying too hard. No one but her seemed to notice.

Adlin darted into the guardroom and returned with an old hand-kerchief wrapped around a hunk of bread and cheese. "Here, Elen."

"Isn't this your own breakfast?"

"Please, with my thanks. I can get more, but I don't know if they'll remember to feed you."

"Convey my thanks to your daughter. I know how well she takes care of you since her mother died."

"I am blessed, indeed. Also, folk came by already and left a few letters, wondering if you could convey them to Orledder Halt. I told them such mundane business would have to wait."

"Thank you. I'll get them when I return. May you and yours be blessed by the High Heavens, Adlin. Ferso."

The wardens reached the gate, and Elen got swept up into the party. The haunt caught her eye so briefly that anyone watching would likely have missed it. He blinked one eye. More likely, it was a sly wink pretending to be a twitch. She gave a little shake of her head and resolutely looked away. Sneaked a glance back again to see he had fixed his gaze on the path ahead, brow clear, chin lifted. But his lips quirked, as if he knew she was looking at him, or as if he was enjoying the theater of it. If a being like him even knew what theater was. She'd have to ask. Not that they could talk to each other again in such a casual way.

Once they were off the bridge, she hurried to take the lead. She liked being out in front, and it also meant she would be less tempted to look back. Yet she did anyway, as the villagers spilled out in their wake and escorted them beyond the stone-lined moat and all the way to the water-filled ditch that ringed the fields and orchards. A great huzzah went up as the prince passed beyond the protected zone, and then Elen lost sight of the village and its environs. The sounds of human life and livestock bells faded. For a while, they walked through woodland cut with pastures and meadows. At length, they entered the wild upland forest, with its rich scent of fallen needles and high-country ground cover of tough gall-leaf, creeping grass, and bitter spike.

The group fell into the same order as yesterday: Elen in the lead, Xilsi and Jirvy behind her, followed by the prince, Fulmo, and Luvi-ara, with Ipis and Kem as rearguard and Simo ranging up and down the line. She set a steady pace. It was better not to dwell on what couldn't be changed. Kem's situation was out of her hands now. It hurt to think of the way he'd angrily muttered, "She's not my aunt." But he was free of Lord Duenn, so it had to be worth it. She had to stop thinking about him and do her job as a guide.

Her gaze roamed the path ahead, the understory of the forest, the familiar rise and fall of the land. Her ears caught the flutter of birds, the scattering noises of wildlife, the click and clatter of branches brushed by the wind, and the occasional rill of a stream. The air was fresh and clean, no trace of the telltale rose-oil scent, but she smelled rain on the way, coming up from the south.

She worked to get the measure of the other wardens. Ipis couldn't have been more than a year or two older than Kem and was apparently Simo's protégé, chosen for the mission because he wanted her to get experience. Xilsi looked quite young, too, and had features of unusually delicate prettiness, at odds with hands calloused from weapons training; she was also the kind of person who kept an eye on everything going on around her, and was quick to have an emphatic opinion. Jirvy was about Elen's age, early thirties, with a stolid, quiet demeanor but a sour tongue when he did speak.

"What's that?" Xilsi demanded, startling at movement glimpsed deep in the trees.

"A deer," said Jirvy. "I forget you grew up in cities. Never seen a deer in the wild, have you?"

"I don't need to be reminded by you thinking you know me."

The others glanced their way and then ignored the exchange, as if they were used to it and wished it would stop, so Elen did too.

The light changed as darker clouds rolled up from the south. The first touch of raindrops spattered, and the group halted so the wardens could don cloaks. Elen had her own style of rain gear: tiered capes, each successively longer, that kept both her and her pack dry on long marches and could be strung up to create a shelter.

She took advantage of the break to go off the path and behind some bushes to pee. From here, concealed, she overheard Ipis speaking in a low voice.

"Do you think the intendant is a spy for Prince Astaylin? And sent the deputy courier to spy on us?"

"The whole crock of pickles looks suspicious." The other speaker was Xilsi. "How could warden messages not get through to an intendant? How could anyone lose a griffin scout? It seems convenient we had to take on a guide just there. But what does the boy say? What's his name?"

"Kem. I like him. He seems level-headed, and learns fast, but I can't figure him out. The Duenn Manor lord claimed him, but he doesn't act Manor-born. He told me he has nothing to say about the deputy courier. Seemed angry when he said it."

"It's a bit of an insult to ask a Manor-born youth about someone so lowborn. Still, there was something going on at Orledder I couldn't figure out. If we'd had more time, I'd have asked around."

"Enough gossip." That was Simo, footfalls crackling on autumn twigs as he walked up. "We're leaving."

They hurried back to the path.

Simo didn't move. He said, "Did you hear all that, Deputy Courier?"

She emerged warily. "As it happens, I did."

"Care to defend yourself from their accusations?"

The viper stirred defensively. She met the captain's gaze squarely, although it was unwise to do so. "Captain, say what you will about me. I'm nothing to you. Nor do I aspire to be more. But the intendant is a good man, who does not involve himself in the palace and whatever goes on there. He doesn't deserve to be spoken of with such suspicion. He is merely doing his best to serve the emperor."

"He has a champion in you, I see."

She pressed a hand to her heart. "He has treated me with respect, and granted me far more than I deserve."

"Ah." Simo gave her a longer look, as if making up his mind about whether she was sincere, then whistled to alert the others. "Let's go on."

"It will rain the rest of the day," she said. "As long you don't mind that, we can keep walking and still hope to reach the Heart Temple I have in mind for our night's lodging. But if you don't mind my saying so, I recommend not using loud whistles for signals. Sound carries a long way up here. Besides swalters, there are desperate people who live outside proper Moats and Ditches, in the hills. They may see a small party like this one as a tempting target."

"Yet you walk alone on these paths."

"I carry nothing of value to them. Well, except my boots."

He looked puzzled as he glanced at her boots, unsure if she was joking. All the wardens wore fine boots of the most elegant leather, next to which hers must appear like poor cousins.

With a gust of wind, the rain began to fall in earnest. Elen made her way back to the path. Kem stood at the rear, hood pulled low. The haunt had his hood thrown back and his face raised to the rain. There was something so sensual about the way he parted his mouth to let raindrops slip past his lips, as if purest elixir. As if the touch of the world was a caress. She could not look away from his closed eyes and ecstatic expression.

The others stood, hesitant, not sure what to do.

At length, Simo said, "Your Highness, best to cover your head, if I may be so bold. The deputy courier says the rain will last the rest of the afternoon."

"Does she?" remarked the haunt in a silky tone, aimed at her, although he so carefully did not look at her that she could almost feel the arrow of his thoughts in her direction.

When all else fails, start walking.

31

TEARS ARE A LUXURY

She led, and they followed, as they must. In the dark days of child-hood she'd always led Ao forward, holding her sister's hand. Very early on, very young, she'd figured out that the atoner who walked in front was slightly less likely to fall afoul of Spore than the ones who walked alongside the main entourage or at the rear. Did the Spore slumber and only stir awake when a tremor of mobile life woke it? Did it have a mind that had to first recognize and then decide to attack its prey? Or was it simply a mindless growth? Perhaps her childhood fancy that she and Ao were better protected by always taking the frightening vanguard was merely something she had trained herself to believe because it made the fear easier to deal with.

Normally, she smelled Verlia Moat and its corrals before she saw the village, but the wind was blowing up from behind her. A steady rain drowned out the telltale blat of goats and sheep that usually welcomed her from a distance. No one was out chopping wood in this weather. So, when the trail swung around Hat Rock to the over-look where the path split, she was surprised to find people standing out in the rain by the holystone post that marked the turnoff to the village. They wore their festival clothes, and all were drenched and shivering. Yet their expressions glowed with excitement. They dropped to their knees onto the wet ground the instant the prince came into sight. Upland villages had no interlocutors; those were a heartland affectation reserved for the palace and the Manor-born. So it was the archon herself who spoke to Luviara.

Would His Exalted Highness not pause for a cup of hot cider in the shelter of the village's market hall? The village archon's house was modest, but she would honor the prince with a feast if he cared to stay overnight, or until the weather cleared. The village's hillside terraces were visible from the overlook, and it seemed every person who lived there had crowded onto the central terrace, in the rain, to greet him, their tiny figures washed by the storm, beneath the gloomy sky.

The prince said nothing as he listened to the archon speaking to Luviara. She supposed he didn't dare. His wardens knew Prince

Gevulin far better than he did. Elen had been shuffled off the path about twenty paces along. From this distance, she could only watch helplessly, could offer no clue to the haunt, not that she had a clue to offer and anyway, she wasn't about to shout.

Simo broke in before Luviara could reply. "I am the warden captain attending His Exalted Highness. We are on urgent palace business and cannot delay."

"But all our people have come out to honor the prince," said the archon with a helpless gesture toward the terraces. "They will never have another chance like this, Your Worthiness. I beg you to consider their humble service and dedication to the emperor."

"We must go on," said Simo curtly. "Luviara, give the archon a token of the prince's esteem."

The theurgist dug into a pouch and handed coins to the archon. "It is decided. I pray you, Worthy Archon, do not argue further."

The woman looked ready to weep, although she took the coin. Behind her, one of her companions spoke to a youth wearing the dirty-white headband of a local runner, not the same boy who had left Sfendia Moat this morning. The runner clasped hands to heart with a bow, then ran off down the main path, ahead of them.

"Deputy Courier! Let us go!" snapped Simo with an impatient wave.

She had to turn her back on the villagers and set out, angry at the wardens, angry at herself. The encounter had taken her by surprise. When the captain came up beside her, she gave in to a rare, reckless impulse.

"Captain, I understand that His Exalted Highness cannot rest overnight at any of these villages, but even a brief stop to take a drink of their cider and a bite of their bread—"

"It is out of the question." His interruption was definitive. He gave her a measuring look. "Unless you're telling me the weather will improve, and the path will get easier from here on out, and the villages will be convenient to our trail."

"No, alas, Captain. The path is challenging even without the rain. Most of the hill villages and hamlets lie on branch trails off this main path."

"That is extra time we cannot allow. Do not mention this again."

He dropped back to walk beside the prince, who was looking off to the right where a pretty little waterfall dropped in a silvery line down a rocky knoll. Could she go behind Simo's back and persuade

Gesavura'alalin to act differently? But the haunt had his own hidden reasons to proceed, and he had to keep up the pretense of being the prince. What were these local people to him, anyway? Whatever it meant to be Shorn, he must feel as distant from villagers as the prince did. In a way, she didn't want to ask because she feared she would find him as removed as the prince, even if he enjoyed sparring with her. Was it just that she didn't want to think ill of him? If so, the fault lay with her.

But she had not accounted for the stubbornness of uplanders. The march toward her intended destination took them past three turnoffs for small communities she normally visited on her courier route. She'd given no thought to the second runner who had raced ahead. The Verlia Moat archon had sent a different message than Elen had expected.

After about an hour, they reached the next holystone post marking a branch path, this one leading to the goat-herding hamlet of Roduran Ditch. Lining either side of the path, beneath dripping trees, the entire population of Roduran Ditch had assembled. The hamlet had an official census population of sixty-three. As Elen came into view, the waiting villagers knelt. A Ditch did not have a proper archon, so their headwoman had brought an offering of a round of goat cheese. Children squirmed, forgetting to cover their faces as they stared in awe at the wardens. Even Elen had to admit that it was difficult to tell the prince apart from the other wardens without knowing how to "read" the meaning of the embroidered badges on his warden's uniform and the arrangement of precious beads dangling from his elaborately braided hair.

"Is that the prince?" one child chirped, pointing at Fulmo. "He's so big! And kind of ugly."

A collective gasp of horror burst from the adults. As one, they cringed, awaiting punishment.

The haunt walked over to the child and set a hand upon the little one's uncovered hair, for despite the rain, every person, old and young alike, had taken off their caps. "May you always be emboldened to ask questions," he said. He looked up and down the path, then proceeded between the line of kneeling villagers, pausing to touch each child on the head. Fulmo accepted the cheese round; Luviara gave a swift blessing; they strode on, leaving the villagers behind.

At the next holystone post, another hour's walk onward, villagers again waited patiently at the side of the path, despite the steady rain. Again, the haunt touched each child upon the head as he passed, leaving what emotions behind him Elen could not know.

The lesson she had learned in childhood was that masters used retainers to work for them and atoners to die for them. Masters had someone else to carry their burdens, so they need never carry it themselves. Because she had not grown up in the empire, she had not prayed every day to honor and praise the emperor whose Shield, granted by the High Heavens, was a blessed shelter for imperial subjects. Here, the villagers revered the distant emperor. While to Elen, the emperor was just another master, of a far bigger territory. The empire simply dressed its power in more flamboyant and complicated clothing. But Elen knew the truth that lay at the root of all: The ones who controlled the witch roads were the only ones who truly had protection against the Pall.

After a while, the rain slackened. Eventually it ceased. The drip and spatter from rain-drenched trees accompanied their squelching footfalls. Midafternoon, they came to the third holystone post of the day. A trail led to Wordia Moat, a good hour's walk each way. This time, she was sure, it would be too far to drag children.

Yet there they waited, the full census of 287 souls, including a frail and incredibly ancient elder who had been carried the whole way on a litter, now set on the cold, wet ground.

The prince knelt beside the elder and, in a shocking act of humility, set his hand upon his own heart in respect. "How many winters have you watched the sun die and be reborn, Esteemed One?"

In a whisper, wheezing with each word, the elder replied. "I was born in Year Ten of the Jasmine Emperor, Exalted Highness. I often wonder why death has spared me for so long. But I now know, it was to see you."

"Or I, to see you, Esteemed One. It is no small thing to touch the past through the lives of those who remember it, each a rare treasure."

The haunt rose and walked down the line, pressing a hand to the head of each child. As he passed, the villagers wept. When Elen could no longer bear to watch, she turned away, walked to the next turn of the path, and waited there. Why was it so painful to see them cry? She did not even know, only that she was relieved to walk on, not because she found the villagers contemptible but because nothing in her life had ever made her cry. Tears were a luxury. Her eyes stayed dry. Or maybe there was something wrong with her, because Aoving had cried all the time; for joy, for sorrow, for anger, for fear, for all of it, tears were Ao's answer. Elen had taught herself to smile through it all, because a smile meant more than happiness. A smile meant she wasn't going to give up, not on herself and not on those she loved. A smile was defiance.

To her surprise, the haunt caught up with her, and they walked at the front with the others far enough behind that they couldn't hear. He stumped along with a strange tension in his body.

At length, he spoke in a low, impassioned voice. "I am unaccountably moved by these people who have waited for hours, in the rain, merely to watch me walk past. Why do they do this? What is it they hope for?"

She could not answer, because she had no answer.

They walked in silence. He seemed content to stride beside her as he waited. But she had to come up with a reply before the wardens became too curious. Their conversation would already be drawing too much attention, since it was unheard of for a prince to converse with a deputy courier.

She said, "A prince of the realm is like a brilliant star, precious and thus out of their grasp. In their ordinary lives, they are too insignificant to be visible to such a divine emanation. Yet here you are. Maybe all they hope for is that you see them for one moment, even in passing. Maybe that is enough."

He did not reply. She wasn't sure if she had offended him, or if he had nothing to say. As she continued on, he fell back to walk beside Fulmo.

They walked deeper into the hills through the cloudy afternoon. Late in the day they broke out of the woodland and ascended to a rocky ridgetop path. In the trees below, she thought she spotted a small red lynx and its shadowy swalter riding astride, but it was only a glimpse, so she couldn't be sure. Nor could she be sure what such a sight portended. Why would a swalter be riding so close to the path? The hill swalters avoided people, unless they were aggressively defending their territory.

A last gasp of rain spat over them, but the weather was moving north, flinging itself against the rising hills. They'd have better weather tomorrow.

Simo came up beside her. "Are you sure we'll reach shelter before dark?"

"We're almost there. Keep your eyes open for swalters. I thought I spotted one."

He didn't even blink to hear this news. "Yes, there are four pacing us."

She gave him a look of sharp surprise.

For the first time, he smiled. "I'm surprised you saw one at all. They're usually impossible to see among the trees. You have keen eyes."

"And you, considering you saw four?"

"I didn't say I saw them. If there are four, there is likely a full family group scouting us."

"There are known to be several unaffiliated packs roaming the Moonrise Hills. But I've never seen one in this area before."

"That's why I'm troubled by their interest."

"Do you think they might attack us?"

He shrugged noncommittally. "How far to the temple?"

She pointed. "Do you see the crag up ahead? The dead tree? That's the turnoff for the Heart Temple."

"I'm surprised the tree hasn't been chopped down for firewood in this Heavens-forsaken place."

"It's a Heavens-sent tree. There's a local story that the pure-water spring was discovered because two journeying venerables witnessed a lightning strike that petrified the tree, as with a bolt of magic. They took it for a sign that they should explore off the path, and thus found the spring below."

Simo shot her a skeptical look and, to her surprise, strode ahead. When Elen and the rest of the party reached the tree, he was already standing before it, with hands on hips, staring as if he, too, had been petrified with wonder or confusion. The tree was stone, in the shape of a stately old oak. It was impossible to imagine anyone could have sculpted a tree down to the detail of each lobed leaf and irregular striations of bark, much less that there could have been a boulder large enough for it to be hewn out of.

The haunt walked past Simo and rested a palm against the trunk.

"Your Highness, are you sure that's safe?" Simo asked.

The haunt raised his other hand to command silence. Closing his eyes, he seemed to be listening. Wind swirled around the crag, growing colder as the clouds cleared off. The star known as Evening's Watch glimmered into view above, warning of night falling fast upon them. The moon hadn't yet risen in the darkening east.

A holystone post marked the split in the path. A tiny shelter housing a bronze bell stood at the top of wooden stair steps laid into the hillside. The steps ran far down into a ragged slot of a narrow valley. Deep in the trees below, lights winked into existence. It would be darker down there than up here.

The haunt's lips moved but no sound came out. What he was saying, she did not know, nor to whom he was speaking. No one interrupted his contemplation. They would stand here all night, if he wished it, and it was never safe to be out at night, but wardens knew that better than most. Elen stood back from the others and scanned the rocky ridge and its slopes, but saw no lynxes, no pale wisps that marked an irruption of Spore, nothing but birds winging past, headed for their night's roost and, once, a curious pika quivering its nose at them, as if they smelled funny, and probably they did.

The haunt opened his eyes and, with a sadly wry smile, removed his hand. "Safe journeys, old friend," he murmured before surveying his companions.

They watched him with what Elen hoped was puzzlement rather than suspicion.

He said, "We have too far to walk for these restrictions on speech to impede us. I will speak to anyone in our party and those we meet as I feel the need. This is in no way intended to criticize your work, Worthy Interlocutor. But it takes too much time and we have a long way to go. Do you all understand?"

Simo stiffened, but tapped his chest in obedience. Ipis scratched her head, looking puzzled, and nudged Kem with an elbow as if to warn him to keep quiet. Xilsi tilted her head to one side, gaze narrowing with a kind of skeptical curiosity. Luviara frowned. Jirvy turned away and scanned the sky for threat. Fulmo had no reaction, simply waiting.

The haunt nodded decisively. "Very good. Deputy Courier, lead on."

Elen rang the bell twice. As its bright resonance faded, they started down into the valley.

32

WISHFUL THINKING

The long descent by stair led them into dense tree cover, the sky barely visible. Soon, Elen could smell the incense of the temple and hear the tinkle of wind chimes and the thump of a waterwheel. They reached the first stone lantern, where a custodian waited by its flickering flame. He bowed in silence and indicated a plank bridge that spanned the outer ditch and its flowing water.

The temple's garden and orchard lay inside the outer ditch. They followed a path lit by small lanterns like toadstools crouched low to the ground. An arch with hanging lamps spanned the approach to the main bridge over an interior ditch. The two runners stood on the other side of the bridge. They bowed, fighting back grins, then jostled each other in shared excitement when the prince deigned to acknowledge them with a dignified nod.

Every Heart Temple had the same basic layout. This one was unusually large, especially for such an isolated place, with a census of 317 living souls and a separate list of the dead whose ashes rested in three-legged urns in the columbarium. The senior venerable bowed in greeting—most of those who served here had taken a vow of silence—and himself conducted the prince to the temple's hostel. The temple residents lined either side of the paths, bowing like grain as the wind passes over it. They stared even as they tried not to, as astonished at Fulmo's presence as at the prince's. As for Elen, she had only ever glimpsed the senior venerable from a distance, but obviously a prince's arrival must be treated with exalted respect and honor.

The hostel was a barnlike barracks space with rope beds and straw mattresses laid end to end and a brick hearth for heating. A separate room held basins for washing, a pipe to bring in water from the temple cistern, and a door onto a latrine courtyard.

"Is there nothing more appropriate for His Highness?" Simo glared at Elen as if this were her fault, and as if the senior venerable, because he was silent, must therefore also be deaf. "Can the senior venerable not courteously give up his own bed for the night?"

"I assure you, Warden, the senior venerable sleeps in less comfort than this."

"These quarters are acceptable," said the haunt. "Simo, we must consider the mission, not our perquisites."

"Of course, Your Highness. The fault is mine."

"You have committed no fault. You are just doing your job, Simo, but I grant pardon regardless, if it eases your mind. I am not offended."

Simo exchanged a startled glance with Jirvy. Elen wondered if she would need to warn the haunt he was skating close to the edge, but he watched the wardens with a steady gaze that took in each least interaction. His right eyebrow quirked, he flashed a glance at her, then turned to the senior priest.

"Pray apprise us of your customary routine, so we do not disrupt your round of worship."

The venerable mimed eating and then tapped his hands together lightly.

Elen said, "A bell will ring when our evening's meal is ready. My thanks, Most Venerable."

The man bowed to the prince and left, his duties discharged.

Fulmo set his big pack by the main door. The wardens chose beds in an array that surrounded the prince. Elen set her pack on an empty bed in the back, then went into the washroom. First, she filled a big water kettle and set it on the hearth to heat. As she was filling the two wash basins with cold water, Kem came in and began washing. In the other room, the haunt was engaging the wardens and Luviara in a discussion, or perhaps Gesavura'alalin was keeping them busy so she could have a moment alone with Kem. Surely that was wishful thinking on her part.

"Kem," she began in a soft voice, surprised at how nervous she was to speak to a child she knew so well and had loved for all his life.

He kept his back turned, shoulders tight, jaw tense, and finished washing his hands. Just when she thought he was going to stalk out without speaking to her, he got the belligerent tilt to his chin that always presaged him starting a fight with his mother.

He turned on her, hands clenched. "You and Mama said my father was dead."

She swallowed, then answered, "Dead to us."

"Is that how you excuse lying to me my whole life?" When his voice dropped into a flat whisper, it meant he was really angry. "When were you going to tell me? Or were you ever going to tell me?"

She looked him in the eye. "Your mother couldn't talk about it.

She got the shakes even to think about it, or about *him*. So I followed her lead."

"What about after she died? What about then?" The pitch of his tone heightened. His cheeks flushed as he trembled in the grip of rage, he who had trained himself to control his reactions because his mother had never been able to control her own.

What could Elen even say?

"I was wrong. I know that. I got in the habit of not saying anything, all those years, and it had been so long, and I thought I would think of a better way later."

He tugged at his mother's ribbon, which he still wore, then pinched his lips together and lifted his chin in challenge. "Is there anything else you should have told me and didn't?"

She hesitated, rubbing her arm. He saw her hesitation. He knew her too well, and he was a smart, observant boy.

"Fuck you."

He stalked out of the washroom, leaving her with the basins of cold water and a lamp whose wick had started to gutter. She poured more oil into the lamp to steady the flame, but that was all she could manage. Instead, she sat in the corner, cleaning her boots, the most calming task she knew. The others came in, washed, and left without speaking to her.

Last came Luviara, who said, "Deputy Courier, are you coming to the dining hall?"

The thought of Kem's anger was like having sand in her throat. Elen didn't feel like eating, but she never refused freely offered food. "Of course."

She accompanied Luviara out of the hostel courtyard. Fulmo stood by the hostel door like a sentry, utterly still.

"Doesn't he come with us? No guards are needed here."

"He's not like us. He eats starlight."

"What?"

Luviara smiled mischievously as she headed after the others, Elen beside her. "It's a tale that started in the villages along the border of the Desolation. All the gagast who serve in the palace come out of the Desolation. I have traveled in the border region and written down whatever accounts I have been able to gather."

"Do you doubt the story? About eating starlight, I mean."

"Stories are complicated. If I had to make a guess, I would say the belief arises from the habit of gagast to stand in perfect stillness at night with their faces turned heavenward. One might think they are absorbing starlight."

"Have you asked Fulmo?"

"Gagast do not speak any human language. Some can read and write, which strikes me as curious. You'll have noted Fulmo has only a thumb and three fingers, but he has a delicate touch and exceptional manual dexterity despite his massive size and clumsy-looking hands. To return to the question of language, it's said the aivur can communicate with the gagast through light."

They made their way along a colonnaded pathway. Ipis had dropped back from the forward group and seemed to be listening.

Elen asked, "What are the aivur truly like? It seems you've met them on your travels."

"So I have."

"Are they humans who were lost when the Pall descended, and who were transformed into something both more and less than human through sorcery?"

"That's what the *Chronicle of the Winter Poet* claims. You've read it?"

"In the intendant's archive. Yes."

"I'm curious to know what else you've read. Most intendants don't offer deputy couriers access to their archives."

Elen ignored this blatant fishing attempt and answered the safer question. "Well, in the play *Flower-Bright Sunrise,* the aivur are depicted as a peaceful and beautiful people who have lived for generations in great tree cities in the distant south. They never eat meat or enact any violence. Naturally a young human man falls in love with one of their noble court. So that makes it seem aivur have always lived in the world. But according to the intendant's daughter, who traveled with her spouse into the east, 'aivur' is just a name for the vicious Blood Wolves and the merciless Sea Wolves. She says they were born in the Pall, because the Pall cannot harm them, and that is why they must be burned. Like Spore."

"The world grants us no easy answers. 'Aivur' is the formal word historians use for a people who look very like us humans, but who have powers and enchantment beyond what is commonly human. It's true many believe the aivur came out of the Desolation seventy years ago. It's also true that the raids of the Sea Wolves and the attacks of the Blood Wolves and their giant spiders in the east only started after the appearance of the Desolation. But it's not clear whether they came out of the Desolation itself, or only seem to have done so. The Desolation was just one of many signs of changes in the land, like famine or plague or a shockingly destructive earthquake, as in the reign of the Orchid Emperor."

"Like the rising of the Pall itself," Elen said. "Although the rising happened about thirty years before the Desolation appeared."

"That's my point. Older chronicles suggest the aivur have always been here, living in their own homelands, apart from humans. In the vast southern forest, for example, a mysterious and rarely seen population of aivur have lived deep in the wild wood for generations. Something about the rising of the Pall caused the aivur to turn their attention to us."

"Are they human, or not?" Elen pressed.

Luviara smiled, amused at the question. "Do you think I know?"

"I wish to hear your learned opinion, Your Worthiness."

"Ah. Well, then. Of the intelligent peoples of the world, the aivur are more easily mistaken for human than are swalter or gagast or fregir. Or dragons, obviously. But it is my considered opinion that, like the other four, they are not human. Indeed, they do not speak of themselves as human. We must never make the mistake of thinking they are like us, or wish to live in harmonious community with us, no matter how much they may look like us, or the charm of their smiles, and by charm I mean sorcery."

"Sorcery? I thought we agreed the practice of sorcery has been eradicated by the order of the emperor. Or, going by the poem in *The Last Flower Withers*, was erased from the world after the fall of the sorcerer-kings, long ago."

"So we must hope," Luviara agreed mildly. "This is more than I like to say, but humans cannot wield sorcery without sacrificing their own life force to do so."

"But theurgists need not do so, with their magic?"

"You have a lot of questions, Deputy Courier. But you are not an acolyte of the Heart Temple, to be granted answers. Ah, here we are. The food smells so appetizing."

A custodian held up a lamp beside an open door. It led into a lovely wood-paneled chamber with a warm brick oven and a long table set with platters.

The table had no chairs, only benches along either side. The wardens hesitated. Obviously, benches stood outside palace protocol. Elen wondered what Prince Gevulin would do, were he here. Would he prove an adaptable man or a rigid one?

But of course, he wasn't here. After a moment's consideration, the haunt seated himself at the middle of one of the benches and gestured for Simo and Luviara to sit on either side of him. Jirvy, Xilsi, Ipis, and Kem sat opposite. Elen hesitated until the custodian gestured to the bench beside Luviara, who nodded. Thus, Elen found herself seated at the same table as a prince, even if he was really the haunt.

The custodian cleared his throat. He was an old man, white-haired and wiry. The prince did not seem to awe him. His hands bore heavy calluses; hard labor or constant war had been his life.

"Worthy Interlocutor, who speaks for His Exalted Highness, I am assigned to serve you and these honored travelers. I am a novice, come lately to the path of custodian."

Luviara said, "We do not eat in the main dining hall with the residents of the temple?"

"This temple is a silent temple. Only a few of us have permission to speak. It is our task to conduct and serve those who overnight in the hostel. I pray you, let me speak the blessing over the food, so you may eat your fill."

The haunt raised a hand to grant permission.

The custodian sang the blessing, then retired to the door. "If you need my services, I will be outside. It is not permitted for me to hear conversation of the world beyond the temple." With a bow, he stepped outside and closed the door.

The hearth beat warmth over them. The world that lay outside these walls had fallen eerily silent, lacking even the whine of wind. The food smelled delicious. However rough the furnishings, the temple denizens ate very well indeed: pears and walnuts stewed with greens; legumes cooked in a creamy goat's milk sauce flavored with onions, bay leaves, and thyme; a leek and cheese pie, hot from the oven; rounds of fresh rye bread; honey-squash pancakes; candied cloudberries that left a sticky sweetness on the lips.

Luviara took upon herself the tearing up and distributing of chunks of bread, but without Fulmo to act as menial, there was some confusion as to how the prince could eat. In the end, Simo tasted all the dishes first, after which the prince served himself in the same manner as his retinue, spooning out portions from the common platters.

After the first edge of hunger was settled, the haunt looked around the table. He was always examining, studying, trying to figure out the others, but also how far he could go.

He said, "Let us go on in the custom of the Warden Hall. Simo?"

"As you wish, Your Highness." Simo nodded at Kem. "Novice Kem, it is our custom to discuss or debate some subject at table, as a means of pedagogy. Do you have a question you wish to ask?"

The boy glanced at Elen with an angry frown. She tensed. Was he going to expose her, condemn her, take his revenge?

He looked away. "I beg your pardon, Captain. After such a long day, I find myself very hungry, and eager to eat more of this delicious food. Might I just listen and thereby learn?"

Simo smiled in an avuncular way. "Of course. This is all new to you. What of you others, then? What shall we speak of?"

33

EVEN IF THEY DO NOT LOOK IT

I have a topic of conversation," said Ipis, leaping in so eagerly that stiff-necked Jirvy looked offended.

"You always do," Jirvy muttered.

"At least she has something to talk about and questions to ask, instead of just offering objections or brooding silence," retorted Xilsi.

Simo tapped a hand emphatically on the tabletop. "His Exalted Highness need not be exposed to our trivial disputes. Pray conduct yourselves with proper dignity in his presence."

They pressed hands to hearts. Kem, seeing the gesture, hurriedly copied it, but the instant they all released their hands, he went back to eating the pancakes with an expression of astonished delight.

Ipis addressed Luviara. "On our walk to the dining hall, I could not help but hear the Worthy Interlocutor speaking of the aivur. When my Manor sent me to Warden Hall, I hoped to see aivur in the City of Heart's Peace. I was so disappointed, I must confess."

Jirvy interrupted, "Our current gracious emperor banned all aivur from the heartland, even the ones that settled in the foreigners' quarter during the reign of the Jasmine Emperor."

"Yes, I think Ipis knows that," said Xilsi with a laugh. She seemed to take pleasure in baiting Jirvy, who scowled at her. "My blessed grandmother was born during the reign of the Jasmine Emperor. She never knew the city without the aivur in it, not until the bans. She always says she thought of them as locals, and not as outsiders."

"How about you?" Ipis asked. "You're born into one of the Six Noble Manors."

"I was raised in a western branch of our Manor. No aivur in Elegant City. But I heard my grandmother's stories every day when I was a child. I was excited that one day I'd get to see, for myself, aivur walking the avenues of the capital. There were aivur ambassadors and merchants and philosophers and artisans and poets and dancers and bards, so she told us. Even grim-faced mercenaries. But then I was sent up to Warden Hall the very same year that the Magnolia Emperor expelled all the aivur from the heartland. So I never got to see them."

"I've heard they are beautiful in the way lynxes and panthers are sleek and handsome," said Ipis breathlessly, "the way griffins and sarpa are glorious in being deadly, the way horses run with a beauty no human can ever match."

"How poetic." Jirvy shook his head wearily. "They're killers. Hunters and warriors."

Ipis ignored him. "But you've traveled a great deal, Worthy Interlocutor, have you not? You've seen and spoken to aivur?"

"That I have." Luviara punctuated the statement by eating a spoonful of candied cloudberries, and the sweetness made her smile. "I have walked in the harbor of North Antinis and spoken to the ones the Sea Wolves call bequeathers. These bequeathers are the ones among them who may speak to outsiders. I have traded stories and songs in the villages, called 'holdings,' where many of the aivur who emerged out of the Desolation settled. I have even spoken to a delegation of forest aivur, the mysterious people called Stalkers."

"Forest Wolves, you mean," muttered Jirvy.

She glanced at him and went on. "They'd come out of the southern forest to trade in Vartic Port, on the shore of Diamond Bay. As for the host of the Blood Wolves, they do not speak to us. They only attack. No imperial soldier or humble farmer captured by them has ever returned."

Simo cleared his throat as a prelude to speaking. The others settled obediently to await his words of wisdom.

The captain spoke in grave tones. "I have traveled in the east and along the contested northern shore. The aivur are wickedly strong and swift because they carry inside themselves the attributes of beasts. That is why they are not like us. We are human in all the ways the High Heavens approve. They are monsters, even if they do not look it."

Elen surreptitiously watched the haunt, who listened with his usual look of intense curiosity. What he thought of all this she could not be sure, nor what was familiar to him and what was new.

"Yet humans can also be monsters, as we learn in the tale of *The Five Cannibal Cousins*," said Xilsi.

"That's just a made-up story," objected Jirvy.

"Who's to say there's no truth to it?" said Luviara good-naturedly. "Are you saying we humans never act wickedly or monstrously? Never lie, or steal, or cheat, or kill without just cause?"

"No, no, of course not," he said hastily.

Xilsi snickered, then fell silent, rubbing her mouth with the back of a hand at a sharp look from Simo.

Luviara went on. "If you wish for my opinion, gleaned from many years of harvesting the fields of the empire, I would tell you that the aivur are no more each alike than any two of us are alike. Among the supposedly peaceful forest folk there may be ill-tempered and violent individuals, and likewise, among the marauding Sea Wolves, there may be those who sail for a boundless love of the sea alone and wish no harm upon anyone. The aivur who now live on the borderland of the Desolation seemed, to me, to wish merely to replant the Desolation so it can grow again. As for the Blood Wolves and their spiders, they are an army. Who's to say what their cities or encampments are like, far from the border where battles are fought?"

"Do you defend their aggression?" Simo demanded. "I have lost friends and kin on the eastern frontier!"

Luviara pressed a hand to her chest. "I beg your pardon, Captain. I do not mean to trouble your heart. It's true I've never found opportunity to speak to any of the aivur who ride in that dreadful host. When I was traveling in the east some years ago, I heard a prisoner from the host had been taken alive. Naturally I hurried to the fort, where it was said the prisoner was being held, but when I got there . . ."

She paused, considered the demolished platters, and eased the last slice of pie onto her plate. Elen could tell she was aware of everyone leaning forward. Like any storyteller, the interlocutor enjoyed their anticipation.

Which was startlingly and rudely interrupted by Xilsi.

"This isn't funny to me. My brother died in the east, fighting the host. In his last letter home, he said their mages cast Spore. We didn't believe it, we thought it was just a story, but then we got a dispatch that he had died after being warped and mangled into a Spore-ridden monster, so his company had to burn what was left of his body in the field and couldn't even send his ashes home. That was what made me decide to Declare to become a warden. So I could learn to fight Spore."

"You didn't always want to be a warden?" Kem asked. Everyone looked at him curiously, since it was the first time he'd spoken since the discussion began.

"Oh, no, not at all." Xilsi grinned, flexing her strong hands, good humor restored. "I wanted to become an embroidery master. Did you always want to become a warden, Kem?"

There was a faraway cast to his gaze. "Yes. It's what I always dreamed of."

The quiet words hit Elen like a slap to the face. He'd never confided this to her or to his mother. *Never*. His words stung, spoken so casually, and to people he barely knew who were now his comrades— for life!—in a way she, who had raised him, could never be. He wouldn't even look at her. Had he discarded her already? Not that she blamed him, yet the moment hit so bitterly, and she was so angry at herself for lacking the courage to tell him the truth.

"You haven't finished your story about the captured prisoner," said the haunt.

Luviara gave him a puzzled look. "I have related this tale to you before, Your Highness."

"Here sit others who have not heard it." He gestured openhandedly, easy to interpret as a command to make an offering. "An unfinished tale is a flight interrupted, is it not?"

Outside, a bell rang, the sound muffled by the walls. The door opened, and the custodian entered and bowed.

"With respect, courteous guests, it is time to douse all lights after the closing prayers. I must ask you to retire to the hostel for the night."

The haunt rose at once, signaling his acceptance of the temple's routine. In silence, their party returned to the barracks room. It was cold outside, the nip of frost in the air. Inside, the brick hearth brought welcome warmth to the long room. Quickly they made ready, washing up, removing boots. Elen tucked herself in under her blanket and cloak fully clothed but for her outer tunic. The custodian waited until all were settled, then pinched out the wicks and shut the door. No one spoke. Elen shut her eyes and dropped into sleep.

A touch to her arm, as brief as a butterfly's alighting and departing, woke her. It was entirely dark, but she knew it was the haunt. She felt his presence like the heat of sunshine on bare skin.

He spoke in a murmur. "I want to show you something."

34

A Slowly Heaving Movement

The barracks room had no windows, so the only light came from a thin line of delicate moonlight that traced the crack beneath the heavy wooden door. She tugged on her boots and followed him past their sleeping companions.

Outside, it was a cloudless night. Fulmo stood next to the door as if turned to stone, face upraised to the stars. The gagast did not stir as they passed, and she wasn't sure if he, too, was under the haunt's enchantment or if he was feeding on starlight and thus frozen to the world.

"There's no lamps," she whispered as they crossed the courtyard beneath the stars and the waning moon.

"You already know you don't need a lamp to see at night, don't you? You never did."

She never had, but she could not bring herself to confirm the statement. Such knowledge was dangerous. It could get a person burned. No wonder Kem was angry. She'd kept so much hidden from him. Because he was too young, that was a good enough reason, or it had been. Nevertheless, Kem had grown old enough to make decisions for himself, to see the world in a complex way, through his own eyes and not just through the gaze of his mother and aunt. Even if she wasn't really his aunt, though she was in every way that mattered. Surely.

"Pay attention," the haunt whispered.

He eased open a gate that let them through into a part of the temple she'd never seen.

"I don't think we're allowed—"

"Princes may walk wherever they will. That much I've learned in my sojourn so far. This way."

He took a circuitous route around the dining hall and kitchen, past the sleeping wing, and all the way to the back of the temple, where a garden courtyard had been paved and planted right up against the cliffside of a steep hill. The air was cold, and yet, beside him, she had a sense of being enveloped in an aura of summer.

At the edge of the courtyard, a bas relief of a tree had been carved into the cliff face. The water oozing down its branches gleamed as if it were starlight turned liquid, sliding into a circular stone basin as wide across as her outstretched arms.

She studied the outlines of the sculpture. "Is this meant to be the same tree as the stone one up on the ridge?"

He raised a hand for silence. They stood together, neither moving, as slow ripples spread across the basin like the wash of time, as the wind soughed in the leaves, as the moon rose high enough that her light caught at last in the basin's shallow waters. The surface turned as if to a sheet of thinnest silver.

Stepping forward, the haunt swept both arms open. The sheen hardened to become a mirror in which the stars twinkled but the moon was not visible, although it was the moon's light that made the mirror.

"Look." He made the word an offer, a request, not a command.

With her first step forward, she could see his reflection although not yet her own. Prince Gevulin's face had fine bones and pleasing eyes. The embroidery that ran along the shoulders and collar of his warden's tunic glowed as if sewn with magic thread, and there was writing down the sleeves of the tunic that wasn't visible, except in the water's mirror. Skeins of protection, perhaps, or secret oaths. She had no idea.

But there was a shadow in the water, a slowly heaving movement that twisted sinuously behind and around the face and figure of the prince. It never fully surfaced, but its shifting flow gave glimpses of the powerful shape of a beast with a long body, half-folded wings, and a narrow, golden head with slender horns and elegant whiskers.

Stepping closer, she stared with both utter delight at its fluid movement and awe at its beauty. She breathed, wonderingly, "Is that a dragon?"

"Come. Another step forward," he said coaxingly.

With the step, her own head and torso appeared in the mirror next to the prince's reflection. Same old El in most ways: round face, green eyes, the wavy, finger's-length scar that ran from beneath her left ear to curl up behind the lobe, out of sight. Of course she was older now than the little girl who had first seen her own reflection in a pure-water pool beneath a full moon so many years ago. She'd gotten tall, but not unusually so; lean from all the walking but with the healthy look of someone who now gets enough to eat every day. Her hair had grown out, black and so tumultuously curly that she

kept it braided back to get it out of her face. As children, her and
Ao's heads had been shaved every full moon. Long hair meant freedom, even if it took a lot longer to care for. The same measuring
gaze, scanning for danger, but a mouth ready to smile because life
was too short not to smile.

But one thing was different, from then to now, from a child of
about five to a woman in her early thirties. In the center of her torso
twined the wispy outline of the viper, clearly visible. Back then, there
had been no viper, only a pale egg-seed tucked next to her heart, like
a Spore. She pressed a hand to her own chest as the viper stirred,
for it could taste the emanation of the pure-water, which was both
poison and cure.

The haunt gave a nod, inviting her to speak.

She said, "The only other time I saw it inside me, it was a seed like
an egg nestled into my heart. I was just a little girl. I didn't know what
it was or that it would—that it could—hatch. How does the mirror
make it visible?"

"The moon mirror shows us our essence. When did you see yourself before?"

The memory slipped free. "It was a long time ago. I had this scar
then, too. I remember noticing it because it was so prominent even
in the reflection, red and raw, but I don't remember getting it. All I
remember is standing on the shore of a pool, under the moon, and
the pool became a mirror like this one, and I saw myself."

"It takes an enchantment to form the mirror, which combines the
essence of moonlight and pure-water, that is, the reflection of truth.
But you don't have that power. Who did?"

She shook her head uneasily. She didn't want to revisit that life
and saw no reason to return, even in memories. "There was someone
standing next to me, a presence, a person. I don't remember seeing
their reflection in the pond, not like yours here beside mine."

"Interesting. We of the Shorn can use spells to hide ourselves
from the mirror, if we so choose. That's why we call it both the heart
mirror and the shadow mirror."

A new thought struck Elen, and she added breathlessly, "The
dragon is your shadow, the heart of you, your essence."

"A handsome fellow, I am sure you will agree. Everyone always
said so. I fear the praise went to my head." His reflection grinned,
and he shot her a cheeky wink.

She rolled her eyes. "Here I stand, an ordinary garden viper. Nothing of beauty or elegance about me."

"Nay, nay, do not say so, for you are everything you should be. Besides that, like all vipers, you have the ability to track your prey."

"What is my prey?"

"You tell me."

"I suppose it is Spore."

"From what hints you've let drop, I suspect that over the years, this instinct for Spore has saved your life time and again, and the lives of others. Am I not correct?"

She sighed, tilting her head to study her sturdy features. Aoving had been pretty in a fragile way that attracted men of a certain type, and, of course, Ao's unusual hair, once it had grown out, had attracted notice as well. In her adolescent years, Elen had sometimes struggled with despair that she could never be the flower to which bees swarmed, that she was the one people treated as a comrade. But Aoving had not prospered because of that interest. Fragile prettiness was a venom in its own fashion, that ate its owner if they were controlled by unkind hands. Being the focus of such attention had badly harmed the vulnerable Ao. After all that, once they'd made a home in Orledder Halt, Elen had no lack of willing partners when she wanted them, while Aoving had never taken a lover again, barely able to bear being touched, except by those in the throes of labor who needed a helping hand to clutch.

The haunt watched her watch her reflection. "The greatest beauty of the world lies in ordinary things. The rising and setting of the sun, on which we depend. The glorious joy of a waterfall. The first flower of spring. A field of ripe grain. The earth it grows in." His reflection gestured upward toward the heavens. "The ordinary stars."

"But the stars aren't ordinary. They're brilliant. They shine."

His eyes half closed as his mouth twitched in a secret little smile. "Yes, it is their shine that draws us to them." He opened his eyes to meet her gaze in the mirror, until suddenly she was sure she'd become so dizzy that she was about to topple into a pool whose undercurrents were threatening to drag her down into unfathomable depths.

She jerked back to get out of range of her own reflection. With that step, a pressure tugged against her skin, as if she were ripping away the veil of truth so she could retreat into the comfort of lies.

"It's not what I expected," she muttered.

"The pure-water spring? The journey through the hills? Life, with all its twists and turns?" A weighty pause, and then, "My attractive smile?"

She laughed, the sound as bright as a bell in the night. The beauty of the night made her reckless. "Maybe you aren't an evil sorcerer after all."

His eyebrows arched in exaggerated surprise, although she heard laughter in his tone. "Did you fear I might be?"

"You must admit a shadowy haunt lurking amid abandoned towers would seem suspicious. Even one with an attractive smile."

"Maybe especially one with an attractive smile." The haunt stepped back from the basin, face falling into shadow, but she could tell he was now smiling. Abruptly, before he could say more, he tensed, going alert. He had heard or sensed something. His posture shifted as he went on guard.

"We'd best return," he began, extending an arm to sweep her back.

The snick of a light object hit the paving stones. A dart skittered across the ground and came to rest by her boot. She jumped back as a pair of sleek lynxes emerged onto an outcropping of rocks from behind a sheet of fountaining water, as if they had emerged out of the hillside itself. The big mountain cats were magnificent creatures large enough to rip off Elen's face, should they attack.

Each was being ridden by a three-horned swalter, crossbows resting on thighs. They were a small people, the tops of their heads reaching no higher than Elen's hip, and were belligerent brawlers or, if the pay was good enough, cunning caravan guards. These two had heads shaven short, with the crescent moon clan markings of one of the Moonrise Hills clans, but she didn't recognize them as individuals.

They weren't looking at her anyway. Their three-eyed faces were turned accusingly, with visible hostility, toward the haunt. He hadn't moved at all and yet, impossibly, he seemed to take up more space, arms slightly raised as if preparing to fling something deadly at the newcomers.

Elen's neck prickled, and she braced herself, ready for violence to break out.

"Speak," said the haunt curtly. He wasn't using the prince's arrogant voice but a tone deeper and more threatening, a sense of expansive power about to break free should he care to let it go.

The swalters did not back down. They clutched their spears more tightly.

"Our Clan Mother sends her greetings, Elder Cousin," said one in a voice like a growl. "You are not welcome in these hills, whose earth has seen the tide rise and fall across the wrath of years. Your kind wracked and ruined the world. And the rest of you were said to be severed, long since, from the land, shorn of your own will and your own doing. So why are you here now? What trouble do you bring in your wake? The beating of your wings is bound to raise turbulence. So speaks the Clan Mother, who has sent us to inquire, having seen and smelled your passage through our territory."

At the mention of the Clan Mother, the haunt settled, as if furling outstretched wings in respect. His reply wasn't mild, but it was neutral. "Younger Cousins, I greet you and send my greetings to your esteemed Clan Mother. I am not a herald. I am but a scout, seeking news of a distant bell. Have you heard its passing toll?"

The two swalters glanced at each other in a shared message. Beyond that, Elen could not discern any features on their faces, even with the moonlight, for they had the knack of making themselves too gauzy to truly see.

"We know nothing of your bell. Nor is it any business of ours. We live here in harmony with the empire and wish only to not be disturbed. We are not interested in negotiations or alliances."

"Then I will offer my respects to your Clan Mother. Give her this message, that I merely pass through these hills on my way into the north. I shall not bother you again, as long as you agree to leave me and those who travel with me alone."

"So shall it be, by the Mother's Beard."

A rattle of wind shook through the garden. The shadows twisted, and the lynxes melted back, disappearing behind the water.

"Is there a lair up there?" Elen asked breathlessly.

"I believe there is," the haunt said in his normal tone, so odd to hear after the tense exchange. "They are a tunneling people, adept at moving through rock."

"Tunneling? Swalters are a forest people."

He cast her a disbelieving look.

She added, "I didn't even know there was a clan at this temple. I didn't know this courtyard existed, even though I've overnighted here every month for ten years. There's another well, in a different courtyard, where travelers can request a drink of pure-water for healing and strength. I never dreamed there was another source."

He raised a hand for silence. She heard a footstep. Together, they retreated behind the prickly evergreen foliage of a winter-bane hedge. Who could possibly be awake? Besides the swalters, that is.

The old custodian padded into the courtyard, lamp in hand. Either the sleep enchantment had worn off, or the man had some kind of protection against it. He held up the lamp, peering around, then saw the dart and, with a grunt of interest, bent to pick it up. With a last glance toward the hillside, he left. The haunt's elbow brushed Elen's, paused, pressed: *Stay still.*

They stood there a while longer, so close she could breathe him in. A yearning caught in her throat, and she wasn't even sure what she was yearning for. A touch. A caress. A kiss, slow and sweet and hot.

He took in a startled breath and, moving swiftly, stepped out from behind the bush. She followed, angry with herself. *Don't get distracted or sloppy. No shortcuts. Stick to the routine. Stay calm.*

She had to focus on the mission, on the here and now, the day to day. But that brought her thoughts back to the washroom and Kem's parting "fuck you." Would Kem ever talk to her again? Could he ever forgive her? Compared to Kem's anger, the rest of this was chaff. Whether the haunt was the prince, or the prince was the haunt, he would walk out of her life and on about the important business of the palace, or the mysterious business of the bell. She would go back to courier duty.

The haunt glanced at her but made no comment about her tense stride and harsh breathing. They returned to the hostel. Fulmo still stood unmoving beneath the starlight. Something tiny rested by his right foot.

It was a dead mouse with a dart stuck in its neck.

The haunt picked it up by the tail, its body dangling limply, empty of life. "A warning. Or a reminder. Not even enough meat to make a meal for the likes of us. What a waste. I'll burn it in the hearth."

"What is the bell?" she asked. "What does it mean?"

He kept his gaze on the dead mouse, as if its corpse contained the answers he sought. "The bell is the trace, the mark, the sign of sorcery. That these swalters know nothing of it is unexpected, for their people lived through the days when sorcery almost destroyed the world."

"That was a long time ago."

"So it seems. Still, their Clan Mother hasn't forgotten the past, has she? I could not tell you what it means that they claim to know nothing of the bell. Either they are lying, or they can't hear it."

"They weren't happy to see you, that's certain. Do you think they might attack us as we travel on? The path grows more isolated from here on out. Maybe you are truly a creature of legend who can wield enchantments, but the human body you wear is fragile enough to kill."

He swung the mouse back and forth by its tail, as if it were a toy and he a beast who played with his prey, which he afterward ate. "They are too wise to attempt it."

35

THE SOBER SEARCH FOR TRUTH

As the sages proclaim, every temple is a heart, and every heart is a temple.

Indeed, where would the Tranquil Empire be without the Heart Temples? The palace and the temples are woven together by the network of imperial roads, into one body.

All Heart Temples follow the same hallowed plan. Any child of the empire recognizes the familiar entry gate, the courtyard and its fountain, an annex where people come to seek healing or help, the hostel where indigent travelers may sleep for three nights, and the holy altar where the temple's custodian places daily offerings. Healers and theurgists serve by the grace of the emperor, their precious skills bound to the temple and thus to the betterment of the empire for the whole of their lives. Those who serve as many years as the beloved Peony Emperor reigned are thereafter addressed as "venerable."

Some poets sing that the Lotus General founded the first Heart Temple where his most beloved consort fell in battle while fighting off an enemy who was about to stab the general in the eye. Playwrights favor a tale of clan treachery and redemption with a blustering cast of rebellious youth and fractious priests brought back into the fold by the general's magnanimity and wisdom.

However, no official records in the palace archives provide evidence for the emperor or his officials commanding the construction of temples in the earliest days of the empire. During the imperial era, all archival documents for temple construction refer only to small local temples built by the order of an intendant or archon, perhaps to burnish the reputation of an overweening minor official. While these edifices are built to the same layout as every temple, they are identifiable by some manner of unique and ostentatious decoration meant to impress, rather than to inspire spiritual reflection through simplicity and familiarity.

The only palace memoranda on the subject come from the early years of the empire. Without exception, they refer to the repair of temples by the imperial engineers, occurring at the same time as sections of deteriorated roads were being rebuilt and restored. Further, chronicles written in the era of the Lotus General and his successor, the Chrysanthemum Emperor, imply that venerables of the Heart Temple fought against the establishment of the empire. As well, there are fragmentary references to Heart Temples found in surviving chronicles from the Seven Golden Kingdoms era, while certain poets of dubious origin write that the first Heart Temple was raised during the age of the sorcerer-kings in order to combat the wicked nature of sorcerers, although this claim is impossible to prove or disprove and caters to the sensationalism of poetic imagination, rather than to the sober search for truth.

Therefore, one thing is clear: the Heart Temples existed before the establishment of the Tranquil Empire and, in one form or another, have knitted together the lives and society of our ancestors for many generations far into the past.

From *The Official's Handbook of the Empire* as compiled by
Luviara, theurgist, working at the behest of the
Inner Chamber of the Heart Temple

36

The Conundrum She Wrestled With

Elen set a hard pace, determined to focus on speed, to stay away from the haunt. Even if he was not a prince, he was a prince. It was the conundrum she wrestled with. Would the wardens kill their prince if they knew a haunt possessed his body? Did Luviara know a way to drive out the haunt, using theurgy? Was Elen willing to stand by and see it done? If it even could be done—and naturally the haunt had said it could not. Wasn't Elen just as bad as the haunt, by saying nothing and letting him continue to use—to steal—the prince's body?

Yet. Yet. Yet.

Gesavura'alalin had claimed he needed the prince only to get to the north, and that he would then depart the body, leaving it unharmed. She believed him, maybe for bad reasons and maybe for good ones and maybe for a tangle of both. Maybe she just liked being able to glance back and see him stroking the bark of trees and picking up stray pebbles to caress them between his fingers, to see him smile to himself if he felt her gaze on him; to see *him* see her. He did not avert his eyes as Kem did every time the lad came close to her. Kem wanted not to see her, as if seeing her wounded him. It was a habit he'd picked up from his mother when she fell into one of her weeks-long sulks, but Elen wasn't about to remind him of that, and anyway, he wasn't speaking to her.

She kept walking. It was easier to be out in front, to leave the messiness behind, where she didn't have to deal with it. Some things couldn't be fixed, so a person had to choose whether to endure or, if the chance arose, to escape. As for Kem, she had to give him space. She had to be patient and wait for an opening.

For four more days they tramped at a hard pace along the upland path. A new runner went out each day. Every village had youths to run messages between the isolated communities.

The first day, their party passed one Moat and two Ditches, the second day two Ditches only, the third day a cluster of three Ditches. Always it was the same: the villagers lining the path, come rain or shine. The fourth day, they passed only one tiny Ditch, whose census of forty-seven souls all knelt at the side of the path. The haunt touched the head of each child who was present, as if he were giving the children a gift. Certainly the locals felt it to be so. How different it must look to them compared to her memory of her own childhood, when the notice of the master upon a lowly atoner meant bad news.

The fifth afternoon, soon after midday, they arrived at Pisgia Moat, a large settlement colloquially known as Fisherman's Rest. Built on stilts along the shore of an upland lake, its many drying sheds gave the village a distinctly fishy smell.

The path led straight to a settlement large enough it might be called a small town. What looked like its entire census of 2,139 souls had gathered at the bridge over the ditch that ringed the landward side of the village. The gate drums beat a merry *bam bam bam boom* in welcome.

"We aren't stopping, are we?" Simo asked. "There's still most of the afternoon left."

"We must stop here. The main path loops northeast on my regular circuit. We'll take a secret turnoff here onto a side trail. On that trail, there's no place to shelter for the night. If we depart at dawn, we can get across the Cut before nightfall."

"If you say so."

His frown annoyed her. "Captain, have I led you wrong?"

"I would be happier to have a surveyor's map, so you can show me where we are."

"I would be happier to carry a surveyor's map. But I am merely a deputy courier, so the map I use is the map in my mind. Have you any other questions for me?"

"I do not."

"I have a question, if I may, Captain."

"Go on."

"What do you mean to tell the archon, about your business?"

Simo looked at her as if she had sprouted two heads. "The prince need tell an archon nothing. Nor will she inquire. If I have any further questions about how we mean to proceed, I shall call for you. But the archon is not to be told anything."

"I understand."

"I hope you do." Shaking his head, he finished, "Let His Exalted Highness be settled in such comfort as we can find in this benighted, primitive place."

"You'll find the town not as primitive as you expect. The archon prides herself on the many luxuries she has been able to afford."

The archon profusely greeted the prince and escorted him to the village's well-appointed hostel, adjacent to its opulently decorated Heart Temple. The lake's rich stock of freshwater fish had brought prosperity to the village, which traded dried fish all around the uplands as a winter food source. The locals were proud of their hostel. It had three separate courtyards and a special suite of rooms for merchants willing to pay for a private garden and private, heated bath. While the archon and the prince's escort made a fuss of installing the prince in the suite, Elen took herself off to the annex where she normally slept.

The annex's tiny courtyard had a tiny fountain with water piped in from the lake, a basin for washing, and a sleeping chamber with a pair of bunk beds and, thank the High Heavens, a good brick hearth.

A familiar woman knelt before the oven, tending the stove. She wore much-mended clothing, and a widow's cap covered her gray hair. The fabric was dingy and discolored by the dirtiness of her daily chores.

She rose, face creased with a nervous smile. "Deputy Courier, is it true a prince has come?"

"It is. Prince Gevulin, the All-Seeing Eye, Prince of the Third Estate. He has other titles, but I see by your expression you have something urgent to relate, so I'll not delay. What is it you have to tell me, Charwoman?"

The woman did not answer, except by wringing her hands.

Elen added, "Oflidu, you have my word that whatever you relate to me here stays between us."

Oflidu sighed. "I know you can keep a secret. Your blessed sister did, may she rest in the glory of the High Heavens. I found something."

She went silent, too afraid to speak more. After a moment, Elen took her pack into the hostel, fetched out the brush, and went back into the courtyard. She sat down, took off her boots, and began to clean the mud-streaked soles. The sheer ordinariness of the chore and the rhythmic *chuff-chuff* of the brush released Oflidu's paralysis.

The woman dipped a hand into the pocket of her skirt and fished out a small brass ornament. It had a broken buckle, with a bit of leather attached. Elen rested the object on her palm. The ornament depicted a griffin's head: eagle's beak, pointed cat ears, a curling crest down the back of a long neck, and stylized feathers. The workmanship was superlative. She'd seen a similar image in the intendant's manifest of the imperial corps. A griffin! Could it be related to the missing scout?

With an effort, Elen tamped down a surge of excitement and dread, and addressed Oflidu in a calm tone.

"This looks like part of the harness worn by an imperial griffin scout. Where did you find this?"

The charwoman fell to her knees, trembling. "I pray you, Deputy Courier—"

"I am Elen to you, am I not? We are not so different, Oflidu."

"Nay, nay, it is not so. You have the courtesy of the intendant. I live on the sufferance of the archon. She has never forgiven me for the death of her child."

"Ah, yes, I remember. My sister told me of the day when four women here in the town were giving birth all at the same time."

"A full moon," Oflidu muttered. "Healer Aoving asked for all four to be taken to the Heart Temple, so she could supervise them together. The archon refused."

"That's right. Aoving told me she delivered the first two in quick succession, easy labors. She went to check on the archon, but her labor was proceeding the most slowly so she came back here because of her concern for your daughter."

Oflidu's hands were gripped to white around the poker. "The fault was mine. It was all my selfish fault."

"How can that be?" Elen said gently.

"I ran to the archon's compound and begged Aoving to hurry back because my daughter was in such pain. If she'd stayed with the archon—"

"That's not what I recall Aoving saying. She related the entire affair to me later." Because the archon's high-handed dealing had angered Aoving, but Elen didn't add that. "The archon's baby had a flaw in its heart. It wouldn't have lived no matter what. That's not your fault."

"The archon says I should have respected authority and not called the healer to attend to my daughter."

"Didn't your daughter have a difficult breech birth? Up to that point, the archon's labor was proceeding normally, and no one knew about the bad heart. A breech birth needs special intervention."

"Yes. A turning. That's what she did. It was the blessing of the High Heavens!"

Or the skill of a good midwife. But Elen didn't say that. "That's why your daughter and your grandchild both survived. Maybe I never told you, but my sister had a few strong words for the archon refusing to lie in with the other women, especially when there was no other midwife available. Does the archon blame the other women too?"

"Yes. She made their lives miserable afterward, too. Both left Fisherman's Rest for other villages. But I have no kin to migrate to. Here I was born, and here I will die. My daughter died from a flux, five years after the birth. She was the only one of my children who survived childhood. Her daughter is all I have left. Ten years now. The bright star of my life. Maybe if my precious grandchild had died, too, the archon would have resented me less."

Elen rubbed the smooth surface of the brass griffin. "What has the archon's resentment to do with this ornament?"

Oflidu swallowed anxiously, but Elen's nod encouraged her to go on. "This time of year, I take my grandchild up to Cloudberry Ridge. There's always late-harvest cloudberries. They dry well. We eat them during the winter season. But I don't have a license to glean there. It's part of the archon's holding."

"I see. You fear the archon will prosecute you out of spite."

"She is justiciar. What if she takes away my child to serve in her household? Or condemns the child to death for theft?"

Elen didn't ask if a justiciar could impose such a cruel sentence. As the intendant had once said, where the law is severe, it is meant to be eased with mercy, and where it is merciful, it is meant to be ruled with a strict observance of justice. But where the justiciar is bent on their own selfish desires, it can be twisted into any wicked form.

"But you have given this to me. Why? Knowing the risk?"

"Because my grandchild sneaked up there on her own. She's old enough to do that."

"To disobey you because she believes you need her help?"

Oflidu wiped tears from her cheek. "She's such a good girl. It will kill me to lose her. But I suppose the archon would be glad of that too. I am just the charwoman. The archon told me she was cheated of the child that should have belonged to her. For you see, she refused to come labor in the temple with the rest of us. It being beneath her consequence. And then—"

Elen saw that the woman was about to repeat her description of the births and death and the archon's selfish anger, so she broke in. "What about the ornament? Who found it? Your grandchild?"

"No, no, I found it. She had gone up the day before."

"Yesterday?"

"No, no, this would have been seven days, maybe six, maybe eight. Just past the fat moon."

Elen choked down an exclamation. "And?" she said as coolly as she could, although her heart pounded.

"She'd gone to see if there were cloudberries left to pick. She came home to tell me there were three ripe patches the archon's people had missed. She told me she'd seen a griffin scout circling above the ruins of Olludia Halt."

37

FIVE BASKETS FULL!

The words hit like a spark, hot with import.

A griffin scout.

Elen's fingers closed over the ornament.

Oflidu went on. "I thought it was childish dreaming. Ever since she first heard stories of the griffin scouts, just a little thing as she was then, she has always said she will grow up to ride a griffin. But that's impossible for a person of our station. So I thought she was telling a tale about seeing a griffin scout, like she does. We went up the next day, sneaked up. There was a rich haul of berries, just as she said. After we'd gleaned them—five baskets full!—I explored down the slope to where I thought was a fresh mound of tufted feather-grass. I can use that to weave—" Her expression changed, and she bent as if waiting to be whipped. In a ragged whisper, she said, "It . . . It . . . It was . . ."

Elen knew the only ending that made sense. "It was a scout and their griffin. Both dead?"

"Oh. Oh." Oflidu clutched her stomach as if in pain. "Dead. Yes. Dead. I didn't look close at the beast. It was so big. So big, and its claws. The scout had been thrown a little ways away. I think the fall killed her. There was so much blood. Head crushed. Brains . . . what was left. Animals had been at it."

"You cut off this ornament? It must have been part of the scout's harness."

"I did. I don't know why. I knew I couldn't sell it." The shadows under her eyes and the exhausted slump of her shoulders betrayed her desperation. "I can't even report it. I've been so afraid. I didn't tell my girl, just told her the feather-grass was too old to be of use. Like me. Please don't let her know. It's better she not know."

Elen had never met Oflidu's grandchild. She only saw the charwoman at the hostel, tending to the fires and the latrines. A sour smell rose from the old woman now, part of it the ash and waste a charwoman dealt with daily, and part of it a miasma of fear. Of vulnerability. Maybe it was the viper in Elen that recognized the scent of prey, she thought with bitter humor, thinking of the haunt and the moon mirror he'd made.

She rested a hand on the woman's shoulder. "Leave the ornament with me. You have done well to confide in me. Go about your business and think no more about this. I'll deal with it. I promise your name and that of your grandchild will never come into it. Do you trust me?"

"Your sister saved my darling girl's life, for a time, anyway, and brought me the one good thing in my life. I pray to the High Heavens that you'll not suffer what your sister did."

Elen rubbed her own face. Even after two years, it hurt to think of Aoving lost beneath the crushing rock. What must her last moments have been like? The crack, the rumble, the change in the air, the mounting dust, the screaming as the first sliding weight of rock hit the upper houses . . .

Elen shut down the spiral of her thoughts. She could not walk that path. It was the way Aoving had lived, always imagining what worst thing might happen even though there was no way to know and usually no way to prevent the unexpected avalanches that engulfed you.

Oflidu was weeping as she got up and went back to the fire. The work had to get done, no matter her tears.

Elen said briskly, "Charwoman, I pray you, let the temple custodian know I will use one of my tokens for a meal this evening. Fish, if you have it."

Oflidu snorted a laugh that broke through her tears. "A bit of fish, yes, I think we here can manage that." Then, in a whisper, not looking up as she placed a log onto the flames, "My thanks."

Elen pocketed the ornament, washed her face and hands, and grabbed her staff and her kit. She turned over options in her mind as she walked back to the entrance to the suite.

Kem and Ipis stood stiffly outside, on guard beside two of the archon's sentinels. From inside Elen heard voices, an awkward laugh, an impatient clap of hands, followed by Luviara saying something she couldn't quite make out.

"Warden Ipis," Elen said, "I beg your leave. I need to speak—wish to speak, on a matter of possible importance—to Warden Captain Simo. I pray you will ask him to meet me here in the courtyard."

Ipis looked Elen up and down with a skeptical grimace. "He's busy with His Exalted Highness. What's so important a deputy courier demands to speak to a warden captain?"

Elen considered the distance from the village to Cloudberry

Ridge, and how much of the afternoon was left. "I can wait until His Exalted Highness is settled."

She took several steps back, finding a patch of sun for warmth, and relaxed into a loose stance that she could hold for some time. Kem studiously did not look at her, standing with rigid correctness, expression stony. Ipis glanced at him with a curious frown, then shrugged, yawned, and crossed her arms, looking bored. She was a big-boned, brawny young woman who walked and talked with the assurance of one who is Manor-born. It was fortunate she seemed to like Kem. In all honesty, Elen was happy enough to keep her own relationship with Kem a secret for now, lest the others scorn him. It was good they'd left Orledder Halt so quickly, before the wardens could hear any gossip about how Lord Duenn had just found his missing child. She didn't want the wardens to question whether the youth deserved to be allowed to Declare for them. Once made, a Declaration could not be revoked, but a person's life could still be made miserable.

Simo appeared at the door, startling Elen because Ipis hadn't gone into the suite to alert him. He spotted her and walked over.

"His Exalted Highness told me that you need to speak to me."

She bit down on a smile. The haunt clearly had exceptional hearing. She'd have to remember that.

"Captain, I wanted to inform you we are within an hour's steep hike of a place known as Cloudberry Ridge. It overlooks the ruins of Olludia Halt and the main avalanche that blocks the road. If you or His Exalted Highness wish to see the barrier from a different angle, that would be the place to do it."

"Would such a trek not be more appropriate for the imperial engineers?"

"Indeed, it would. In the past two years I have escorted three separate groups of engineers up there to observe and measure the damage. I thought His Highness might be interested."

"Why would you think that?" Simo glanced toward the door, then back at her with narrowed eyes.

"Captain, I am merely a provincial deputy courier, but I have ears. It seems curious to me that the intendant received no message of the prince's imminent arrival. It also seems curious that His Exalted Highness had no knowledge of the barrier that has been blocking the road for almost two years. That's a long time for an exalted highness, especially one with such an impressive list of accomplishments, not to know."

"He was elevated to all-seeing eye only recently," said Simo, sounding defensive. "Before that he had been traveling extensively around the empire and would have had no reason to be kept up to date on that sort of news."

"I pray forgiveness for asking, but did *you* not know about the avalanche, Captain?"

"I am not chief warden. That position belongs to another, senior to me, appointed by the emperor. I was recalled from the eastern frontier to serve Prince Gevulin, at the specific request of the Elegant Consort, his blessed mother."

"So, you were also kept in the dark about the road being blocked," said Elen, seeing a crack in his armor. "Then you may be particularly interested in seeing the avalanche."

"I don't see what benefit it serves. From the carriages, we saw the road buried under rock. It's difficult to imagine it can be shifted. Theurgists may be able to command spirits of air, but air cannot lift boulders. There's no way across Grinder's Cut, is there?"

Elen quickly rubbed a hand across her lips, reminding him that the archon's sentinels stood nearby and could possibly hear.

"Yes, exactly," he added awkwardly, catching her signal. "So I ask again, what is the point of going to see this barrier?"

She rubbed a hand along her pocket, feeling the hard shape of the ornament. It would be hard to explain without naming Oflidu, but Simo waved a hand in curt dismissal and turned back. Just then, the haunt appeared in the doorway. He paused to make sure everyone was looking before he strolled out with all the haughty posture and languid grace appropriate to a prince.

"Simo! Is there news?"

The warden pressed hands to heart. "Your Highness."

"What news?" His impatience snapped like a whip.

"Nothing to bother yourself with, Your Highness."

"Let me be the judge of that. Go on."

A pause.

A long pause.

"Ah, eh, uh." Simo really did not want to tell him. How odd. Elen cleared her throat softly, and the sound spurred the captain on. "It seems an hour's walk from here there is a ridge from which one can survey the more severe of the two avalanches that block the road."

"The avalanche that buried a village? Not the avalanche we saw from the road? Yes, let's go at once. I need to stretch my legs and

take the air. The incense inside those rooms is making me sneeze."
He punctuated his words with a healthy sneeze, then laughed as if he
found the reflex of sneezing to be absurdly amusing.

Simo stared at him. "Your Highness? Are you well?"

"I am ready to depart!"

38

SOMEWHERE AMONG THE ROCKS

The archon emerged, desperately trying to explain to Luviara that nothing was too good for the prince if he would only let her know his needs, and there were two licensed courtesans in town who knew all the heartland customs and could cater to any taste, and if that was not sufficient then she had a daughter of fourteen, never touched, who would be honored to accept the prince's attentions.

The haunt kept his back to the archon as his expression twisted with distaste. He said, "Simo, at once. Just you, me, and the deputy courier. The others will remain here."

Simo knew his business, which was to get a party together swiftly and yet also with the prince's safety in mind. "Of course, Your Highness. But I insist we take Xilsi and Jirvy. Ipis, you will use the afternoon to train Kem. Your Worthiness, it will be a steep climb, so best you stay with Fulmo and make sure the archon knows what will suit His Highness the best."

"A child!" muttered the haunt with disgust.

Xilsi and Jirvy emerged with their weapons, handing Simo his own kit. Fulmo handed out leather bottles, filled to the brim and sealed with caps. Besides being able to carry three times as much as anyone else, he tasted everything for the prince. As everyone knew from *The Crafty Cannibal Cooks and the Sweet Little Girl*, poison was the most commonplace murder weapon used in the palace to eliminate rivals.

The five of them made good time climbing out of the valley of the lake on a path that twisted and turned up the western face of Olu Ridge. Xilsi easily kept pace scrambling up at the front with Elen. The warden was a strong and energetic woman. Elen had thought her as young as Ipis but, over the days, had realized Xilsi had one of those piquant faces that make a person look younger than they really are.

The two women halted at a switchback to await the others. Simo had paused on the path below because the haunt had stopped to admire a towering tuft of late-flowering feather-grass. Jirvy stood lower down, bow in hand, scanning the hillside. His gaze flickered upward, toward the two women.

Xilsi stiffened. "What a relief to walk alongside a calm-minded person like yourself, Deputy Courier."

Elen glanced between the two wardens, so far apart and yet clearly, intensely aware of each other, and said neutrally, "It must seem a rougher path than the well-paved witch roads you usually travel."

"We wardens don't call them witch roads."

"My apologies."

"I know provincials call them witch roads because they're able to withstand the Pall and its Spore, and I certainly don't care what you provincials call them, but some who walk around with sticks up their asses"—Xilsi gave a careless wave in the direction of Jirvy— "will sourly protest they are properly known as imperial roads, as opposed to ordinary roads. Not to change the subject, but I thought up here in the hills during the moon-bright, we'd see Spore."

"Irruptions are rare in this area. Maybe the composition of the dirt, or the type of rock that builds the bones of these hills. Maybe just the elevation."

Xilsi looked her up and down. "You're a strange one, for a deputy courier."

"Am I?"

"You know a lot. You don't seem afraid of much. You speak freely to everyone, even to me. Even to the prince, now he's released you from the requirement to speak through Luviara."

"I'm surprised she hasn't turned back yet."

Xilsi grinned with what appeared to be genuine delight. "That old coot! She's as tough as they come. She's been all over the empire and outside it, too. I swear by the High Heavens, she has walked more in her life than all the rest of us put together can ever hope to manage. She'll never turn back, not at a chance like this."

What manner of chance is that? Elen wanted to ask but held her tongue and let Xilsi go on.

"A different interlocutor had been assigned to His Highness when he was raised to the seat of all-seeing eye. He sent that one back because he said the man was a spy for Prince Astaylin. He asked for Theurgist Luviara by name."

"Did he? Is it common for a prince of the Third Estate to know the names of theurgists?"

Xilsi flicked her fingers as if brushing dirt off her shoulder. "His Highness is the smartest person at court, for all he's only twenty-six. Six years younger than me, if you can credit it."

"You look younger than him."

"It's my face," Xilsi said. "My mother was the same. She looked twenty until she was fifty."

"And after she was fifty?"

Xilsi grinned. "Then she looked twenty-one."

Elen laughed.

"That's what puzzles me about you," Xilsi went on. "I've been a warden since I was seventeen. Like our Kem."

Elen couldn't help but wince—Kem confiding in everyone already—as Xilsi went on.

"I've never met a provincial official, much less a mere deputy courier, who would talk and laugh with a Manor-born soul like me the way you do. Ipis thinks you're the intendant's child by a courtesan, secretly raised in his household. Kem said you aren't. Although if he's of Duenn Manor, I don't know how he would know, but he seemed certain."

"I'm not the intendant's by-blow, I assure you."

"Prince Astaylin's spy, then?" Xilsi asked, so casually that Elen realized this entire seemingly friendly conversation might have been engineered to spring the question on her.

She shook her head with an amused smile. "Warden, I assure you, I have never been to the heartland nor farther south than the one time I traveled to Ilvewind Cross with the intendant's retinue. I have walked the Moonrise Hills circuit every month for the last ten years. If you doubt the truth of my statement, you will find the transmission logs of my passage at every village and temple along the route, as well as in more detail at Map Hall in the Residence at Orledder Halt."

Xilsi crossed her arms. "Don't you get bored with the same routine, over and over?"

"The path is never the same from one month to the next, just as people are never the same from one year to the next, even if only in small ways. I am content."

It was even true, except for her nagging worry about Kem. Who would she be now that Kem was leaving her? She didn't know, and as she stared over the lake and its highland valley, she wondered if the circuit would become a burden once she had no one waiting at home. Still, Captain Jinyan had recommended her for surveyor's training. That would be something. Wouldn't it?

"Here they are," said Xilsi as Simo and the haunt caught up to them. Simo was winded by the steepness of the slope, puffing and blowing, while the haunt wasn't even breathing hard. After all, the haunt had the use of the prince's very fit body, honed through climbing the ten peaks and mastering the graceful eloquence of the Wind Dance.

"We're almost there," said Elen to Simo, who glared at her.

"Then why are you waiting?" he demanded.

She headed up.

"You shouldn't say such things to the captain," said Xilsi, keeping pace.

"What things?"

"You've insulted Simo by suggesting he will be relieved to reach the top of the ridge."

"Won't he be? He's out of breath."

"Yes, but it's impertinent for you to say it aloud. Now, if you were to say the same to Jirvy, I would applaud."

"I see," said Elen, deciding this was dangerously slippery ground. "Here we are, just this last climb over these rocks. Careful of that crevice. There're nettles."

She clambered atop a flat rock and halted with the world laid like a platter before her. Xilsi leaped up beside Elen and, eyes widening, exclaimed aloud. They looked over a rocky slope. Bristling cloud-berry thickets, yellowing stands of sedge, and tall drifts of hill-grass grew among the many outcroppings that littered the slope. A fair distance away, there was, indeed, a massive tuft of what looked like feather-grass, but because she knew it was a dead griffin, Elen could only see it as spiky wing feathers in the early stages of fading and decay. The body would be wedged among the rocks.

Farther down, the slope cut abruptly away into a stark cliff face. A few pine trees still dangled over the precipice created by part of the slope peeling off as an entire section had come crashing down. The view was tremendous.

If a person could walk vertically through the air, they would descend a thousand paces or more from the top of the cliff to the rubble at its base. The land below the cliff was a canyon, wider in the south and narrowing as it ran north past the Halt. Its far side was a steep ridge, like this one with a sheer escarpment. To the north, the high, rocky ridges flattened into the characteristic plateau through which wound the river canyon known as Grinder's Cut. Olu Canyon was one of the side canyons that made up Grinder's Cut. Olu Canyon had a stream at its base. Early in the empire, imperial engineers had refurbished Olludia Halt for travelers needing extra time to get through the grueling ups and downs of the rest of the canyon route.

The massive rockslide that had torn away part of the cliff face had buried the village and rolled onward to block the entire canyon. A row of six undamaged houses stood in a line just above the unstable rock.

"What are those anchoring posts?" Xilsi asked. She pointed to a set of iron spikes driven into the ground near the upper edge of the cliff.

"Do you see those intact houses? People were trapped there after the avalanche, with no way up or down. Rescuers drove in the spikes so they could lower down harnesses and bring people up, one by one. It was the only way to get them out. They were the only survivors from Olludia Halt. Even so, five of the survivors died before they were all rescued."

"Incredible to think of attempting such an operation. Look there! Down in the scree. Isn't that the circular roof of the Heart Temple? I think there's a better angle to see it from down by the anchoring spikes."

Elen rubbed her eyes. She did not want to look. The main temple building had been only half buried, its custodian miraculously spared, but its lower buildings were gone, hidden beneath slabs of crazily tilted rock and the massive debris slide. Aoving sometimes assisted laboring women in their homes, but more commonly their kin brought them to the Heart Temple's annex, which had beds and heated water and other useful accoutrements for delivering children and healing wounds and illnesses, and whose courtyard offered a meditative sanctuary for a person who needed time to pray, or grieve. Now Ao's body lay, unrecoverable, alongside that of the woman she'd been assisting. Elen's grief lay buried there, too.

She hadn't had time to grieve. The rescues had taken weeks. There'd been frantic meetings, more storms, and a second avalanche that had covered another section of road, a bit farther south.

There'd been Kem, mourning his mother. It was especially complicated for a child to mourn a parent they had both loved and been so very angry with. Worst of all, Kem's last exchange of words with his mother had been in argument.

"You can discuss Kema's—*Kem's*—Declaration later," Elen had said to them both that day, thinking they just needed time to cool off. She would never cease regretting that she had let Aoving leave with the conversation unresolved, without even a hug for the growing youth Aoving didn't quite know how to accept for who he was becoming, because his growing desire to speak to his own needs had scared Ao. Everything had scared her. Of course it had.

Just as she had hoped, the haunt strolled up beside her.

"Are you all right, Deputy Courier? You seem . . . preoccupied."

39

THE MORNING OF THEIR DEATH

He shaded his eyes with a hand. Xilsi had walked down to the anchoring posts and was testing their strength by trying to shift them. Simo stood about fifty paces to the right, trying to get the best view of the track of the avalanche across the canyon that allowed him to also see where the road emerged on either side of the rockfall. If a person knew where to stand, two of the five bridges were visible in the distance, spectacular feats of engineering. Simo had a notebook out and was sketching the scene. Jirvy remained out of sight on the other side of the ridge, keeping a sentry's eye on the trail they'd climbed.

"I understand better now," the haunt remarked. "The road lies beneath the rubble, so physical traffic can't move along it until the rock has been cleared. If it even can be cleared. But whatever magic is built into the road lies in its deepest foundation. So the magic wasn't affected, because the avalanche merely covers the roadbed. Do you know what manner of magic it is?"

"People say it is a protective magic created by the bones of the holy venerables of ancient days, whose purpose in life was to protect the vulnerable and the lowly."

"Is that what the wardens say?"

"The wardens claim the empire created the magic to protect the roads. But the real question is how old the original roads are. Luviara seems to think they are older than the empire."

"Hm. There were roads, long past, in my day, although I never had reason to use them, nor did I ever see them being built, so I can't be sure they are the same ones. I'd like to ask about warden magic, but they would find that suspicious since I am meant to know all. Yet I have so many questions."

"Like what?"

"Why do the witch roads repel the Pall? Perhaps I'll have a better sense when I finally touch a road. Also, the wardens speak of a swift form of communication that is tied to all the imperial roads, both to the witch roads and the other imperial roads, the ones that apparently don't protect against the Pall. What is this swift form of communication?"

"I don't know. Only wardens know. Maybe Kem will find out and tell me. For that matter, you might ask Ipis to explain the history of the roads and their magic to Kem. Then you could listen in."

"Ah! That I shall! There's another thing I'm curious about. Did you know all the wardens have a rather weak spirit of metal bound to them? All but Kem, I mean."

"A spirit?"

"Yes. Can't you feel its presence when they grip a shrive-steel sword?"

"No. But I also can't tell Luviara has spirits of air bound to her, not as you can."

"Ah. Well. My senses are peculiarly exquisite at sniffing out spirits. They're very tasty, after all," he finished with a sly, sidelong glance at her.

She grimaced. "That's a little disturbing."

He raised an eyebrow. "Interesting you would say so, since you do not object to eating flesh any more than I do."

"I meant no offense," she said hastily.

"I take no offense. I do not apologize for what I am. But I can see this topic bothers you."

"Well, then, Your Highness, I am peculiarly exquisite at changing the subject when needs be. Have you figured out what the prince's mission is?"

"Do you mean to ask if I had a headache one evening?"

She smiled. "Did you?"

"In fact, I did. It was so debilitating I asked Simo to entertain me quietly by mellifluously reading aloud, in a soft tone, all the correspondence and dispatches in our possession. By fortunate chance, it seems this request made no one suspicious. It's not clear whether this means the prince is a meticulous thinker and planner, or a rank fool who can't hold a thought in his handsome head." He paused, striking a noble pose to accentuate his attractive profile.

"Yes, very handsome. But what did you find out?"

He flashed her an accusatory look. "It is really the outside of enough to not receive the appreciation this body deserves."

"I fear the praise would go to your head."

He laughed. Fortunately, the others were too far away to hear. "Stung by my own arrow! Very well. I learned the prince received one of these express communications from the Vigil warden who serves at a Vigil tower called South Flat Vigil."

"No hint from Simo of how these express communications work?"

"Alas not, and I haven't figured out how to ask without creating suspicion. If I may go on with fewer interruptions—"

"I beg your pardon."

"As well you might, so I grant you my imperial and very handsome pardon." He didn't look at her, but his charming smile flashed, and his amusement made her heart do such a flip-turn that she had to bite her lower lip to focus as he went on. "The South Flat Vigil warden received a communication from the North Flat Vigil warden. What does this mean? North Flat, South Flat?"

"There is a Vigil tower on each side of a Pall, where the road meets the Pall. That's why they're called Vigils."

"They are vigilant in keeping watch on the Pall?"

"That's one reason, yes."

"I'm quite clever. I hope you've noticed."

"You've made it difficult not to. May I go on?"

"You have my permission, since I know you've been waiting for it."

She snorted. "Anyway, that's not the main reason for Vigil towers. The empire staffs sentinel towers all along the shoreline of a Pall to keep watch in case the Pall expands like water rising or a tide coming in. So people can be warned. A Vigil tower also keeps watch on the road and any traffic that comes and goes along the road where it crosses a Pall."

"The imperial roads cross the Pall?"

"Yes, because the Pall can't touch the witch roads, so the roads act as causeways across the Palls. The Vigils seem to have been built after the Pall rose. A Vigil isn't just a watchtower. It's also a gate through which one must pass to enter and leave a Pall. Your cargo is searched. People and living creatures are examined for signs of Spore. Imperial officials mark their date of passage so the palace knows where they are. And so on."

"You're saying humans and other animals can safely cross a Pall as long as they stay on the road?"

"That's correct. The road protects them."

"Thus the witchery. I see."

"Don't wardens carry a map of the empire and its roads?"

"Yes, Simo does. I got a look at it. But I can only learn the writing system if I can follow along as people are reading it out loud. I wasn't able to make out the names of places. Not yet. Go on, if you please."

"South Flat Vigil is in Ilvewind Province, at the southern shore of Flat Pall. North Flat Vigil is on the north side of Flat Pall, in Woodfall Province."

"This gives me a better picture of the matter. The North Flat Vigil warden informed the South Flat Vigil warden they had lost all contact with the Far Boundary Vigil warden. I did figure out that Far Boundary Vigil is the last working Vigil tower on this road. As far as I can tell, it stands on the frontier of the empire."

"And this is the incident—the loss of contact with the Far Boundary Vigil warden—that caused the prince to leave in haste for the north?"

"So it seems. But it's difficult to understand what the prince thinks is going on, since nothing lies north of Far Boundary Vigil except what is apparently named Far Boundary Pall. No road. No imperial lands. Perhaps no habitable land at all."

Elen rubbed her arm.

The haunt's gaze dropped to the gesture. "You have something else you might say, do you not? What are you clutching so tightly in your other hand? Wait, here comes Xilsi."

The warden strode up, cheeks chafed by the wind. "Your Highness! It's quite a view!"

He said, "Xilsi, are those cloudberry bushes over there? The archon told me all about her special cloudberry brew and wished me to try some to refresh my palate. Yet I had barely taken a tiny sip when Fulmo gave a hand signal, and at once, Luviara insisted loudly that cloudberries are best when eaten fresh from the vine. It was a curious interaction. But regardless, now I wonder, since I set down the cup without drinking further, in order to come on this expedition."

"Shall I pick some, Your Highness? I hear that upland cloudberries plucked in autumn are the sweetest."

"I saw ripe berries over the ridge, near where Jirvy is keeping watch," said Elen helpfully.

"No doubt he's eaten all for himself by now." Xilsi flapped a dismissive hand, but she obediently walked off out of sight in pursuit of cloudberries.

"Why do those two squabble all the time?" Elen murmured.

She hadn't meant it as a real question, but he answered, "I've discovered they were lovers and had an unpleasant dissolution of love and trust just before the prince took up the position of all-seeing eye, or maybe just after, or maybe because of it." He waggled a hand back and forth. "I'm not sure. What I haven't figured out is who thought it would be a good idea to bring them on this mission together."

"Maybe someone did it on purpose to create strife within your party."

"An interesting proposal. But Simo may finish his sketch at any time so we can't discuss it now. Why did you want us to come up here?"

Shockingly, she'd briefly forgotten she'd engineered this expedition to the ridge. After a last look around to make sure no one was within hearing, she spoke in an undertone.

"I am going to walk ahead and drop a brass ornament on the ground. You are going to discover it and share it with Simo. Let it draw your attention to the unusual tuft of what looks like a thick growth of feather-grass. Down there. Do you see it? Yes. Go yourself or send Simo, but you or another warden need to discover the corpses of a griffin and its scout."

Only when she paused for breath did she realize how foolish it was to trust this creature who wore a dragon's shadow, a haunt who had stolen a man's body for its own purposes, who spoke casually of hunting down and eating spirits. Who hadn't actually ever answered when she'd wondered aloud if he was a sorcerer. Yet she hadn't hesitated to trust him.

"A griffin scout? How intriguing! I heard there is one missing."

Elen blew out a breath in relief, collected herself, and went on in what she hoped was her usual pragmatic tone. "Presumably, this is the griffin scout meant to bring word to the intendant of your arrival. Let it seem your discovery is happening by chance."

"Why? Did you kill the griffin and scout and need me to cover it up?"

She laughed. "Very kind, I'm sure. But no. I'm not in the habit of killing griffins or their riders, since I doubt I could if I wanted to. Which I don't."

"Oh, you could," he remarked as easily as if commenting upon the weather. "Your viper is deadly to all living creatures, except you. Did you not know?"

She rubbed her arm, thinking of the Duenn Manor captain who had assaulted Ao. After her viper had bitten him, Roel had died in agony, unable even to scream. But she knew better than to fall down

this abyss into a past she was better off never revisiting. She stubbornly veered back to the matter at hand.

"I never knew a griffin scout was in the area. I only heard the
prince had sent one when the prince told the intendant. I am hiding
the identity of the person who revealed the truth to me, since their
involvement will bring unjustified punishment on their head."

"Who was it?"

"I am hiding the identity of—"

"Very well. It shall be as you say." He clasped his hands behind
his back and surveyed the canyon, the far rim, the line of the road,
the uneven heaps of scree caught among the shattered buildings of
the buried town. In a louder tone, he said, as if to the High Heavens, "What a lovely view except for the terrible fate visited upon the
humble folk who lived below all unknowing on the morning of their
death."

The words hit as knives to Elen's heart. She hurried forward,
suddenly wanting nothing more than to escape the burst of pain.
She wasn't even sure she knew how to grieve. She just had to keep
moving, lest they stumble into Spore and be eaten by the very poison
that wanted only to consume lives.

Ten steps forward, she opened her hand and let the brass ornament drop with a barely audible thump onto the ground. Then she
went down to the spikes as if to test their strength, as Xilsi had.
Gripping one of the metal posts, she pushed and pulled, but it was
set stout and solid. Nevertheless, to have something to do, she kept
a hand on it. Behind her, there came an interval of silence, followed
by voices in sharp discussion, fading as the two men explored.

The light winked, caught on something shiny down in the canyon, amid the rubble. She blinked, looked again, and got out her
spyglass. With a slow scan, she studied the road, following it back
to the place where the avalanche had poured across in a great pile of
stone and dirt. There was something strange about the slope. Was
that a path cutting up the unstable incline? Had the light winked
just where the flattened trail-like ribbon vanished out of sight, over
the top of the debris pile?

A dark shape moved just beyond the crest. She knelt, sharply alert,
and fixed her spyglass to the spot. A moment later, a goat nosed over
with delicate steps, testing the ground. It raised its head as if hearing
something behind it, then trotted down onto the road and made a
beeline for the village's untended gardens and their rich, unguarded

harvest. A second goat appeared, followed by a third. Elen chuckled. If goats had found a way through, then surely the engineers could not be far behind. Whatever was going on with the princes in the palace, Orledder Intendancy needed the road to be reopened.

From down by the feather-grass tuft came exclamations of surprise and shock. When she saw Xilsi and Jirvy come running with bows at the ready, she, too, hastened to the prince.

The dead griffin lay half hidden by the rocky unevenness of the ground, close to the crumbling edge. A few ells more and the beast would have toppled over the side, perhaps never to be found. The rider lay about twenty paces away, skull crushed and face unrecognizable, just as Oflidu had said. A sad sight, and a grim end. By the state of decomposition, bloating, and smell, the corpse hadn't died yesterday nor a month ago but sometime in between. As Elen came up, Simo rose from his examination of the rider's body and shook his head.

"I see no sign of attack. But I don't understand how her shoulder ornament came to be so far away, and up the slope. Look here. Its leather band has been cut by a blade."

The haunt said nothing.

Simo added, "Perhaps the rider feared they would plunge over the edge, and she was trying to get down, or to leave a sign."

The griffin was a noble beast even in death, twice the size of a cart horse, wings spread open where it had crashed into the rocks. Its wingspan was what made the corpse appear as feather-grass from a distance. The body and head were hidden by being jammed down between the rocks.

Jirvy stood at the breast of the griffin, between its massive forelegs and wicked claws, not that the claws would ever hurt anyone again. He shouted, "I found it."

Coming up, Xilsi said, "I hope you checked for Spore first."

"Leave off your carping, will you?" Jirvy snapped. "Spore can't take hold in dead things." Then, in an altered tone of respect, "Your Highness. I've found a crossbow bolt."

He stepped back and held out the bolt, a gloved hand closed over the fletching.

The haunt bent forward to examine the shaft and the head smeared with dried fluids. He took a few sniffs. "Any other weapon?"

"None I could find."

"Wrap the point carefully, and don't touch it. Fulmo must examine it."

"Do you think the griffin was poisoned, Your Highness?" asked Simo.

"Does it not appear strange to you? A single bolt to bring down a griffin? By the evidence of this scene, I would say the beast plummeted out of the sky and the rider had no recourse. But perhaps I am reading too much into the evidence."

"If it pierced the heart," said Simo.

"I don't think this bolt penetrated far enough to reach the griffin's heart," said Jirvy. He set down the bolt, stripped off his warden's coat and tabard, and removed his undershirt to display a well-honed torso, although it was impossible for Elen to ignore the whip scars on the man's back and a raggedly healed scar above his hip. Xilsi moved abruptly away to examine the contents of the rider's travel pouch.

After pulling on tabard and coat, Jirvy wrapped the point and shaft in the undershirt and secured it with a leather cord. "The fletching's interesting too," he noted. "It's southern, commonly found among the hunters of Makepeace Forest. They borrowed the rounded, low-cut tail feather fletching from the Forest Wolves who live farther south. It's quieter for hunting."

Xilsi looked up and gestured to get everyone's attention. "Someone's robbed this corpse!"

Elen's hand convulsed, and she carefully looked at the ground.

"What do you mean?" said the haunt, who was still holding the brass ornament.

"My sister is a griffin rider. They recruited her because she's small, light, and utterly fearless." Her smile was so bright it altered her face with an unexpectedly sweet affection. Then she frowned down at the body. The rider was a small, slender person dressed in the wool-and-leather uniform of the griffin corps. "Riders carry two pouches. One is their personal pouch for a few necessaries. They have to travel light. The other is their official corps pouch. The official pouch isn't here. Furthermore, its buckles are here and intact, which means it wasn't severed or cut loose. It was unbuckled and taken. Which means someone knew this body was here and took the official pouch but left the personal pouch. Look here."

She held up a gorgeous necklace of tiny gemstones.

Jirvy colored and looked away uncomfortably.

Simo said, "That's a tryst necklace."

"Yes. There's nothing valuable in an imperial pouch except its contents, which are written in cipher. But this necklace would be worth a month's living up here."

"More like ten years," said Elen, "if those are lapis lazuli and serpentine and amethyst."

"Jade, not serpentine," said Xilsi. "There's also this gold ring. A pair of beautiful griffin-leather gloves impossible to obtain on the open market. And a change of clothes, but these undergarments are expensive silk—again, quite valuable."

"The jewelry and gloves would be difficult to sell," said Simo. "Especially in the uplands. It would draw attention."

"Not more difficult or attention-drawing than ciphered palace communications," Xilsi countered.

The captain frowned. "That's true enough. It's baffling. And disturbing."

The haunt said, "We'd best go back. It's getting late. We'll stand a double guard tonight and leave at dawn. Tell no one except Ipis—and Kem—of what we found. Am I understood?"

40

Once they had returned to Fisherman's Rest, the haunt sent a message to the archon that he would not be able to eat supper at her table. He informed Elen she was to sleep in the suite, not in the annex, and set Ipis and Kem to guard the suite's entrance. Taking a seat in the parlor, he had Jirvy unwrap the bolt. Fulmo took the shaft in one hand, sniffed it, then pressed the metal to his lips and stood as if lifeless for what felt like forever. His gray-brown complexion shifted color. Waves of blushing and fading flowed beneath his skin.

Finally, the gagast stirred. Luviara brought him pencil and paper, on which he wrote his findings.

He'd found traces of three toxins on the crossbow bolt's point. One was the plant known as fleshbane, the second was the venom of the red-stripe snake, and a third was a toxin he did not recognize but that was potent enough, in combination with the other two, to kill a large animal without inhalation or ingestion, merely through contact with its blood, in this case even a shallow wound.

Luviara said, "Your Highness, where did this deadly bolt come from?"

"We discovered it on our walk up the ridge."

"Are you saying someone shot at you?"

"I am saying we need to tread very carefully indeed." He did not mention the dead griffin or its scout.

A knock came at the door.

Ipis stuck her head in, looking around the parlor curiously, as if wondering what they had been doing. She said, "The archon has sent supper, with her compliments."

A procession of servers entered bearing sixteen platters of food, half of which were fish: steamed fish, stewed fish, sauced fish, minced fish, baked fish, fishcakes, fish soup, and, on a flat ceramic tray, fish and vegetables cunningly arranged as the famous sculpture, *The Death of the Holy Compassionate Healer Surrounded by Her Heart Venerables*. The rest of the meal consisted of baked, roasted, and stewed turnips, with one dish of fried turnip greens, bitter from autumn frost, an apple and parsnip compote, hot bread, and a covered pitcher of the archon's vaunted cloudberry brew.

Once the servers had arranged the table, they retreated to stand attentively at the wall.

"They may go," said the haunt with a peremptory wave of his hand.

"Interlocutor," said the eldest of the servers, "the archon has graciously asked that we do all we can to facilitate the feast for His Exalted Highness."

Luviara rose from the bench on which she'd been seated. "His Exalted Highness has dismissed you. That is all."

The senior server cleared his throat, looking unaccountably nervous, but he led the rest out, not that they had any choice.

Elen had remained standing the entire time. She still felt uneasy about sitting in the presence of a man the others thought of as the prince, and would have preferred to return to the small annex where she normally slept, but the discovery of the dead griffin and its rider had altered the nature of the expedition. No longer was their party on an inconvenient detour caused by a terrible but unpredictable natural disaster. Now there was deliberate malice on their trail.

The haunt raised a hand and, rising, circled the parlor. He halted to listen every few steps, checked beneath and behind every piece of furniture, every wall hanging, ran a hand along the baseboard, and had Fulmo run a finger along the join of wall and ceiling to make sure there were no secret spy holes. Simo ran one more circuit of the surrounding rooms, which were empty. After locking the entrance doors, he brought Ipis and Kem into the parlor. Thus sealed in, they sat at the table. Elen was given a place at the far end, away from the prince.

Fulmo tasted each dish and indicated each was clear of contamination, until the cloudberry brew, which received a shake of his blocky head.

"The same as the other brew you were offered," said Luviara. "Not poison, it seems, but drugged."

The haunt nodded. "Then let us pour out the brew as if we have consumed it and satiate ourselves with the rest. Although it is tiresome to always have to assume no food and drink can be trusted."

"None better than a gagast as a food taster, Your Highness," said Luviara. "But I never heard the story of how you came to bring Fulmo into your service."

"No, I suppose you did not," he remarked, and set to his food.

The archon had done her best with fish and turnips. Elen had never before eaten so well in this town, not in ten years of stopping here every month. The bread was particularly good, soft inside with a crisp crust, and baked from wheat flour with no coarse millet for filler.

At first, they ate in silence, dedicated to the food. As people began to heap seconds upon their plates, Simo opened the table for discussion.

"This bolt must concern us deeply. Now what, Your Highness?"

"We go on," said the haunt. "Armed with the knowledge that someone is hunting us."

"Shouldn't we demand answers from the archon?" Simo asked.

"I think not. For now, the archon doesn't know what we've found. We can't be sure she's involved with Prince Astaylin."

"What about Lord Duenn?" Elen asked. "Could the archon be involved with him, with Woodfall Province?"

Simo hissed angrily. Kem glowered. The other wardens looked at the haunt, waiting for his reaction to this unseemly interruption.

"What about Lord Duenn?" the haunt said lightly. "How likely do you think it is that he could have tendrils that reach so far, farther than a prince's?"

"Not likely," said Simo, ending that branch of the discussion.

The haunt cleared his throat and went on. "The attempted drugging with the brew suggests the archon is involved with someone, or something. Unless she's just a common thief, but it makes no sense to attack a prince of the Third Estate without being sure of protection from inside the palace."

"What if we're followed when we leave?" asked Simo.

"I trust the deputy courier to know a way around that."

"I do, Your Highness," said Elen, feeling it safe to answer.

"Oh, I know what you're going to do," said Kem with his usual grin. Then he remembered how mad he was at her, and blew out a sharp exhalation, clenched his hands, and pretended he hadn't said anything. He said to Ipis, in a tight voice, "Thanks for the lessons today. I learned a lot of things I never knew before."

"Your Highness, our novice is a quick learner," said Ipis. "As well, Kem knows a great deal about mountain craft and even a bit of surveyor lore."

"I am pleased to hear of the novice's good progress," said the haunt loftily. "A very promising start to what it is hoped will be a long and loyal life as a warden in service of the empire."

Flushed about the ears, Kem set back to his food.

The haunt examined the last hunk of bread and, with great seriousness, plucked it off its platter and consumed the whole in three neat bites, but with an expression of mild distaste. "I don't understand the appeal of this manner of food," he remarked before turning back to the fish.

Forgetting herself, and angry on behalf of the unheralded baker, Elen said, "The bread is the best thing here! Uh. Your Highness."

Everyone stared, except Kem, who pressed fingers to his forehead and pretended he hadn't heard or seen her appalling rudeness.

The haunt blinked, surveying the varying expressions of the wardens: Simo offended, Ipis shocked, Xilsi torn between amusement and distaste, Jirvy puzzled. Luviara's gnomic smile. Fulmo's indifference. He cleared his throat. "It pleases me to remind you all that if the archon is indeed involved with someone who has the power to urge her to violent deeds, she will not attack us in the village with so many potential witnesses. Rather she will wait to strike until we are out on the path again, isolated and alone. Anything else?"

"Your Highness, as a distraction, mention the copper mines as we're leaving," said Elen.

"Copper mines?"

"To one of us, as if continuing a conversation. But not to the archon."

"I see. Very well. We leave at dawn."

41

THEIR PURSUERS

They marched out the gate and over the moat at dawn, onto a path that led onward into the eastern region of the Moonrise Hills. The archon and a number of local officials and favored hangers-on trailed them. Lesser folk were chased away by sentinels, but they tagged along as close as they were able, eager to watch the departure of the exalted highness. Not for them the touch of a prince's hand upon the heads of their precious children. The archon didn't allow it, a woman jealous of her privileges. She even brought out her daughter in a pretty garment, all ribbons and pearls like a bauble, but Elen saw anxiety in the girl's face and wondered what it was, exactly, that the girl feared.

She couldn't solve every problem. Right now, she had enough on her platter, even if she would have gladly eaten that last hunk of excellent bread. Fortunately, they'd been supplied with bread and cheese for the day's journey, so there was hope for a decent repast later in the day. There was another bottle of cloudberry brew, too, which Fulmo stowed in his pack.

The haunt said something to Simo about the copper mines and shushed him when he tried to answer, as if he'd just noticed they were within hearing of their escort. The archon and her escort halted when they reached the sheds that stank of fish. Perhaps the archon couldn't bear the smell, although she had to be used to it by now.

After the drying sheds, they passed empty sheds where winter-caught fish would be filleted, hung to freeze, and stored in sealed pots underground. The gardens had been turned over for the winter and vulnerable perennials covered with straw. The air was brisk but the sky clear; no snow tonight, but the first falls would come soon.

A long boardwalk crossed a strip of marshy ground at the eastern end of the valley. Past this stood a waypost with a census marker. They were now officially outside the archon's jurisdiction, as Luviara remarked to the others.

"That may be true as written," said Elen, "but her reach extends pretty far in these hills. There's not much out here except hamlets with goats and sheep who depend on Fisherman's Rest for winter and early-spring supplies. Two days on from here there are copper mines. It's so isolated it's difficult to feed and house the miners, so the operations have stayed small. Or maybe the archon likes it that way. Pisgia Moat has a smaller census population than Orledder Halt, but she retains a larger force of sentinels. I don't think it's because of brigands or swalters. In my observation, it's to control the mines."

The holystone post also marked a crossroads where a secondary path headed east up a notch, into the surrounding hills. The main path swung southeast along the base of the valley, toward a pass farther south. Elen took the secondary path.

For an hour, they walked at a brisk pace, keeping the party close together. She listened for telltale signs that someone was following but heard no voices, no tramp of feet. The path unfolded with its familiar landmarks: the foundation of a brick oven where a house had once stood, the bricks long since carried away to build other structures; stone steps set into a steep slope and, at the top, beneath a rocky outcrop, an overhang where a person could shelter in the event of a storm; beyond it, a path through dense forest.

They passed an ancient spruce so large its carpet of decaying needles kept the ground clear of new growth in a circle around it. Without a word, she led them around to the back of the spruce and showed them where to duck through its scratchy branches, into a gap of space where one of the lower branches was missing. Here she had once waited out a blizzard. She left them beneath the pungent branches. After checking the ground around the tree to make sure they'd not dropped anything, she scuffed the path ahead for a ways before circling back.

Just in time. As she slid beneath the branches into where the others hunkered in silence, they heard the tramp of feet, a big party approaching. By feel, she climbed to a spot where she could see over the path without being seen. As far as she knew, no one else had ever sussed out this shelter.

A group of twenty-two people passed in a file. They were armed with long bows, crossbows, swords, spears, and one brutish-looking halberd. About half had faces she recognized from the archon's household. The others wore stylish heartland caps and less elaborate approximations of the fly-whisk braids that looked so handsome on the prince. One wore the yellow headband of an official palace messenger, as well as a brass ring around their upper arm to mark their service to the palace. She scanned them closely, thinking she might see Duenn's militia captain or maybe the man she thought of as Gloves. But she saw no one she recognized from Lord Duenn's entourage. She was stamping her own fears, her own history, onto something that had nothing to do with her and Kem's past.

In truth, it made sense to speculate that these heartlanders might be Prince Astaylin's agents. For all she knew, Prince Gevulin was the instigator of a feud that the other prince had been forced to respond to. Or maybe the archon's goals had nothing to do with a feud for power. Maybe it was just about money. Underutilized copper mines might be of interest to a prince eager to expand sources of personal revenue, and the archon might simply be protecting her monopoly over them, or some deal she'd made with an official. If that was the case, then the archon's party would walk on to the mines and not trouble them further. Yet, the first attempt to drug them had come soon after they'd arrived, surely alerted by the palace messenger.

Elen waited for the group to pass out of sight, then waited yet more. Below her, no one spoke. Finally, she climbed down and, in an undertone, said, "There are heartlanders marching with the archon's group. They're all armed. Whatever her reasons, it sure looks as if the archon intends to harm His Exalted Highness somewhere in these hills. Afterward, she can claim he vanished and was never seen again."

"Now what?" asked Simo.

"We retrace our path."

"Isn't the cutoff to the trail that leads to the rope bridge about four miles farther on? That's the way you and I went," Kem asked. His suspicious tone stung. As if he suspected she might be misleading them on purpose.

She kept her tone bland, to disguise the hurt she felt. "So we did. But this time we are taking a steep shortcut with a lot of climbing. I hope the archon's people are headed to the mines. But even if they are, they'll soon discover we didn't go there and figure we turned north to the smugglers' crossing. We need to beat the other group to the rope bridge. If we can do that, we'll make it over."

"If we can't?" Simo asked.

"Then I guess we'll find out how well you wardens can fight." She grinned.

"Excellent," said the haunt, sounding invigorated at the prospect of fighting.

They crawled back out, Xilsi rubbing her cheeks where the prickly scrape of the spruce had reddened her skin. Elen could feel Kem's unasked questions like a weight, his accusing gaze on her back, but he followed orders and said nothing. They walked at speed, descended the stone steps at a jog, and turned aside by the ruins of the oven. Beyond lay a silted-in depression marking a circular ditch around the collapsed remains of a livestock shed, a longhouse, and a pile of stones that marked a well. Inside the ditch no new growth had sprouted except for a single white-needle pine that towered like an angry ghost. It was a haunted place, not because of ancient statues, as with the Spires, but because local legend said there had been a terrible murder here, driven by jealousy, and ending with a lover dumped into the well so the corpse permanently poisoned its waters.

The presence of the white pine suggested the hamlet had been overtaken by Spore, not by jealousy. Or maybe both, since both were poisonous. Regardless, the outbreak had taken place three or more generations in the past, although Elen sniffed the air and smelled nothing off.

Beyond the ruins lay a trail up to open, grassy ground where the hamlet's sheep had once grazed and, beyond that, a steep climb up a ridge. If their pursuers turned this way, they would have to come around by a long trail, past a different herder's hamlet, census sixteen, known as Fifen Ditch. There, the sentinels would question the locals and discover the prince and his wardens had never passed through.

At the top of the ridge, the blustering wind flung the promise of winter into their faces.

Elen had to raise her voice to be heard. "Luviara, can you manage climbing a cliff?"

"Are you calling me old?" said the interlocutor with an amused smile.

"I am," agreed Elen cheerfully.

The theurgist chuckled. "I can scarcely argue, Deputy Courier, since I am old. But I think you'll find I will not be the last to reach the top of the cliff. Lead on. This is a most illuminating detour. I shall delight in recording our adventures in my journal."

"I'd rather you not reveal the presence of the rope bridge," said Elen.

"It seems the archon and her people know of it. How secret can it be?"

"With respect, Your Worthiness, and since you have raised the subject, the intendant is concerned to discover who set it up and who is using it for smuggling. That's best done quietly."

"You have an exaggerated idea of how many people read my journal."

"How many?" Elen asked, suddenly curious.

"Just two. Besides myself, I mean. I assure you, the intendant need not worry that his investigation will be impeded by my record."

The haunt said, "This is all very interesting, I am sure, but under the circumstances, we must move on."

"Of course, Your Highness." Elen took a swig from her bottle and headed out.

They descended into a wooded defile and along its rugged ground until they reached a dead end. Here, the dregs of a waterfall dribbled down a sheer rock face. In the spring and early summer, it was a thundering fall with a large pool beneath, perfect for cooling off after a hard hike. This late in the season, with autumn's slackening of rains, the pool was mostly mud and stones except for a deep crescent where the central fall concentrated, still strong enough to churn the water. On either side, rocky scree lay in slopes too unstable to climb. The only way out was to go back up the defile.

42

A SWALTER DELVING

Kem tipped his head back. "We can't get up that!" he objected when before—just days before!—he would have waited for her to show him what her intention was instead of instantly finding fault.

Everyone looked at her as if they were thinking the same thing. Everyone except the haunt. He paced out the pebbled rim of the pool until he reached the cliff, slick with oozing water. He set a hand on the rock, swiped up a few drops, and set them to his lips. The steady splash of the falls wasn't too loud to drown out his voice.

"Of course," he said as he turned to give Elen a knowing look. "It's a swalter delving. The entrance must be hidden behind the waterfall. It is certainly abandoned. Had you ventured to enter a swalter delving where swalters were currently living, they'd have shot you with their paralyzing arrows, eaten out your eyes and tongue, and left you to crawl blind and mute back the way you came, while being gnawed on by rats. Their lynxes don't eat human flesh."

Everyone stared at him, speechless. Even Elen. His tone was perfectly straightforward, as with accepted fact.

However, Luviara recovered quickly. "Swalter delvings are simply old folk stories. Swalters live in forest lairs, often near caves, it's true, but never permanently beneath the rock."

The haunt said, "Maybe they live so in these days, but swalters existed long before the empire. You didn't see it, but there was such a delving at—"

He broke off, remembering that the others didn't know he and Elen had gone exploring in the Heart Temple while the rest slept.

Elen jumped in. "Our pursuers are miles behind us, but that doesn't mean they can't catch up. This way."

Around the other side of the pool, several ledges created narrow terraces up the rock wall. Although it wasn't obvious to the naked eye, not unless you knew what you were looking at, these ledges created a perilous stairway into a cave hidden behind the waterfall. They ducked through the falling water and stumbled on damp rock made slippery by algae. Xilsi flailed, and Jirvy caught her before she fell, but she shoved him off and stumped after Elen, up into the back of the cave and onto drier ground, where not enough light reached for algae to grow.

The large cave bore no signs of recent habitation. Instead, in the very back, rose square pillars surrounding a six-sided beehive-like structure. They weren't ruins, precisely, but so old they seemed instead like the bones of a long-dead creature. Luviara flitted around them like a moth to flames.

"Look here!" she cried. "This is no beehive. The structure surrounds a shaft. Perhaps it is a well? Can it be climbed down? No, never mind. I think it's blocked by fallen stones."

"Wow! Have you ever seen such a thing?" said Kem to Ipis as they surveyed the musty depths.

"Did swalters really delve this? I thought they were more like unusually intelligent animals, not builders like us." Ipis traced the curve of a rusted iron wheel. "This looks like it could have been part of a well winch."

Simo said, "Ipis, don't touch anything."

Elen got out her lantern and tinder box, and lit a wick. By the flickering light, she led them into the darkest recess of the cave, which led into a tunnel just wide enough and tall enough to fit Fulmo's body, as long as he hunched his shoulders to keep his head down and tucked his arms against his chest. As they ascended along a curving tunnel hewn through the rock, spiraling upward, he had at intervals to turn sideways to squeeze through.

Luviara crowded up behind Elen to get the best use of the light. She was beside herself with excitement. They came to a handsomely carved archway of floral vines and gamboling lynx cubs. Without warning, Luviara turned aside and entered.

"Interlocutor, I pray you, stop," said Elen.

Luviara paid her no attention as she strode toward a farther intersection barely visible at the edge of the lantern's aura. She called back, "But this is astonishing. An entire warren of rooms and more rooms and yet more rooms, a village carved inside the cliff!"

Jirvy shoved past Elen. "Interlocutor! Halt! There's a trap right ahead of you. A thread across the tunnel. Take a step back!"

For a tense moment, Elen feared Luviara would stubbornly keep walking, but then the theurgist took a slow step back.

"Keep moving," said Jirvy.

She backed up until she reached the main passage. He set an arrow to his bow, took aim, and loosed. The arrow cracked against the rock wall, followed by a twang as of a plucked string. A gusty grunt sounded, followed by a patter of darts filling the tunnel. They fell short of Luviara, but she leaped back anyway.

"Good shot, Jirvy," remarked the haunt amiably. "As I was saying, I recommend we keep moving. Yet tell me, Deputy Courier, how is it you survived your investigation of this delving?"

"I stuck to the main passage. Most of these side tunnels exude a disturbing scent. I stuck to where the air smells fresh."

Undaunted by her narrow escape, Luviara quivered with excitement as they continued upward, passing yet more branching corridors. "This place could house hundreds. I didn't know swalters congregated in such large numbers. My observations suggest they never tolerate clans larger than twelve."

"If we survive this mission," the haunt replied sardonically, "then I will grant you a most gracious princely writ to explore at your leisure."

She cleared her throat. "Only the emperor can do that, Your Exalted Highness."

"Of course."

"How is it you know all this hidden lore, Your Highness? I've never come across it, and I thought I had read everything."

"It seems you have not," he said drily. "Now, *move*."

It was a stiff climb and a long one due to the twisting and strenuous nature of the route. The tunnel ended in a room like the bottom of a large well. Its shaft opened onto the cloudy sky, about twenty ells above.

"How do we get up that?" Xilsi asked with a skeptical snort. "Fly?"

Elen pointed. "It's hard to make out, but there's a ladder-like route built into the shaft. You have to have a good grip and strength for climbing. And a head for heights. I'll go first. There's a place I can rig my rope at the top." She turned to the theurgist. "The rope can be tied about your chest, Your Worthiness, for added support, and to catch you if you fall."

Luviara smiled. "I shan't need any such consideration, but I thank you for your concern, Deputy Courier. I admire your deep knowledge of this region. It's unexpected."

"I have walked this route for ten years. Like you, I'm not averse to exploring when I have the time. There's much to discover, if one knows how to look."

"I should know better than to judge the provinces by the prejudices of the heartland. Old habits die hard. I hope you and I have more time to talk."

The haunt shifted restlessly, and Elen wondered if he disliked being confined within a place where swalters had once lived. "To that end, I urge you, Deputy Courier, to lead the way."

The "ladder" was a cunning network of jutting stonework that made use of the shaft's irregular walls to create an upward path. To her surprise, Xilsi followed right after her, adept at negotiating the climb. Elen did not look down—she wasn't fond of heights—so when she scrambled over the rim and out onto the flat ground, she was surprised when first Xilsi, then Ipis, and then Kem emerged in quick succession.

"What is this place?" asked Ipis as she looked around with the bright eyes and youthful curiosity of a person who has never before walked in the wide world.

Kem straightened his shoulders, looking a little cocky now that he had information to impart to his trainer. "We have walked through the Moonrise Hills, which now lie south and east of us. This is the tableland north of the hills. And that—see there, that hazy line—that's the north wall of Grinder's Cut."

The shaft was hidden by large boulders, like sentries surrounding it. Beyond the boulders lay a flat plateau that stretched north for many leagues. From here, they could hazily see the rim of the north wall of Grinder's Cut, although it was difficult to perceive the rim of the closer south wall, which was obscured by the rising slope of the land and straggling lines of pine, juniper, and bitter oak.

The haunt emerged from the shaft. He was sweating, even a little sallow, and he strode away, without speaking, into the shade of a boulder and stood there with his face turned away from them. Fulmo pulled himself up and over, followed by Simo, whose grimace suggested he'd found the ascent difficult.

Xilsi stuck her head over the shaft and shouted down, "You going to stay down there, eh, Jirv?"

Simo wagged a scolding finger at her. "He stayed behind to assist the interlocutor. Let go of this, Xilsi. You know better."

She flushed. "He knows better too."

"Are you assuming I haven't spoken to him as well?"

She stalked off to stand by Kem and Ipis and pretend she was interested in the path ahead.

Elen walked over to Simo, by the shaft. "Is the interlocutor going to be able to make it up?"

From below, Jirvy's laugh echoed incongruously. He shouted up, "Stand back."

There came a whooshing sound, almost like the flutter of wings, accompanied by a gust of wind that sparkled as with twinkling embers. Elen skipped back, blinking what felt like ash out of her eyes. Simo cast an arm in front of his face.

There, on the rim of the shaft, stood Luviara, with her scarf and knee-length robes settling around her as if they'd just been whirled in a windstorm.

Elen was too shocked to speak. Kem turned, looking puzzled and then astonished. The wardens did not appear surprised, but when Kem murmured a question to Ipis, she shook her head with a tilt of her chin toward Elen, as if to say she couldn't tell him here, where the deputy courier might hear.

Luviara straightened her clothing and said, "Is there somewhere private I might relieve myself? I didn't want to do so while in the swalters' delving. I have it on good authority they skewer intruders, and mutilate trespassers, and how better to discern a trespasser than by smelling their piss?"

Elen nodded. "Yes, yes, of course, we should all take a quick pee among the rocks before we go on our way. Your Worthiness, may I ask—?"

"Not now," said the haunt, strolling up. His gaze on Luviara was so unusually aggressive that the theurgist, for once, appeared flustered. "How many can you keep bound to you at a time? Do they do your bidding in exchange for release?"

"Your Highness, we theurgists are not required to speak of our art even to the palace."

"Of course you aren't *required* to, but my question stands."

"I beg your pardon and mean no disrespect, Your Highness, but we are enjoined to never disclose the secrets of our craft."

His blistering frown made him look as angry as a thunderous storm sliding across the lowlands. The displeasure radiating off him was sobering and unpleasant. Luviara's eyes widened with alarm. The wardens glanced warily at him. All took a step away. His gaze flickered, noticing their reactions. As if by magic, his expression cleared to its usual sardonic amusement.

"Yes, yes, of course you are so enjoined. Make haste. We'll go as soon as Jirvy is with us."

Despite Xilsi's insinuation about Jirvy's inability to climb, the man reached the top quickly and without any sign of being winded or distressed. By then, the others had done their business over behind a shield of rocks. The scent of fresh urine dissipated in the ever-blowing wind as Elen led them at an easy jog into the uneven shadow and light beneath the trees, headed toward the rim of Grinder's Cut.

43

THE ROPE BRIDGE

The rim of Grinder's Cut was like an illusion. They walked for several hours through airy forests and rocky clearings and back into forest when, with no change in the landscape, the great canyon cut the ground open at their feet. At night, a person could stumble off the edge all unknowing and plunge a thousand ells to their death. If the fall didn't kill them, then they would surely roll into the thread of Pall that ran parallel to the river that flowed along the bottom of the canyon. Death by smashing their head open on the rocks would be preferable.

The wardens stared across the gap between the southern rim and the northern rim.

"How are we meant to get across that?" Simo demanded. "Fly?"

"Perhaps the Worthy Interlocutor could aid with that," remarked the haunt with a dour side-eye.

"Your Exalted Highness," replied Luviara with a tartness that surprised Elen, "this humble theurgist holds not enough in strength to convey even one person across that distance, nor enough in numbers to convey all."

"So, fewer than nine air spirits left who are bound to you, and weak ones at that."

At this, Luviara lost her temper. "If you knew, then why did you ask before, Your Highness?"

Simo snapped, "Interlocutor! You speak out of turn!"

The haunt raised a hand to silence the captain. "It is a fair question. And I have a fair answer. I like to know exactly what tools I have at my disposal. But I believe the deputy courier has a plan."

"Yes, I do," said Elen briskly, thinking it best to smooth over the little confrontation. "But we are too visible out here, so let's keep moving. A league south, there's a turning where the rims run closer together. That's where the rope bridge is. This way."

They proceeded in silence. Perhaps Luviara was fuming, but the woman seemed more thoughtful than anything. The wardens stayed alert, gazes often turned back the way they'd come.

At a gnarled juniper tree, Elen led everyone over the rim and through a notch between two jutting promontories. They made their way along a track that hugged the side of the upper slope, slowly descending like a very long ramp. On one side, her shoulder scraped the rock face and, on the other side, her hand dangled over the drop-off. It was dizzying, if you looked down.

She had worried for Fulmo. He was so large that he appeared ungainly, incongruous, ready to topple over the side, yet he was so sure-footed that she wondered if gagast had something of a goat's balance and spatial acuity. The haunt managed easily as well, but the wardens had a harder time, tentative when the track narrowed and gaining speed where it widened. Still, they followed gamely enough. They were tough, and they would never leave their prince.

For once, Luviara seemed unsure, lagging farther behind, until Kem came forward from his place in the rearguard to give her what assistance he could. He had a good head for heights, and he and Joef really had practiced slack rope obsessively back when they'd decided they were going to join a traveling theatrical troupe. Elen wasn't worried about him except for all the ways she was worried about him.

Their group made slow progress, however. As the sun sank toward the west, the shadows got longer, covering the bottom of the canyon. Down there, the pale thread of the Pall gleamed as if woven with threads of moonlight or with the writhing souls of the living creatures it had captured and absorbed.

"Did you hear that?" The haunt raised a hand. "A shout. From back the way we came."

"Most likely our pursuers," said Elen as she kept moving. The mine gambit hadn't worked. This meant the archon was almost certainly working with someone from the palace who knew where the prince was headed, possibly the same person who had stolen the griffin scout's message pouch—or ordered it stolen.

"Maybe they'll fall off," muttered Xilsi. She gave a choked-off cry and said, shakily, "Curse it, I looked down."

"Keep moving," said Elen. "We're almost there. We'll make it."

At a switchback, a secondary trail headed up, instead of down, and Elen took the ascending trail. It led to a rocky point thrust out from the south wall of the canyon. Their party gathered on what was essentially a wide ledge about one hundred ells from the bottom. The walls towered above them.

"I feel trapped," muttered Jirvy.

"I've heard that song before," said Xilsi with a contemptuous curl of her upper lip.

Simo snapped, "Enough!"

Ipis murmured, as if to the air, "Why will they not let it go?"

Kem said, "Let what go?"

Luviara said, "May I sit for just a moment?"

"You may rest," said Elen, "but you'll need to be ready to go as soon as I'm across."

The haunt said nothing. He was studying the scene with intense interest, as if he'd been here before, but surely that was impossible.

They were now so close to the bottom that the river was audible, burbling in counterpoint to the whine of the wind. At this time of year the waters ran low, but even if a person could climb all the way to the bottom of the canyon, which in theory they could, they could not cross without wading through the Pall. And that would be the end of them.

Beyond the rocky point the big canyon split, as if an axe blow had splintered the high plateau with extra cracks. Two tributary rivers fed into the main river, creating a kind of intersection with a wider gap. The ground was quite rugged but included shelves of higher ground rising like islands into the air, like stepping stones. The sides of the big cut were layered with terraces and ledges. In other words, it was one of the few places for a hundred leagues in either direction where it was plausible to span the canyon with a bridge.

Whoever had built the road had attempted to bridge this specific gap, perhaps first, although eventually they had abandoned it and farther to the west had built the more feasible but much longer sequence of Five Bridges.

Five massive piers remained from the original attempt, pillar-like support structures on which the arches and roadbed of the bridge would have been laid. They looked like square towers set in a row across the canyon. They were so tall they appeared strangely frail despite their girth and solidity. The one closest to the ledge had collapsed, bricks broken and scattered over the floor of the canyon to create a partial dam that had allowed a pool of water to gather and then the river to run out in a cataract down the debris. The other four piers were intact. A rickety-looking rope-and-plank bridge connected the farther piers to the north rim.

Luviara said, "I've read about this. Incredible to see it! It's said the Orchid Emperor spent one thousand seven hundred and sixty-five lives trying to complete it before finally giving up."

"That's a lot of lives before giving up," said Elen. "Why try at all?"

Luviara glanced at the prince. "It is not my place to speculate on an emperor's decisions. But the poets say it was pride. My apologies, Your Highness."

He wasn't listening, because he was conferring with Simo.

The captain said, "I see a rope bridge starting from the first intact pier. But it isn't connected to this ledge. How are we to reach the bridge? It's too far to jump."

"Look down," said Elen.

Four iron rings had been hammered into the rock face, two just below the ledge and the other two below the upper pair. A thick rope was secured to the right lower ring. This taut rope spanned the gulf of air between the ledge and the first pier, a distance of about twenty paces. But it wasn't the horizontal distance. It was the hundred-ells drop that made the passage dizzying and daunting.

"Are we meant to shimmy across, one by one?" Simo demanded. "That will take too long, and might not even be possible with our equipment."

"Only one person needs to shimmy," said Elen, "and that will be me, or Novice Warden Kem."

"Why him?" asked Simo suspiciously.

"He's got the strength and balance to manage it. Also, he's made this crossing before, not long ago."

"You have?" said Ipis. "Oh, merciful Heavens, Kem. That looks terrifying. How brave of you!"

Kem's expression warred between sullen anger that Elen dared to speak of him after her lifetime of lying, and the cocky youthful need to show off in front of people he wanted to impress so they'd accept him as worthy to be one of their number.

Nevertheless, he shot Elen a look. "Of course I'll go."

"Then go," said Simo. "I, for one, would like to cross before our pursuers reach us, especially because the way the canyon curves means we won't be able to see them until they're right on us."

"Or they could make better time along the rim and come down from above," said Elen.

The haunt laughed. Simo muttered words under his breath.

Luviara eyed the cliff face that rose above them. "Could they?"

"It's climbable, so sure, they could, depending on how deter-mined they are to murder an exalted highness and whether they have a theurgist with them." The last part of the comment was a guess on Elen's part.

"Unlikely," muttered Luviara. Elen could only hope the interlocutor was correct.

Jirvy pulled off his indigo scarf, deftly unknotted it, and reknotted it with the other side of the scarf showing: this a bland yellow-brown-green fabric that gave his head some camouflage. "Your Highness, I'll set up a perimeter watch."

The haunt grinned in a way that made him look like a hungry man who'd just been told there's a grand feast waiting. "I'll come with you, Jirvy."

"Your Highness, that's not wise," objected Simo.

"I do believe it is, since I have it on the best authority that I am an adept of the bow and the spear. By which authority I mean *my own*. Do you doubt my prowess?"

Simo hesitated, unwilling to send the prince into danger and yet unable to question his skills.

"You'll act as decoys. They won't see me or Jirvy." The haunt's expression grew serious, even grim. "If I cannot defend those who serve me, then why should they serve me? Xilsi, set yourself up among the rocks, in case any get past us."

Jirvy flashed a glance at Xilsi, with a twitch like a sneer of triumph that he was chosen to attend the prince, while she was left behind. He and the haunt scrambled up the back of the ledge and made their way back by climbing above the path. Where the rock face curved away, they vanished from sight. Xilsi found an overhang where she could crouch, bow in hand, with an open line of sight to where the path reached the ledge.

Elen turned to Kem. "Are you ready?"

He looked her straight in the eye. "I'll do what I must, as a warden, and to save the prince."

"As if you don't relish the challenge," she added with a quirk of her lips, but he just shrugged, rejecting her overture. No matter. She was patient.

She added, "I'll take the upper rope and fix it at the pier. You'll follow with the securing ropes."

He shook his head in his usual know-it-all fashion. "I should go first. It's not that you're not strong—you can walk for days without faltering—but I'm stronger in the upper body. I've been training with Joef on the boulders, and taking winter cherry to bulk up my muscles."

She knew all this but kept her mouth shut, glad to hear him lecture her because it meant he was talking to her. Anyway, it was the outcome she'd aimed for, because he would be better at the first crossing. "All right. I have a safety loop."

He hitched a shoulder in refusal. "It'll just slow me down. I'm not going to fall."

"How are you going to do it?" Ipis asked. "That rope's just . . . stretched there and if you fall . . . your head'll crack open."

Kem gave Ipis a saucy look. "Watch me."

He set down his pack, took off his boots, and secured them by their laces to the pack. Without a glance at Elen, he swung down to set his feet on the rope. For an instant she thought he was going to balance his way across, as he and Joef often did on a rope strung an arm's length above the ground, but he knew his business. Elen and Kem had indeed made this crossing not ten days ago—although with the safety loop—because she'd wanted him to understand he was capable of so many things, whatever life brought to his doorstep. And here they were.

A thirty-ells-long coil of rope was securely fastened to and tucked beneath the right upper ring. He slung it over his shoulder and chest, then swung down to hang by his knees as he loosened the rope so it could unspool. Hand over hand, he crawled backward across the gap, pausing every time he needed to let out more loops of the rope. Despite the constant tug of the wind, his movements remained deft and sure, legs anchoring him in case his hands slipped. But they never did. As the new rope extended behind him, he reached the first intact pier and its iron anchors. He clambered onto the pier, which had iron posts and rings driven into it. He looped the new rope through the two rings and tugged until it was taut, then fastened it with secure knots.

He waved. Now it was Elen's turn.

44

DON'T LOOK DOWN

Elen's task was to haul two more ropes over, the ones fixed to the two other rings. It was tricky because, while she now had two fixed ropes for her crossing rather than one, she had to trust that Kem had fully secured the lower rope. If he hadn't, she'd fall.

The setup was deliberately meant to make it hard to get across. While Elen suspected the archon of Fisherman's Rest knew of and profited by the smugglers' bridge, she could not ask, nor did she want the archon to know she knew. So much for that, with the archon's people in pursuit.

She'd already set down her pack and taken off her boots. The air was cold on her feet, a risk since cold feet got stiff and clumsy, but the distance wasn't far. She had the benefit of two ropes, one for her feet and one overhead to hold on to. She looped the safety rope so it would drag along the upper rope in case she lost her grip, and set the two ropes to unspool behind her as she crossed.

The wind running down the canyon pushed at her back as she grimly edged forward. The tough fiber of the rope ground into the soles of her feet as she rocked unsteadily, ignoring the flashes of pain. Her hand on the upper rope gripped as she swayed. It was so far down.

Don't look.

A shout rang out in the distance, back along the path. Elen's right foot slipped, dangling over the air, and part of her weight dragged on the safety loop. Teeth gritted, hands gripped so tight they ached, she struggled to regain her calm, her looseness.

"Relax!" shouted Kem. "Breathe! In, slow. Out, slow. Slide one step, right foot, left foot. There you go. I'll count down. Twenty. Nineteen."

Eighteen. Seventeen.

The wind snarled in her hair, rumbled at the loose ropes, pushed and pushed and pushed so unforgivingly. The wind wanted her to fall. The air was malevolent. But she held on to Kem's voice. He was using the exact same brightly neutral tone he'd learned from her, that blessed child.

"Thirteen. Twelve."

More shouts were followed by a shriek, but there was nothing she could do for those she'd left behind. She had to cross. Ten. Nine.

Another shout, this one turning into a falling scream, but it was all taking place behind her back, so she couldn't see.

She mustn't look back.

Ipis whooped with triumph. Simo shouted, "Head down!"

Elen ducked her head. An arrow wobbled past, close enough that she might have grabbed it, had she good enough balance. *Damn!* She caught sight of the river below. So far below. A spurt of nausea destabilized her.

"Don't look!" called Kem. "Eyes on your hands. Four. Three."

A gust of wind shuddered her hard. Both her feet slipped off the rope. She hung by her fingers, most of her weight dangling in the safety loop. Kicking back, she desperately tried to get her feet back on the rope, but she couldn't catch it.

A strong hand grasped her right arm. Kem swung her back to the rope, she got purchase, and with a heave and a "Ho!" she dropped onto the ledge, kneeling, panting.

"Don't think I don't know why you did it like that," he scolded. "Like you were testing me to make sure I secured the rope. I wouldn't have let you fall."

"I know."

"Here, get this rope strung through."

He took the other rope. She didn't have enough breath to speak, but she could pull her rope through its double ring. Working together, they got the rope structure into place, with its two upper and two lower ropes pulled taut and secured.

The ledge had a little cave cut into it, where a person could tuck in tight out of the rain. The space was half-filled with an object rolled up inside an oiled canvas. Kem uncovered it as Elen caught her breath. She stared, aghast, back across the gap at the stark unfolding of a skirmish.

Xilsi stood, back against the rock face, bowstring drawn as she sighted on the empty path. From the pier, Elen could see farther back along the path. To her surprise, while she'd crossed, Fulmo had moved away from the others and placed himself on the path like a roadblock, so hunched in on himself that he seemed more like a boulder than a living creature. Beyond him, the path curved out of sight around a bend before curving back into Elen's view.

Several hundred paces from the rope bridge's ledge, the pursuers had stalled, forced to take shelter to avoid arrows loosed from on high. It took her a bit to find Jirvy, where he was wedged into a rocky gap above. Two of the pursuers were climbing toward him. An arrow struck one in the shoulder, bringing the climber to a halt. From the rear of the column, archers took aim, but their arrows broke against rock on either side of the warden.

Kem moved past her with the bundle. He wasn't stuck staring. He was doing his job.

But she couldn't stop looking. Where was the haunt?

She caught movement at the rim of the south wall. Another group of pursuers were gathering up there, seeking a way to climb down to the ledge. From up on the rim they had a clear shot at the ropes. A vivid image of Kem falling to his death with an arrow stuck in his chest flashed in her mind.

"Wait! Kem! I'll go."

"Shut up, I'm faster." His curtness caught her so off guard that he got past her while she was still blinking.

Horribly, he was correct. Having to watch him go churned up every feeling of helplessness she'd ever scoured from her heart after she and Ao had escaped their childhood servitude. It made her twitch as shadows of the past bubbled up in her mind. Because she'd left her gear and her weapons, even her bow, on the ledge, she couldn't guard him. She just had to stand, sick in her heart and scared—and how she hated being scared without having a single thing she could do except watch.

The remaining part of the bridge was a rolled-up length of planks strung together with wire. Kem secured one end to the two iron posts and began unrolling the bundle across the bottom pair of ropes, securing the planks at intervals as he went. He was fast, so sure of himself it left her breathless even as the wind pushed and tugged at his body. But he was in his element; he was young and brash because the world hadn't hurt him. His mother had hurt him more with her sulks and outbursts and her initial, reflexive, frightened refusal to accept that he was the person he knew himself to be. Elen had never cared, no more than the empire did, so long as every newly fledged adult Declared a place for themselves within the imperial order and obeyed imperial law.

An arrow flew past, too close to his head! A second arrow drew a dark line toward Kem's exposed figure, but spun away as the wind caught it. A line of archers stood at the rim, readying to pick him off.

They weren't alone.

A shadow expanded behind the pursuers. All at once, without warning, a soldier went spinning off the rim, arms pinwheeling, screaming as he fell kicking and twisting past the ledge. A second body came head over heels, this one silent and limp. Then a third, shot by Xilsi as the body fell past, even though it was an arrow wasted because the fall would kill him. All this followed by an outbreak of shouting and a sound like the roar of thunder, booming and beating in waves against the air.

Kem reached the other side. She'd missed half his crossing, holding her breath while time had jumped ahead. He grabbed his gear and her gear and headed back without hesitation, not even holding the upper ropes as he made haste in a loose, bent-kneed, even stride that kept the plank walkway from rocking too hard. Once across, he waved to the others. Ipis came first, clutching at the upper ropes, sweating, ashen, jaw set, the planks rocking crazily because she was nervously jerky as she crossed. The instant Ipis reached the solidity of the pier, Luviara gamely set out.

Xilsi came down from her position in the rocks, unable to get a line on the skirmish above. Yet the pursuers retreated in confusion from the rim. They were being chased by a rumbling, swirling shadow that, from this angle, looked like a dragon made of smoke writhing through the sky. After they'd vanished from Elen's sight, she heard shouts, a scream, a clatter of weapons; then silence.

Surely that had been the haunt who had tossed the bodies over the cliff. Yet how, and what was he, and how could a human body make such a beastly roar? Turn into smoke and still be flesh and bone?

Yells of triumph broke from the path. One of the archers had hit Jirvy in the shoulder. The shaft of the arrow stuck out of the warden's flesh, blocking the movement of his left arm. He wedged his bow between his thighs and, his entire posture a scream of pain, snapped the shaft in two. Despite the head of the arrow still stuck in him, he drew his bow and nocked another arrow.

The pursuers sped another flight of arrows upward. An arrow buried its head deep in Jirvy's thigh and another struck his chest below the already wounded shoulder. Even so, he held on to his bow and loosed an arrow. Then he slumped forward.

"Jirvy's down," Elen shouted.

Xilsi ran down the path to Fulmo. Using the gagast as her shield, she commenced loosing arrows at the soldiers exposed on the path. They shot back, but their arrows hit the rock or the gagast, who might as well have been rock himself as the metal points bounced off him. Xilsi hit two of the enemy before the pursuers retreated.

Luviara reached the far side. She knelt, heaving and trembling. In a whisper, she said, "Had I known, I'd have let you rig the rope around me and haul me up that cursed shaft, dignity be damned. Then I could have used my last strong air spirit for this cursed crossing."

"Better if you had a means to get Jirvy across," said Elen, before shouting, "Simo! Come now!"

"I can't leave the prince!" he called back.

She pointed above him, and he looked up just as the haunt leaped down and onto the ledge. Or flew down. Elen couldn't be sure; she'd been watching Jirvy, so if the haunt had climbed down the cliff face, she'd missed it. How he had managed it so quickly she couldn't know, because she saw no trace of wings or smoke. He said something to Simo and ran down to where Fulmo blocked the path. He and Xilsi squeezed past the gagast. With Xilsi covering him with her bow, the haunt climbed up to Jirvy and, impossibly, got the groaning, half-conscious warden down to the path. Once on level ground, even as narrow as it was, he draped the warden across his shoulders as easily as if Jirvy were a child. He and Xilsi retreated back to the ledge. A scattershot of arrows followed as the pursuers realized their prey was fleeing. A shouted order from their leader demanded the troop advance. Fulmo did not shift, still blocking the path.

Simo crossed the bridge, followed by the haunt, who balanced as deftly on the planks as if he were on solid ground, even with Jirvy hanging across his shoulders and the bridge sagging alarmingly from the extra weight. Xilsi careened after them like a wild drunk and was sobbing by the time she reached the pier.

"I hate heights," she wheezed out to Elen.

Kem had shepherded the others on to the next pier. Xilsi staggered up and followed Ipis, Luviara, and the haunt to the sturdier spans of the permanent rope bridge that reached from pier to pier and on to the north wall, where steps led up to the north rim.

On the other side, the enemy soldiers closed cautiously in on Fulmo.

"Fulmo!" Elen shouted. "Cross now!"

Simo came up behind her. "He's too heavy to cross."

"We can't just leave him."

"Fulmo won't leave the prince. There's another path for him, one only he can take."

"What path is that?"

Fulmo tipped sideways off the path and twisted, brawny arms and tree-trunk legs tucked tight. He crashed and bounced down the rock face, the noise echoing. He thudded hard where the ground leveled out at the base of the cliffs. His momentum rolled him into the streaming thread of Pall that oozed along the bottom of the canyon.

"Merciful Heavens," Elen breathed. Had he killed himself rather than be taken prisoner?

An arrow thumped down a body's length from her as the pursuers began to shoot at her and Simo. A few arrows arched toward the far rope bridges, where the others were hurrying toward safety.

"You need to move out of range," said Simo. He knelt and set knife to rope.

"No!" Kem's voice startled her. She'd been so fixed on Fulmo she'd not noticed the boy return. "Warden, let me loosen the ropes. If they're smart, they won't try to cross, but if they aren't, the ropes will give way when they're partway across."

Simo slapped Kem on the shoulder. "Good thinking."

Elen was still staring at Fulmo's body. It had rolled all the way through the thread of Pall to fetch up in the shallows of the river. His form lay as still as if he had turned into stone, in truth. Water rushed over him as over a mostly submerged rock.

"Hey!" Kem barked at her. "Go!"

She moved in a daze. It was so difficult to absorb it all. But she had to keep moving. That was how you survived.

45

THE MOST EFFICIENT WAY

For so long she had walked in the lead, the first line of defense. She was the protector, the responsible one. Now, most of the party was ahead of her while Kem, with Simo, were the rearguard, making sure their pursuers couldn't get over the gap. She crossed the first of the fixed rope bridges, glancing down at intervals even though she knew not to look down because it made her dizzy, made her fathom the depths, the fall, the crack and splatter a body made when it hit from a height. An old memory, locked away as in a chest. What was the name of the woman who'd fallen? She didn't recall now if she'd ever known, only the tumble, the smack of flesh hitting stone. Ao sobbing. Screams and yells as a rising Pall swept closer to people cornered by its eerie movements.

Elen shoved the memory back down into the darkness. Her palms were damp, and she didn't dare slip or falter. There was nothing she could do to help Fulmo. Still, it was odd he'd thrown himself over like that. What had Simo meant?

She reached the third pier. Kem and Simo came running across the bridge behind her, catching up. Kem was laughing and Simo grinning, and all because a foolish soldier was starting to creep out over the temporary rope bridge, determined to get across. Nothing about the situation pleased Elen, though. She'd seen too much of death to enjoy the suffering of others. So she resolutely set her face forward and started over the next rope bridge. It was the longest of the bridges, one hundred paces of swaying length with the wind blustering about her. Her clothes rippled, her pack shifted, her boots drummed against her back because she hadn't had time to put them back on.

A shout of warning from the other side. A frantic shriek. The wind's rumble in her ears. One foot before the next. Her left big toe oozed blood from a scrape. When had that happened? Did it even matter? She glanced back to make sure Kem and Simo were safe behind her.

When Elen reached the north rim, Xilsi clapped her on the back. "There's a gamble that paid off! Did you see them fall? Two of them! What idiots!"

Elen trudged past, not answering. Luviara was seated, looking windblown and exhausted. Jirvy lay on the ground, on his back, eyes open. A blot of blood darkened his indigo tabard.

"How is he?" she asked Ipis, who was crouched beside the injured warden.

Jirvy himself answered with a wan but determined smile. "I've suffered worse."

"You got hit in the chest," she objected.

"It was shallow. I hit my head. That's why I passed out. The shoulder wound is a tough one, though. The prince already got the arrow out."

"That was fast."

Ipis said, "No one ever mentioned His Exalted Highness trained as a healer."

"I'm glad to see you alert and awake, Jirvy," said Elen, to change the subject.

"You more than some," he remarked with a sidelong glance toward Xilsi, who was waiting at the end of the bridge to greet Simo.

Ipis said, "What is it with you two?"

Jirvy shut his eyes.

Elen didn't want to know, so she said, "Where is the prince?"

"He scouted ahead," said Ipis. "Said to wait for Simo and follow."

Elen found an open patch of ground, sat, pulled on socks over numb toes, and laced up her boots. There was a lot of congratulatory back-slapping as Kem and Simo arrived, and then everyone had to discuss how to get Jirvy up the steps to the rim.

Elen left the wardens to it and started up, so she was surprised to reach the first switchback and find that the haunt had halted there instead of continuing the ascent. He was gazing into the canyon's depths.

"Here you are," he said. "Will you come with me? I need to fetch Fulmo. I could use your help."

"Isn't he . . . dead?"

The haunt gave her a disbelieving look. She might as well have suggested the sky was green. "Why would you say that? Are you coming?"

The rock face on this side was steep but not a sheer escarpment the way the cliff face was on the south rim. There was even an old trace of a trackway leading down, worn by goats or sheep or maybe by locals brave or desperate enough to hunt among the shrubs and stunted trees on the north side of the river, which animals and people could do because the stream of Pall flowed on the south bank of the river.

The haunt began scrambling down. Elen left her pack on the landing and headed after him. She'd been down this way only once before, exploring. It was a climb, but not dangerous if you kept your foot- and handholds steady.

Without looking back at her, he added, "A gagast can harden their outer skin to make themself impervious to physical damage taken from metal or rock. The fall won't have hurt him. Not in any way we understand such falls."

"How do you know so much about gagast?"

"Why would I not? They are people too."

People who had been around back when he'd been around, but why would that be surprising?

She sighed. "What I mean is, even if he survived the fall, he rolled through the Pall before he reached the water. And while the water will wash some of it away, the river is shallow this time of year, and he wasn't ever fully submerged. So he's got Spore still on him."

He tilted his head back to look up at her, examining her as if she had become a stranger in his eyes. "I don't understand how you know so little about yourself. He's like to you and to me, the real me, I mean, not the prince. You and I aren't eaten up by the Pall. Neither is he."

"Then why hasn't he gotten up?"

"Ah, that would be the water. We have to haul him out before he can shed his shell."

"You and I can shift him?"

"I can shift him. Your viper will be able to make sure he doesn't bring any Spore with him that might have lodged in his nostrils or fastened to his epidermis. That way he won't inadvertently spread Spore beyond the Pall."

"What will you tell the others?"

"They know Fulmo is immune to the touch of the Pall because he is a gagast, if I am reading correctly between the lines of remarks they've made."

"You seem to be getting good at that."

"I am, aren't I? Quite the clever fellow." His cheeky grin made her snort-laugh, an incongruous sound she was suddenly ashamed of as her gaze lifted to take in the ground at the base of the south wall, the ropes and planks of the first bridge hanging down the rock face, and three visible bodies lying among the rocks, one within an arm's length of the Pall. The thread of Pall itself lay as still as a ribbon of dawn fog on a windless day, unmoving. Was the body nearest the Pall dead? Or just out of reach?

Then the fallen man stirred with a gasp. Choking, he tried to drag himself up, but his legs were broken. In a spasm of pain, he rolled the wrong way. A foot touched the Pall.

Elen's voice stuck in her throat.

The mist churned. A ripple spread to engulf the man's foot. Life, life, life. A tower of Spore bubbled up, building a grotesquely elongated foot that split the seams of the man's leather boot with a hundred seething tendrils. The man heaved and huffed, fingers scrambling frantically for the knife at his belt. The Spore hissed with eager whispers as it began to boil up his leg. He couldn't get a grip on the hilt. Something inside him broke. He spasmed. Spittle and pink foam leaked from his mouth until finally he slumped, going limp. Dead. She knew it at once, felt its finality. The Spore gave a despairing puff and collapsed, retreating back into the Pall.

The mist settled. All lay still.

Elen pressed a hand against her face to suppress a flash of memory: a horse, stumbling. No, not that. She did not want to see that again, so she shut away the distressing image and, with a determined exhalation, lowered her hand.

Had this man and the others deserved death? She was not the emperor, nor the court of the High Heavens, to pass judgment, nor did she want to be.

"How fortunate that he died quickly," said the haunt in a casual tone. He had kept his gaze on the Pall all this time, but now he looked at her. "As I was saying, as far as I can tell, from what the others have said and haven't said, it seems Fulmo was brought into Prince Gevulin's service by Hemerlin."

"Hemerlin?" She had to drag her thoughts back to the here and the now. A soldier was dead, along with at least four others, all because they'd tried to kill the prince. The haunt had saved the prince's party. That was what mattered. She was adept at walling things off. It was how she'd survived.

He went on as if their conversation had not just been interrupted by a grisly death he had himself caused. "I suspect a gagast's immunity to Pall has to do with their ability to sense poisons in food and drink. But I couldn't say for sure. There are so many mysteries yet to be unwound! I'm quite agog at wondering what we'll discover when we reach Far Boundary Vigil. If we reach it. Truly, the prince has determined enemies. I almost admire them."

He started down again. She climbed after him, mulling over his words. It made sense that a chief menial would seek any means to protect the prince he served.

"I heard the gagast send small tributary groups to the palace. Do you suppose every prince gets one?" she asked.

"I wasn't aware the gagast of these benighted days distributed their own kin as tribute. They're a very independent people."

"All I know of gagast is that they walked out of the Desolation."

He glanced at her as he picked his way down. "I don't quite understand this *Desolation*."

"The Desolation used to be a Pall. It covered most of Wheathome Province, which ran from the northern coast south into the heartland. The Pall that rose there was really large, like a sea. Then, about thirty years after its rising, it vanished. In just a few months, so the chroniclers write. As if it were being drained. Like—I don't know—out of a hole in the bottom of a tub."

"What lies in this Desolation now?"

"In its outer borderlands, there is nothing alive, no animals, no plants, just bare ground and rocks. But no Spore either. After a few years, aivur and gagast began emerging from the interior. They were almost like refugees racing ahead of a storm."

"You've seen this—the Desolation—with your own eyes?"

"No, not me. I read the chronicles and way-sheets compiled from the reports of imperial surveyors."

"Where within the Desolation do the aivur and gagast come from? How had they survived, if there is no life because the Pall devoured it?"

"No one knows. Surveyors who went in either never came out or had to turn back before they got very far. The borderlands are mapped, but the interior of the Desolation remains a blank region that runs from the northern sea all the way south, well into the heartland."

They descended the last, steepest, and thus trickiest part of the path in silence. She was feeling an ache in her fingers, the way loose stone could slip beneath her boots and send her plunging. An hour before, the cold wind had shivered down her neck; now, she was sweating. The bottom of the canyon lay in shadow. Compared to the south face, there was little rockfall below the north face and much more plant growth, vegetation grasping at every chance to flourish where water separated it from the Pall. The shallow autumn river burbled noisily as its flow spilled and played along exposed rocks.

The haunt waved at her to remain on the shore. He splashed out to the sprawled figure of the gagast. She looked over her shoulder to see the wardens climbing toward the rim, intent on aiding Jirvy and Luviara. Kem peered down, looking for them in the shadows. Simo got his attention and sent him up, then waved at her, as if to let her know she should proceed with whatever plan the prince had.

Had something like this happened before with Fulmo? Wardens were expert Spore killers, after all, so Prince Gevulin would have that much protection once he got the gagast out of the water.

It was getting darker, the shadows stretching ominously. Or were these shadows emanating from the prince's body, more of the smoky essence she'd glimpsed before, now twisting along the surface of the water? The haunt got hold of the gagast's big ankles and tugged the body across the rocky shallows with a grinding noise. Maybe the prince was that strong, or maybe the gagast did not weigh as much as a bulky creature ought to. Or maybe the haunt's shadow, like uncanny limbs, was assisting.

The smoke shifted, seeming to coalesce back into the prince's flesh. With a striking burst of strength, the haunt hauled the gagast up onto shore and, after one last grunting tug, sat back on his behind with a laugh. Fulmo's body was entirely out of the water, although it did not move.

"The viper!" said the haunt with a snap of anger. "Where's the viper? I told you there might be Spore—"

A mist-pale movement flashed atop the body. A tiny hill mouse staggered out from the fold of Fulmo's neck, having somehow gotten caught in the tumble down through the Pall. One of the mouse's forelimbs was already torturously transforming into a wicked-looking claw, while its ears were flowering like dandelions ready to burst.

Elen cursed, kneeling, and set her hand on the ground as she rolled up her sleeve. The viper stirred, uncoiling from her heart but not yet emerged. The Spore-ridden mouse hopped from Fulmo's neck to his shoulder and scurried down his motionless arm toward the ground and the plants and the life, the life, the life that it would burst upon and thus trigger an irruption to race, unchecked, along the canyon floor.

The haunt plucked up the mouse by the tail. It struggled, writhing and twisting, and its body elongated in multiple directions as it tried to escape his grip. It hissed in the malignant manner of Spore everywhere. The haunt merely opened his mouth wide, dropped the mouse in, and closed his lips over it, sucking in the tip of its tail.

Pain burned like hot ash through Elen's skin as the viper finally emerged from her arm. It slithered eagerly across the rocks to investigate Fulmo's body. For once, Elen scarcely noticed the pain, because she was staring at the haunt. She couldn't be sure whether she was horrified or entertained or maybe both, because she'd never seen anything like this.

He munched and he crunched with an expression of delight, and, still masticating, he pointed at the viper as if to remind her to keep an eye on its hunt. It had discovered a seedling Spore nestled in one of the gagast's armpits. The viper sucked down the wisp and kept on searching as the haunt swallowed, once, twice, and a third time. He wiped his mouth with the back of a hand and sighed with pleasure.

"So much texture," he said. "I do miss that. The Heart Temple was the worst. There was no flesh at all to be had."

"At a Heart Temple, they don't eat the flesh of animals." She didn't know what else to say.

He looked at her quizzically, eyebrows spiked upward. "Is something wrong?"

She waved a hand, aware she was grimacing, and choked out, "You ate it whole, fur and guts and bones and all."

"It seemed the most efficient way to be rid of it."

"Won't the Spore infest you? Eat you out from the inside?"

"Didn't we already have this discussion? It can't eat me faster than I can repair the damage it causes me."

"But you don't have a viper to eat the Spore."

"I do not, it's true! My healing power is of a different capacity. As long as I inhabit the prince's body, he benefits from that which my people take for granted, but which so many other creatures—like humans!—sorely lack. Good fortune for him!"

"I can scarcely argue otherwise," she agreed. "But I should warn you not to do that in front of any of the others. They'll think you have taken leave of your senses."

"Oh, I see." He nodded. "That's useful to know."

"The prince's status gives you a great deal of slack. By which I mean, an exalted prince can get away with things that others can't."

"I do notice how they are reluctant to question me, much less countermand anything I say I want. It has proven useful."

"Yes," she said drily. "The prince is much better for your needs than Kem."

"You would say so, since you care a great deal about the boy and nothing about the prince. Well." He tilted his head to one side as he gave her a sidelong look, his eyes bright and his gaze teasing. "Perhaps you find the prince's handsome figure to be of interest."

She chuckled because she hadn't expected him to be so forthright. "Maybe I do, but in any other circumstance, I would not be sitting here and speaking to a prince. No, wait, that's the wrong way round. He wouldn't be speaking to me."

His rascal smile flashed as he leaned toward her invitingly. "Ah. So you *do* find this body attractive?"

"Are you *flirting* with me, Gesavura'alalin?" A flush hit her hard, cheeks heating not with embarrassment, not precisely, but because the absurdity of the situation—of him—delighted her. He delighted her, in a way the prince never would, even in the same body. Yet what a terrible, terrible idea it would be. It couldn't even be considered.

He pressed a finger to his lips with thoughtful repose. "Is it allowed?"

"No!" she said too emphatically. "It is certainly not allowed. A prince has palace concubines to fulfill princely sexual needs."

He winced. "Yes, I recall those two now. They fluttered a great deal, and they wore heavy layers of scent, quite enough to make me sneeze. The worst part was that the perfume could not disguise the smell of their desperation."

"Desperation?" The sweetness of their carefree flirtation vanished like a dazzling snowflake dissolving in a draft of hot wind.

"I can't explain it. When an individual desires to please another only because they believe that to please is their only way to be safe. Isn't that a form of desperation?"

She thought of Aoving at Duenn Manor. "Yes, it is. Aren't the wardens that way with you, as well?"

"Not in the same way. The wardens are . . . soldiers under my command. They know their skills and their worth. The wardens don't need me to have a purpose in life. To patrol the roads and to serve the empire. To feel they have freedom of movement and choices they can themselves make. From what I saw of the menials and the concubines, they serve only the body and whim of the prince. If the prince's displeasure turns on them, then what is to become of them? Do you know? Is it something awful?"

"I don't know what goes on in the palace."

He raised a hand, waving a finger to emphasize his point. "That's what I meant about Hemerlin. These menials and concubines are so dependent upon the one they serve that they must observe and know that person better than anyone. Maybe better than the person knows themselves. Besides how unpleasantly obsequious it is, it's also very dangerous in my situation. As I'm sure you can see."

"I can. But what about Fulmo, then? You kept him on, and he's a menial."

"A gagast cannot be coerced, not as humans can, which is why his arrangement with the palace puzzles me. How Hemerlin is involved is a question I can't answer. And I've no way to ask that doesn't reveal my ignorance. Still, we've made it this far, you and I, have we not? Working together."

His gaze had its own enchantment, inviting her in, offering her a partnership. It was impossible not to incline toward him. His hand crept toward hers, across the stony ground, as if he meant to take hold. What would that even mean? She imagined how it might proceed: the brush of warm fingers over her own, the twining of hands, the way bodies lean toward each other as toward fate—

Movement caught in the periphery of her gaze, and she jolted back. *Don't get distracted!*

But the movement was the viper, which had finished its circuit and, racing back to her, slid up beneath her hand and, with the familiar burn, poured itself back into her flesh.

"Here we go," he said, looking past her. "To break the shell, a gagast needs the touch of an ally so they know it is safe to emerge. Me hauling him out will have triggered the change."

On the river's stony shoreline, Fulmo's body shuddered as a tremor passed through it. A series of pops sounded in snapping, sizzling bursts. Elen leaped to her feet.

The gagast's skin crackled, a thousand tiny lines spreading across his body. With a loud crack, his epidermis shattered like ceramic splintering. It fell away in a thousand pieces, spilling onto the ground in a clatter of shards. A new, fresh Fulmo emerged, slightly smaller and with a brighter, more coppery skin tone, but otherwise apparently the same.

Rising, he looked first at the haunt and then at her. She glanced down at her bare arm, but the viper had tucked itself safely away inside her. Fulmo hadn't seen, although she couldn't be sure he didn't already know. He could taste poisons and toxins, after all. Wasn't it possible he could sense the presence of the viper? If so, he had said nothing. Likewise, if he knew a disembodied soul possessed the prince's body, he'd not given the haunt away.

Elen sat there, still stunned by all she had witnessed in such quick succession. But Fulmo and the haunt rose and walked together to the north face. They started climbing.

The haunt called merrily back, "Best to get out of here while we can still see to climb. Our pursuers will happily take potshots at us once they regroup."

All at once she felt parched, exhausted by all the surprises. She cupped a hand into the cold water of the streaming river and drank. Its icy sweetness was as bracing as a draught of pure-water. Local tradition said the river was partly fed by pure-water springs rising in these hills.

Refreshed, although still shaken, she rose and followed, questions like swarming wasps in her mind.

46

A MORE COMPLICATED STORY

ACCORDING TO THE imperial archives, the imperial roads were built in the early years of the empire, commanded into being through the foresight and wisdom of the Lotus General and his heirs. It is certain that a number of roads were built at this time to accommodate the armies of the Lotus Clan as they moved swiftly to bring order and peace to lands riven by strife and disorder. It is also known the imperial roads allow the wardens, then and now, to communicate by means swifter even than griffin scouts. This secret is not shared outside the Imperial Order of Wardens.

However, extensive travels along the so-called witch roads and the other primary imperial routes, combined with the discovery of fragmentary evidence gathered from locally held scrolls not found and burned by the imperial censors, suggest a more complicated story.

The witch roads differ from the other imperial roads because of their ability to fend off the Pall. Yet the Pall had not yet risen when the Lotus Clan established the Tranquil Empire.

It would be two hundred years after the founding of the empire before a white mist seeped upward out of the ground to form shallow seas and rivers of deadly fog and irrupting Spore that inundated large swathes of land and one entire province. The records show that the Azalea Emperor and his officials had no warning and no prior knowledge of that which came to be called the Pall.

Because of this, I believe it most likely the roads were not deliberately constructed with protection against the Pall. How could the imperial engineers have done so if they did not know what was coming and what it would do? Why only some of the roads and not all of them?

So, how did the witch roads come about?

Perhaps there is an accidental quality to the witch roads that the other main military and secondary roads lack. Maybe they truly do contain mortar ground from the bones of the holy venerables who rebelled against the Lotus Clan.

Or perhaps the witch roads were constructed long before the

empire to guard against a threat that our wise ancestors feared might come to pass, in a future that would have seemed distant to them but is the world we live in now.

From *The Official's Handbook of the Empire* as compiled by
Luviara, theurgist, working at the behest of the
Inner Chamber of the Heart Temple

47

It was dusk by the time Elen reached the rim of the north face. She had lagged behind the haunt and Fulmo, trying to settle the churn of emotions that battered like the wings of a bird trapped inside a cage.

Their exchange by the river had the elusive quality of a flower's lovely scent: attractive, and yet nothing one could hold. Petals could be distilled by a perfumer into an oil, leaves gathered by an herbalist to make a tisane, but, unlike these, the haunt was a temporary passenger who would ultimately vanish and leave nothing of himself behind. She had to be pragmatic. Regardless, if any in their party came to believe the prince had an "interest" in her, she couldn't imagine what would happen. Princes didn't consort with deputy couriers, didn't even speak to them. It was an unfathomable gulf. She had to keep reminding herself that she was speaking to another person entirely. She had to protect herself and Kem, and the haunt, too. He might not be innocent; he might be anything; but he had a mission and she intended to help him keep to it.

Yet flirtation was only one fragment of what surged and whirl-pooled in her tumultuous thoughts. The fight at the bridge kept crashing back in.

As an atoner in the nameless land, she'd seen death. But not like this.

As a sentinel in Duenn Manor's militia, she'd trained with weapons and ridden patrols but had never fought, never struck anyone with naked steel, although a few times the troop had chased frightened and desperate people out of Duenn territory. As a deputy courier, she'd walked with a measure of protection, mostly because she carried nothing valuable for brigands, except her boots and hardy garments, and also because, in the early years of his intendancy, the intendant had made it brutally clear, with a series of public executions, that his officials were not to be tampered with. It was a lesson he'd never had to repeat. Imperial couriers walked with the "shield" of the empire on their backs because couriers were a crucial element in the empire's control of its vast territories.

Over the years, she'd learned to cope with the trauma she'd survived, each incident bad enough in its own particular way. Open a chest, set the memories inside, and close the lid.

She'd not been prepared for facing death in this specifically brutal way.

Her thoughts kept skittering back to the falling bodies, to the screams, to the blood on Jirvy's tabard. To the dying man on the shore. To the smoky emanation, coming from the haunt, that she hadn't been able to see clearly. Their pursuers hadn't really had a chance, had they? The haunt had enjoyed unleashing his power. Whatever that power was. What if part of his power was the charm he turned on her, the rascal smile, the sardonic wit, the ease with which he engaged with her and lured her in.

He was a puzzle, truly. Dangerous and unknowable. Yet so alluring.

Ought she to fear him? She couldn't find it in herself to do so.

Life had an odd sense of humor.

Where the steps reached the tableland, she spotted campfires against the lowering dusk and made her way toward the light.

The others had set up camp on a slab of bedrock amid an undulation of boulders worn away by eons of wind and rain. They had built a campfire at each cardinal direction, with room to sleep inside. It was standard wilderness camping protocol for surveyors or couriers or anyone caught outside a protective ring, whether that ring be a Halt or some manner of water-filled moat or ditch. Stone and fire were the best protection if there was nothing else.

Four fires burned. Xilsi and Kem were clearing out any scraps of plants that might attract Spore. Ipis quartered the ground using her shrive-steel sword for signs of the deadly substance.

Elen took in a deep breath, seeking any sign of Spore, but felt and smelled nothing. There was no Spore nearby, not that she could sniff out.

Luviara sat cross-legged on a ground cloth, writing in her journal.

Fulmo had gotten a pot of food going, his movements slowing as twilight settled. He looked no different from before. If she had not witnessed the cracking shell, she'd probably not notice he was a bit smaller.

The haunt was kneeling beside Jirvy, with a hand on the warden's injured thigh. Was there a pale golden haze gleaming around his hand? Or was it just firelight glinting on the three lineage rings a prince wore?

A shadow emerged from behind a boulder and approached her.

"Here you are, Deputy Courier." Simo blocked her path, so she had to stop.

"Yes, here I am, Captain." She eyed his aggressive stance.

From inside the ring of campfires, Kem laughed at something Ipis said. It hurt that he still was so angry at her and yet could laugh and joke with others. But she had to put it aside. He had the right to be angry. It wasn't her place to require him to react or respond in any specific way. Still, it hurt because he'd never been mad at her before, ever, not like this.

Simo cleared his throat portentously to grab her wandering attention. "Deputy Courier, you will have observed the situation with the gagast. I assure you, we who serve His Exalted Highness are aware of Fulmo's unusual characteristics."

"If you mean he is immune to Spore, and how he protects himself against steel and afterward cracks open a new skin, then yes, I am aware. Is there something else you are concerned about, Captain?"

His mouth worked. His shoulders tensed.

She added, "One of our pursuers survived the fall, but he died before Spore could escape through him." Not that she was about to mention the mouse! Or her viper!

He nodded, satisfied by her answer. "Do you know this countryside?"

"North of the Cut? Not really. I've been over Five Bridges with the intendant. That was five years ago, when the intendant escorted a newly appointed intendant to Farledder Intendancy. There was a lot of brigandage in Farledder Intendancy at the time because . . . well, that's local gossip that won't interest you. I've studied the surveyor maps of the area. If we leave here at dawn and head overland, west-northwest, we should reach the road by midafternoon, north of the fifth bridge. From there, we can make it to the next Halt by nightfall."

"Do you happen to recall the name of the Farledder intendant?"

She caught the flutter of his eyes, the curl of his mouth. The defensive posture. "Are you concerned the Farledder intendant might be an ally of Prince Astaylin?"

"Surely you understand why we must be on full alert."

"I do. Her name is Berel Karissar. She is a distant cousin of the Orledder intendant. That's why the intendant was asked to escort her when she first came north."

Simo relaxed. "That's good, then. Karis Manor is one of the Six Noble Manors, the first clans who stood in support of the new empire, in case you didn't know."

She knew, but she kept her mouth closed.

"They have remained loyal to the emperor, and don't involve themselves in factional struggles."

"As Duenn Manor has decided to do?"

"Lesser Manors often struggle to elevate their place amid the ranks. It's even more true for the provincial, meritorious Manors like Duenn, since they are not much to speak of, after all," he went on with the patronizing tone of a man raised in a more prestigious Manor. "So they must pin their hopes of greater status upon a prince, most especially a prince of the Third Estate."

"You mean one who can aspire to become crown prince. But there's already a crown prince. The emperor's son."

Simo shrugged dismissively and, curiously, did not answer. Did his silence suggest the crown prince's existence was tolerated rather than admired?

"Is there anything else, Captain?"

"You are disrespectful," he remarked, "but you got us here, as the Orledder intendant said you would. So I will overlook your faults, which have been on such prominent display. But I give you this warning, Deputy Courier. You are not a member of this party. You are neither a menial nor an official to the prince. He may condescend to speak to you, but it does not mean you may take liberties and believe you can speak to him, or to any of us, as if you stand as our equal."

"I am well aware I am but a minor provincial deputy courier who lacks a Manor-born lineage or any other mark of distinction. I'll not offend further. You'll be rid of me as soon as we reach the road."

Yet, to say the words caused a twinge in her heart. They'd leave her behind because they would no longer need her. She glanced toward the camp. The glow of fires limned the prince's body as if painting his form into her memory. It was perilous to slide down that slippery slope. Not infatuation, precisely; in its clumsy, eager way, infatuation was far less dangerous, because it was fleeting. She felt drawn to him, his pleasing face and form but, more than that, to his wit, his snarky asides, the way he found things amusing, the mischievous spark, the odd ways he viewed the world as if he'd never seen it through human eyes. The way he looked at her as if the viper made her whole, rather than made her a monster.

Even the haunt was but a passing traveler in her life. There was Kem, standing side by side with Ipis. Kem, who wouldn't talk to her now. But she had to be patient. She'd find a way to speak to him, out of earshot of the others. She had to. She couldn't bear to let him go on with the others while he was so angry with her, nothing resolved, just his sense of betrayal. She couldn't bear it.

"Yes, we will be rid of you soon enough," agreed Simo with a grimace of satisfaction.

How on this earth had she offended the captain so greatly? She'd only done her job. But she knew better than to beat her head bloody against this kind of rock.

"If it please you, Captain, may I settle at the fire? My feet hurt. It's been a long day, with quite a bit more excitement than I am used to. And by excitement I mean to say a skirmish. It has exhausted me."

Unexpectedly, his expression softened. "Ah. Yes. I was stationed for years on the eastern frontier. I remember my first battle. It wasn't even a battle, just an encounter in an abandoned village that surprised everyone involved, the enemy as much as us. Your service is noted. I give you leave to be free of duties until dawn." He stepped out of her way.

As she approached the fire, Kem looked over and saw her. Because he stood inside the circle of fires, she could see the disapproving press of his mouth, succeeded by the defensive hunch of his shoulders and a flare in his eyes as he made a decision. He turned back to Ipis, and ignored Elen as she entered the circle. The gesture stung, as he meant it to. Nevertheless, she spread out her ground cloth and sat, relieved to be off her feet.

The haunt hadn't moved from beside Jirvy. The warden had his eyes closed; Elen thought the man was awake but quiescent. Enchanted? Bespelled? An almost indiscernible golden mist still played about the haunt's hand, like captured light oozing into the wounded man's body. The light seemed to be moving sluggishly, hypnotically, circling, calming . . .

Her head nodded forward.

She startled up when Fulmo appeared before her with a pot. His movements by now were grindingly slow and yet, somehow, he was determined to feed her before night paralyzed him. She hastily got bowl and spoon from her pack and accepted a ladleful of chewy turnip and goat cheese stew, spiced with humble fennel. He creaked back toward the fire, tilted his head up, and went still.

Against a cloudless night, the stars glittered in a cold sky. The moon had not yet risen. She checked out the others. Kem and Ipis were seated, chatting with Luviara as they ate. Jirvy had finally fallen asleep, covered with a blanket. The haunt stood alone by the northern fire, facing north as if trying to see into the darkness. He held a bowl in one hand, but he wasn't eating. Simo must have been on watch because she couldn't see him.

Xilsi plopped down beside Elen with her own bowl and began to eat with the relish of a person who is fulsomely hungry. Her face was still bright from the lingering effects of the skirmish and crossing.

"I'll say this for you, Deputy Courier . . . Can I just call you by your name? Elen, isn't it?"

48

I t is," said Elen cautiously. In general, she tried to avoid the attention of people who had the authority to arbitrarily punish her on whatever grounds they wished.

Xilsi nodded enthusiastically. "Well, then, now we're companions. You've got a cool head and an impressive store of knowledge and skill. You ever thought of asking to join the wardens?"

"As a menial, do you mean?"

Xilsi flashed her a look, then laughed. "Fair enough. You don't strike me as the type to manage a menial's life, not like Hemerlin. To be honest, I had a feeling you manipulated the prince into getting rid of the old man. Hemerlin knows his work, it's true, but he acts as if he owns the prince. Been with him since the exalted highness was but a child."

"So I have heard."

"He couldn't have kept up anyway, so it was just as well. I'm sorry about Jirvy, by the way." Xilsi spoke so casually that Elen hadn't a clue what she meant.

"Sorry he was injured?"

"Since he'll live, I'm kind of glad he's hurting. Sorry I complained to you, I mean. It's not meant to be your business. I shouldn't have brought others into it."

Elen studied the other woman's expression. "I pray you, Warden—"

"Xilsi." It was a tone of command, of a woman of high status used to being obeyed.

"Xilsi. I pray you, let me know if I overstep, but it seems you two aren't married. I would gently ask if you were lovers who've had a hostile parting—"

"Yes!" Xilsi lifted her chin with fierce flush of anger. "It was a shock. That motherfucker. Not his mother, I mean. She's a mere fifth-rank administrator out of Novra Manor. His father is merely a captain in the army. So it stood to reason it would happen eventually."

"What would happen eventually?"

"Oh! Oh, yes, I suppose you don't know about that. They made a marriage alliance for him to try to improve their lineage's standing. He didn't have the courage to tell me. Coward! Maybe he hoped we could just keep shagging as usual, but I'll tell you something, I'm not about to be the scraps after someone else's feast. I have my pride!" Xilsi looked Elen up and down, and Elen took the opportunity to eat more of the hearty stew. She was so hungry, and also eating helped her to not hear the word "coward" as if it were Kem saying it to her. "It's odd how comfortable I feel with you."

"Why is that odd?"

"Because you're not Manor-born. Yet you almost act as if you were. Well, no one would ever mistake you for being Manor-born. But I'm used to folk acting differently around me than you do. It's curious, don't you think?"

"I've never been around Manor-born people except for the intendant and his family." Yet that wasn't true, was it? Joef's mother was Manor-born, and the lad had been raised by his mother's sister. It was just that all the Manor-born folk in a place like Orledder Halt were minor relatives of minor cousin branches, not important people like the heartland Manor-born. Except for the intendant. "Now that you mention it, I do have a question."

"What's that?"

"I don't understand the intricacies of the Manors. But if it stood to reason his family would make a marriage alliance for him eventually, then isn't that also true for you?"

"His Manor doesn't have enough status to marry into mine. So he and I would never have made a match of it."

"I see, but that wasn't what I meant. Aren't you to be assigned a marriage alliance, as someone who is Manor-born?"

"Oh! Of course. Yes. No. My cohort of siblings is large. Some of us had to volunteer to never marry. I was at the front of that line!"

"You never wanted to marry?"

"My twin has given birth four times, no . . . five. No, wait, there's been a sixth! I wasn't interested in that at all. But you and I are about the same age, I'd wager. I'm thirty-two."

"Yes, that seems right," said Elen, to say something.

"Have you been married?"

"I have not."

"So, you see, we're not so different."

"I think we are so different, Xilsi. I never had the opportunity to marry. I didn't dare ever get pregnant. It wasn't a matter of what I wanted or didn't want. I had a sister to protect. She had enough trouble with her pregnancy, and after that, the baby to raise and shield. It simply wasn't possible to even think of marriage, so I didn't think about it. I'd rather enjoy what life has to offer to the likes of me than resent what lies out of my reach."

"What an astounding philosophy!"

"I suppose there isn't much that lies out of your reach."

Xilsi set down her bowl and crossed her arms, examining Elen with an expression that wasn't hostile, exactly, but lacked any sense that this direct a stare might be intrusive and rude.

"I just never thought of it like that," she remarked, then picked up bowl and spoon and went back to eating. She had a way of savoring each spoonful that suggested no one had ever snatched scraps out of her hands to leave her hungry and, thus, to cause her to eat quickly so as to leave no opening.

Kem, Ipis, and Luviara sat about ten paces away, chatting. Elen had been studiously ignoring them, not wanting to seem to be eavesdropping. But Xilsi, as she ate, turned her attention toward the trio with a look of lively interest.

"And how did you know?" the theurgist was asking Kem. "When did you realize? If you don't mind my asking, I mean. I've been told before I can be a bit intrusive and rude, but I never get tired of asking questions about the world. How else are we to understand it?"

"Is it knowing, though?" Kem asked. "Or accepting?"

"You tell me!" The theurgist always sounded so excited, as if the world were a huge pastry and she the delighted child offered bite after delicious bite.

"It was something Joef said to me."

"That's the archivist's nephew? You were always friends?"

"He was always around with the other children. But we really started spending time together when I got sent to the upper school in the Residency, so I must have been ten."

"The upper school?"

"It's for Manor-born children. But the intendant admits any pupil from the Halt school who shows promise."

"I see," said Luviara with an odd tone flattening her voice. "So, it seems some local officials still follow the directive of the Willow Emperor, in this regard. But let me not digress, as I surely could. Go on."

"I just always felt easy with Joef, like I didn't so much with my mother. May she be blessed in our memories."

Ipis broke in. "Hold on. You're Duenn Manor, though. Isn't that Joef boy born and raised in Orledder Halt? The intendant there is Karis Manor, so it makes sense that the officials and administrators the intendant settled around him are also Karis, not Duenn."

"Oh. Ah. That's right." Kem was nothing if not quick on his feet. "My mother was sent away from Duenn Manor for political reasons. She settled at Orledder Halt. So that's where I was raised. It's complicated."

"I am sure it is," said the theurgist soothingly.

Elen caught the old woman glancing her way. She ducked her head back to her bowl, pretending she hadn't noticed, but she kept listening. Kem had never talked to her about what had led up to him telling his mother one day, seemingly out of the blue, that he was a boy. Elen had stayed out of the arguments between them, and then Ao had died, and Kem had made his Declaration legally public, and they'd gone on with life. Or done their best to do so, even if now she saw the cracks she'd ignored because she hadn't wanted to see them.

He went on. "My mother had healing hands. She was a respected midwife. She was patient with people in labor in a way she never was with me. I admired that, but she wanted me to be a midwife too. She took me along all the time, and I didn't mind helping but . . . it wasn't what I wanted."

"Are you saying you Declared so your mother couldn't pressure you into being a midwife?" asked Ipis.

"I don't think that's what he's saying," said Luviara. "Even though it also happens to be true that he couldn't become a midwife if he wasn't a woman."

"It was bigger than that," said Kem. "I guess it always is, isn't it? I never felt comfortable in myself, not since I was little. But I guess when I look back, I realize I didn't have any way to think about it that helped me figure it out. It wasn't something we would talk about at home. Not with my mother. And my . . . well, the other person I would have wanted to talk to always shut down any conversation that might upset my mother."

Ouch. That was a barb punched straight in through her skin, she who had always been so sure she was such a good aunt, such a good caretaker, such a good protector. Kem did not look at her but by now she was sure he knew she was listening. Probably he wanted to cast her a pointed look that said, *You ought to have been listening*, but he didn't dare alert the others. There'd be too many questions if the other wardens learned the truth.

"What was it your friend Joef said to you?" Luviara asked.

Kem had the sweetest smile, touched by fondness for his great good friend, Joef, best buddies and true comrades. "One time we were out fishing, just quiet-like. We could sit for hours that way. And he said, 'You're the brother I always wanted to have.' And I realized I could be the brother, that I wanted to be the brother, that it all made sense to me when he said that. We were brothers. I don't know." He shrugged. "It was like nothing and everything at the same time."

"That's sweet," said Ipis. "I've never fished. Can you teach me?"

"Sure," said Kem. "How can it be you never learned to fish?"

She shrugged. "Someone else made the food. We started our training early for officialdom."

Elen snorted softly. Ah, the Manor-born. Someone else to make the food. Xilsi cast a glance her way as if unsure of what amused her.

The theurgist said, to Kem, "It's a rare gift to share something so close to your heart. I thank you for the trust you show in us. I feel I know the world a tiny bit better for knowing something of your journey."

For knowing something. Luviara, a virtual stranger, had asked. Elen never had asked, at first because it had upset Aoving and after . . . because she had accepted him as he was. To her, acceptance was a sign of respect. Not to query or probe. But what if he'd wanted her to ask? What if he had wanted to share but wasn't sure if she wanted to hear him, not after all the time she'd changed the subject on his mother's behalf?

Kem's head twitched as if he almost looked her way, to gauge her expression, but stopped himself just in time. He said, "I hope I'm barely started on my journey. I always dreamed of being a warden, but I didn't think . . . well, now here I am. And my thanks to you, Ipis."

"Me? You should thank His Exalted Highness. He's the one who hates Prince Astaylin so much he snapped you up just to slap the face of one of Astaylin's lesser lords. It's exactly the kind of thing the prince would do."

"Is that so?" Luviara had a way of sharpening her tone when her interest was piqued. "That's what puzzles me. I wasn't aware there was hostility between the two princes. Does he speak of it often?"

Ipis tensed. She rose and gave the polite hand-to-heart owed to elders. "I've said too much. It isn't my place to comment on the palace or the all-seeing eye, who serves at the pleasure of the emperor. May we serve as we are bidden. Come on, Kem. We need to sleep. We'll take second watch."

"He's an odd one, don't you think?" said Xilsi in a low voice.

"Who?" Elen asked, pretending to misunderstand.

"Something about the boy's story doesn't quite add up, but never mind. I suppose we all have secrets we'd rather keep hidden. He'll make a good warden if we survive this breakneck journey. Getting shot at today was a shock. One of the reasons I joined the wardens was because it is the best way to stay out of princely feuds. Wardens serve the empire, not a faction. Here."

She held out her bowl toward Elen.

For a moment, Elen was confused, until the gesture fell into place. No time like the present to test the temperature of these new waters. "Xilsi, I'm not a menial."

The warden blinked in surprise, then grinned. Oddly enough, the moment wasn't even awkward. "So you aren't. I'm not used to the gagast doing that work yet. So accustomed to Hemerlin and his crew. They'd have come by and taken the bowl without me asking. But I don't mind the extra burden of fieldwork. I can even cook! I don't need to be waited on, not like some." Her head tilted toward Jirvy, but she didn't look at his sleeping figure. Instead, she got to her feet. "I've got last watch. Lucky you. Simo says you get to sleep all night as your reward for a task well done."

"I'll take the sleep with thanks," said Elen in an exaggeratedly vivacious tone.

Xilsi laughed like it was a great joke between friends.

Elen cleaned out her own bowl and spoon and got out her bedroll. The haunt remained standing at the edge of the firelight. Was he listening for bells in the night?

Kem, Ipis, Luviara, and Xilsi settled onto ground cloths, wrapping themselves in cloaks and blankets against the chill. Jirvy lay at their center like the stone in a ring. Maybe it was because she was so tired, but Elen could have sworn the injured warden was still limned by that misty veil of sparkling gold. But no one else gave him a second look, and that made her wonder if only she could see it.

49

A Douse of Icy Water

Elen woke at dawn to find Jirvy up and eating voraciously. Xilsi was standing behind him, hands propped belligerently on her hips.

"I thought you were dead," she said in a low voice.

"You wished I were dead," he said between bites of flatbread.

"I didn't *wish* anything. Well, not anything that would delay or harm the mission. Anyway, you're not the center of my life, even if you wish you were."

He cast a glance at Xilsi, and it was still too dim for Elen to catch the look's nuances. His tone mingled anger and something else, maybe shame. "I said I was sorry, but that will never be enough for you, will it?"

"I used to think you cared enough to know."

The haunt appeared out of the darkness. "I pray you, wardens, let go of this dispute, however entertaining you may find it, for I assure you, it is not so entertaining to the rest of us."

The two wardens stiffened as if turned to salt.

"What is it you have there, Fulmo? Ah, more bread. So shall it be, bread yesterday, bread today, bread tomorrow." He sighed wearily as he accepted flatbread rolled up into a tube and took a bite, paused with a startled expression, and took a second bite. "But what is this? There's something soft smeared inside."

"I believe it is liver paste, Your Highness," said Jirvy. "Goat's liver, if I don't mistake the flavor."

"Delightful." His gaze flicked toward Elen as if to make sure she was still present.

Alongside the others, she ate, after which they broke camp, doused the embers, and headed out in a neat file.

Elen led the way, using a compass and her general knowledge of the land to set a route to the west-northwest. The plateau country here was lightly wooded, with grassy stretches. They were now in Farledder Intendancy, the most sparsely populated intendancy of Ilvewind Province. If they walked far enough, they would intercept the road.

Jirvy limped only slightly as they walked.

"How are your wounds?" the captain asked. "I thought they'd cause you more trouble today, given you passed out. His Exalted Highness learned field medicine at the palace school, so I must suppose he was able to clean and bind them most effectively."

"I thought I wouldn't be able to sleep, but I went right out," Jirvy answered, gingerly testing the movement of his shoulder. "Odd how well-rested I feel, despite everything."

"The gashes weren't too deep," said the haunt. "They'll heal soon enough if you get enough rest, they're kept clean, and not too much stress is placed on them."

"That's good news," Simo agreed.

The wardens said no more. They were eager to keep moving. But Elen thought Luviara skeptical, even suspicious. As a theurgist, had she been able to see the golden glow? Yet a prince could not be questioned.

As for herself, Elen was sure the haunt had used a targeted version of sleep magic to cast Jirvy into such a deep slumber. But that wasn't all. Magic was the only explanation she could find for the skirmish she'd caught glimpses of atop the south rim of Grinder's Cut. That hadn't been sorcery, had it? Sorcery sucked the life force out of its victims; that's why it was wicked. The soldiers had been very much alive when they'd fallen flailing and terrified to their deaths.

Her thoughts circled back to the conversation she'd overheard between Kem, Ipis, and Luviara. Why had Kem never told her he dreamed of being a warden? Because she'd have told him not to hope for something he couldn't have? Was she just a douse of icy water on his dreams?

As if drawn by her thoughts, Kem came up beside her. "I saw you listening last night at supper," he said, like a challenge.

"I thought you were on rearguard today," she said, a little angry he'd glided up on her without her noticing.

"Don't get distracted," he said nastily, as if he would rather have pinched her in the hopes of getting a rise out of her.

How she wanted to tell him she loved him. That she was sorry, or should have done something differently. But platitudes, even keenly felt ones, would just anger him. So, she kept her mouth shut.

They walked for a while in silence. As she expected, he gave in to whatever impulse had driven him to walk with her. "I got permission to walk vanguard today. Simo liked the way I handled myself at the rope bridge."

A safe subject! "You handled yourself well."

"Yeah."

Again, she held her tongue. The crunch of their feet made a nice counterpoint to the silence between them. They were about the same height and had always been able to match their strides, whereas Ao was always hurrying or dawdling. Elen had never minded; Ao was who she was. But as Kem got older and came more into himself, and argued more with his mother, Ao's quirks had started to annoy him. He wasn't wrong that Elen had shut down any conversation that upset his mother. She'd thought she was being compassionate toward them both, but maybe she was just tired.

This time they walked for quite some distance before she decided he wasn't going to bite, so she'd have to.

"I never heard that story about you and Joef before, about being brothers."

"Yeah, well, you never asked, did you?" This was the opening he'd been waiting for. "You never asked, and you never told. Why didn't you tell me the truth about my father and where I came from?"

"I told you—"

"Even if I get why you never talked about it while Mama was alive—I'm not saying it was okay!—but even if I get why you might have made that choice to protect her or to protect yourself, then why not after she died?"

"I didn't know how. I wasn't sure when."

"What garbage! And from you. You! I expect more from you! You weren't the one who—" He broke off and glanced back.

The rest had fallen back to cluster around their prince, who had found something of interest along the trail that he wanted them to discuss. The haunt was giving her space; she was sure of it. How did the haunt know? How could he tell? Or could he simply hear better than the others?

Kem turned back to her. "You were the one I could rely on. Now I find out that was a lie. You were a lie."

His distrust was worse than his anger, and yet strangely, unexpectedly, she found she was angry too. Angry on her own behalf. "I wasn't a lie, Kem. You didn't suffer the things your mother did. I was protecting you."

"Maybe I don't want to be protected. I'm not a baby anymore."

"That's for sure." She went to lightly punch him on the shoulder, then pulled it. He glared at her, and she couldn't tell whether he was mad that she'd tried to joke with him or that she'd stopped herself from giving him a friendly thump.

Her heart pounded as she struggled through her tangled thoughts. He stumped along, each thud of a footfall like an accusation that she'd betrayed him.

Let him think what he would think. She couldn't change what had happened. But she was here now.

"I had palpitations when you ran the plank walkway back across the rope bridge. You were fearless. Your balance and strength are incredible. You took charge when you needed to. You got it done. It's no wonder Simo was impressed. I don't think any of his people, even with all their years of experience, could have done it."

He shrugged as if to blow off her words, but a little smirk played about his mouth, a sure sign he was pleased at her praise. Confidence made him go for the throat.

"So, is it true? Are you a thief and a murderer?"

Time to jump in with both feet.

"Yes, I am."

He missed a step and had to stagger to catch his balance, then took two longer strides to catch up because she hadn't faltered in her steady pace.

"Fuck me," he muttered. And to her, belligerently, "What did you steal?"

She caught his gaze, made sure to hold it for a breath, hard and sure. "You, Kem. Your mother and I stole you from Duenn Manor."

"Oh, fuck," he breathed.

That was one way to turn his anger upside down. Not her preferred way, but she'd started, so she had to go on. "Now you've met Lord Duenn, are you sorry not to have been raised by him?"

He clamped his lips shut and refused to answer. She didn't see it as a victory, but it was a beginning.

They walked on. The others had started up again, following the track she'd found, an old deer trail that wound through stands of pine and spruce.

Finally, he said, "What about the other thing?"

She glanced back. The others were lost to sight among the trees.

"Yes, Kem. I killed the Duenn Manor captain who was raping your mother."

He flinched, as she'd meant him to.

"If I could have killed Lord Duenn and gotten away with it, I'd have done that too. But I couldn't. Running was our only option."

His face got very red, blood rushing to his cheeks. He huffed, catching his breath, then demanded, "What else are you hiding from me?"

She rubbed her forearm.

"Why do you always do that with your arm when you're nervous? 'An old injury,' that's what you always say. What does it really mean?"

This time it was she who didn't know what to say. How to proceed. Where to go with this. It was too much. Too soon. Too late.

"See! You still won't trust me. Whatever it is."

For the first time, she saw tears on his face.

Her beloved child was crying, and it was she who had hurt him.

"No, no, listen, Kem. I'll show you. But it has to be in secret."

"In secret? Why?"

"I have to show you. It's not something that can be explained."

He scrubbed impatiently at his damp cheeks with the back of a hand. "You're just putting me off, but I guess that's how you operate."

"Yes, I did put it off too long." Once started, she found she didn't want to stop, too much bottled up all these years. "I loved your mother so much. It's true, it was hard to be her sister some of the time. She was difficult one day and generous the next. Oh, by the High Heavens, she deserved better. Here's the thing I want you to understand, Kem. I'd do it again."

"Do what again?" he said sullenly. "Murder a man?"

"Yes. If you can't live with that, then so be it. I didn't even know she'd been sent down to the barracks until I was walking back from the latrines late in the evening and I heard her crying out from the shed the men called 'Cock's-a-Walking.'" Her voice got flatter, harsher. "I blame myself."

"How can you blame yourself? You were, what, the lowest rank of sentinel?"

"Militia, not sentinel, because we were the Manor's guard, not imperial. But, yes, I was the lowest rank."

"And you weren't even Manor-born, just brought in because the Manor lost so many of their people to a plague and had to bring in outsiders even though they didn't want to. That's what Lord Duenn said." When Elen looked at him in surprise, he muttered, "He was ranting and ranting, so I heard a lot of disjointed ranting. I mean, what could you have done?"

"I could have convinced your mother to escape Duenn Manor before the worst happened, not that the worst hadn't already happened to her, I mean. It's not like she was with Lord Duenn because she wanted to be with him. He was lord. He took what he wanted." The words flooded. "If I had tried to convince her to run away sooner, then maybe . . . but we ate every single day, and she could wash every day, and wear clean clothes, and she hated him—Lord Duenn, I mean—but there's only so much time a man like Duenn can spend walking his cock inside one specific woman, so most of the time she could sit in peace in the herb garden, with a platter of food and just herself for company. She liked some of the other women, the ones who were kind to her. I don't think any of his concubines liked him. They mostly held on to each other, because the women of the Manor lineage didn't like that he kept so many lowborn concubines. You know your mother was gifted with healing. She taught herself a lot, even as a child, about herbs and wounds and illnesses, and how to treat them. One of the older aunt-wives in Duenn Manor took a liking to her and trained her. She got a reputation as someone good to have during labor. It was one of the things Manor-born women in a place like Woodfall Province are allowed to do freely, to midwife and to heal. The rest of the time, she tended the garden. Plants grew for her. They loved her tender care."

"She wasn't so tender with me," he muttered.

"She was when you were a baby. She would sing to you. Do you remember that one lullaby about the moon—" She broke off, seeing a flush of anger—or grief—flood his face again, and so she let the memory go. "It's just you started to assert yourself and even talk back sometimes, when things weren't the way you thought they should be. Nothing wrong with that! But she never knew how to deal with it."

"That's for sure," he mumbled.

"Anyway, Lord Duenn got tired of her. Maybe she forgot to smile and pretend to enjoy it one time while he was fucking her."

He winced.

"I never asked why," she went on hoarsely, "and she never talked about it because it made her cry. Anyway, he sent her to the barracks, to punish her, I suppose. He knew what they would do."

"Why were you safe there, if she wasn't?"

She shrugged angrily. "I was militia. That was the same as being a man, in their eyes. Even the ones who didn't like me, didn't like me because I was an outsider, not because I was a woman. Also, I was meaner than all of them put together, in my sunshiny way. I kicked more than one butt when I had to, let me tell you."

"I'll bet you did," he muttered without looking at her.

"No means too underhanded to employ," she added with a cheery smile. He didn't answer or smile in return, so she sighed and went on. "Besides that, Captain Roel made sure everyone stayed professional among the ranks. All that time I thought he was a decent man, but when I looked back on it afterward, I realized it wasn't protecting me that he cared about. It was that breaking discipline would undercut his authority over the troop. But that's not what you asked me."

She took a breath. Took another as they walked onward, boots meeting the ground with a heavy tread. Finally, she went on.

"Yes, Kem, I would do it again. And again, and again. I walked in on the captain raping your mother, and I killed him, and we stole you, and we ran."

He looked away, at the sky, at the ground, at the trees and the grass, breathing raggedly, troubled, halfway to tears but holding them back. At length, still walking, he looked at her, finding refuge in anger.

"You say this all now because you're backed into a corner. Why couldn't you tell me before? Did you think I wouldn't understand? That it wouldn't have helped me understand her better, and love her better. Maybe I wouldn't have said those things I said to her that last day right before she left for Olludia Halt—" His voice broke. The tears spilled, and he furiously wiped his nose with his wrist.

Oh, Kem. Blaming himself now. It was just like him to do so.

"You know your mother, Kem. I loved her, she was all I had to love my entire childhood. She couldn't endure thinking even for a moment of any of the things that happened to us before we reached Orledder Halt. So I let it go, even though it meant you never knew the story. I'm sorry it has hurt you. I can't tell you how sorry. You're everything to me. You know that. And I also know you're young and resilient. I trust you. I believe in you—"

"Fuck off! Just fuck the fuck off. I'm so mad. I'm so mad."

She closed her mouth.

He wiped his eyes and sniffed, and sniffed again and wiped his nose again. But he kept walking alongside her. Not speaking. Not looking at her. Just there, sullen, angry, stumping along—*bam bam bam bam*—as if his footsteps could hammer the world into becoming a different place than it was.

It was enough, for now. As long as he didn't turn his back on her and walk away.

50

❖

MORE LIKE A JOKE

Kem had said not one more word. His silence hurt her, and it also soothed her, and the sun was out, and the world was radiant. The air was crisp and dry, with no trace of rose-oil scent. The trees smelled of sap and needles. A meadow bloomed with late purple fan flowers in clusters of bright promise that lightened her heart. Two rabbits grazing amid grass raised their ears and watched her and Kem pass with alert interest. She and Kem weren't the predators they feared. Then, with a flash of white tail, they leaped away into the brush.

Both she and Kem glanced back reflexively, to see why the rabbits had fled. The haunt had appeared out of the woodland, closing the gap while the wardens scrambled at his heels to keep up with his brisk stride. Was the prince beautiful when he danced, all grace and power? Wasn't he already beautiful? His willow-leaf eyes, broad forehead, narrow chin, and lips that flashed through so many emotions as if he were restraining words he wanted to say.

The haunt's gaze found her. She had to turn away and keep walking lest she blush and stammer, the way youths in the throes of first love did in the plays, although she had never been so innocent nor so free.

Kem brushed her arm with his hand to signal that she should halt, so she did, a little flushed as she turned back. He took a step away from her, leaving room for the prince to come up.

The weight of the haunt's presence hit her as something more than physical, like the crackling in the air as a storm blows in. He stopped in front of her. The wardens halted behind him. All had weapons out and ready. Jirvy scanned the open woodland with an arrow set to his bow's string.

"Is there something out there?" Elen asked. Had she been so intent on speaking to Kem that she'd been oblivious? *Don't get distracted!*

Simo displayed some scraps of leather cordage. "We found what looks like a temporary campsite, and bits of debris like this cordage as well as shells and peels from a meal. Not more than a day ago, Jirvy reckons."

"Smugglers?" said Elen.

"Perhaps." The haunt shaded his eyes to look onward. "Yet I wonder. We are almost at the road. I feel its presence in my bones."

"That's a fine figure of speech, Your Highness," said Luviara. "If a curious one."

"I am a curious fellow," he said with a mocking lift of his eyebrows.

The wardens looked at each other and looked at him. He was getting too relaxed.

Elen said, "What do you mean, Your Highness?"

"This is a route smugglers would take if they were going to or from the crossing, yes. But what about bandits who might lurk in this area, meaning to prey on passing wagons?"

"Something's off," said Jirvy.

At his quiet words, everyone peered around as if expecting a crowd of bandits to jump out of thin air.

Simo rearranged the order of march. He and Elen walked at the front, with Jirvy and Xilsi bringing up the rear, and the others in the middle. They moved cautiously, pausing often to make little side trips to check out places where people might be hiding. Many signs indicated that they were coming closer to the road: an area where small-scale logging had left stumps, an old charcoal-making site, the marks of recent grazing in a meadow. There was a crude shelter for shepherd and sheep, which was ringed by a hallow-wood-lined ditch that could be filled with water but whose bottom was only a slimy mess of mud. The shelter's gate was secured, and the interior was tidy, but empty of everything except a neat pile of firewood stacked beside a crude stone hearth. Jirvy thought the place hadn't been used for several months.

Soon after, Elen and the captain saw, farther off, the remains of overgrown gardens around an old village foundation, surely abandoned. Simo pointed toward the tumbledown buildings, some lacking roofs. Was that a thread of smoke winding heavenward from out of a broken window of one of the still-roofed cottages?

"How many?" she whispered, thinking of the spirit Simo had used to see swalters when they were in the hill country.

He held up three fingers.

Coming up beside Simo, the haunt followed the captain's gaze, and smiled in a predatory fashion. He indicated himself, Simo, Jirvy, and Xilsi.

Simo said to Elen, "You and the others take cover back behind those trees."

Elen did not argue. The wardens had training and weapons she lacked. Deputy couriers relied on their connections, familiarity, and the threat of the intendant's authority to avoid trouble. None of those would work here. She, Luviara, Fulmo, Ipis, and Kem retreated in silence. Ipis set up Kem and herself as guards, keeping an eye on the other directions in case there were other hostile people prowling about. Elen wedged herself up a tree, trying to get a better look.

For a long time she saw only glimpses of the haunt and the three wardens circling in from different directions toward the cluster of buildings. There, Jirvy at the outer edge of the village. Simo, crouched by the well.

Luviara stared up at Elen, wanting to ask but knowing—for once—that she must remain silent. Fulmo waited unmoving, statuelike.

Ipis hissed softly, and when Elen looked that way she saw nothing at first, then movement in the grass: a green snake slithered past, seeming unaware of how close it was to Ipis, who stood completely still, watching it with wide eyes.

Kem murmured, "That kind isn't venomous, you can tell by the black dots on the back of its head," and Ipis relaxed slightly.

A startled shout rang out from the abandoned village. Elen whipped her gaze back that way in time to see Xilsi darting behind a half-fallen shed, sword in hand. A man burst out of the door of a cottage. In the blink of an eye, an arrow sprouted in his shoulder. He staggered forward, sprinting for the forest, and Simo tackled him from the side, the two crashing together to the dirt. From inside the cottage came a burst of noise, then silence, too distant for her to know what was going on.

The haunt appeared in the doorway, dusting off his hands. Simo rose, keeping one foot on the fallen man's back, and set two fingers to his lips. A sharp birdcall pierced the air.

"Let's go," said Ipis.

They hurried over. Based on the deteriorating condition of the buildings' roofs and walls, the village had been empty for at least one generation and possibly more. When Elen and the others arrived, the wardens had corralled three rough-looking men inside the target cottage. Elen went in, leaving Ipis, Kem, Fulmo, and Luviara outside.

Jirvy was tying up the last of the captives, the wounded one, and lashing all three to a heavy wooden pillar. The man with the arrow in his shoulder was pale and in pain. The other two had the look of people who are thinking very, very fast about what to say next. They looked less dirty and thin than Elen had expected, as if they had a place where they washed and ate like normal people.

One said, belligerently, "We never did anything wrong. We're just woodcutters."

Xilsi retorted, "The stamped sacks of wheat, turnips, and dried nuts in the next-door shed say otherwise. You've been raiding local produce wagons on their way to the intendancy storehouse, haven't you?"

"You can't prove it was us," said the belligerent one.

Simo gave a sarcastic laugh as he picked up their fallen weapons: three long knives, a spear, and two old militia swords. "If you are woodcutters, then where are your axes?" he asked lightly. He looked unusually pleased with the outcome of their altercation.

Elen pulled a shutter aside to spill light into the dim interior, revealing coils of rope and three sturdy leather packs half hidden in a shadowy corner. Opening the packs, she discovered two heavy copper ingots in each pack, and, besides that, a small pouch of unpolished gems, a box neatly stuffed with bright feathers from rare hill-country birds that were suitable for decorating fancy hats, and a finely tooled leather pouch incised with the badge of the Griffin Corps.

Xilsi whistled angrily. "The missing pouch."

Elen unbuckled the flap. "It's empty."

Xilsi got right up into the face of the man who had spoken. "Where'd you get this? What happened to the contents?"

Seeing the packs opened, he deflated, losing all his bluster. "It came with the rest we were given to haul, just as it is. We walk things over the gap and onward, that's all."

"And steal food intended for the imperial storehouses, for winter rations." Xilsi gave him a hard shove with her boot. He pitched to one side, the movement jostling the man with the arrow in his shoulder, who whimpered, and then shut up when Xilsi shifted her glare to him.

"To whom do you deliver the goods?" Simo asked.

The man shrugged. "We leave it in a depository. That's all. We never see who picks it up."

"I'll take that," said the haunt to Elen. She handed him the corps pouch. He, in his turn, gave it to Simo. "Keep it as evidence, Captain."

Then he went outside, and the wardens followed. Luviara had been trying to get a look inside, but she retreated as the others emerged.

"What do you intend to do with them, Your Highness?" the interlocutor asked him.

"Bandits are a problem for the intendant of this area to solve, not my jurisdiction. Fulmo"—he gestured to the gagast—"don't you still have that cloudberry brew? If we drug them, they won't be able to wriggle free before we can alert the nearest authorities to pick up them and their contraband."

Ipis grinned and nudged Kem.

Xilsi said, "An elegant solution, Your Highness. Worthy of a wineshop poem about the ironies of fortune and the unexpected uses of ordinary gifts."

The haunt's gaze slid to touch on Elen's face, then swiftly away as he addressed the others. "I am a great connoisseur of the ordinary and thus precious gift that may arrive unannounced and unexpected."

Elen had to turn away, to go stick her head into the other empty cottages, so forlorn and slowly collapsing, the fading traces of lives once lived here. Restless, she walked onward, knowing the others would come after her. Past the ruined village stood rows of quince, pear, and apple trees that could have used pruning but were still bearing fruit. Once she got beyond the orchard, she saw the road.

From a distance, the imperial road looked like a low wall cutting through the countryside. Its pavement ran atop a foundation built of stone and in-fill, about three ells in height. The side of the road was sloped, not vertical, and easy to climb up on foot, although a cart or carriage had a harder time of it without the ramps present at villages, crossroads, and Halts.

The wardens, even Simo, grinned with relief as they climbed the embankment. Xilsi gave a whoop when she reached the pavement at the top.

Ipis did a funny little dance, all jerky knees and elbows, then called Kem over and said, "I'll teach it to you. 'A Bee Got in My Shirt!' is the most popular song in the wineshops this year."

Under the young warden's attention, Kem's cloudy expression cleared.

Elen waited at the base, bracing herself. The haunt had not yet ascended either. He shaded his eyes as he examined the workmanship that had survived generations of wind, rain, snow, heat, ice, and steady traffic.

"Your Highness?" Simo called down. "Do you need assistance?"

The haunt spoke in a low voice, not looking at her. "Does it sting you too?"

"Only when I'm walking directly on the pavement. It won't damage you. It just hurts."

"So we must hope," he remarked. "Shall we climb together?"

"It would not be seemly, Your Highness. You must go first, not because you or I care, but because they do."

He set his jaw and scrambled up to the roadbed where the others waited. Elen sighed and followed. Because the others hadn't started walking north, she halted with her feet still on the embankment, on quiescent stone. She would wait as long as possible before touching the road. Even so, its buzzing tremor hummed in her bones, making the viper curl up more tightly around her heart, a sensation that made her short of breath.

Kem was staring up and down the road with an expression of astonishment. "There's no traffic! I've never seen the road with no traffic at all. But I guess south of Farledder Halt there's nowhere to go."

"What's that?" asked Ipis, pointing south along the road. "Is that a wagon? Two wagons?"

"There are two villages between here and Five Bridges," said Elen.

Xilsi said, "I'll bet those bandits were waiting here for this. Good fortune for these drovers that we came along first."

"Wagons!" cried the haunt, as if the humble vehicles were a treasure house on wheels. "Worthy Interlocutor, come with me. Jirvy, you as well. The rest of you stay here."

He set out at a jog for the wagons, Luviara hastening to keep up. Jirvy followed, although he was favoring his injured leg more than he had at the beginning of their walk.

"I thought you'd only been here once before," said Simo to Elen.

"Yes, and I recall passing through both villages. One is Gested Moat, and the other Gesfol Ditch. But that's not why I know they're there, or their names. As a deputy courier, I have access to Map Hall in the Residency. As a loyal provincial official of the empire, even humblest of deputy couriers as I am, I consider it my duty to be well-versed in the routes that link together the empire. It is part of my duty to know all possible havens for travelers, should I need that information myself or to pass on to another courier or palace official. As now."

Xilsi snorted, elbowing Elen as if letting her know her overly detailed explanation was a good joke, a little gnat up the captain's nose.

"I am not accustomed to being mocked by the likes of you," Simo said with a glance toward the haunt who, fortunately, was by now too far away to have heard.

"I do not mock, Captain. I am forever grateful to the intendant for the trust he has shown me. Because of that, I will ever strive to serve him."

"Not the emperor?" asked Simo sharply.

"The intendant serves the emperor, so by serving the intendant, I serve the empire and its emperor, who stands far above the likes of me. I am but a small fish."

"A small fish with a big mouth," he muttered.

She pressed hand to heart. "So I have been told. It is my greatest failing."

"I like your frankness," said Xilsi. "I grew up in a Manor filled with people who use flowery speeches to say anything except what they are really thinking. The better you can flatter, the higher you can rise. That's why I escaped to the wardens, because wardens have to be good at what they do to carry out their duties effectively. Why, our fine Simo comes from a lesser heartland lineage, nothing as grand as mine. Yet he has risen to personally attend on the all-seeing eye, our most gracious and exalted Prince Gevulin." She tilted her head to one side. "The prince chose you himself, did he not, Captain?"

Simo looked annoyed. Instead of replying, he walked after the prince.

Elen was struck by the realization that there was more than one layer to the internal ranking of the wardens. Simo was captain of this operation, definitely. But Xilsi came from such a high-status Manor—whichever one it might be—that she could say anything she wanted and not be punished for insubordination or disrespect.

"What?" said Xilsi, looking at her. "I'm starting to get your expressions. You're thinking something."

"I should hope I am always thinking *something*," said Elen, making Xilsi snort again. "But I do have a question, now that we are comrades."

Xilsi brightened, as if no one had ever called her a comrade before. "Go on!"

"Did you ever wonder if your superior Manor lineage might have placed Jirvy in a difficult situation? To be lovers is to be intimate, is it not? To be true lovers is to be equals. What if your elevated status was a third presence in the bed with you?"

Xilsi rubbed her chin, frowning. "He still didn't tell me about the betrothal, and he let it go on as if nothing had changed. He has a *child*. Did I mention the child? And another on the way!"

"Ouch. That would make me angry too. Not to be told, I mean. I don't know anything about how Manors make marriages."

"Did he think I wouldn't find out? That I don't know people, and that people don't talk?"

All Elen could think was that Jirvy must have been married a rather long time if he had one child and another on the way, and if so, why had it taken Xilsi so long to figure it out, or to be told?

"Yes," Elen agreed carefully, "I would think people would talk. Just maybe not where you could hear."

Xilsi grunted thoughtfully, then sighed gustily, clearly making ready to complain some more.

"Will you look at that!" cried Ipis, pointing south, as if toward a miraculous rescue.

Here came the two wagons, now commandeered. Jirvy sat in the back of one, while Luviara had evidently decided to stick with walking instead of jolting atop a load of late-harvest squash. The haunt had taken a seat on the driver's bench beside a man who, judging by his tiller's garb, was a farmer taking his produce to market in Farledder Halt. The two of them seemed to be chatting, which made the wardens stare. The ears of the oxen flicked back and forth, and they snorted with unease now and again, but kept plodding obediently forward.

As the wagons rolled up, the haunt announced, "Tiller Mekel and his uncle, Drover Neset, will gladly convey us the rest of the way to the Halt in exchange for protection. It seems bandits have been operating in these parts, stealing produce from local farmers."

He met Elen's gaze with a tip of his head toward the second vehicle, to let her know that she might ride, not walk. Simo signaled to Xilsi to walk ahead as vanguard. Elen made a dash for the second wagon. The road stung through the soles of her boots, but she ignored the pain as she ran. The oxen plodded quite slowly, so it was easy to grab the side and swing over into its bed. This wagon carried burlap sacks full to bursting, outsides flecked with unhusked barley.

As she settled in, the driver glanced back at her. Since Kem and Ipis had fallen back to walk the rearguard, she was its only passenger.

"May the High Heavens shine good fortune upon you, Drover," she said politely.

"Huh." He was an old man with a long face and a stolid expression. "You're not a warden."

"I'm a deputy courier out of Orledder Halt."

"Is that really a prince?" he asked. "Or are these wardens just funning us?"

"It's really a prince," she said, thinking of the haunt.

He caught her hesitation. "Likely story. More like a joke among yon Manor-born. They think us snail-witted, we villagers. I don't know if it's worse to think you, lass, are in on it, or taken in by it. Huh."

He turned his back on her and spoke not one more word for the rest of the journey. She took the opportunity to nap, lulled to sleep by the steady grind of the wheels against the road and the *clop clop clop* of the steadfast beasts.

51

AS THE EMPIRE DECREES

When Elen woke, it was late afternoon, the setting sun bleeding gold-red majesty over the westering clouds. They had reached tended fields, orchards, and livestock pens, as well as small tanneries and dye-works. There was a stream with a working mill and, downstream from the mill, a smoking furnace. Just ahead, the road split to create a Halt.

Farledder Halt was more modest than Orledder Halt but set up in the same quartered district pattern, so any traveler could know where to go and be assured of receiving the services they needed. The wagons descended the south ramp, and stopped at the gate to the Residency. The prince descended with a gracious farewell to the dazzled farmer, thanking the man for describing to him—in such detail!—the rainfall patterns, crop yields, and livestock prices of the local area. Luviara handed the man a bag of coins that made the farmer gasp and the cousin mutter, "I'll be spackled and turniped. Thought he were putting us on."

The haunt swanned in through the gate, ignoring the challenge of the Halt sentinels. The Residency plaza was small, and its pavement freshly swept and neatly kept, but it was obvious no one knew a prince might be arriving, since the statues of the emperors were not adorned with flower necklaces. Even this late in the season, bright-wheel or bluebeard or star-thistle could be found in the meadows, and any well-run Residency would have a flower garden that included chrysanthemum.

"Hey!" An elderly woman wearing warden blue was seated on the tiny portico of the Warden Hall, tucked into one corner of the plaza. Leaning on her broomstick, she rose creakily and shook a scolding hand at them. "You need to sign in at the gate, not just dance in like you're a prince—!"

Breaking off, she squinted, then called over her shoulder to someone inside.

After that, everything happened very quickly. Shouts of alarm. The pound of running feet. Raised voices in the distance. The appearance of the flustered intendant, looking as mussed and fussed as if she'd been woken from a nap.

Elen recognized Intendant Berel from the journey she'd made with the Orledder intendant. She was a mousey cousin, wearing the wreath badge of Karis Manor, striped with the colors of her junior lineage to set her apart from people like the Orledder intendant, who had been born into Karis's ruling lineage and thus need not wear any stripes on his badge.

Berel rushed forward, attended by a pair of glamorously painted and garbed concubines. Dropping to her knees, she struck her forehead repeatedly with the palms of her hands.

"Your Exalted Highness, the fault is mine. Pray do not excuse me for the lapse. I should have greeted you properly. I deserve punishment."

The haunt sighed, looking put out. "Yes, yes, of course you should have known, if only I could have gotten word to you of my imminent arrival. Yet here we are."

"You are too gracious."

"I am, that," he murmured, and cursed to the High Heavens if he did not slide his gaze to light upon Elen watching him. "Haven't I always said so?"

"Everything shall be as you desire, Your Highness. My Residency is at your disposal. Tea and cakes are being prepared even as I speak. What is your command?"

"Immediately send sentinels to collect a group of smugglers. Captain Simo will explain where we left them." He tugged at his fly-whisk braids, by now frayed and out of sorts, and scratched at the nape of his neck. "I desire a bath, and a skilled individual to wash and rebraid my hair. Clean clothes. Our gear cleaned and mended. My people tended. Warden Jirvy needs the attention of your Heart Temple healer. A decent meal. Then we will discuss transportation to South Flat Vigil."

Berel was beginning to recover her poise, although she remained humbly on her knees. "All shall be as you wish, Your Highness."

She beckoned over her sentinel captain, who went aside with Simo to discuss the smugglers. That begun, she went on.

"You may retire to our imperial suite, where you shall be bathed and feasted in whatever manner you desire. My younger sister is particularly skilled with . . . hair. Your wardens will be welcome in the Warden Hall. By her badge, your worthy interlocutor is also a theurgist. Our Heart Hostel is modest but well appointed. And . . ." Her gaze faltered on the gagast.

The haunt said, "Fulmo is my personal menial. He will attend me at all times."

"Of course. Of course." She bobbed several times, then straightened to give Elen a piercing look. "Oh, yes, I recall this deputy courier. She's from Orledder, is she not? The intendant's pet, that's what they called her."

Xilsi broke in abruptly. "She's not a dog. She's a person."

Berel stiffened, looking ready to do battle with what appeared to her to be an ordinary warden.

The haunt spoke before the intendant could. "The deputy courier guided my party across the Cut. No more discussion is needed on this matter."

"To aid you is my only responsibility, Your Highness. The deputy courier can be housed here until my blessed cousin finds a way to retrieve her. Or perhaps she has orders to return by the path you used to get here, although I confess I am puzzled how it was managed. Her information will be of great value to my surveyor, so after you are gone I will have my people interview her—"

"*No!*"

Half the people jumped and the other half cowered. His anger hit like a pressure pushing outward. His thunderous glower was certainly worthy of the prince Elen had first encountered. He looked exactly like someone who had the means to destroy you if you tried to cross him. A prince in full flood, unstoppable, their will irresistible. But something more than that too, a sense he was somehow larger and more powerful than his physical body. That he was restraining himself.

Simo cautiously cleared his throat. "Your Highness, we no longer require the services of the deputy courier, and given your mission—"

"*No.* The deputy courier remains with me—" He broke off, took a breath, and went on. "The deputy courier will remain with this party."

His tone allowed no argument, so no one argued, but the wardens didn't know where to look. His insistence surprised them. All but Luviara, who studied him thoughtfully. Elen didn't know where to look or what expression she ought to attempt to paste onto her face. She had a knack for looking the way she thought people wanted her to look; to appear unthreatening, or vaguely confused, or surly and tough, as the situation warranted. What did that *no* mean?

The haunt blinked several times, as if reviewing his impassioned speech and the reactions of those around him. Finally, he said, in a milder tone, "We may need a courier."

The statement was odd, in itself, because a prince need never explain his reasons. Explaining made you look weak.

Emboldened, Simo said, "She is just a provincial courier, not an imperial courier, much less a palace courier. Intendant Berel will have couriers of her own, who know this intendancy better—"

"She is the courier we have, and know, and furthermore"—he jutted out his chin belligerently, warming to the subject—"we shall need her assistance returning the way we came, shall we not?"

"I sketched out our passage, so we can retrace it," said Simo. "But I expect the route is closed to us because of the archon's hostility—"

"Furthermore!" The word was the snap of a whip, cutting off Simo. "If my adversary's agents happen upon her, they will kill her. What manner of imperial shield am I, if I carelessly and uncaringly allow those who have assisted me to be tossed aside into the path of knives? Is this what you desire, Simo? That instead of protecting the people who serve me, I dishonorably discard them?"

"The fault is mine, Your Highness." Simo dropped to his knees and hid his face behind his hands. The other wardens followed. Elen knelt too, stunned by the unspooling sense that the force of his anger, the explosion of his temper, was tied to something she feared to think too closely about.

Yet she could not help but wonder. Did he genuinely care about her?

He surveyed the plaza and the kneeling people, all of them, even the Manor-born, for all were his servants because all were servants of the palace, of the empire, and he the only person in this place whose body had been born into the imperial lineage within the Flower Court.

"Enough of this! Have I not made my wishes clear to all of you?"

Berel's attendants cowered, trembling. The taut silence stretched out. Drifting on the air came the unexceptional sounds of life in the Halt beyond the Residency's wall: wheels on stone, a shrill whistle, water splashing as it was poured, the hustle and bustle of a community closing down their day's activities and making ready for the night. The wall that separated the rest of the Halt from the Residency was the barrier of custom and privilege that separated anyone not palace-born, or in service within the palace, from the emperor. The locals had no reason to enter the Residency except the day they Declared a profession, or if they were required to stand before the justiciary. Every person's birth token and death token resided in the census hall of each intendancy, the scant record of a life.

All but El, who existed nowhere that anyone could find, because she had no birth token. Elen the courier might have left her mark in the many transmission logs of her monthly courier routes. But when El died, she would, like a butterfly, vanish forever from the memory of the world. Maybe she already had, since Kem did not know El, only Aunt Elen. Now that Ao was gone, only the haunt knew that name.

The haunt did not look at her again. Perhaps he had realized his mistake, that people would wonder why an exalted prince had leaped to retain a deputy courier and made so many excuses for doing so when he need only demand to be obeyed.

Raising a hand, he said, in a more princely drawl, "Intendant, my bath!"

The intendant escorted him away. The wardens retreated to the Warden Hall, Kem casting one last look back at Elen with his eyebrows stuck in his most quizzical expression. She gave him the little hand sign that meant *Later* and he signed a quick *Okay* back. The exchange so heartened her that she thought she could manage anything as long as he didn't hate her.

Luviara lingered, looking her up and down. "That was interesting. A pity Chief Menial Hemerlin isn't here to offer an opinion, which I am sure we would find illuminating. Where shall you go for the night, Deputy Courier?"

Heat rose in Elen's cheeks, as if the theurgist's words were an innuendo. "There'll be a courier barracks next to their Map Hall."

"Of course. Each to our place, as the empire decrees. You will be here at dawn when we make ready to depart for the north?"

"Do you think I will not?"

The old woman pressed her journal to her chest. "I think the world is a fascinating place, full of secrets whose depths we may never plumb, however thoroughly we may probe. May you rest easy this night, Deputy Courier. I am sure I will, for the first time in many days."

52

IF THAT IS YOUR PREFERENCE

In the morning, Intendant Berel insisted on escorting Prince Gevulin herself in her personal carriage. She traveled with her younger sister, who was dressed as if for court in resplendent orange-and-gold silk. After all, Xilsi remarked to Elen as Berel and her sister got into the carriage, it was well known that Prince Gevulin had but one legal consort, a man with the same equipment he had, and no children yet by any of his concubines.

"I didn't know that."

"Why would you? The intendant hopes to lure him into having sex with the sister and getting her pregnant."

"Then what?"

"He will have to acknowledge the child before the Heart Temple. Then the emperor will acknowledge the child as a grandchild, to be entered on the rolls of the palace lineage as a prince of the Fifth Estate. A trifling rank among princes, to be sure. But the mother will be given her own suite of rooms in the Flower Court and the title of Blossoming Consort. That gives her a chance to give birth to a prince of the Fourth Estate."

"To be born into the Fourth Estate you have to be born *in* the Flower Court?"

"That's right. You can see why this is an opportunity a grasping person like Intendant Berel cannot pass up. But the prince is too smart to get a Karis Manor scion pregnant."

"Why is that?"

"Whew. You really don't know anything, do you?"

"I knew enough to get you across Grinder's Cut."

"Riposted! Karis Manor is one of the Six Noble Manors in the empire, didn't you know that? Your intendant surely does. If Karis Manor has a child in the palace, that gives them power to influence the child through its mother. My Manor is deep in the palace, a finger in every sausage and every pie, if you know what I mean."

"Around here, that's a saying about who people are having sex with."

Xilsi snorted. "You're always good for a laugh. It's true enough.

My grandmother was the favorite consort of the Hibiscus Emperor, in his old age. Everyone says I look just like her."

"So you're saying she was a piquant beauty who looked younger than her years?"

Xilsi gave Elen a startled look, then laughed out loud. "If you're trying to get into my bed, I warn you, I only eat sausage, never pie. Even if it is a troublesome business to not get pregnant. I got pregnant once during training. The medicine the temple healer gave me to get my bleeding to start back up made me weak for months. I had to be sent down to the next year cohort. My family was outraged."

"At the wardens for sending you back a year?"

"No, at me for getting pregnant. If I didn't like sex so much, I'd give it up, but here we are." Her gaze darted to Jirvy and away, as if she did not want to be caught looking.

"I know a few effective ways to prevent pregnancy," said Elen.

"That's what the palace physician told me, and look how that worked out."

"Maybe the palace physicians don't know everything. My sister was a midwife and herbalist. She spent years figuring out how to help people, especially—"

Especially menials and other lowborn persons who weren't allowed to say no. As Aoving hadn't been allowed to say no to Lord Duenn, or to Captain Roel.

"Especially who?"

The explanation felt a bridge too far for highborn Xilsi, so Elen said, "Especially for desperate people. There are all kinds of reasons."

"I know that feeling! Tell me all."

The carriage doors slammed shut once the last covered tray of journey food was handed in to the carriage.

"Later," Xilsi added. "It seems we're finally off."

Mounts were brought round for the wardens and an accompanying troop of six sentinels. They set out. Fulmo had no trouble keeping up at a steady lope. His energy seemed inexhaustible. Maybe he did feast on starlight.

Racing north, they made good time, their general direction a long, slow descent off the plateau. No messengers raced ahead to warn the villagers, so people out in the fields gave the cavalcade only a passing glance, as if the intendant traveled along this route so frequently her presence had become commonplace. Intendant Berel was proud of her posting houses, where they stopped over the course of each day's journey to change out horses so as to keep up a fast pace. Farledder Intendancy was horse country, supplying much of the imperial needs in the northern provinces. By the many horses available, the care taken with their stabling, and the luxurious private salons in the posting houses, it was clear Berel had enriched herself on the horse trade.

Each night, they stopped at the next Halt. Although none were as large and prosperous as Farledder Halt, each Halt included lodging for imperial officials, as well as an imperial suite, although none had ever hosted an actual prince, not in living memory.

Elen was never admitted into the imperial suite, not as the wardens were. She ate her meals and slept at night in the barracks set aside for lesser officials. To her surprise, she missed the camaraderie of their expedition through the hills.

The third night on the road, she sat at the end of one of the long tables in the salon reserved for lesser officials. There were only two other officials in the room, seated at a different table where they discussed weights and measures in pedantic, half-drunk tones. A Residence menial brought her a plate neatly arranged with crispy eel, salted beans, green onion pancake, and a bowl of spar-flower soup, a commonplace autumn dish in the northern provinces.

"Rice wine, honey beer, pale fire, or peach juice?" the woman asked.

"I'll take the juice, if it's fresh," said Elen. "My thanks. What's your name? I'm Deputy Courier Elen."

"I'm Cavna." The woman gave her a long look. "They say you're with His Exalted Highness's party."

Elen smiled politely. "I am, that. Nice to have a quiet, relaxed meal in here."

Cavna laughed. "I can imagine. I'll get that juice."

Elen set to the food, enjoying the crispness of the eel and the saltiness of the beans, although the green onions tasted old and the flour used for the pancakes was a musty barley, not freshly ground wheat; tasty enough, and plenty of it, but definitely not what a prince and an intendant would be eating in the imperial suite. Cavna brought a mug of juice, chatted in a friendly way about the weather, and left again when the weights-and-measures officials called her over for something.

Elen had just started in on the peppery tartness of the soup when the door to the outside opened. A man wearing a surveyor's uniform entered. He went at once to Cavna. After speaking to her, he gave a show of spotting Elen and made his way over.

He looked windblown, hair back in a bun but strands flying everywhere. His uniform was rumpled and stained, as if he'd spent too many nights sleeping on the dirt. That wasn't unusual for surveyors. What was unusual about him was the way he set down his pack, pulled out the chair opposite her, and sat, leaning toward her too eagerly.

"I heard you crossed Grinder's Cut, even though Five Bridges is blocked." He paused, shook his head as if to dislodge a fly in his brain, and added, "I'm Berri. Imperial Order of Surveyors, if you can't tell. I hear you're Deputy Courier Elen, out of Orledder Halt."

"I am she."

His grin was awkward. Elen couldn't tell if his smiles were out of practice, or if he was faking it because he wanted something from her. "That's Captain Jinyan there, still, right?"

Elen stayed on her guard. "It is."

"I know her from way back." He gave no specifics.

"What brings you to these parts?" Elen asked.

Berri pulled an oiled leather tube out of his pack and, to Elen's astonishment, unrolled his surveyor's map right there on the table beside her unfinished soup, which might splatter over it. The weights-and-measures officials didn't notice or display any interest in this marvel, and a marvel the map was, heavily marked with years' worth of signs and symbols that only surveyors could interpret.

"Can you show me where you got across?" he asked.

She had already spotted the wiggle of the great canyon, the split where the rope bridge could be unspooled, but she merely said, "I'm under the orders of the exalted highness and the Orledder intendant."

He bobbed his head, looking disappointed. "Yes, I see. Of course. Can't argue with that."

Cavna came up and set a mug of honey beer down in front of Berri.

"You're not eating?" Elen asked him.

"Oh." The question stymied him. "I suppose I should."

Cavna shared a look with Elen, a spark of fellow feeling, and the menial said, "I'll bring him a plate. Not just ale, like he normally does."

Berri was so intent on staring at the map that he missed the exchange.

As Cavna walked away, Elen said to Berri, "Have you been at this Halt long?"

"A bit. I've been under the weather." He spoke the words evasively and took a nervous swig of beer. "I'm on my way back from Woodfall Province."

Was he a spy? A shadow warden pretending to be a surveyor? On the trail of Prince Gevulin? But she studied surveyor maps at Map Hall, and this one looked legitimate. Well-loved, even. More carefully tended than the man himself.

"Have you been out for a while?" Elen asked.

Now he grinned with real excitement. "I can tell you because you're a deputy courier. Look here! I was sent out to remap the extent of Far Boundary Pall."

Where the prince was going, but she wasn't about to tell him that. Maybe he was fishing.

But as he went on, his awkward manner dissolved as he pointed out features on the map. "Now and again Palls develop what we call 'spurs.' They grow like a tendril out of the main Pall. But I guess you know that . . ."

Before she could answer in the affirmative, he rushed on.

"Far Boundary Pall developed a fast-moving spur about ten years ago. See it here, this narrow thread? Its inlet departs the Pall here, to the east of Far Boundary Vigil. It runs for tens of leagues south through Woodfall Province, more like a river than anything. Like a snake winding through the countryside! It's cut off several ordinary roads. That's forced the locals to take long detours, and it's disrupted trade and harvest in the eastern region of the province. If you're headed into Woodfall, and you pass Pelis Manor North, you'll be able to see it from their watchtower. It cuts that close to the Manor compound. You going that way?"

Here it came, the probing for information.

Elen said, "I'm impressed by how you surveyors are out walking the land all the time. The intendant receives a new set of imperial maps every three years, and there's always something new."

Berri's grin widened. "Yes! We never stop, because the Pall never stops. Except for one." He indicated the Pall nearest them, another few days north of where they were sitting at a table with crispy eel and honey beer. "Did you know the boundaries of Flat Pall haven't shifted at all in one hundred years? It's the only Pall never to have grown or shrunk since the first rising, that we know of. No one knows why."

Her refusal to answer seemed to have slid right past him. Curious, she tried her own probe. "I only know of one Pall that has vanished completely. The Desolation."

His grin snapped into a morose frown. He sat back, shoulders slumping, and all at once looked too weary to sit up straight. Grabbing the mug, he slugged down the rest of the beer, clapped it on the table, and called, "Cavna! More beer!"

The woman looked over and visibly sighed. She didn't hurry over. Something was off. Elen said, "Have you been to the Desolation?"

Berri wiped his hands carefully on a handkerchief—his cleanest item besides the map—and set his hands, palms down and separated, to frame an area of the map whose boundaries were elaborately filled in and whose central region was blank.

"I lost my best friend there," he said in a low voice. He picked up the mug, saw it was empty, and set it down again. He hadn't touched his food.

"Ah." She had uncovered something she hadn't expected, something raw and wounded. Its echo resonated in her own heart.

He mumbled on without prompting. "That scar on your neck—not to be rude—but it reminds me of him."

"Why is that?" she asked carefully.

He seemed not to hear the question. "He was fascinated by the Desolation. Kept going in, even though everyone knew it was dangerous. It's a terrible place, you know. Wild and disordered. Landmarks don't stay in one place. I only went in twice, but he went back again and again. Then the last time, he never returned. I had sworn never to go back in, but I had to follow the trail he left. We leave signs other surveyors can read."

A thing Elen hadn't known!

"The trail he left dead-ended at a blank cliff face. I found this there, the last piece of him in the whole wide world."

He pulled out a brass disk strung on a leather cord that he wore around his neck. Strangely, the disk held a scent that made her think of fields of dream-flower drowsing under the summer sun. It was incised like a stylized lightning bolt. The line was jagged, not wavy like her scar, but there were about the same number of angles. It wasn't that big of a leap for a drunken, grieving man to see the two as alike.

"The lightning bolt is our mark. We used it for messages when we were boys, planning mischief." He leaned closer, breath sodden with the smell of beer. "He's still alive, I'm sure of it. He left the disk to mark his path. He went into the cliff and wasn't sure if he'd be able to get out again. Everyone says I'm deluded. No one wants to talk about him anymore. They say it's ill fortune to do so. He's the last surveyor known to have been lost in the Desolation. I'm the last one who went in and came out alive."

"What is his name?" she asked.

Berri's pained smile held a grief still so fresh it hurt to see it in his face. "Rotho. What a goof. Always tripping over his own feet. I love that man."

Her viper stirred. Was it Berri's exhausted longing for his missing friend that roused it? Or did his still-living sorrow resonate in her heart, for didn't she herself smile in just such a way when her grief for Ao rose sharply to the surface of her thoughts?

Yet his story made her wonder: Could her viper hunt down a missing man like Rotho through a shifting and deadly landscape?

"Will you ever go search for him again?" she asked.

Berri shrugged resignedly. "I'd have gone ten times, or a hundred. But it's no longer allowed. All told, our order lost nineteen surveyors to the Desolation before the ban."

"That's an astounding number. How did that happen?"

"Our maps were wrong, the ones that were drawn of that province before the rise of the Pall."

"How can maps be wrong?"

"It's uncanny. I say that as the last known surveyor who went in and got out again, when I went to look for Rotho. Wherever an old map showed a hill, there was no hill but some other feature, a canyon, a lake, a mire, a pile of monstrous bones. Sometimes terrible creatures would crawl out of the wilderness, creatures never before seen or recorded in the archives. Or so it was claimed, but no one who saw the monsters survived for long, after their report of the encounter. Almost as if seeing a monster was enough to curse a person into an early death. I never saw any such creatures. The Hibiscus Emperor allowed aivur to settle along the border of the Desolation, thinking to protect the borderland with their presence. In the last year of his reign, the Lily Emperor put a stop to all surveyor explorations because of the death toll. When the Magnolia Emperor banished the aivur from the heartland and the provinces, she signed a treaty with a council of aivur. The treaty allows aivur communities to remain in the border country around the Desolation so long as they never pass the Whispering Fence. Some say the aivur patrol the dead lands, that they hunt monsters, or search for ancient treasure. We stay out."

"A Whispering Fence! Huh. I'd like to see the Desolation."

"No, you wouldn't." He rubbed his face wearily.

Elen recognized now that the loss of his old friend—brother, lover, whatever the man had been to him—had broken him.

Elen called Cavna over and asked for more drinks, then a second round, and managed Berri into eating a bit. Eventually she got him laughing over a famous comedic play they'd both seen. How many full buckets had the despicable captain tripped over in the course of the play? Seven, or eight? What had been in each one, and in which order? Wine. Water. Fermented apple peelings. Coals. Urine. Feces. Spiders. They couldn't remember the eighth. Not Spore, because that wouldn't have been funny.

That night, in the lesser officials' barracks, a body slipped as if by accident into Elen's bunk while she was in it. She punched hard at the stranger's belly, and he choked, then burst into tears, for it was Berri, sobbing over his lost friend. So she let him lie there with her, both clothed, because he just wanted comfort, like puppies in a basket. So small a thing, and so hard to find. In the morning, when she woke, he was already gone.

At dawn on the fifth day, Elen and the wardens gathered in the courtyard of quiet Itumiel Halt's hostel, waiting for their horses. The carriages were pulled up, ready to go. Xilsi grinned as the prince emerged from the imperial bower, looking stormy. Remarkably, even after several days, his hair had not yet been rebraided. It was getting more flyaway and shiny. Sometimes, when he thought no one was looking, he would scratch.

Intendant Berel hustled along behind him, bowing as she walked. "I pray you, Your Exalted Highness, I meant no offense. Such exalted attention would be a mark of honor for my sister. I have a young male cousin, if that is your preference. I did not mean to presume."

He halted to look down his nose at her, a whirlwind of shadow in his face, as if his anger had taken wing. "Of course you meant to presume. You and your party will leave us. Now."

Berel shrank back, clearly scared, but she had an avaricious streak and, in a wheedling tone, went on stubbornly. "But Your Highness, we will reach South Flat Vigil today."

"*I* will reach South Flat Vigil today. You, on the other hand, may return to Farledder Halt or, frankly, ride into the Pall, if that is your preference."

His gaze flashed to the portico. Berel's sister had appeared in the doorway, her shoulders heaving with suppressed sobs as the handsome prince rode out of her life.

"That is all. You are dismissed."

The wardens looked so pleased at this turn of events that Elen had to wonder what life had been like for them the last four days. As they rode out, Simo took the lead beside the haunt, who seemed restless and impatient, even snappish if anyone was foolish enough to try to talk to him. Maybe it was because they were nearing Flat Pall. Elen felt the inexorable pull of a powerful current tugging her body into darkness. Water, dragging her into its opaque depths.

Where did that memory of water come from? She shut her eyes, trying to remember, but all that was left was a vague impression of a night sky, brilliant with stars, and the salty slosh of water against her bare skin. It was an old memory from the nameless land, strange and troubling.

The viper stirred, wanting out. It sensed the Pall, the same as a horse heads for its stable, as a pigeon flies to its roost, as the heart brings the traveler home, time and again, to the people it loves.

Late in the afternoon, the road crested a low rise. They looked over what must once have been a wide valley, now nothing but a flat sea of pale mist.

The Vigil tower, built of pale holystone, rose in the distance, at the edge of the Pall. It was supported by a cluster of stone buildings, ringed by a holystone wall and a garden, all surrounded by a moat crossed by a gated bridge. All other signs of habitation had ceased an hour or more ago. No one who wasn't required to chose to live this close to the Pall.

The Pall had a distinct shoreline. On one side, soil had been cleared of vegetation and salted for about fifty paces back. On the other, like a blanket laid down, the Pall. No waves troubled it. The wind carved no scallops across its surface. It just lay there, inert, like low-lying fog on a windless day.

Beyond the Vigil, the road cut straight through Flat Pall. It was easy to see because the white mist was pulled back on either side, about a hand's breadth from the foundation stones. A witch road, in truth, its magic powerful enough to fend off the Pall.

The higher ground of Woodfall Province was visible on the other side, about two leagues away. She had never wanted to return to Woodfall Province. Never, ever.

Yet now, after so many days with the wardens—with the haunt— she realized that she was willing to risk the crossing into Woodfall if it meant she could find out what was going on. Why was the prince rushing to Far Boundary Pall? What awaited him there? And why was it so crucial for him to keep it a secret?

53

The Vigil

The intendant's carriage carried a traveler's horn like the one the party had left behind with the palace vehicles, that announced its princely visitation. The horn's high, harsh call blasted out five times as they crossed the final league to the Vigil.

By the time their carriages reached the bridge over the moat, wardens awaited them on the bridge in disciplined formation. They bowed as the carriages rolled past, then fell in behind as an honor guard. A pack of Spore-hunting dogs trotted at the rear in good order, intently sniffing as if they could scent the entire journey.

Past the moat lay gardens. These had been turned over for the winter and covered with straw. In the orchard, even the quince had been harvested. Smoke was rising from a sealed shed where, by the smell, meat was being smoked for the winter.

In the countryside, the imperial road was wide enough for two carriages to pass. As it approached the holystone wall that surrounded the inner buildings, it narrowed to the width of a single lane. It was an effective way to control traffic in and out. Their carriages passed beneath an arch in the outer wall.

Elen had never been to either South Flat or North Flat Vigil. She and Ao had fled from Woodfall far to the southwest, via a different road that crossed Flat Pall in a different place. But the layout of every Vigil was much the same. In order to proceed on a road across a Pall, travelers had to check in with the magistrates, show their travel permit, and have their cargo approved according to its manifest. Those coming out of a Pall had to have their vehicles and livestock inspected for Spore before being granted permission to go on.

Inside the wall, the road became a single-lane street. It led past an inn, a stable, a carriage house, a magistrate's office, a hostel for officials, and finally to a plaza.

Here, the carriages halted. Everyone disembarked. Elen looked around, getting her bearings. To the left, and thus the west, rose a Heart Temple with its usual courtyard and fountain. To her right, and thus the east, stood a large kitchen and storehouse compound. Directly ahead, the plaza ended in the northernmost side of the holystone wall, its gleaming stones rising to the height of a two-story building. Planted at the centerpoint of the wall was the Vigil tower, a blocky edifice that rose a full six stories.

Kem craned his head back to stare all the way to the top of the tower, mouth agape. The west wall of the tower glowed softly where the rays of the setting sun painted a shimmering glamor along its holystone. His gaze dropped and, instinctively, he looked over to Elen with a grin, wanting to share his delight and amazement with her, as they always shared the wondrous nature of the world. She nodded, allowing herself a small smile in answer. He was too astonished to remember that he was so very angry with her.

Maybe the most astonishing thing about the Vigil tower wasn't its impressive height but the way the road ran directly beneath—through—the massive base story of the tower, as if through an arched tunnel. A lowered portcullis currently blocked the tunnel.

To get to the main entrance into the tower, a visitor had to climb a ramp to a terrace, where double doors led into the second floor. The Vigil's warden captain waited on this ramp, flanked by more wardens and high-ranking menials.

Except for Kem, the wardens in their own party had taken the arrival in stride. The haunt tried to hide his curiosity, but Elen could see the way his gaze took in the position of every person in the plaza, how he held one hand slightly forward, palm open, as if to feel something through the air. He waited by the carriage as the Vigil captain and her people descended from the ramp and knelt to greet him.

"I, Cweles, captain of this Vigil, greet you with my loyal wardens. You honor us with your presence, Your Highness. We are amazed and gratified by your swift arrival, considering the Five Bridges region is blocked. If you wish to cross Flat Pall today there is still time before sundown. We can have the horses changed out, or our own travel carriages made ready immediately."

The haunt's outstretched hand twitched. He took in a deep breath, let it out slowly. "No need. We will remain here for the night and depart at dawn."

The words surprised Elen. Weren't they in a hurry? Why linger? His expression gave nothing away.

The Vigil captain bowed. "As you wish, Your Highness."

"Arise," he said. "No need for you to stay on your knees."

Cweles was not as spry as she must once have been, as was obvious when she took the hand of her chief menial to help her back to her feet. A Vigil was a good posting for a warden who was still competent but not as physically capable of long journeying. "Your Highness, you are gracious and generous."

"So everyone assures me, time and again," he said drily. By now, his wardens no longer looked startled at these odd asides. The Vigil wardens didn't know him, so they bowed to indicate agreement.

Cweles indicated the open doors on the terrace above. "May it please you to enter, the comfort of the imperial suite awaits you, Your Highness. Once you have settled your things and bathed, if that is your wish, a supper will be ready in the hall. We can discuss the latest information I have received."

"Ah, indeed. Yes. It will be best if all my people hear the news."

Fulmo and the wardens took only the gear they'd brought overland, leaving the carriages and the intendant's luxuries to be driven away by the Farledder coachmen. As they headed up the ramp into the tower, Elen was taken aside by the Vigil's chief menial and escorted to the kitchen building. Inside, menials were bustling to put together a meal acceptable for an imperial palate. The cook was shouting, and there didn't seem to be enough hands to get all the necessary jobs done.

One young person was sobbing in a corner, overwhelmed at the thought of having to enter the same room as an exalted prince. "I'll drop something, I just know it!"

"Deputy courier, you may rest on that bench, out of the way," said the chief menial, a tall man with gray hair and a dour face.

"Perhaps I can help," she said as she set her pack down by the bench. "I can chop up turnips as well as anyone. Or I can carry a tray to the hall, if you'd like. I see one of your servers is a bit overset. Perhaps it leaves you shorthanded, and for a prince's exalted visit, at that!"

His deep frown quirked slightly. "I suppose you won't be overwhelmed by the prince, since you've been traveling with him. Your uniform is cleaner than I expected."

"I've been able to brush it every night, thanks to the luxurious Halts managed by Intendant Berel Karissar," she said, sensing humor behind his forbidding expression. "They're all quite well appointed and cater to the most refined sensibilities."

He gave a snort of amusement. "They are, indeed. Intendant Berel will accept nothing less than the best for herself. She has visited here many times, to sell us horses at an inflated price. Very well. I like you. What's your name?"

"Elen."

"Very well, Elen. Wash your hands. Your face too. That basin over there, by the back door."

She washed her hands and face, a good scrub with lavender-scented soap that she thoroughly enjoyed. The chief menial had gone over to supervise the table where the platters were being readied. She offered herself up for inspection.

He looked her up and down. "You'll do. I'm surprised to see a deputy courier with the prince's party, but I suppose you were chosen for your looks. They say the prince has an eye for what pleases him."

"Do they?" she said, amused by the comment. She couldn't help but think of the prince's lovely concubines, whom he apparently couldn't bear to travel without, even when he was in a desperate hurry. "But I did not come from the heartland with the wardens. I serve the intendant of Orledder Halt. I was only assigned to His Exalted Highness's party when Prince Gevulin reached there."

"Orledder Halt. But the road is blocked at Five Bridges." He bent closer and, in an undertone, said, "How did you get here so fast? We thought the prince would be weeks on the road, once we heard he was coming."

She pressed her hands together and gave him an innocent look. "I beg your pardon, Chief Menial. I am not at liberty to disclose any details of our journey. You will have to apply to your Vigil captain or to the prince himself."

He nodded approvingly. "Saucy, too. I know your type. Good thing I'll be in the hall to hear all about it. I feel sure it will prove an entertaining story."

She laughed.

At that, he clapped his hands. "Take up your trays and platters! Follow me! No looking around! Keep your eyes to yourselves! No staring at His Exalted Highness! Do not dishonor your service in this Vigil with any disreputable behavior!"

Elen took a tray and fell in at the rear of the group. They processed single file along a covered walkway and entered the tower. The lower half was blocky, large enough to fit four rooms per level. They ascended to the fifth level, a single chamber with glass windows and sentry balconies on every side. The view was spectacular. Kem stood next to Ipis by the north-facing windows, the two staring across the Pall toward the countryside of Woodfall Province, the view fading as the day dimmed toward dusk.

Half the room was a parlor furnished with reading chairs and reading lamps, while the other half was taken up with a long table. The prince was seated in the grandest of the reading chairs, the one most appropriate to his exalted status. The Vigil captain had seated herself on a humble stool to his right. She'd set down a basket of message scrolls on a table in front of him.

"—as you can see, Your Highness, these are all the messages we received and sent onward according to the usual protocol. I personally transcribed everything, so these are my own copies of the original messages. They have remained in my sole custody."

"What is the most recent news?"

"Nothing has changed from the dispatch I sent ten days ago, Your Highness."

"I did not receive that dispatch because we were not on the road. We came overland, across Grinder's Cut."

"How can that be possible?" she asked, amazed.

The haunt's gaze flicked toward the door, where Elen stood with the menials as they waited for permission to serve. To the warden, he said, "A story for later."

"Of course, Your Highness. Let the meal be served." She gestured an order.

The chief menial presided over the setting of the table and the lighting of the oil lamps. Once the prince and wardens were seated at the table, the chief menial himself set drink and food before Fulmo. After the gagast approved the dishes, the chief served the prince, after which the rest of the table was served. Elen's entire task had been to set her tray on a side table and keep out of the way. This vantage allowed her to listen, and that was what she wanted.

The wardens ate and drank in silence at first.

Eventually, the prince set down a drained cup. "Let us discuss the mission. Speed is of the essence. There is much to be considered. Indeed, I wish to review all of the messages again."

"All of them?" The request startled Cweles.

"Perhaps by considering them all together, instead of piecemeal, I can shake loose some detail I missed before."

"I am sure you miss nothing, Your Highness."

The lift of his chin signaled his displeasure. "Reserve your flattery for those who desire it. I am not one of them. Read them to me, in order."

"Your Highness?"

He made a business of rubbing his brows with a pained expression. "I have a headache. If the task is not appropriate for you, Captain, then my interlocutor shall do it."

"A theurgist, Your Highness?" She looked even more baffled.

"She has a melodious voice, as interlocutors must do. Luviara, start from the first, and read them straight through."

"Of course, Your Highness." Luviara rose from her chair and fetched the basket. She was either pleased to be singled out or perhaps eager to scry warden secrets. After pushing her plate aside, she set out the messages in a row. The haunt leaned forward as Luviara examined the dates written on the outside of the scrolls, lined them up in order, and unrolled the earliest dated message.

As she scanned the calligraphy, she raised her eyebrows with a delighted expression. "I do not recognize this script! It is true you wardens use your own cipher."

Cweles gave the haunt a long look, brow furrowed, as if she hadn't yet puzzled out an answer and wasn't happy with the need to do so. "Your Highness?"

He blinked. Elen could almost see his thoughts scrambling as he decided what to do.

He rubbed his forehead again, grimacing with a pained frown. "As I have already stated, Captain, I have a headache. Waste no further time!"

Cweles covered her face with her hands, bobbed once, and lowered her hands. "The fault is mine."

"Yes, yes. Now, go on. I wish to go to my rest early, so there will be no delay at dawn for our departure."

Cweles gestured to the chief menial. "Clear the room."

The haunt nodded at Luviara and Fulmo. They obediently went out—although Luviara's expression was clouded by frustration—and the menials followed them, leaving only Captain Cweles, the haunt, and his wardens. Elen stood as still as she could, pretending she was the wall. The chief menial, last to go, halted in the doorway and gestured for her to come.

Without looking over, the haunt said, "The deputy courier stays."

"Your Highness," objected Cweles. "As warden captain, I beg

leave to remind you this is sensitive warden business! Not courier business."

He turned a hard gaze on her. "Yet the deputy courier stays. Need I repeat myself?"

"Your Highness," murmured Cweles in a low voice. "The fault is mine."

The chief menial's eyebrows raised, but he said nothing, just closed the door behind him, leaving Elen in the room.

54

No Answer

Her mouth pinched in disapproval, Vigil Captain Cweles cast a glance toward Elen. Even the wardens who knew Elen looked puzzled, even skeptical. But none could countermand a prince.

"Go on, Captain," said the haunt, well aware of these roiling undercurrents.

Cweles unrolled each message in order and read aloud in a clipped heartland accent while the prince studied the writing, following along as she spoke.

"Year Seventeen of the Blessed Reign of the Magnolia Emperor, Month of Iron, from His Exalted Highness Prince Gevulin, Prince-Warden and All-Seeing Eye in command of the Imperial Order of the Wardens, to Warden Captain Mekvo in command of Far Boundary Vigil, these words: As of this day, I, Prince Gevulin, rise in command as All-Seeing Eye. Let all wardens confirm their obedience.

"Year Seventeen of the Blessed Reign of the Magnolia Emperor, Month of Iron, from Warden Captain Mekvo to His Exalted Highness Prince Gevulin, these words: May His Exalted Highness be blessed. So is it confirmed at Far Boundary Vigil.

"Year Eighteen of the Blessed Reign of the Magnolia Emperor, Month of Gold, Day One, from Warden Captain Mekvo to His Exalted Highness Prince Gevulin, these words: May His Exalted Highness be blessed. With the new year, Far Boundary Pall confirms all is quiet.

"Year Eighteen of the Blessed Reign of the Magnolia Emperor, Month of Gold, from His Exalted Highness Prince Gevulin, Prince-Warden and All-Seeing Eye in command of the Imperial Order of the Wardens, to Warden Captain Mekvo in command of Far Boundary Vigil, these words: Report received. Remain vigilant."

Cweles paused. "These next are all part of a single message, sent in stages, according to the normal protocol. With your permission, Your Exalted Highness, I'll read them as one."

"Go on."

"Year Eighteen of the Reign of the Magnolia Emperor, Month of Copper, Day Sixteen, from Warden Captain Mekvo to His Exalted

Highness Prince Gevulin, these words: Urgent news. Need immediate response. A man has appeared overnight at the Vigil. Hard to
understand. May be some mistranslation. Claims to have crossed
Far Boundary Pall, although we know this to be impossible. Claims
to be an envoy of a far land and its lady-king of the far north."

A pulse of staggering adrenaline flooded Elen's body, so sharp
she swayed. Had she misheard?

The captain read onward in her same bland tone. "Seeks an audience with Prince Gevulin, by name, saying he speaks on behalf
of the lady-king, 'according to the mutual assistance pact sealed and
sworn at Storm Port on Witch-Tower Island,' and that her message
is intended for the prince alone, not to be conveyed via others, only
by him. How do we proceed?"

Xilsi snorted. "What a wild, ridiculous tale!"

The haunt raised a hand, and Xilsi cleared her throat and settled.
His gaze flicked toward Elen, standing there painfully alert, before
he said coolly, to Cweles, "Go on."

The Vigil captain continued. "Year Eighteen of the Reign of the
Magnolia Emperor, Month of Copper, from His Exalted Highness
Prince Gevulin, Prince-Warden and All-Seeing Eye in command
of the Imperial Order of the Wardens, to Warden Captain Mekvo
in command of Far Boundary Vigil, these words: Detain man as a
prisoner. Keep him isolated, no contact with others. Do not speak of
this to anyone. His Exalted Highness will depart immediately and
travel via the Northern Road. Expect arrival at Far Boundary Vigil
in eighteen days."

The words pounded into Elen's head. *Keep him isolated. No contact
with others. His Exalted Highness will depart immediately.*

Was this truly the prince's secret mission? It stunned her.

"Month of Copper, from His Exalted Highness Prince Gevulin,
to Captain Mekvo, these words: Have arrived in Ilvewind Cross.
Please confirm receipt, as have heard no further word."

Cweles halted. At first, no one spoke, although Xilsi was shaking
her head with a sort of resigned disgust at the folly of the world.

"What then?" the haunt asked.

"Your Highness, there came no reply from Captain Mekvo. On
my own authority as Vigil captain, I sent a further message to Mekvo,
who I happen to know well. He is a responsible and loyal man. To
that query, no answer has been received."

Only now did Xilsi's expression shift from eye-rolling to concern.

She clenched a hand and mouthed a word Elen couldn't read from her lips.

"No answer from Captain Mekvo at all?" the haunt asked.

"None. Silence."

Simo and Jirvy, too, became taut with interest at this news. Ipis and Kem simply looked confused. In Elen's heart, the viper stirred, alert to signs of trouble.

"What then?" the haunt asked.

"I sent a message to you, Your Highness, informing you that Far Boundary Vigil had gone silent, and that I was sending one of my wardens to the Vigil to scout out the situation."

"My answer to your message? Can you read that?"

"I cannot because you did not answer. That was ten days ago."

"Of course. We had already departed Orledder Halt. What of your investigation into Captain Mekvo's silence?"

She picked up the second-to-last scroll. "Month of Copper, Day Twenty-Three, from Warden Captain Cweles in command of South Flat Vigil to Warden Captain Mekvo, these words: I have sent Warden Enshi to confirm all is well at your Vigil. Please confirm Warden Enshi has arrived."

"What answer did you receive?"

"I received no answer."

At these calmly stated words, the skin at the back of Elen's neck prickled. Here blew an ill wind.

The haunt stood. "I will personally investigate the situation at Far Boundary Vigil. What is your advice on carriages? Must I continue on in the Farledder carriages? I dislike being beholden to that woman."

The words had an icy tone that made Cweles smile cynically.

"Indeed, Your Highness, while I am sure we must all thank Intendant Berel for her efforts, she does encroach."

He muttered something under his breath, looking genuinely angry, before arranging his expression into something blander. "What do you recommend?"

"The Sun Chasers will do better than our battle carriages. However, while our horses are of the highest quality, they are not tireless like the palace beasts. The eastern half of Woodfall Province is more sparsely populated than its western half, so I am not sure how often you will be able to change out horses. There is one other limitation. Our Sun Chasers can't carry more than four people each, and you have nine in your party. The deputy courier can remain here."

Kem glanced toward her with a look of alarm, but the other wardens kept their gazes fixed on the haunt.

"That would be a good solution, Your Highness," said Simo.

The haunt flicked a hand dismissively. "Fulmo can keep up on foot. My entire party is staying together."

Cweles took this in with obvious surprise. "As you wish, Your Highness. I will assign a squad of wardens to go with you on horseback, Your Highness, all eight that I have here. I fear bandits may have attacked Far Boundary Vigil. I should never have sent Enshi there alone."

"I need only my own people. We are an efficient fighting force. I'm not concerned about bandits. Simo, who can drive a carriage?"

"Besides you, Your Highness?"

"Let me rephrase. I will not be driving. Who can manage the horses in my place?"

Simo tapped his own chest. "I will do so, Your Highness, as is my duty. I'd say Jirvy for the other carriage but better to not jostle his injuries. So, Xilsi will drive."

"That's settled."

The haunt stood, and all stood, although Kem filched a savory roll off the table and slipped it up his sleeve, a skill he and Joef had perfected in the Residency kitchens.

Outside, seen through open windows, night had fallen. Clouds covered the stars. The Pall was touched by flares of phosphorescence, like a woolly blanket dusted with imprisoned fireflies. The road cut across as a slash of darkness. A distant light marked North Flat Vigil on the far side.

The haunt strode to the door, reached for the latch, but paused before he touched it. With a wry smile, he withdrew his hand, and waited for Captain Cweles to open the door for him.

"All will be ready at dawn, Your Highness," Cweles assured him.

"Of course it will. I know you will not fail me, Captain."

The imperial suite was one floor below, outer door left open into its formal receiving parlor. Luviara was seated at a table, writing in her journal by the light of an oil lamp. She looked cross, irritated to have been left out. As the others filed into the parlor, Elen hurried down the stairs before the interlocutor could look up and see her, lest Luviara wonder why Elen hadn't left with the menials.

Below, the kitchen was bustling as the cook and her assistants assembled a supply of journey food appropriate for a prince.

The chief menial took Elen aside. "The barracks are out of the way, and the annex bunks are cold at night. If you wish, there is a pallet behind the hearth in one of the storerooms. It will be quiet there. I will wake you personally before dawn, so you can be ready."

"That's very kind. Might I thank you by name, Chief Menial?"

He smiled in the genial way of an elder remembering their youthful days of flirtation. "Kind? I'm not so sure of that. You may address me as Navru. I suppose we may see you on the return journey."

"So it is to be hoped, if the High Heavens smile upon us."

His smile faded as he turned somber. "I believe you are one of the fortunate blessed."

The words made her uneasy. "Do you? Why so?"

"Just a feeling I have. I got the gift of side-seeing from my grandfather." Navru's expression turned inward; his gaze had fixed onto a shore that Elen could not see. "You have survived things that killed others, have you not? Yet there is joy in you, despite these stormy tides that would have scoured others into oblivion."

When he fell silent, she stood there, unsure what to say.

After a moment, he shook himself, as if returning from a long journey. "I do not mean to embarrass you. Tread carefully. Help may come from an unlooked-for direction."

She pressed a hand to her heart in respect, then made her way to the storeroom. The pallet was tucked into a warm corner, with a curtain. She slung her pack down, took off her boots and outer gear, and lay down. Her thoughts raced in frantic circles. A far land. A lady-king. Beyond all that, what had this to do with Prince Gevulin specifically, rather than the empire in general?

But she could solve nothing here on her pallet. She focused on her breathing, the whole world inhaled and then exhaled, steady onward, calming her galloping thoughts and hammering pulse. The clatter of busywork and murmured chatter from the kitchen soothed her. She fell asleep.

An unknown time later, she woke to an uncanny silence. Something was very off kilter.

All she could think was: Had the past caught up to her at last?

55

A WILD AND ALLURING STORY

At her back, the bricks of the hearth were warm. It was night, everything dark and hushed. Had the menials finished their tasks and gone to bed? Yet it wasn't the quiet that had woken her. A weight pressed on her, as if the air had grown heavy and torpid. She had felt this eerie intrusion before. *Magic.*

Was it the haunt's doing? Or something else? Something terrible? Something she couldn't escape? She certainly wasn't going to lie here and wait until the threat leaped on her!

She swung her feet out, tucked them into her boots, pulled on her cloak, and crept out to the kitchen. The lamps still burned. By their light she saw the cook, assistants, servers, and charwoman, all draped across tables, slumped on the floor, sleeping peacefully. Elen added wood to the fire, which was starting to die down.

Slipping outside, she scanned the plaza. There was no moon, but some of the clouds had cleared off, and stars shone in patches. Lamps burned: one at the entrance into the Heart Temple, one at the portcullis, and one by the closed doors into the tower. Two sentries lay slumped on the ramp, fast asleep. She padded over and tucked their cloaks more tightly around them to keep in their body heat. The doors into the Vigil were locked, so she descended to discover that, in her visual search, she'd missed Fulmo. The gagast stood at the gap where the road reached the wall. His face was once again lifted toward the sky, and he did not stir or seem to see her. Not unlike the statues at the Spires, Elen realized. Why hadn't she noticed the similarity before?

Most importantly, the iron portcullis had been raised, and one of its thick metal pickets was lodged on a large block of stone high enough that a person could crawl beneath it. What human could have managed this feat alone?

The road's witchery hummed in her bones. Here in the Vigil compound, the road lay almost level to the ground, with a narrow edge of foundation stone laid a hand's span lower. This edge was just wide enough for her body. She was able to wiggle through along its narrow width rather than squirm painfully along on the road itself.

Once past the portcullis, she stood up within the dim confines of the passage, trapped on the road. The arched tunnel ran about twenty paces. She hurried along, aware of the road as a sting in the air, an itch nagging at her flesh, but the holystone of the walls and the foundation absorbed some of the sting, and she moved fast, eager to get out. Overhead, the arched ceiling was cut by murder holes, slits where defenders could drop missiles and hot oil and other deadly things onto attackers below. The precautions seemed strange to her, since what was most deadly here, at the shore of a Pall, was the possibility of an outbreak of Spore. Here in the north there'd been no war for generations because of the presence of Far Boundary Pall. The Sea Wolves confined their raids to the far west, while the frontier war against the Blood Wolves raged in the outer east. There were occasional border skirmishes with brigands on the Tranquil Sea and the forest nations to the south, those that hadn't been absorbed into the empire as outlying provinces. The heartland itself remained at peace.

There was a second portcullis at the other end of the tunnel, this one also raised and kept propped up on a stone. Crawling under, Elen emerged onto what was commonly called the port of entry. This wide plaza ran all the way to the edge of the Pall and was paved in holystone, in which Spore could get no grasp. On either side were inspection chambers and, more ominously, two large shrive-steel cages surrounding iron pillars, the burning ground for hapless Spore-corrupted people, or on the rare occasions when an aivur spy, passing as human, got caught by a keen-eyed warden.

Once past the tower, the road widened back to its usual two-wagon width, and its foundation rose, ramping up from ground height. Thus raised, the road met the edge of the Pall as a pier meets a languid sea. It continued on across the fog-like expanse as a causeway. Lampposts ran along the road out into the Pall. One of the jobs of Vigil-assigned wardens was to keep the lamps filled with oil and burning, day and night.

A figure knelt at the base of the road, where its foundation stones met the Pall. He had a hand in the mist, as if in shallows of water. He moved his hand through the Pall. An eerie, pale light followed his movements as he stirred the unmoving mist to create a swirl of current.

The haunt removed his hand from the Pall and rose to greet her.

Embroidered eyes glimmered along the hem of his warden's tabard, the mark of the all-seeing eye.

The starlight—and the distant lamps—didn't really offer enough light to see more than shadows, yet his face shone as if gilded by the majesty of the High Heavens. He was very attractive, both in the human body he wore and because there was more to him, the whisper of the violent shadow Elen had seen at the canyon's rim, that sense of an ancient power that could be capricious or compassionate, murderous or mischievous, depending on its mood.

He smiled sweetly, yet there was an edge of challenge in his expression. He surely sensed the possibility of the moment as much as she did. "I had hoped you would come out and find me."

"I'm just surprised you're wearing clothes," she said in her most deadpan tone.

He laughed with delight, then grimaced and tapped a palm to his forehead as if to mime beating his head against a wall. "I didn't dare get my hair rebraided, much less take off my underclothes, for the entire journey with that intendant and her grasping sister. The sister tried to intrude into the bathing chamber more than once. She would just walk in at any time I was alone—the late evening, the middle night, just before dawn—always seeking to insinuate herself into my bed and my amorous attentions, not that I myself felt the least trace of interest in her. The prince might have had other ideas—his body is certainly reactive—but I was not about to indulge them. It was frightful."

"Don't you like sex?" Elen asked, trying not to laugh because he spoke as if the situation was ridiculous and absurdly funny. Yet, beneath the mockery, his distress did not seem feigned.

He puffed a bit, offended. "That's quite a personal question. Anyway, I am only borrowing this body. As an honorable person, I must respect its autonomy in matters pertaining to personal and intimate consent."

"Well, except for possessing the prince, who didn't understand what he was consenting to."

"True enough, but if you wish me to say I regret standing here, then I do not and I will not."

"Yes, you have your mission to accomplish." All at once she was struck by a dreadful foreboding. The questions raised by the messages the Vigil captain had read out loud mattered to Prince Gevulin, not to the haunt. What if the haunt had found what he needed already? A little choked, she said, "Is this Pall what you journeyed north to find?"

He looked away from her, north over the mist. The flat surface did not stir. The currents he'd drawn had faded. Only those distant firefly lights sparked and vanished in erratic intervals, like cries for help or the random popping of embers in a dying fire. His expression changed, going still and serious. She tensed.

Without looking at her, he said, "I wasn't thinking of my mission when I said I do not regret standing here. I was thinking of meeting you."

All speech died on her tongue. Her entire existence felt washed as by a current that threatened to drag her out beyond hope of return. She would not ask what he meant because she knew it herself, that strange and inexplicable sense when two people discover that, tangled into their souls, twists the connection of an invisible thread that weaves their fates one to the other, that asks their hearts to speak whether in silence or in words, in action or in thought.

The haunt smiled wryly and turned his dark gaze upon her, an expression as much regret as longing. "I shall now attempt to smooth over this awkward moment. It is true, I am seeking signs of a living threat. But this Pall isn't it. This Pall has no tides, no currents, no inflow or outflow. It is stagnant, and thus it is dying."

"Dying?" That word she could say. It was easier than revealing the vulnerability in her heart. But the word hooked her to the memory of Berri's anguished tears.

"'Dying' is the wrong word." He mulled for a bit, having the gift of quiet.

She waited.

He raised a hand to touch his lips. "It tastes like ashes. Flat Pall has no living existence of its own. More like residue left over after combustion. Do you know if the Pall has risen elsewhere in the wide world, beyond the empire? In an earlier era, perhaps?"

She temporized. "I don't know. What are you looking for?"

He sighed. "Listening, more like. Sorcery has a tone. A bell. You and I both heard it. I don't know what it means that its resonance has caught in the Spires now, in these days. It's coming from somewhere. My task is to find it."

"There really were sorcerer-kings, in ancient times?"

"There was sorcery, yes. There were people who used their wicked power to rule. Well, not even to rule, but to take and to trample, to blight and to bleed life out of living things in order to extend and expand their own. As long as they shone brightly in their own eyes, in their own fastnesses, they cared not if they cast the world into darkness and despair and disorder."

"And then what happened?"

"The usual story. Those who opposed them, fought them, even though it must have seemed a futile war. Still, honorable people will stand up when they must. In the end, the honorable people won, although at a terrible cost."

"You were one of those honorable people."

He laughed bitterly. "No, I was not. I am the least of the Shorn, late to the party but eager to feast on the praise given to the brave and the bold, which I never deserved. Yet look at me now, reduced to walking in another's body as I hope to redeem myself in some small way for what I refused to do in the hard days, when my help was most needed."

It was painful to hear that sardonic tone turned on himself. But reassuring him that surely, *surely*, he was wrong about his assessment of himself was definitely not the way to proceed.

"Where is Prince Gevulin?" she asked instead. "Are you sure he isn't seeing and hearing all?"

"Oh, no! That is not how the passage spell works. First, as I said before, the host must agree to carry one of the Shorn for a specific mission or task. When we enter, the host's mind retreats as behind a veil. They do not see or hear anything that happens. It's as if they sleep while we walk in their body. They trust the traveler will treat their body with respect and in no way violate any bounds of intimacy or violence that aren't absolutely necessary for survival. Thus . . ." He extended a hand toward her, as one would if meaning to take hold of another person's hand, but drew it back without touching her.

"I see." Her fingers closed over empty air. "What are the Shorn, exactly?"

"We who were shorn of our bodies in order to survive natural death and become . . . what shall I say? . . . to become guardians and warriors and caretakers, set aside so we might be released in a time of need. We retain our sense of self and our knowledge and memory, and some of the inherent gifts we wielded in the time before being shorn."

"Magical gifts?"

"It might be so," he said evasively. "But after being shorn, we have no bodies, so we need the passage spell to enter a physical body. Only then can we move about the world, which is otherwise closed to us. But after touching the Pall here, I believe my soul can move into and within the Pall."

"Like a fish swimming in the ocean?"

"I would scarcely compare my glorious self to a *fish*. But something like that, yes. I believe the Pall would act as a soft shell harboring my soul in the same way the hard shell of a statue did for so long." A flicker of disquiet troubled his expression. "Yet, were I to become trapped in a stagnant Pall like this one, I would eventually wither away and die with it. Sparks fade as ashes grow cold."

Elen swallowed past a thickness in her throat. "What will happen when you reach a living Pall?"

"If there is such a thing, I will release the prince and descend into the Pall. In a living Pall, I may hope to find the answers I seek about those you call the sorcerer-kings—if they remain dead, or have somehow returned to life and become a wicked enemy to vanquish yet again. I might even find one of my Shorn compatriots, should any survive. Yet having touched this Pall, and hearing about the Desolation, I wonder if any living Pall survives."

"Far Boundary Pall is a living Pall, if by that you mean a place with tides and currents."

"How can you know this? Is that what the surveyors say?"

She had never admitted this before to another living being, except Ao, who already knew. "I crossed it."

He tilted his head, the gesture almost birdlike. "Did you, now? My wardens tell me Far Boundary Pall is at the northern edge of the world. Nothing lies beyond it except, eventually, an ocean. And salt ocean is more of a barrier to the Pall than a witch road."

"Yes, that is why the message Captain Cweles read made Xilsi say it was ridiculous."

"It was not ridiculous?"

"There is a far land lying beyond Far Boundary Pall. Twenty years ago, its southern quarter was ruled by a lady-king. She might still be alive. And at that time, her heir was her daughter."

"You know this, how?"

It was the secret she and Ao had kept most carefully, fearing what would happen if the truth became known. Yet she'd told the haunt her childhood name. He'd told her more about his past and his true mission. Most importantly, the prince would never know. It was time to let go of the fear.

"It's where Ao and I came from originally, years ago. We were children when we escaped. Not that we knew what we were doing, mind you. It seems neither the wardens nor the surveyors know there is an entire country beyond Far Boundary Pall. But apparently Prince Gevulin does. Because why else would he have received that message from Captain Mekvo and immediately set out, in such a rush, to race north to get to Far Boundary Vigil. While meanwhile ordering Mekvo to keep the mysterious man in isolation so no one else could talk to him until Prince Gevulin got there. How does he know? *Why* does he know? What does it mean?"

"Put like that, it is a curious puzzle. Although it answers the question of what Prince Gevulin's mission is, if it is to interview, or silence, the messenger." The haunt rubbed his forehead as if he really did have a headache. "I don't understand how the wardens don't know. They're the ones with the map."

"A map of the *roads*. At Far Boundary Vigil the road is broken. Literally broken. Severed. That's why the wardens think it is the end of the road. Even the surveyors believe that. That's what everyone says, that the road was built that far and no farther."

"But it isn't?"

"Beyond the broken edge, there lies a gap of Pall. Beyond that gap, the witch road continues. But you can't see the continuation of the road from Far Boundary's Vigil tower. To reach the next part of the road, you have to wade through the Pall."

"Which humans can't do. So how could a messenger have passed across? You and Kem's mother did truly make this crossing?"

"Coming from the north, yes. There's a long stretch of intact witch road through the middle of the Pall. Far Boundary Pall is very wide, it's more of a sound than a lake. It takes days to walk that causeway. And it takes courage to do it, with Pall all around you and no sight or scent of land. Even then, while you're still in the Pall, there's yet another break in the road that has to be crossed. Beyond all that lies a nameless land. Maybe before the Pall it was part of the empire. Or maybe it was the last of the Seven Golden Kingdoms that came before the empire. I don't know."

"What are the Seven Golden Kingdoms?"

"The Tranquil Empire was founded by the Lotus Clan three

hundred years ago. They overthrew the corrupt rulers of the Seven Golden Kingdoms to bring order and peace to the land."

"Exactly the kind of story a new empire tells," he said with a sarcastic lift of his brows.

"Yes, the world is full of stories," she agreed with a smile. "Some true, some false, some meant to make you believe one thing instead of another, some brutal, some funny, some sad, and some brim-full of the most irresistible joy."

He almost winced, but it wasn't a wince, it was a powerful emotion struck through his heart.

"You are a story," he said, his tone so warm that she flushed, as if the cold air had burst into flame around her.

She pressed a hand to her chest.

He said, softly, gently, "A wild and alluring story, whose mysteries I adore."

What sweet bliss is this, she thought, *that I look at him and want to do nothing but smile? Well, maybe rather more. Maybe that, too.*

But she made no move. She, too, had to respect the code of the passage spell.

Beneath the sky, they stood together, side by side, not speaking, because what was there to say? He did not try to touch her, and she was content to be close enough to feel his presence beside her, whatever it meant. How could anyone know what would come to pass in this world? That he and she had met at all was a wonder beyond imagining. That they would part, she knew. He'd already told her so.

Why dwell on what had not yet come? Why wrestle with a future no one could predict? It was enough to be here, in this place, on this night, as the clouds ran on the winds above, and the Pall lay motionless, and the Vigil slept. The world held them in its tenderest embrace. *Life is so brief,* the wind murmured. *Let your heart swell to fill the moments you have.*

56

THE PULSE OF THE EMPIRE

They set off as the sun's rim cut the horizon. Its rising light gleamed along the east-facing wall of the holystone tower, bright enough to be seen for a great distance, which was another reason Vigils were built from holystone. They acted as beacons to people crossing a Pall, a reminder there was an end to their fear.

Wardens traveled in various types of conveyance. Captain Cweles had given them the use of two light carriages, called Sun Chasers because of a famous incident from the reign of the Azalea Emperor when a pair of wardens had outraced a slow-moving Spore irruption by never letting the sun set on their path.

A driver's bench and a back bench were fixed over what was little more than a shrive-steel framework holding together four big wheels. The Sun Chaser was built for speed, not safety nor comfort nor cargo. Chief Menial Navru buckled panniers of food and drink into each carriage. Everyone's packs were wedged into wire cages beneath their feet.

Simo took charge of the first carriage. "Your Highness," he said, indicating the driver's bench beside him. The haunt glanced toward Elen, his sly half smile an invitation for her to join him. But Luviara was already pulling herself up into the back bench next to Jirvy and his bow. It would have been exceedingly awkward to throw Luviara out once she'd settled in. So Elen dipped her chin, and the haunt sighed resignedly and turned to look forward.

Xilsi jumped up to the driver's seat of the second carriage. She was all smiles as she called down, "Elen, up with me! Let the young ones crowd into the back. I should have been a coachman!"

"As if a Manor-born scion like yourself would ever have become a coachman," Elen retorted as she climbed up beside Xilsi, who laughed.

Kem was so excited that he grinned at Elen as he crowded in next to Ipis. Simo, and then Xilsi, gave the command to walk, and the horses flicked their ears eagerly. Elen gripped the bench's railing as the carriages rolled forward.

"Not used to traveling by carriage?" Xilsi asked without taking her eyes off her pair of horses.

"No. I'm used to my own two feet. I've never ridden in a Sun Chaser."

"These are good goers. Just wait until we open up into a trot."

All the barriers to control movement into and out of the Pall had been opened. They passed the final gate and were saluted by wardens standing atop hallow-wood sentry boxes. Then there was nothing but the road running ahead in a long, straight line, with the Pall on either side.

Kem said to Ipis, "Have you traveled across a Pall?"

"Sure, three times," said Ipis in a boastful tone. "Twice on training runs. Haven't you?"

"I've never," he said, then added in a sharper tone, his mood shifting with mercurial swiftness, "or not that I remember, anyway."

Elen felt his accusing gaze on her like pinpricks.

Xilsi was grinning like a fool as she urged the horses into a high-stepping trot. The carriage ran smoothly, and while it wasn't fast like the imperial carriages, it was definitely faster than walking—unless, of course, one was a gagast. Fulmo loped along behind the second carriage, easily keeping pace.

After a while, Xilsi said, "I've never been out this way. What a weird Pall. Do you feel it? Can you hear it? They each have their own distinct miasma. But this is strange, even for a Pall. Blunted. Dull. No wonder they call it 'flat.'"

They lapsed into a silence broken only by the rumbling hum of the wheels and the rhythmic clip of hooves, soothing in their constancy. The countryside covered by the Pall was a lowland plain, but it was hard to know how level the land was beneath. The mist that stretched away to either side of the elevated roadbed lay entirely still, as if stiffened and ironed flat, with not a single ripple, nothing but the occasional burst of a spark-like glimmer that as quickly vanished. Like a cry for help no one could hear, Elen thought, then wished she hadn't because she wondered if it were true. No human or animal who walked or fell into a Pall survived, unless the haunt was correct in saying a soul—the breath of the High Heavens that animated the bodies of people and animals—might survive in some attenuated, trapped form, and wouldn't that be the worst thing of all?

After a while, Kem whispered, "There's no wind."

"Shh, it's bad luck to talk," Ipis murmured.

"Oh, it is not," scoffed Xilsi. "Don't tell the novice such nonsense. People don't talk when crossing Palls because they feel uneasy, that's all."

"It is strange there is no wind," said Elen, "because the clouds are moving, and there was a breeze at the Vigil."

It *was* strange, stranger even than she could explain to the others. Fifteen years ago, Elen and Aoving had crossed Flat Pall with toddler Kem. At that time, they had crossed Flat Pall a hundred or more miles to the southwest of South Flat Vigil. They had crossed on the Feldspar Spur, the witch road that ran closest to Duenn Manor. The southwestern stretch of Flat Pall had been flat, like this, but she recalled it as not quite this still and not quite this empty. She recalled seeing ripples in the mist, as if unseen creatures swam within its dense bank of foggy white. The movements had intrigued her so much that, once or twice during their crossing, she had halted to stare in wonder. Graceful curves and patterns ran like a language being written beneath the surface of a page. Aoving had wept in fear for the entire crossing, but she had kept walking despite how frightened she was. That was Aoving all over: everything scared her, but she kept walking straight into the heart of what terrified her most because she refused to give in to death. She'd been so fragile and so stubborn, and Kem had gotten all of her stubbornness, thank goodness, even if he had become impatient with Ao's fragility as he got older. Maybe if Elen had helped him understand where it came from, he'd have found more peace with his mother in the months before the avalanche had taken her, but she'd respected Aoving's wishes and said nothing of a past that Aoving had not wanted to revisit ever again.

Now, remembering, she puzzled over the silent Pall. Why the difference between the southern stretch of Flat Pall and this northern region? Had this part of Flat Pall always been emptier, always a backwater? Or had all of Flat Pall undergone changes in the last fifteen years? Could it be the haunt had sensed the Pall's impending death? Could Palls actually die? Were they alive in any meaningful sense? Yet, something had happened during the reign of the Mulberry Emperor that had drained the inland Pall then known as Imperial Pall. That had turned it into a desolation, *the* Desolation, a land empty of life, all of it devoured—and yet now free of the Pall that had once covered it. More strangely still, if Berri was correct, its contours no longer fit the pre-Pall maps of how the topography had looked before the Pall had inundated it. Had the Pall transformed the land itself into a new landscape? Spore transformed things, even if most people thought of it as distorting ordinary creatures into monsters.

The viper pulsed at her heart, awake, alert, but not restless or uneasy. Content, perhaps. The Pall did not scare the viper, nor did it arouse the viper's hunger. That was strange, too, given that the viper hunted Spore. Was there no Spore in Flat Pall? Nothing with enough energy to irrupt?

Xilsi's enthusiasm at being the coachman had cooled, and she'd turned her attention fully to the horses, looking a bit strained. They, at least, had been bred and chosen for a steady temperament and followed the lead carriage with no signs of distress or nervousness.

Kem coughed anxiously. "What's that noise?"

Elen thought it might be the wind rising, but it was a rushing burble, plopping and splashing.

"It's a river," Xilsi said with a chuckle.

The tone of the roadbed changed beneath them as the elevated embankment became an arched bridge. Water rushed below, a wide, powerful river with high banks.

"That's a big river," said Kem.

Even silent Ipis exclaimed, "Wow!"

They stared at the churn of the rushing waters flowing below the long span of the bridge. The difference between the road and the river was that the Pall did not touch the water but stretched over it, like a wispy canopy, which was why they had not seen the river ahead. All was hidden beneath the Pall, only the high causeway of the road left exposed, while the river ran as if beneath an extended archway formed by the deadly toxin.

The sound of the wheels changed as the bridge reached solid ground and the piers and arches became, again, an embankment.

Xilsi said, "Did you ever hear the story about a prince who took a dare and found the headwaters of a river, and got in a boat and pushed off and floated into the Pall?"

"And was never seen again?" Elen said.

"Oh, no, not at all. She survived the journey, returned to the palace, murdered her uncle, the Oak Emperor, for being completely inept, and placed herself on the throne."

"The Willow Emperor!" said Kem. "I mean, I didn't know about the boat, but my friend Joef told me all about the murder. There are at least twenty plays written about it, as well as five chronicles and two histories and more poems than can be counted. 'She who was kindest to me now sets the poisoned cup to my lips.'"

"That's right, she poisoned him," said Xilsi. "But maybe the High Heavens had a hand in it."

"How's that?" Kem asked.

"Because the Willow Emperor is the one who set in place all the new protocols that allow the empire to survive, and even thrive, despite the Pall."

"Is the story about the river true?" Elen asked skeptically.

"Do you think it's not possible?"

"I think that on the river, on a boat, a person can remain untouched by Spore, so yes, it's possible."

"Then why do you doubt the story?"

"I doubt an exalted prince would take such a chance."

"Do you not? I think it might even change such a prince's life, their view, and cause them to decide to mount a coup and murder their uncle and place themselves on the throne. Prince Gevulin would do it in a heartbeat if he thought it would gain him the throne."

Ipis hissed. "Xilsi! That's treason to speak so."

Xilsi snorted. "I can tell you've never set foot in the inner palace, or even talked to anyone who has. Besides me, I mean. Never cross a prince or a prince's mother. Or at least, not if they have any power. If they don't have any power within the palace, then you can do as you please to them, and the sooner the better, in case they decide to support someone else's bid for power."

"Prince Gevulin wants power?" Elen asked.

Xilsi gave Elen a cold look. "Haven't you figured him out yet? He pays an unusual amount of attention to you. Since you're not his bed type, there's something else going on."

This was not the direction Elen wanted the conversation to go, so she affected a puzzled air. "Xilsi, I don't know anything about the palace. Except what I see in the plays and read in wineshop poems."

Xilsi chuckled. "That's fair enough. Let me explain about Gevulin. Although if I hear any of you repeating this to someone else, I'll write a wineshop poem about you, and you'll be bitterly sorry. As for the prince, there's always been something else going on with him. In all the palace school competitions, he hated it if he didn't come in first, but he hated it even worse if he thought people were letting him win. Lots of people in the palace thought the Magnolia Emperor—may she live long and in peace—was trying to get rid of him when she sent him on a fact-finding tour of the borders of the empire, figuring he would get killed."

Kem nodded wisely. "Joef says—"

"Hey!" Xilsi cut him off. "I'm talking, not your friend Joef, who has never set foot in the palace either. Anyway, who knows? That was about four years ago. After Gevulin returned, the Magnolia Emperor appointed him as all-seeing eye. Which happened at the same time she appointed Prince Astaylin as General of the Imperial Order of Engineers. And raised them both to become Princes of the Third Estate."

"I heard whispers in the barracks," said Ipis in a low, enthralled tone. "That Crown Prince Minaylin—may the High Heavens forgive me for speaking with such disrespect—is rumored to be spoiled and indulged and spends his days gambling and drinking instead of studying the classics and learning how to administer the empire, as is his duty. That some ministers have begun grumbling that the crown prince is not fit to become emperor. That a different prince should be raised to the Second Estate."

"Yes. That's why Gevulin and Astaylin have become rivals. Because they each see an opening."

"So the way this mission has played out, the prince not being told of the avalanche and the blocked road, and maybe even the death of the griffin scout, has to do with their rivalry?" Elen asked.

"I'd hate to think of Astaylin agreeing to the murder of a griffin and scout. But her concealing the blocked road to make her brother look bad, yes, that is definitely the kind of play Astaylin would make in this game." She cast an assaying look at Elen. "Your knowledge of this back-door route gives Gevulin a chance to pike Astaylin in the eye and gain advantage. I suppose that might be explanation enough for why he favors you."

Yet her considering frown suggested she wasn't convinced.

Elen felt it time to dramatically change the subject so it couldn't possibly slide back to her and the haunt. She chose her words with particular care. "Who is the mysterious envoy mentioned in the messages from Far Boundary Vigil? The one from a far land, speaking for a lady-king? Whatever that might be."

"I have no idea," said Xilsi. "It surprised me, I'll tell you that."

"His Exalted Highness did not fill you in on the specifics of the mission?"

"No. I'm just an ordinary warden, not one of his inner circle."

"Who are his inner circle?"

"Of those of us here? Only Simo. Besides Simo, Gevulin's mother, the Elegant Consort. Her, more than anyone. Her most trusted kinfolk, who benefit from her status as the mother of a Prince of the Third Estate, and their confidantes. Hemerlin, obviously. Fulmo, possibly, since Hemerlin is the one who brought the gagast into the prince's service, which he'd never have done if he didn't have reason to trust Fulmo."

"Why Simo?" Elen asked. "Meaning nothing against Simo! I'm just trying to sort it out."

"Remember that fact-finding tour the emperor sent Gevulin on? Simo accompanied him for the entire journey and was elevated to captain of Gevulin's personal escort after the prince was appointed as all-seeing eye. Simo doesn't have the backing of a high-status Manor, so he couldn't ever have expected to gain the rank of captain without the prince's support. Not that I think Simo doesn't deserve it. He's one of the best wardens in the order. It's just that the promotion makes him personally beholden to the prince, rather than to the order."

"I heard you've been offered a captaincy twice," said Ipis, "and turned it down both times."

"Three times," said Xilsi flatly, as if the topic annoyed her. "And you can be cursed sure I won't let anyone put that target on my back."

"What target?" Elen asked.

"Maybe I've said too much. It's one of the reasons I Declared for the wardens. And for the road wardens, not the shadow wardens."

"The shadow wardens?"

"Forget I said that. The point is, wardens aren't meant to dabble our toes in the dirty bathwater of palace affairs. But that doesn't mean we only guard the roads. If you think of the roads as the blood vessels of the empire, then we are listeners of a different kind. We listen to the pulse of the empire."

"What does the pulse tell you?" Elen asked, remembering the intendant's fear of spies.

Xilsi peered ahead. They could see the back of the haunt as he sat straight and proud, looking ahead. As if sensing Xilsi's gaze, Luviara turned to look back. Elen raised a cheerful hand. The theurgist answered with a lively wave of her own.

"That one," muttered Xilsi. "I wonder about her."

"Luviara? What do you wonder?" Ipis asked. "She seems harmless. Like a magpie, always looking for treasure. Chirp chirp chirp."

"I wonder a lot of things," said Xilsi. "Crown Prince Minaylin is the only living child of the Magnolia Emperor. He's about the same age as our Kem, here. No longer a boy, and not quite yet a man. The emperor is barely forty, so the crown prince has time to grow and learn, however he may behave now. Still, it's said character shows early. The Lily Emperor would have weeded out such an undisciplined child from the ranks of eligible princes. Instead, the Magnolia Emperor named him as her crown prince when he was only twelve. She could have named one of her younger siblings, like Astaylin or Gevulin. They are competent adults. They survived the strict regimen of their exalted parent, the Lily Emperor. But the Magnolia Emperor didn't name either of her siblings. Instead, she placed them in a position to become rivals. I, for one, wonder if it was deliberate on her part to set them at odds. That, Deputy Courier, is the pulse of the empire."

57

HALF-TOLD LIES AND FRAGMENTS OF TRUTH

When they reached the port of entry at North Flat Vigil, leaving the Pall behind, they grabbed their packs and disembarked from the carriages. The horses were led away to be quarantined before being returned to the roster. A pair of wardens traced the framework of the two carriages with the flats of their shrive-steel swords. The travelers lined up in order of rank to go through the inspection chambers.

Elen went last into a chamber that was paneled, ceiling to floor, with hallow-wood planks. She disrobed and laid out her clothing on a hallow-wood table. The contents of her pack as well: her courier's kit, a change of clothing, a clean pair of socks, pot, bowl, spoon, and knife, menstrual kit, soap and comb and linen towel. She could name the person who had crafted each item, like her one-time lover and regular friend, Baima, who had made the oatmeal honey soap.

A bell rang. The farther door opened. She walked into the next chamber, built entirely of holystone on which Spore could get no purchase. Steps took her down into a bath-like area that made her think of the bath the prince had taken at the Residency. Had the haunt stood here, arms extended decoratively, while a menial poured pure-water through the overhead hatch and onto his head?

Thinking of him, she couldn't help but smile as water showered down from above, drenching her. She'd long been grateful that the touch of pure-water did not sting as the road did. If anything, it coaxed the viper toward slumber. She waited, dripping and shivering. If Spore had lodged itself somewhere about a traveler's body, then it would now slide free to get away from the pure-water.

Of course, they'd been on the road, where Spore never gained purchase. Still, according to the dictates of the Willow Emperor, no exceptions could be made. After all, it was also a good way for the empire to keep track of people's movements and manifests.

The next door led into a changing room, where all her gear had been brought over. She dried off, dressed, packed up her things, and rang a handbell. A menial opened the last door and escorted her down a passageway to the forecourt of the Vigil tower. Here, the Sun Chasers waited with a change of horses and the wardens seated, ready to go. As she clambered up onto the second carriage beside Xilsi, she heard the Vigil captain speaking earnestly by the first one.

"Your Highness, you're sure you won't take a brief repast before you go on?"

"We will not."

Xilsi sighed and muttered, "Astaylin would consider it time well spent to indulge officials for an hour, and certainly over a meal, to sound out their loyalties and offer quiet favors. The exalted Gevulin never waits around for anything or anyone."

The Vigil captain had not yet released the side of the carriage. "Then I must pass on this warning now. There's been trouble nearby."

Simo looked over sharply. "What manner of trouble?"

"Mischief in the hallow-wood plantations. Cutting down saplings. Salting the soil. The troublemakers do their business at night. You'll have to push hard to reach Pelis Manor North by sunset today. There's nowhere else secure where you can halt between here and there."

The haunt marked Elen seated beside Xilsi before turning back to the Vigil captain. "Your warning is noted. Simo, let us proceed."

The gates opened. They swept out of the courtyard, down the avenue, through the gardens, past the moat, and into Woodfall Province. Where Elen had not set foot in fifteen years.

The first thing that struck her was the distinctive spicy-sweet scent of hallow-wood. She'd loved that smell once. Now, it made her uneasy, as if Lord Duenn might burst into view at any instant with a ledger in hand, toting up his riches.

Ipis gave a great sniff. "Is that hallow-wood? I've never smelled it out in the open!"

Kem said, a bit tendentiously, "Hallow-wood forests cover much of the western half of Woodfall Province. In fact, harvesting hallow-wood logs and shipping them to the heartland is the primary source of wealth for Woodfall Province's three meritorious Manors, Lolunn, Czeyi, and—uh—Duenn." He cleared his throat self-consciously, then added, "No one but those Manors is allowed to cut and sell it."

Xilsi shot Elen the look of an elder amused by the antics of the youth. "Are you showing off, Novice Kem?" she said over her shoulder.

"Oh, uh—" He flushed.

"No, it's all right. You've been very patient with Ipis bossing you around for days now."

Ipis snorted. "Like you weren't one of *my* trainers? I learned the bossy method from you."

"That's my girl!" said Xilsi with a chuckle. "You're both all right, you two. Work hard enough, and someday you might become warden captains, like Simo."

"Do you think so?" Kem's expression was eager as he contemplated the prospect of a life far from Orledder Halt.

Elen pressed a hand to her belly, feeling hollow. It was for the best, of course it was, but it was so hard to envision a life without him in it: a flat, silent, empty Pall stretching into an unknown distance.

"Look at all this!" cried Ipis as the carriages rolled past a vast field of recently planted hallow-wood saplings, none taller than Fulmo. The air was redolent of fresh growth. "Which Manor controls this plantation?"

"Likely Pelis Manor," said Xilsi.

"Aren't they one of the Six Noble Manors?" Kem asked. "Why would they be in the provinces?"

"Pelis Manor decided to get involved in the hallow-wood trade. They got imperial permission to open a branch Manor in the eastern half of Woodfall. Pelis Manor North is where we'll halt for the night. If we get there by nightfall!"

After about a league, the landscape began to rumple into gently rolling hills. The young plantations were overtaken by mature forest, thick with black birch, sandy oak, and the occasional white pine. Ground cover flourished: purple thistle, cone-shrub, and the last yellow blossoms of sunspark. As they passed through a wide meadow, the drowsy fragrance of blue sap-bloom struck Elen like a blow. She hadn't smelled sap-bloom since they'd escaped Duenn Manor. Aoving had woven wreaths of sap-bloom to decorate her hair whenever she was called to the lord's chamber for the night. Lord Duenn had thought it was decorative and pretty, but Aoving used the blooms to make him fall asleep faster. It was the kind of hedge healer's knowledge that the wealthy and elegant Manors knew nothing of and thus could not protect themselves against. By such small ways people made life just a tiny bit more endurable, day by day.

Amid fields, a small village appeared, sitting behind a shallow ditch half full of a muddy sludge that barely passed as water.

"Someone is getting sloppy," said Xilsi. "Elen, can you note this down in your transmission log? It needs to be recorded for Map Hall."

"I only have authority to record possible infractions in Orledder Intendancy."

"I don't care about that. Make the report through your intendant. It looks to me like people are getting lazy. Maybe there's been no Spore in recent years, and they think the threat has vanished."

"Maybe Flat Pall is dying," Elen said, "and doesn't have any Spore left to cast into the winds."

"Huh." Xilsi cast her a measuring look. "That's an interesting thought. Go on."

Without mentioning her conversation with the haunt, Elen explained about the surveyor she'd spoken to, the appearance of the Desolation where a Pall had disappeared, and Berri's idea that if Flat Pall was dying then it, too, might simply drain away, leaving empty land behind it, devoid of life, with possibly altered contours, but potentially re-habitable territory.

"An intriguing notion," said Xilsi. "You should train as a surveyor. I'll mention it to Simo, and he can mention it to the exalted highness. Not that Prince Gevulin has any influence over the surveyors, mind you. The Inspector General of the Imperial Order of Surveyors is an old coot, the last surviving sibling of the Hibiscus Emperor, if you can believe it."

"How can that be possible?" Kem asked. "Joef made me memorize all the reign years of the eighteen emperors. The Hibiscus Emperor ascended the Lotus Throne eighty-six years ago."

"Yes, and Prince Darolin was a babe in arms at the time. So would have been about forty when the Hibiscus Emperor died. He must be ninety now. He tried to slap my ass once, the lecher, but I was quicker and I slapped his ass first, which amused him more. But I can bore you for hours with tales of the palace, the more lurid the better."

"Can you?" Kem asked excitedly. "If only Joef were here. He would love it."

Xilsi laughed. "Joef and I would close down the wineshops with our gossiping."

"Is it true the Peony Emperor had three wives and four husbands?" Kem asked.

"Are you referring to the famous sex manuals?"

"Sex manuals?" cried Ipis. "Are there really imperial sex manuals? Kem, you are blushing!"

"This is a subject best left to the classroom," said Xilsi. "Not that I haven't leafed through copies with the greatest interest. I was much intrigued by the turnip sculptures."

Kem awkwardly cleared his throat. Elen puckered up her face so as not to laugh.

Xilsi grinned. "Ask me another one, just not sex manuals or bedroom secrets."

"What about the Scalt War in the reign of the Orchid Emperor?"

"Oho! General Sakor is one of my ancestors!"

"The legendary hero who carried the snake-headed spear?"

"The very one! Let me tell you how he got that spear. It's not in any of the official histories."

The friendly conversation eased Elen's heart. She could manage anything as long as she knew Kem was going to be all right.

Xilsi's story was a long and convoluted tale. When they halted at midday to change horses and use the latrine, Elen switched places with Kem so the lad didn't have to crane his neck to ask yet more questions.

As Elen crammed in beside Ipis, the young warden sighed. "I'm going to die of boredom."

"Don't you like history?"

"No. I like routine. I like knowing all the pieces of each thing we need to do, in the order we need to do it. Histories and chronicles are too messy, bits of truth amid half-told lies. No one agrees on anything."

The words made Elen think of standing on the shore of the Pall beside the haunt. *You are a story,* he had said, as if it were a gift, a treasure. But Ipis was right too: Elen was a messy story, half-told lies and fragments of truth, patched garments and holes she never meant to fill. She had to figure out how to respect Ao's demand that they never speak of the past. Or was it El who had shut that door?

Was it right to offer Kem only scraps? Surely Ao also deserved her son knowing that she'd loved him even when she hadn't always known how to show it, except through criticism. As children, El and Ao had never been warned, never been taught, never been corrected or scolded, never anything, because they were only atoners, sacrifices who would be consumed, sooner or later, by Spore. So why bother?

Warning him, correcting him, scolding him: those were Ao's ways of letting her child know she cared.

The Sun Chasers rolled onward through Woodfall Province. Despite everything—the speed of the carriages, the wardens around her, the viper in her heart—she winced to see the dusky green and orangey-brown dyes of the villagers' clothing, colors she never saw around Orledder. The snatches of local songs and the rhythm of speech of the local dialect made her twitch. She kept looking for people to charge out of the forest on their bull elks and demand she be turned over to the harsh justice of Duenn Manor and Kem dragged off, despite everything. She was grateful they were in the northeast region, far from the southwest where Lord Duenn ruled. She was glad they had left him in Orledder Halt. Let him rant and spew. He was stuck behind the blocked road. The trap had sprung on the hunter instead of the prey.

Late in the afternoon, they passed the wrecked remains of a hallow-wood plantation: young trees hacked down; charred greenwood. It even smelled as if the vandals had taken a shit by the road to show their contempt. About ten laborers were raking debris. They jolted nervously at the sound of the carriages and called out. Three armed men appeared, bows ready. When they recognized the warden banner, they waved the laborers back to work.

"Things aren't looking so peaceful at Pelis Manor North," said Xilsi with an unusually grim frown. "But I guess we're about to find out."

58

The Great Lineages

THE GREAT LINEAGES have always influenced imperial policy and, at times, have dictated the decisions made by the emperor.

In the days of the Seven Golden Kingdoms, these lineages called themselves *clans* and spread their kin and clan-homes widely throughout all seven kingdoms. Thus, as the clans grew in power, it scarcely mattered if a clan member spoke Forsi or Indical, if they wore west country plain-garb or southron glitter-cloth, if Ghorsim was at war with Asdiria. The clans welcomed their own into their clan-homes, no matter where they'd come from or how far they'd traveled. A clan member might be born in the west, with a westerner's accent and name and looks, but would be welcomed in an eastern or southern hall as easily as if she had been born there alongside her clan-cousins.

In this way, the boundaries between the seven kingdoms became blurred. People became more loyal to their clan than to their local king. So the kings began to persecute the clans.

Therefore, when the Lotus Clan rose up to conquer the Seven Golden Kingdoms and create the Tranquil Empire, many of the clans supported the Lotus rebels.

While it is true some venerables among the Heart Temple theurgists warned against the impure ambition of the Lotus Clan, other theurgists were all too happy to aid the general known as the Guardian of the Lotus Fountain, he who was to become the founder of the empire, even if he was never a named emperor. As a reward for their support, the Heart Temple was granted a certain autonomy over internal matters of temple rule, as long as all theurgists served the empire. In exchange, they gifted to the palace full oversight of and authority over the rare and difficult magic known as theurgy.

In its turn, the palace rewarded the loyal clans with one of the benefits of that magic. The palace gave permission for each large clan compound to be invested with and thus protected by one of the earth spirits known as *geniuses,* whose function as guardians of physical buildings is described in more detail within the chapter on Manors. The favored clans were renamed *Manors,* in honor of their grand new domiciles.

It is these Manors who have subsequently provided ministers, magistrates, justiciars, administrators, captains and generals, financiers, councilors, favored consorts, and secret informers to the palace. The foundation of the empire stands upon the bricks and backs of the Manors. No wise emperor forgets that fundamental truth. Woe betide any cunning and ambitious prince who neglects to build and nurture these crucial alliances.

> From *The Official's Handbook of the Empire* as compiled by
> Luviara, theurgist, working at the behest of the
> Inner Chamber of the Heart Temple

59

A FUNNEL CLOUD

Pelis Manor was tucked into a little valley nestled amid a hilly countryside cut with new planting, all under guard. A watchtower stood at the top of a hill behind the manor house. Outbuildings, a small griffin mews, and livestock stockades stood farther out, inside an encircling moat. These included a big rectangular structure that Elen recognized as a sarpa pen, like the one outside Orledder Halt.

The main compound, shaped like a blocky trident, wasn't particularly large or impressive, but it was a Manor all the same, built atop bedrock, into which Spore could get no hold, and linked to the imperial road by a spur of holystone-paved road. The lead carriage halted at the moat. The bridge across was barred by a railing. The militia on guard gave the wardens the appropriate salute for imperial officials. As per protocol, the militia did not speak first. Puzzlingly, their stoic expressions did not change, as anyone might think they would when they found themselves unexpectedly faced with one of the great princes of the land.

The haunt raised a hand languidly to acknowledge their presence.

Luviara stood to speak. "Inform the Manor's lord that His Exalted Highness Gevulin, Prince-Warden of the Imperial Order of Wardens, Exalted General of the All-Seeing Eye, Captain of a Thousand, Adept of the Bow and the Spear . . ."

As Luviara rang down through all the prince's titles, Elen's attention caught on the Manor's burning ground. Its circular pavement of holystone lay about one hundred paces to the left of the bridge. An iron pillar stood at the center of the pavement, with a shrive-steel cage built around it. No burning ground in Orledder Intendancy had been lit since the Wormwood Irruption.

Shockingly, this burning ground held a fresh corpse, collapsed against the pillar to which it had been fastened by wire. Bones peeked whitely from the soot-blackened remains of flesh. There was no sign of incinerated Spore, which often showed up as a crackling ice-like crust that, over several days, would be absorbed by the holystone. The executed individual had not been Spore-ridden, which meant they had been burned to death for a different reason.

Ipis shuddered, her whole body shaking. "That's a Sea Wolf."

Kem gasped as he stared at the grimly contorted remains. "A Sea Wolf! How do you know?"

"The white chain around its neck. They all wear them. The links are carved out of the bones of their ancestors. They don't burn. But why would a Sea Wolf be here?"

"A spy," said Xilsi. "Aivur send the ones who look human enough."

"Where would such a spy have come from? Woodfall Province has got no ports, no beaches, no rivers connected to ocean. No way for them to sail in. It's months of travel to walk all the way from the far west."

"That's what spies do, gather information by risking themselves for months or years in enemy territory," said Xilsi. "Now, hush. Luviara is finally finished. We're going in."

The guards shifted the railing to allow them access over the bridge and into the protected zone. But the forward carriage didn't move. Instead, the haunt jumped down and, signing for the others to stay where they were, paced out to the burning ground. Hands clasped behind his back, he circled the holystone sun-wise, then circled back counter-sun-wise, then walked onto the pavement as everyone stared. What was he doing? No one dared ask.

He opened the cage's door, approached the remains, and knelt an arm's length from their twisted jumble. With a gloved hand, he picked up something from the ground, studied it, then tucked it into a pocket. For a while longer, he crouched in contemplation, then rose and returned to the carriage. Without a word, he climbed back up and waved his fingers to show he was ready to proceed.

"What was that all about?" Ipis whispered.

"Quiet," said Xilsi as they started forward.

What *had* it been about? Kem glanced back, sharing a look, and Elen shrugged. Then he remembered he was mad at her and turned to face forward.

The carriages drove past fields, gardens, and outbuildings. The exterior of the Manor had the look of an old fortress, with high stone walls, palisade and wall walks, towers at each corner, and a reinforced entry gate. The great gates stood open. Simo halted the forward carriage before it. It was customary to wait for the genius to manifest before entering a Manor.

The air beneath the gates began to swirl and grow dark, as if a whirlpool of ash were being sucked through a crack from out of a land of grit and darkness and into the ordinary world. It coalesced into a funnel cloud: the genius of the Manor, a protective spirit called out of stone to guard the compound and its occupants.

A smoky voice spoke out of the ash-colored cloud. "Who seeks entry? What is your business?"

"I am Interlocutor Luviara. My respects to you, Ervis."

"You know my name," the genius rumbled as the cloud seethed, although Elen couldn't tell if the seething was irritation or approval.

"As a theurgist, Honored Spirit, I know the name of every genius."

The funnel cloud's churning slowed with an emotion Elen, again, could not interpret, then returned to its restless swirl.

Luviara took the silence as her cue to go on. "His Exalted Highness Prince Gevulin seeks entry. His party will overnight at the Manor and go on their way in the morning. His business is his concern alone."

"He and his party may pass." The funnel spun apart as if an unfelt wind had torn it to pieces, and the ashy cloud streaked into the stones of the wall and vanished from sight.

Their party crossed under the wall in silence. A Manor was sentient in a way other buildings never could be. It wasn't that the stones were aware; it was the genius bound to the Manor who was aware and ever-present.

Kem whispered, "Joef told me geniuses look like people. Why did that one look like a cloud of ash?"

Ipis said, a bit sourly, "Yeah, I don't think your great good friend Joef knows everything he thinks he knows."

Xilsi looked amused. "Some geniuses do appear in a human form. Just like that Sea Wolf who was executed out on the burning ground, who probably looked perfectly human but is aivur. Well, not just like. Spirits are the breath of the High Heavens, cast upon the lower world. Thus they don't have physical form or physical substance. But they can appear pretty much however they want since their substance is . . . fluid. A genius can observe and hear pretty much anything going on anywhere in the Manor they inhabit, can't they, Honored Ervis?"

A puff of ashy smoke popped in the air about the carriage.

Kem gaped as the wind dissolved it. *"Anything?"*

Ipis laughed. "Yes! Even the privies! And your sex manuals!"

A grinning Xilsi brought the carriage to a stop next to the other vehicle. "Don't mind her teasing, Kem. A genius can't be everywhere at once at every moment. And that's even if they cared to be, which I doubt they do. But naturally Ervis is keeping an eye on us newcomers."

Beyond the gate lay a wide courtyard with three arched entrances. Grooms waited on the left to receive the horses and carriages. Militia stood at attention on the right. On the entry steps of the main building stood the white-haired lord of the Manor, identifiable by a silver circlet and formal sash, from which dangled the keys to the Manor's treasury. She was attended by an interlocutor and a respectful collection of kinsfolk, all wearing Manor embroidery on their sleeves, cuffs, collars, and hems.

Luviara spoke so all could hear. "His Exalted Highness recognizes your presence. You may announce yourself. If the records are correct, you are Lord Genia, known as a woman of wisdom, once tutor to the Magnolia Emperor, and now living in quiet retirement here in the north. Make yourself known."

Assisted by a menial, the lord of Pelis Manor went down on one knee. "Exalted Highness, you are well come. You do me too much honor. I offer my humblest greetings, and pray that our modest hospitality may embrace you as you deserve."

The haunt gave a languid wave. "You may arise, Lord Genia. We've come a long way, and will accept a bath, a meal, and a bed. We depart at dawn tomorrow."

"Of course, Exalted Highness. Your pleasure is my duty. All is in readiness."

"I'm curious," said Luviara. "You don't seem surprised to see us."

"Why should I be surprised, when His Exalted Highness himself alerted me he was coming?" The old woman smiled, relaxing now that the formalities had been observed. "It is good to see you again, Gevulin. I pray you, come inside at once."

Lord Genia not only knew the prince but was well enough acquainted to be casual with him. In an instant, Pelis Manor North no longer seemed like a haven but rather a dangerous trap waiting to be sprung. What if Genia realized the haunt wasn't Gevulin?

60

The haunt made a show of getting down from the forward carriage. Menials rushed to assist, but he waved them off. He turned his attention to the old woman, adopting an unexpectedly confiding manner. He pressed a hand to his chest dramatically.

"Lord Genia, I have had difficulty on my journey. There has even been an attempt on my life."

She nodded sagely. "It is as we feared, Your Highness. Your rival will stop at nothing."

"Indeed," he agreed smoothly. Elen admired the speed at which he could pivot. Her tight breathing settled. "Which message got through?"

"The griffin scout, Your Highness. Then she flew back south to meet you. Are you telling me she never reported in? She seemed a capable individual."

"She was murdered. Her griffin with her. I found the bodies in the Moonrise Hills."

The shock of hearing these tidings fell like lightning upon the gathered people. Who would kill a griffin, those rare and precious creatures? Even sarpa were more commonplace, although harder to control. And the scout, too; an imperial official!

But the Manor-folk weren't the only people who were shocked at the news. Luviara's usual expression of clever confidence spasmed into a look of stunned disbelief, followed swiftly by a flash of anger and then something more calculating. She muttered, "The crossbow bolt at Pisgia Moat," then said nothing more.

Lord Genia leaned heavily on her young interlocutor as she replied in a trembling voice. "Your Highness, I am quite shaken to hear this news. I entertained the scout at my own table, showing her great honor. She was out of Xorras Manor, the great-niece of an old friend of mine, who I served with in the magisterial offices. That was before I retired from the palace to head the hallow-wood operation here, at your gracious mother's urging."

"Such a crime must shake us all," he agreed. "But first, a bath, then supper, after which we shall discuss the whole in a private meeting, you and I. Not out here in front of all."

"Of course. The fault is mine. You are entirely correct that we live in disturbed times."

"I saw the damaged plantation by the road."

"Indeed! It is not the only one that has been attacked. Let you and your wardens be settled and fed." Genia's discerning gaze caught on Elen in her humble garb. "A deputy courier can be sent to the stables. She'll be fed and housed there."

"No. My entire party stays with me, no exceptions. I have not gotten over the shock of being attacked in the Moonrise Hills by militia meant to be loyal subjects of the emperor."

"Attacked! These are shocking tidings, indeed."

"One of my wardens was injured."

"I will myself inspect his wound!"

"Ah. Yes. So you shall. You'll understand why I prefer to keep my people close rather than to risk losing even one."

Lord Genia pressed a hand to her chest. "It seems trouble is stalking farther afield than I had realized. As you say, we can discuss this at more length in private."

The prince was escorted to the imperial bathing suite with Fulmo, Simo, and Luviara in attendance. Elen accompanied Xilsi, Ipis, Kem, and Jirvy to an opulent bathing suite quite at odds with the Manor's modest exterior. It was laid out in a tangle of rooms that included both private and communal washing rooms, a hot-soak room, a steam room, a cold-plunge room, and rooms where folk could be massaged and oiled.

"We never had anything like this where I grew up," said Ipis. "I don't know where to go first."

"Follow me and learn, little cub," said Xilsi with a laugh. "We're a friendly group here, most of us."

She shaded a sneer toward Jirvy. He went aside into a private room, closing its curtains behind him.

"Coward," muttered Xilsi.

Ipis sighed and exchanged a conspiratorially long-suffering look with Kem.

Elen said, "Isn't Lord Genia meant to examine his wound?"

"I suppose she is, and I guess it's best she does," Xilsi agreed grudgingly. "In her youth, she was a surgeon in the army."

They entered a large communal washing chamber with separate

ceramic pipes for cold and hot water, a luxury not available even at the Orledder Residency. Here they stripped and handed their clothing over to menials to be brushed or cleaned overnight. Elen wondered if Kem would show any reserve in front of the others but, of course, they already knew; they'd bathed together at the Halts, so there was nothing to explain. His earlier Declaration had been recorded and sealed by the magistrate two years ago. That was all that mattered to the empire.

Xilsi chased out the menials who had remained behind to assist. They doused each other with water, laughing, and washed with scented soap. There were different fragrances and textures of soap, as if it were ordinary to have so much choice. Kem's eyes were as big as saucers. He kept holding a particular blue-striped bar of soap to his nose.

"What is this? It's got lavender, but something else. Usually I can tell."

Xilsi sniffed, shrugged, then handed the soap to Ipis, who rubbed her nose and sneezed, then hastily handed it to Elen with a muttered, "Too strong for me."

Elen inhaled, and was struck by the hammer of a memory. A hot night when she and Ao had found a secret trove of uncollected bitternuts, that they'd hidden by twisting the nuts into the hems of their hand-me-down tunics. Later, at night, they'd secretly ground down the bitternuts for their nourishing oil. They'd never been caught, although it was a crime to possess them. All had to be turned over to the master, since the oil was valuable.

"Are you all right?" Kem said anxiously.

They were all staring at her as if her face had melted. But as the shock wore off, the situation struck her as funny: all of them naked, dripping, consumed by an interest in soap.

She handed the soap back to Kem and was about to say she couldn't place the scent when he said, combatively, "You recognize it. I can tell."

Xilsi looked between Elen and Kem, curious at the interplay.

"It's bitternut oil," said Elen. "It doesn't grow in Orledder Intendancy, only farther north. But it's rare."

In fact, she'd never found or heard of it in the lands controlled by Duenn Manor, not in the five years she and Ao had lived there. Only in the Nameless Land. In which case, how had it come here?

"The locals claimed it kept Spore away, but I don't know if that's true," she added. Vials of the precious oil had been a common reward to thanes for their service and loyalty. Retainers weren't given oil; they were more likely to be gifted a portion of meat or a still usable wool tunic or a pair of old boots the retainer could call their own. Atoners had nothing of their own.

"I never heard of any oil that keeps away Spore," said Xilsi, still with furrowed brow, as if she'd seen a chink of light where she expected only darkness. "Maybe the theurgist knows, since she seems to know everything."

"Is Luviara allowed to wash up in the imperial baths?" Ipis asked.

"She will be kept close to the prince in case anyone besides Lord Genia has to talk to him, so she won't wash up until after he's had his bath and his dinner and private meeting."

"She'll enjoy the show, at least," Elen said with a chuckle, remembering Luviara's wink during the prince's first bath.

"What show?" asked Ipis.

Xilsi's eyes narrowed. "You two, Ipis, Kem. Get rinsed. Out."

They hastily rinsed off and hustled out. Xilsi sat on a wooden bench and gave her nails a thorough scrubbing with a brush. Elen sat next to her, doing the same. It was a rare treat to have such an abundance of warm water and coarse, clean brushes. Sitting beside Xilsi felt pleasingly comfortable, the way she felt with the local women at the community bathhouse in Orledder.

"Listen," said Xilsi in a low voice, gaze flicking around the empty chamber as if checking for secret hidey-holes or shadow wardens. "I don't know what you and the prince are up to, and I hope it is just about his rivalry with Astaylin. But in case it isn't, you must understand that whatever did or didn't happen with Intendant Berel's good-looking sister, you are too lowborn to be taken into the palace."

Elen laughed merrily.

"What's so funny?" demanded Xilsi.

"Believe me, Xilsi, I have no desire to be taken into the palace. His Exalted Highness hasn't touched me, nor have I touched him, although I admit to you personally, since you and I are friends and comrades . . . we are, right?"

Xilsi smiled, looking so genuinely pleased that Elen wondered how few people the warden had to call friends. Not surprising, perhaps. She didn't make it easy for people. Or maybe she didn't know how to make it easy for herself. "Sure. Go on."

"I did see him naked at the baths at Orledder Residency. Just between you and me, he has a very attractive body, no doubt from all that dancing and running up and down peaks."

"Elen!"

"Yes, it's disrespectful, but I have eyes, and I'm not dead. Anyway, the theurgist saw him, too, and she has eyes, and she's not dead either. So let's never mention it again."

"Huh. I've never seen him naked and I don't want to."

"Why not?"

"For me, it would be a threat."

"How so? Because your grandmother was an imperial consort?"

"Yes. I'm not a menial or a concubine, available for passing sexual interludes. For me to see a prince naked means there is the possibility of a marriage or, if the prince is a sausage, then a pregnancy. That's the last thing I want. But regardless, don't talk about his looks and especially never talk about him being naked. People will consider it disrespectful. And I'm not interested in gossip about him. The prince is not a very pleasant man, you know."

"Ah," said Elen as blandly as possible, biting down on a smile.

"I admit, he's been more pleasant on this journey than I've ever experienced. Maybe being released from the hothouse of the palace has loosened him up. Or maybe when he fainted he hit his head and it affected his mind. But don't think he won't throw all of us into the Pall if he needs to, to get his way. I admire his skill and discipline and intelligence, and he's as fair an official as any I've served under, but he's an ambitious prince, which is a dangerous thing. You heard Lord Genia. There's more going on even than I know."

"Is Lord Genia part of his inner circle?"

"Apparently, she is. Hemerlin would know more. But I sure don't like not knowing what's going on."

The curtain into the chamber rippled. From behind its concealing drape, Jirvy said drily, "Best hurry, His Exalted Highness won't want us to dawdle."

"Fuck off," said Xilsi. Then, in a low voice to Elen, "I hope he didn't hear us."

Elen whispered, "You think he'll rat on us?"

"Jirvy? A rat? Never. I'd bet my life on it. I'm just done with him knowing my private thoughts. I confided way too much to him over the years." Xilsi shook her head, hands clenched in her lap, then, with an effort, relaxed, tossed the used brush into a basket, and dumped a bucket of cold water over her head. "To be fair, he didn't want to come on this mission when he found out I was assigned to it, but he's the best archer in the order. When the all-seeing eye gives a command, we obey. This is the only time you'll hear me say a single nice thing about that motherfucker."

"The prince?"

Xilsi snorted, grinning. "Ha! No, Jirvy. Come on."

In the next chamber, they dried off and dressed in clothing dyed with Pelis Manor's distinctive gray and green. A menial led them into the central part of the Manor. This far north, autumn nights could get quite cold, but the interior was saturated in warmth, heated by multiple brick ovens, showcasing a measure of the Manor's wealth. Elen was sweating by the time they were shown into a dining hall. Here the prince was already seated at the high table beside Lord Genia and what appeared to be several of her relatives, ranging in age from a palsy-ridden, elderly man to a boy of about ten who was too overawed by the prince to eat.

The food was delicious and plentiful. Elen sat with the wardens at a lower table while Simo attended the prince at the high table. Luviara had to be on duty, standing beside the prince's chair. As Xilsi had said, the interlocutor would eat and bathe later, as would Simo. Fulmo wasn't there, as it was now night, but Lord Genia employed a human food taster who sampled each dish before it was offered to the prince.

After the meal, they retired to a parlor where the prince sat in the imperial chair while Genia sat opposite, in the lord's chair. The wardens were brought stools so they could sit as well. Genia dismissed all her people except her interlocutor, a retired general named Murli who was in charge of the Manor's militia, her chief steward, her chief archivist, and a lively young woman who was Genia's granddaughter, recently returned from the capital city and years of training in Pelis's heartland Manor.

"You're Xilsi Bakassar, aren't you?" said the granddaughter, whose name was Worvua.

Jirvy made a soft noise.

Xilsi said, suspiciously, "I am. Why do you ask?"

"You're still famous in the wineshops, if you wanted to know."

"I know what I am," said Xilsi with cool hauteur.

"You are beautiful, just as the songs say," agreed the young woman. "Is it true, what they say about you refusing to enter the Flower Court as a consort?"

For the first time, a spasm of uncertainty twisted Xilsi's usually confident features, as if the memory made her uncomfortable. Her gaze flashed nervously toward the haunt.

He was watching the byplay, as always, and he raised a hand. "You have my permission to gossip another time with my warden, Sar Worvua. For now, I require Lord Genia's report."

The young woman slipped off her stool and knelt, covering her face. "The fault is mine, Your Highness."

He glanced at Elen, and she gave a quick shake of her head. He cleared his throat and flicked his fingers in that way he had, as if brushing away a nuisance of flies. "Gossip is like honey, hard to resist when it lies right out there in the open to be licked up by every tongue. But this is not the place or time. Sit. Sit."

Worvua scrambled back up to a stool as her grandmother gave her a look that would have killed anyone else. "You are gracious, Your Highness."

With another sigh, he rubbed his forehead. "So everyone feels obliged to tell me," he muttered before lowering his hand. "Lord Genia, do you have the message the scout left?"

"It was verbal, Your Highness, according to your usual protocol."

In the company of others, they retained a formal relationship, Elen noted, and she supposed the haunt was glad of it, since it gave him less chance to slip up with someone familiar with him.

"Of course. I am relieved to know my protocol is being followed faithfully." Yet his eyes narrowed in a way that made Elen guess he was annoyed, not relieved. A physical message could have been read for more information about the prince's mission.

Simo said, "The scout must have delivered the message and flown directly toward Orledder Halt, only to be shot down near the ruins of Olludia Halt."

Lord Genia shook her head with a grim frown. "It's so difficult to believe that to be true. A dead griffin!"

"All too true," said the haunt. "Were I ever to find the criminal who murdered that beautiful creature, I would tear them limb from limb."

He rose and took a turn around the room while the others waited in respectful silence. Luviara had her journal out, and she wrote with swift strokes. Her expression had a stony blankness that worried Elen. Why had the haunt said to tell only Ipis and Kem about the dead scout and griffin, not Luviara?

The haunt sat back down. "The scout, too, of course. Appalling treason to murder a loyal servant of the emperor. But that investigation will have to wait until my return to the palace. Lord Genia, tell me of the remains on the burning ground."

"Remains? Ah, that's a strange story, Your Highness. One of my patrols caught a man hurrying south alongside the road. He was not walking *on* the road, which is always suspicious."

The haunt's gaze flickered. Elen thought he was purposefully not looking her way, where she sat at the back of the group.

Genia went on. "The man claimed to be an envoy from a northern kingdom, the name of which sounded like Far Land. There is no such place north of here. A search revealed him to be a Sea Wolf, bearing a Sea Wolf's ancestral chain. Thus, we burned him, according to the dictates of the Magnolia Emperor."

Elen saw the haunt's hand drift to touch the pocket where he'd slipped whatever object he'd picked up from the burning ground.

Luviara said, "Your Highness, if I may."

He waved a hand in agreement.

"Lord Genia, did you inquire at Far Boundary Vigil?"

"I sent a messenger, yes, but the messenger has not yet returned."

"Is the messenger delayed?"

"Now that you mention it, we did expect the messenger back yesterday, but there's been no sign yet. Should I be alarmed, Your Highness?"

"I will endeavor to find the messenger and send them back to you," said the haunt. "To that end, we will sleep now and leave as soon as it is light."

"All will be in readiness at dawn, Your Highness."

"Yes. Is there any other private business you have with me before I go?" he asked.

She indicated the steward. "My clerks have just finished preparing the most recent report from the hallow-wood operations that your gracious mother urged you to sponsor on our behalf, which you graciously did despite the disputes your petition caused in the palace."

"Ah, yes, but for my gracious mother, what would I not attempt?"

Genia smiled indulgently. "You are a famously devoted son. Do you wish to read the report now? A copy has been made for you."

The steward produced a thick scroll.

The haunt's look of alarm was not feigned. "I shall peruse the report on the journey. Is there anything else?"

She exchanged a glance with her granddaughter, who rubbed a shoulder as if touching an old bruise. "As it happens, Your Highness, there is. It touches on this matter of hallow-wood plantations."

"Do you know who is burning and despoiling them?"

"We don't know for sure, but we have our suspicions about who might be behind it. Lord Duenn can't like that we are setting up extensive hallow-wood operations that will compete with his once the trees are mature. And there's more to the matter even than that. On behalf of my son-in-law, who is away from the Manor, I received an overture from Duenn Manor for a marriage alliance between Lord Duenn's eldest son and our dear Worvua."

"Refuse it," said the haunt.

Genia blinked. "I did not expect such a swift and declarative answer."

"You must refuse it," he repeated, sounding heated.

The granddaughter relaxed, a smile flashing. "Grandmother, I told you that's what Father would have said if he had been here." The smile shifted from relief to one of sour amusement. "Instead of out hunting, as usual."

"Worvua! Do not interrupt." Genia inclined her head to the prince. "As you wish, Your Highness. That is my preference, regardless."

"You did not feel able to refuse outright?" asked the haunt with a smile meant to coax out more information.

"Naturally, Lord Duenn's overture was unwelcome since Duenn Manor is only a meritorious Manor and shouldn't expect to marry into a noble Manor like ours. It would have been easy to refuse outright had Prince Nwelin been in residence instead of out hunting. I could simply have forwarded his princely edict. No one can contest that! However, for myself, as newly appointed lord of a small branch Manor that was only established fifteen years ago, it is not so simple to summarily reject the offer, given the wealth and power Lord Duenn wields here in Woodfall Province. Since I had no princely edict to offer, I chose for the time being to hedge my bets, if you will forgive such a common turn of phrase."

"A hedge acts as a fence," the haunt murmured. Elen could practically see his mind turning over the phrase, trying to grasp its meaning.

Genia had gone on, however, her emotions running in a high simmer. "Besides that, I have received gossip from my brethren in the heartland that Duenn Manor is hitching its carriage to horses pulled by Prince Astaylin. It is said Prince Astaylin has spoken critical words about the crown prince."

"Is it said thus!" the haunt exclaimed, with a sardonic smile.

"The emperor cannot look kindly upon those who criticize her child and heir."

"One would think not," he agreed.

"Well, your firm answer gives me the means to decline the Duenn offer at once. I'll send a messenger with appropriately dismissive gifts. My thanks, Your Highness."

"What a relief!" breathed Worvua, pressing a hand to her heart.

Genia smiled dotingly on the young woman, then addressed the haunt again. "As for the morning, I can assemble a force of militia to send onward with you."

"No, we shall continue on as we have done. I intend to move without alerting the countryside. A troop of soldiers will slow us down if they cannot change out their mounts at every stop, as we can. That is, if the road's services are being maintained here."

"Your Highness!" It was clear she took offense at the suggestion but could not say so. "All will be in order as you proceed. The road that lies within the purview of Pelis Manor is well-guarded and maintained."

As he rose, he smiled as if in jest, but his hand again brushed his pocket as he said, "I shall remember you said so."

The prince was escorted to the imperial suite. Elen was sent to the barracks.

She asked around and found a militiaman willing to walk her up the stony path to the watchtower, a steep and invigorating climb in the cold night air.

Torges was a flirt. "We call this the snogging tower," he said, but with a wink to make it clear he wasn't applying any pressure.

Elen gave him a friendly smile. "Another time, I hope! I heard you can see an inlet of Pall from here."

"Yes! Even at night."

They greeted the guard on duty at the base of the elaborate wood construction and ascended by ladder three stories to the watch-platform. A militiaman draped in a heavy winter cloak was pacing in the brisk wind. He seemed happy to crouch in a sheltered corner to warm up with a smoke of sharp-leaf while Elen scanned the landscape.

Torges pointed out the sights. "There's the griffin mews, rebuilt two years ago. The sarpa pen is off there. You can just see the roof, with the white tiles. You'd be surprised that we get sarpa through here every season, but that's because of Prince Nwelin—he's long had an interest in sarpa." Before Elen could ask more about Worvua's absent father, the militiaman kept going. "Livestock corrals over there, well away from feasting griffins and sarpa acid. You know how it is. And . . . There! Do you see the inlet?"

Off to the northeast, though not so far away, she caught sight of a pearly gleam, like a thread woven out of moonlight twisting through a dark countryside.

"It's eerie how it shows up at night," Torges said.

"Do you fear it might come this way?"

"Sometimes I do! I swear to you, it's like a sluggish giant viper headed for the-High-Heavens-knows-where. Some say it's got a mind of its own. Me, I think it's hemmed in by the hallow-wood saplings the lord's been planting, our thanks to her good governance. What do you think?"

"Pall usually rises on lower ground. If a stream can't flow from there into this valley, then this Pall isn't likely to either."

"I didn't think of it like that. I guess that's why you're a deputy courier and I just stand guard with as much curiosity as an old stone." He offered her a swig from a leather bottle filled with alcoholic cider.

She drank, and he laughed when she winced at its vinegary tartness. "Did Surveyor Berri stop by here?" she asked.

"Yes, he was here, off and on for over two months. Got drunk every night and walked out to map every morning with a hangover. I'm surprised Spore didn't eat him up. Half the time he was stumbling over his own feet. It's a lonely life, being a surveyor. I'd hate it. No wonder he drank too much."

"I met him on the road here. He told me this inlet runs all the way north to Far Boundary Pall. That it flows out of Far Boundary Pall."

"That's what he told Lord Genia, may she live long. She had this watchtower built so we can keep our eyes on it, day and night."

"Not to watch for bandits or enemies? People sneaking around at night to burn hallow-wood?"

"That, too. We'll beat the shit out of them when we catch them, may they be cursed to the hell of knives." He rubbed his hands together to warm them, then went to crouch next to his comrade and take a smoke.

Elen stood at the railing, watching the thread of Pall. It lay like a ribbon against the earth, oddly beautiful. But the most disturbing part was that, seen from a distance and just as Torges had said, it reminded her of the color and gleam of her viper.

61

A Pinch of Jealousy

At dawn, the entire household of several hundred people assembled to pay their respects. As they approached the waiting carriages, the haunt managed to walk briefly beside Elen and, in a low voice, said, "Find out how far we have to go, how many stops along the way. And so on."

She gave no acknowledgment but made sure to climb up beside Xilsi on the driver's bench, leaving Kem and Ipis in back, again. Which was fine, because the two young ones were digging excitedly into a pouch a menial had given them that contained non-astringent soap, linen menstrual cloths and papyrus plugs, a small hallowwood bowl for washing out, and dried ginger root to make a tisane for cramps.

"With you and the deputy courier along I thought we would run out of supplies," said Ipis to Kem. "What a lovely gesture on the part of the Manor. I think that fancy Worvua has a crush on Xilsi."

Xilsi's jaw tightened but, before she could snap back, Elen said, "Too much pie," which made the warden grin.

The morning was cold, and clouds crowded the northern horizon with the threat of rain or sleet, but it was cheering to be on the move.

Elen asked, "How close are we? A day? Two days? Ten days? Will there be stages all along the route? It seems strange there would be."

"Why?" asked Xilsi.

"Because Far Boundary Vigil is the end of the road. Surely people don't go there very often."

"They don't. A terminus Vigil doesn't even have a full complement of wardens. There's no port of entry, so all they do is keep an eye on the Pall. The staff there is six wardens, twelve menials, and one Vigil captain."

"Isn't the Vigil captain a cohort friend of yours?" Ipis asked.

"Yes."

Ipis said, to Kem, "I told you so," and then, to Xilsi, "I thought end-of-road Vigils went to old-timers who couldn't handle anything more strenuous."

"Mekvo got injured in the east. Far Boundary Vigil is a quiet place to recover. He sends me letters about how he goes fishing and berry picking. He even caught three hatchling sarpa."

"There are sarpa in the north?" Kem asked. "Joef says—"

"Here we go," drawled Ipis.

"—they are desert creatures and need hot sand to hatch their eggs. Is that wrong?" he finished, sounding defensive.

"No argument from me," said Xilsi. "Maybe Mekky was just pulling my leg. Sarpa scare the fuck out of me, and that's with them being on our side. Or, at least, sarpa riders claim they can control them. I would rather face one of the giant spiders the Blood Wolves ride. Well. Maybe not. Anyway, Elen, to answer your question, if we were still in the palace carriages, we could reach the Vigil by dusk today. Since we aren't, I figure three days, depending on the quality of the horses we get the farther north we go. Today we'll get good replacements because we'll be in Pelis Manor territory. But after that we'll be back in a regular intendancy under backwater provincial rule. According to Mekvo, there's not much up here except poor farmers growing oats, rye, and turnips, and shepherds with endless flocks of sheep."

They drove for most of the day in silence. The gloomy weather weighed heavily. Kem didn't even ask for stories. The forest ran on and on through rolling hills thick with trees. The distinctive sweet-sour aroma of hallow-wood acted as a balm to restless thoughts. Hallow-wood protected against Spore, and it also soothed, so Ao had often said. She would add shavings of hallow-wood bark to tisanes to help people through labor. Not because it eased the pain, she'd told Elen, but because it made the pain easier to bear.

Or maybe the wardens weren't talking because, the closer they got to their destination, the more guarded and anxious they became. No one knew what they would find there, or even what the prince *expected* to find. The dead Sea Wolf, who had claimed to be an envoy from a "far land," complicated the situation. Could it be possible the Sea Wolf was the same "envoy" who had arrived at the Vigil? Had he murdered everyone there before setting off south? Probably Xilsi was worried for her friend, on top of everything else.

They changed horses twice that day. Elen used the first change-off to whisper Xilsi's information to the haunt. Healthy, well-kept pacers allowed them to make such good time that, in early afternoon, they passed a small Halt at the edge of Pelis Manor territory but continued after a change of horses. The haunt was ruthless in pressing on.

At sunset, the Sun Chasers rolled into Norvest Halt. The intendant wasn't in residence, they were informed by an overawed official, preferring an easterly town by a lake, about half a day's ride away.

No change of carriage horses was available so, in the morning, they had to proceed with the same teams from yesterday. A pair of riding horses, not yet saddled, had been brought out as well, drawing puzzled looks from the wardens.

The haunt leaped up onto the driver's seat of the forward carriage, taking the reins before Simo could.

"Your Highness!" Simo protested.

"I'll drive. The deputy courier may ride with me. Simo, you will drive the other carriage with Jirvy, Luviara, and Kem. Xilsi and Ipis will ride."

"Ride, Your Highness?"

"They can better guard us from horseback."

Simo's mouth twitched as if he disagreed. "Of course, Your Highness. But Ipis is still young, on her first full patrol, and it might be better if she—"

"Is she not trained in bow craft and sword craft?"

"She is, but—"

"Is Jirvy completely healed? His injuries no longer troubling him?"

"Not entirely, but—"

"Therefore, do as I say. Deputy Courier, attend me."

Elen stowed her pack in the wire frame and climbed up beside him. Before her butt could even touch the bench, he set the horses forward. They were good goers, as Xilsi had said. They rolled through the small Halt's central street as folk stared at this wonder, a prince driving an open carriage for all to see. A ramp led them up on the road, headed north. Elen looked back to see the other carriage a good ways behind.

"You caught them by surprise."

He said nothing, his gaze on the horses. The light of the rising sun fell on the side of his face, a sheen that made his complexion gleam like polished bronze. His mouth looked prim, disapproving, but those lips held promise, as if the right words would loosen their tight lines into the mischievous smile that delighted her. She studied his fly-whisk braids, now remarkably neat and tidy, looking quite splendid and noble as they dangled pleasingly past his shoulders, swaying with the motion of the carriage.

"Did someone at Pelis Manor rebraid your hair?"

A hint of color shaded his cheeks. "My scalp was itching. Yet I could have endured even that, until I saw myself in a mirror. I couldn't bear how flyaway and disorderly everything looked."

"High Heavens above, that would ill-serve the world for you to be seen one day longer in such a terrible state."

The jest teased out a hint of that smile. "Had you not guessed before? I am a callow creature who loves nothing more than to see the shine of my wings."

"Who did it?" she asked, thinking of the good-looking and well-dressed granddaughter, Worvua, who had the calm confidence of a highborn scion, one who knew the way of the world and wasn't desperate to ingratiate herself. That quality could be very attractive to someone who tired of false praise and clumsy attempts to climb into his bed. Maybe Worvua was now eligible to become a palace consort.

The haunt's smile slid headlong into rascal, or maybe smugness. A smug rascal. "Can it be I hear a pinch of jealousy in your tone?"

Is that what this tight feeling in her chest was? By the High Heavens, this would not do!

Elen gave a sniff of disdain. "It is no business of a deputy courier who braids a prince's exalted hair."

"Indeed, it is not." His gaze flashed to her, then back to the road and the horses. "But I'll tell you anyway. It was the lord herself, Genia. She has a deft hand with braids, I'll tell you that. It appears she is the one who arranged for Hemerlin to be assigned to the prince's household, back when Gevulin was a child. Rather than being a menial assigned to the palace and thus belonging to the emperor, Hemerlin's devotion was therefore transferred solely to the child."

"That's quite a gift. How did that come about?"

"In an agreement with the prince's mother, the Elegant Consort."

"Genia and the Elegant Consort are kin?"

"Yes, as it turns out, they are. By marriage, not by blood. I had to figure out the truth between Genia's words, because the prince clearly knows the whole. The prince is famous in the palace for his devotion to his mother, who is the architect of his rise."

"How does Lord Genia fit into this?"

"From what hints I caught, Genia and the Elegant Consort's mother—"

"Gevulin's grandmother?"

"Yes. They were intimate friends in their youth. Lovers, most likely. Genia stands in some measure as a nest guardian."

"Like a great-aunt, only without the blood connection."

"The relationship explains Pelis Manor's allegiance to Gevulin."

"She wasn't at all suspicious of you? If she knows the prince so well?"

"I asked her more questions than she asked me. The price of hallow-wood. How the harvest has been. The health of her people. How she likes living in Woodfall Province. She was eager to be listened to."

"People usually are."

"When she did get around to asking me questions, I said I had a headache."

Elen laughed. "This journey has been quite a headache for the prince."

"For the prince, perhaps," he murmured, eyes on the road, "but not for me."

She didn't know what to say to that, but she felt his presence keenly beside her on the bench, a bare hand's breadth separating their bodies. It was so hard not to touch him, to test the strength of his arm, the curve of his shoulder, the pressure of his leg.

Instead, she looked back. Fulmo was loping along about one hundred paces back, in the middle of the road, so the second carriage could not pass him. Either he was oblivious, or he was keeping the carriages apart on purpose. Xilsi and Ipis hadn't yet appeared. How long did it take for horses to get saddled?

"I'm surprised you took this chance," she said. "The others find it very odd when you show me preference. The only reason they're not suspicious of you is because they have no idea you could even exist."

"It doesn't matter, you see," he said in a dull tone.

"How can it not matter? It's playing with fire. You saw the corpse on the burning ground. Even an emperor would be chained to the iron pillars and burned if they were found to be contaminated by Spore. That's how the Mallow Emperor died. How much more likely a haunt, who people will fear is tainted by an ancient and evil sorcery?"

His hands tightened on the reins, but he forced them to relax before the horses took the wrong measure of his mood. "I can already feel it. Can't you?"

"Feel what?"

"Far Boundary Pall. I couldn't feel Flat Pall until we reached it. Even then when I drew my hand through the mist, I felt nothing, just ashes. Don't you see?"

He swallowed, and the movement of his throat became the most interesting thing in the world. The stubborn tilt of his chin. His willow-leaf eyes were brown, as deep as any mystery, and his frown made him look angry, but it wasn't anger. When he spoke again, his voice had turned harsh.

"It doesn't matter what they think. I will be leaving, departing this body to go into the Pall. Then the prince can deal with their questions. I'll be gone."

She choked, unable to speak.

Gone.

He shifted on the bench as one might adjust to the jostling of any swift-rolling carriage. By doing so, his thigh came to rest along the length of hers, the warmth of his flesh pressed against the cool line of hers. It wasn't a caress. It was just two people seated close on a narrow bench. That was all.

But it was everything. It was what he could give her.

She said hoarsely, "What are you, really? If you name yourself Gesavura'alalin, and we remove Gevulin, then are you not Sara'ala? Who were you before? Who will you become, when you depart the prince's body?"

His smile was a brush of sorrow. "I was a feckless, vain, charming fellow. And very handsome, I assure you. Everyone said so."

She laughed, as he meant her to.

"After the wars, some were ordered to enter the ranks of the Shorn. They obeyed because our circumstances were desperate. Others volunteered out of duty, or because they had noble hearts who sought only to serve by saving us from the Shivering Tide and the Hollow Wind. But I, El, I did it on a lark. Because I was bored. Because everyone was praising those who volunteered, and I wanted to be praised too. For a long time, trapped in the Spires, I regretted my choice. I panicked at being trapped. But we were all taught a calming spell, one to take away pain for a time, to ease the heart. That got me through the desperate patches."

"Oh. Is that what you use to put people to sleep? And on Jirvy, at Grinder's Cut?"

"Indeed. Clever of you to see the link. It allowed him to walk without pain for a time."

"I thought it was a healing spell."

"I cannot heal another's body."

"Can you heal your own?"

He shrugged. "That is part of what I am. Wings, shine, and all the rest."

"A dragon," she breathed wonderingly. She did not make it a question.

A faint smile ghosted his face, then faded. "In the Spires, in those bad times, the spell would ease my heart enough to get through it. Even so, for a long time I despaired and even lapsed into lethargy. Eventually I became resigned. Then, a stupid young human man came to the Spires and thought he was sparring with a ghost, and my comrade—"

"Your comrade? Oh, you mean the statue standing opposite you?"

"Yes. The human man hadn't heard of passage spells, of the Shorn, of our history, of any of it. Which was a shocking realization for the likes of me, I'll tell you. Thinking I would be trapped there forever because the world had forgotten who we are and what we meant for the safety of all. He could scarcely volunteer to aid us, as we'd been promised would happen, if he knew nothing of us or our selfless calling."

"You'd been promised that people would remember."

"Yes. But my comrade was not so dull-witted and shocked as I was. She had the wit, and the lack of honesty, to twist her words so as to get the lad to agree to the passage spell. That's how she left in his body. I don't even know what became of her. By the time the prince arrived, all I could think about was that I too could get out of the prison I agreed to walk into."

"You tried it on me and Kem!"

Without smiling, he said, "I admired you for refusing, although I didn't know you then. And now, here we are."

She shifted restlessly, overcome by an unexpected emotion blended of bright hope and cruel loss. "What about your duty? What about the bell?"

"I am doing my duty. I seek the source of the bell so as to discover if some wicked meddler has unearthed the secrets of sorcery and is trying to raise the dreaded sorcerer-kings back into the world. Perhaps I may even discover if there are others of my kind who are awake and abroad on the same task, if they heard what I heard. But I fear I can only find those answers in a living Pall. If nothing else, perhaps I can come to understand what these Palls truly are. What it means that they have risen into the world at this time. There's so much I don't know."

He fell silent. The horses clipped along. The wheels rolled on and on. The landscape was mixed woodland and grassland.

"What *do* you know?" Elen asked breezily, to lighten the mood.

His smile grew wry, even bitter.

"I know the world is beautiful," he said softly. "That's what I didn't understand before. My petty grievances and useless envies flew alongside me, wrapped tightly around me. I was charming when I needed to be, and sulked when I didn't get my way. Only after I endured all those generations, locked in the Spires, did I realize I had never appreciated all the tiny miracles of living. The astonishment that is a tree. The simple pleasure of being amazed by the sky. Dazzled by the wonderment that surrounds us. Why do you already understand this, El? How are you so wise? How can you see the best in things? Take a hopeful view? Smile because of a raindrop? Laugh at the bounding of a rabbit into the brush? Love the boy without asking anything in return?"

"Maybe a little in return," she said. "Love can be selfish. He's so mad at me right now."

"Less mad than you fear," he remarked.

Sharply, she said, "What do you know?"

"He watches you more than you realize. As if he's trying to figure out how to put back together a shattered pot. Or is that too humble an example?"

"No, no, it's a wonderful example. A pot is a fine and precious item. It can store grain or oil, carry water or vinegar, be peed in, if need be! So many uses! How could I possibly scorn a humble pot? Our lives are immeasurably better because of humble pots."

"See, there it is. Before, had any compared me to a humble pot, I'd have huffed and puffed and flown away in a great, simmering sulk. But you see the gift in it. You smile to hear it. Why?"

"I don't know."

She settled her hands in her lap as an old memory rose.

Glancing at her, he said, "You do know. You have an idea, anyway."

She pressed a hand to her chest, feeling the viper stir. Years ago, she had bundled up her memories of her childhood and packed them neatly away into a chest; not a real chest, of course, but one that the viper wrapped around as a seal. It had been the best way forward at the time. Ao had never been able to let go of the past. Memory and fear had nipped at Ao's heels all her life, had given her nightmares, abrupt gusts of stormy sobbing, stretches of weary calm; had given her love for a child who Ao adored and yet in whom she also saw the man who had assaulted her repeatedly. How did a person live with so many contradictions?

"I do know," she admitted. "I know exactly when it happened."

How strange it was to feel a sense of relief at speaking those simple words. To know he wanted to know. That he cared. That he saw her not as the stubbornly fearless sister who protected, the capable aunt who guarded, the intelligent young woman who reminded a grief-stricken old man of his lost daughter, the friendly deputy courier who asked the humblest people how they were and listened to their answers while saying so little about herself. He saw *her*. He saw El.

His silence was invitation. She had guarded herself for so long. It was astonishing to realize the warm feeling in her heart was the daring presumption of hope. She could tell him.

She could tell him, and he would honor her truth.

"Your Highness!" The shout came from behind them.

62

TOO MANY BLANK SPOTS

The haunt gave a soft groan, but it was too late. The two riders cantered up, having caught them at last.

In the countryside, grassy meadows were interspersed with isolated copses, the trees clustered about ponds or along streams. No hallow-wood grew here. Instead, the open ground was dotted with flocks of sheep. Shepherds shaded their eyes to stare at the distant road and the passing carriages and riders.

"So many sheep!" Ipis exclaimed with a big, broad grin.

Xilsi looked annoyed. For the first time, she spoke tartly, exactly like a woman who has grown up so assured of her status in the world that she might even think to scold a prince. "Your Highness, if we are to guard you, it means we must ride alongside and ahead of you to make sure you are not turned into a pincushion by bandits hiding behind bushes or setting an ambush in that copse up ahead."

A sulky grimace flashed across his face. Was this a glimpse of the self-centered personality he claimed to have had before he had become one of the Shorn, stuffed away by a spell to await his chance to walk again in the world?

"Can no one get an hour of privacy in this benighted world?" he muttered.

"I beg your pardon, Your Highness," said Xilsi in a sharp tone. "I missed that."

Hastily, Elen said, "Where do we stop next?"

Xilsi waved at Ipis to ride ahead to scout a copse growing next to the road, while she settled her mount into an easy trot beside the carriage, allowing her to converse without shouting. "The last Halt on the road. On the map, it's called Urwine Halt, but Mekvo says the locals call it Sheep Bladder Halt."

"Sheep Bladder Halt?" Elen glanced at the haunt, who had fixed a haughty look upon his handsome face. He made no attempt to enter the conversation. He seemed genuinely upset that their private exchange had been so rudely interrupted, even if Xilsi was right.

"There's got to be a story behind that!" Elen urged.

"Indeed, there must be," drawled the haunt sardonically.

"Ah, well," temporized Xilsi, "it was just a local story Mekky wrote to me, because he knows I love a good tale."

"I am eager to hear it," said the haunt, clearly still annoyed at the interruption, but knowing he couldn't chase Xilsi off without arousing even more questions.

"Of course, Your Highness. There's a large river that runs north, eventually through the Pall and into the northern ocean, I believe, all of that out of our reach now. Here in the Woodfall Province, the lands east of that river used to be the most populous in the region, rich with farming, fishing, and quarries. Before the Pall, farmers brought their produce to Urwine Halt, which had a bustling market. One year there were catastrophic rains that washed out the only bridge. People had to float their produce and grains across on sheep bladders to get to market. The name stuck."

Elen scanned the countryside. She saw not a single habitation. "It doesn't seem very populated now."

"When a Pall covered all that northern region, the trade died out. A few people still live in the Halt, farmers and shepherds and such, but besides a magistrate, it's not even got a Warden Hall."

"It must have a Heart Temple," said Elen.

"Yes, according to our maps. That's where we'll stay."

The haunt said, "If we push through, we can reach Far Boundary Vigil today."

"Not before sunset, Your Highness."

"We are safe on the road, even at night."

"If there is a change of horses available."

"We'll push through," he said. "I am alarmed that Lord Genia's messenger never returned. I am alarmed we have heard nothing from Captain Mekvo himself. Are you not alarmed for your comrade, Xilsi?"

She was silent for a stretch, then said somberly, "It's why I volunteered for this mission, Your Highness."

He looked at her with a flicker of amusement in his eyes. "What, not for me?"

She frowned. "Your Highness, can it be that the deputy courier has taught you how to make a joke?"

"Alas, I fear not. I am quite an unhumorous fellow."

Xilsi looked astonished, then puzzled, then cast a searching glance at Elen.

She offered her sweetest smile in return. "I told His Exalted

Highness that humor is like honey, known to catch more flies than does vinegar."

The haunt said drily, "Are you comparing my loyal wardens to flies?"

Here, now, as they approached the end of their journey, with her heart singed and a powerful anger surging in her breast—it was so unfair!—she gave in to her worst impulse.

She said, "Not at all, Your Highness, for your wardens are skilled and trustworthy individuals who willingly follow their all-seeing eye, regardless of how their prince general treats them. I was thinking, instead, of all the interested parties a prince must convince were he to wish to change the nature of his circumstances. A man who wields wit strikes me as far more persuasive than one who merely has a golden rod stuck up his ass to make him stand tall, as well as the means to allow his servants to whip those who get in his way."

"Deputy Courier, you are out of line!" Xilsi barked the words. Her horse shied, startled by the shift of tension in the warden's body.

The haunt saw it all. "Out of line she may be, Xilsi, but is she wrong?"

Xilsi bottled up her anger. "Everyone respects you, Your Highness."

"Yes, but they don't like me."

Xilsi said nothing.

"That's an answer," he said with a mocking smile. "Is it better to be loved, or to be powerful? I ask you."

"Who are you asking?" Xilsi retorted, another unexpected reproof. "A Bakassar heir or this deputy courier who has not even one ancestor to her name she has ever mentioned?"

"I thought we were friends," said Elen, taken aback.

"Of course we are friends!" snapped Xilsi. "I can still be mad at you. You shouldn't have said it."

"Because I'm not highborn?"

"Because a prince will be executed on the burning ground for the least whisper of treason against the emperor. All of us who ride with him will be executed alongside him if we are found to be complicit. That's what you don't understand! Forgive me, Your Highness."

"There is nothing to forgive," he said mildly. "Are you wrong, Xilsi?"

"No, I am right, as you know perfectly well. Don't think I haven't guessed the purpose of this mission, even as I've kept my mouth shut. A mysterious envoy can't have come as a surprise to you, nor would you have hastened north if you didn't know what it might mean. If Mekvo has gotten mixed up in your trouble, then I need to help him. It's exactly the kind of reckless thing he would do."

"Treason against the emperor?"

"Not against the emperor. She's a harsh taskmaster for harsh times, except for her one weakness."

"Which is?" Elen asked, curious to see what a Xilsi in this mood would spill.

"Everyone knows the crown prince is unsuitable. Everyone except his mother, the emperor. So, the palace and the Manors are forced into a corner. They must back you, Your Highness, or they must back Prince Astaylin, in the hope that one or the other will rise in the emperor's esteem. Yet, at the same time, they must be seen in every public way to support the crown prince. That must be why the griffin scout was murdered. Prince Astaylin knew you were going north and wanted to block you. But why north? That's what I didn't understand. Far Boundary Vigil is a dead end. What is there that matters so much? Who is the envoy, and what does it mean? I finally asked Simo point-blank this morning after you raced away. He refused to answer. I think not even he knows."

"No one knows," said the haunt with a smile that Xilsi no doubt saw as the smug triumph of an ambitious, arrogant man who has kept a treasonous plot hidden all this time. But Elen knew it was genuine amusement on his part. He was simply telling the truth.

No one knew, if the prince hadn't told them. No one knew, because the haunt had no access to the prince's thoughts or memories.

Except Elen was finally starting to put the pieces together herself. A race to a terminus Vigil, past which lay no land but only an ocean of Pall. Or so people thought.

But a nameless land did lie beyond the Pall. A land filled with too many people in a too-small country; with too many soldiers whose masters fought endless, if small, wars with each other and with the raiders—the Sea Wolves—who harried the stormy coast. As a child, she'd not understood what it all meant, only that soldiers did not kill atoners in skirmishes because atoners were needed as bait for Spore. If a master was killed, their atoners were captured and put to work for a new master. In a way, she and Ao had been lucky. Their lives could have been much worse.

Luviara fit into the prince's puzzle, too, but Elen couldn't figure out how. She was missing too much information. Her map had too many blank spots.

Ahead, by the copse of trees, Ipis shouted an all clear. Behind, Fulmo began to close the gap between him and the prince's carriage. The second carriage kept pace with the gagast.

The horses trotted onward. The haunt handled the reins deftly. Had he learned by watching Simo, or had he some kind of unconscious access to the prince's physical muscular memory, as in the way he held out his arms so people might wash, and admire, his body?

Now, he said, "Why else would Prince Astaylin send Lord Duenn to spy, hinder, burn hallow-wood, and worse? Why murder a valuable scout and a rare and wondrous griffin? Why would an archon at an isolated lake town take such a bold chance against a prince, knowing the punishment for failure would be death? So you can see, Xilsi, given all this, why a prince like myself would be keen to reach the Vigil in haste, tonight. Especially since we have strong horses who can make one long last run."

Xilsi frowned. Considered. At length, she bent, making a bow from the saddle. "Your Highness. It shall be as you command."

63

THE LAST VIGIL

They arrived at Sheep Bladder Halt in midafternoon, having pushed the horses hard all day. Traffic into the Halt was unusually heavy, people arriving from its hinterlands aboard wagons piled with homely goods. They reminded Elen of birds flocking to winter nests, since a Halt was the safest place to hunker down through a cold northern winter.

The very young and excessively flustered provincial magistrate knelt in terror to see a prince. Hands covering his face, he confessed that the Residency had been partitioned into apartments for the winter season. Worse, the imperial suite was shuttered, since no one dared live in rooms meant for a prince. Dust lay so thick on its covered furniture that it was entirely unsuitable even to lay out a passing meal. Only death, he croaked, would be a suitable reward for his dereliction of duty.

"The fault is mine." He cringed, awaiting punishment.

"We need only change horses, so make haste," said Simo to the trembling magistrate.

Luviara stood back by the carriage, not speaking, even though speaking was her duty. Elen hadn't heard a single word from the interlocutor since Pelis Manor North.

The magistrate offered a pair of carriage horses, as well as his personal mount, and the riding horse left by the Pelis messenger a few days earlier, which had not been collected because the messenger had yet to return. The haunt paced as the town was scoured for more horses. Several locals brought mounts to the residency.

Elen had to act as interpreter because none of the heartlanders could understand the local dialect, not even Luviara. Elen slid easily back into the Woodfall Province rhythm and cant.

In the end, they found no more carriage horses but were able to commandeer two more decent riding horses. They had to leave one of the Sun Chasers behind. Jirvy declared himself fit to ride. Elen took the other horse because she sensed the haunt did not want to ride. The closest he ever came to any of the horses was while seated on the driver's bench. Any time he got too close otherwise, the beasts flicked their ears nervously.

As for her, horses did not love her, but they didn't hate her either. They seemed to sense the existence of the viper but, because they could not see any slithering movement, they did not associate it with Elen, not as dogs often did, which was why dogs avoided her. She asked to ride a phlegmatic older mare who seemed unlikely to balk and, on this sturdy mount, rode directly behind the carriage. Fulmo and Jirvy took the rearguard, with Ipis and Xilsi in the vanguard. They pushed on as the sun sank into the west.

The countryside got flatter. Oxbow lakes suggested a great river had once wound westward through this region. Perhaps it now flowed beneath Far Boundary Pall.

As the sun set, Fulmo's steps slowed. He fell behind as the light faded.

"Your Highness, shouldn't we halt?" Xilsi asked.

The haunt glanced back. Fulmo had come to a stop in the middle of the road, stiff as a statue, head upturned toward the night sky, frozen by the stars.

"No. He will follow once the sun rises. Nothing physical can harm him, so he is in no danger."

They left the gagast behind, his motionless figure vanishing in the gloom.

Darkness descended but for the delicate witchery of the road itself, barely more than a will-o'-the-wisp glow and usually only visible on moonless nights. In the nameless land, there had been a road that gleamed like this at night. As a child, she'd been told the road was a holy avenue, reserved for masters, they who were anointed by the white-haired god to stand above all other people.

Riding along the witch road now, she was grateful for its magic. It was dangerous to walk abroad at night because one could not see Spore growing out of plants, could not spot hollows where fresh Pall had gathered as tendrils of deadly mist—not until it was too late. The road's glamor reminded her of moonlight, comforting and gentle, offering a helping hand in darkness. This evening, a waxing crescent moon accompanied them like a pale lantern held on high. The bite of coming winter numbed her lips. The landscape slumbered to either side, awaiting its spring flowering months hence.

Crammed into the carriage's back bench, next to Luviara, Kem raised an arm. "Look!" he cried, his voice a crack in the night's shell of silence. "Is that the Vigil?"

The land was so level, and the trees so scattered, that it was possible to see landmarks a fair distance away. A diffuse, vertical line of soft white stuck up like a knife, still leagues away. The road speared directly toward it.

As the evening passed, and the moon sank into the west, the tower grew in size. Yet no lamps marked the bridge over the moat or the gate in the compound's wall, as they should have done. More ominous still, the beacon light that ought to be clearly visible at the top of the tower was absent. The Vigil lay dark except for the eerie sheen of its holystone walls.

Near midnight, guided by a lamp hung from the Sun Chaser, the exhausted horses clattered across the bridge that spanned the moat. Their party passed gardens, and entered the Vigil compound through an open, unguarded gate.

The Vigil towers and their compounds were said to be as old as the roads, built to be checkpoints and watchtowers. It wasn't the towers themselves but the layout of the ports-of-entry that dated from the reign of the Willow Emperor. As a terminal Vigil, Far Boundary Vigil had no street of administrative offices to keep track of merchants and travelers. Its buildings were military in look, suggesting it had once housed a large garrison rather than the small numbers Xilsi had mentioned. All of the outer buildings were boarded up, although a few had shutters hanging loose. There was a pervasive scent of ashy char.

The sound of their passage echoed strangely until they passed the inner gate into the inner plaza. Simo pulled up the carriage in the courtyard, and the riders came to a halt around it.

The lamps that should have been lit on either side of the door into the tower's interior were dark. Everything was dark and still: the tower's windows, the temple's gate, the kitchen's smokeless chimney and main door left ajar. No one came to greet them.

Simo raised a hand. Those in the carriage climbed down to the ground and the riders dismounted, weapons drawn as they scanned the courtyard, the surrounding buildings, the sky and the clouds. No sound penetrated the night except the soughing of a light breeze, the erratic tapping of a loose shutter, and a strange murmuring *shush-shoom* that Elen had not heard for years but recognized instantly, with a shudder. The viper licked at her heart. It wanted out. It sensed how close it was, after so long, to its birth Pall.

Kem whispered, "What is that sound? It's creepy."

"It's the Pall," said Simo gravely.

"The other Pall didn't sound like that. It didn't sound like anything."

"This Pall marks the end of the world," said the captain. "You may think of it as if we have reached an ocean's shore."

"I've never been to an ocean," said Kem.

"Someday you will, by the grace of the High Heavens," said Simo, then turned to the haunt. "Your Highness? What now?"

The haunt paced the limits of the courtyard, head cocked as if listening, or as if something was hurting him and he was trying to shake it loose. He didn't answer, so Simo went on.

"With your permission, Your Highness, we will search the tower and the outbuildings while you wait here."

"You won't find anyone," said the haunt in a tone that rang like a threat. "I sense no living people here except us."

"Of course, Your Highness. But we'll search regardless. Jirvy, light three lamps. Xilsi and Ipis, take the tower. Jirvy and I will search the outbuildings. Kem, care for the horses."

"Should I stable them, get them under shelter in case it rains?" Kem asked.

Slowly, Simo turned a full circle, alert to any possible hint of light, sound, or movement. If any of the Vigil's garrison was alive, they had to be unconscious or hidden somewhere farther away, because they certainly could not have missed the noise of their arrival.

"I don't like this at all," Simo said, "so for now just keep them warm. Let them drink and eat a little, but sparingly, in case we need to leave quickly. I hope it doesn't come to that." He paused, watching the man he knew as his prince.

The haunt's pacing hadn't slackened. If anything, he was picking up speed as if goaded by an unseen spirit. As if he could not rest, or even stand still, so close to the Pall. Was it calling to him in the same way it called to the viper?

A crushing weight settled on Elen's chest.

He meant to leave.

He had to leave.

The captain cleared his throat to get the prince's attention, and the haunt swung around to look at him. "Your Highness, if you'll remain here with the horses and the others . . ."

The haunt said nothing, went back to his pacing.

The four wardens readied their weapons and headed out, Xilsi and Ipis up the ramp into the tower and Jirvy and Simo into the area that held the kitchen, barracks, stable, and storerooms.

"Deputy Courier," said Kem in his most courteous voice, "perhaps you might help me with the horses." He handed her four blankets but made no further comment as he walked away to drape and tie the blankets he'd kept over the carriage horses, who were beginning to shiver. Elen did the same with the riding mounts. She hung the lamp from a post and went to examine the watering trough outside the entrance to the stable. The trough had water in it that looked clean enough; she broke its skin of ice with a few taps from her knife. Kem took a bucket of water to each horse in turn—not too much!—while Elen parceled oats into feedbags. Tension made her stiff and clumsy, or perhaps she was clumsy because she kept turning her head to check on the pacing haunt.

"Your Highness, I request an audience." Luviara's voice startled her, coming as it did from out of the darkness by the carriage.

The haunt's footsteps did not alter or slow. "What is it?" he said curtly.

"If it please you, Your Highness, why did you not tell me about the attack on the griffin scout?"

"Because you are not a warden."

"Young Kem here is not a warden."

"He is a novice warden." The haunt's tone was hard, even dismissive.

Kem shot a nervous look at Elen as if to say, *What do I do?* She gave the hand sign that meant to let it go, often used in years past when he had started an argument with his mother over some trivial dispute. Giving Elen a nod, he dipped the empty bucket into the trough and headed back to another horse.

"So, I am the only one who did not know?" Luviara's tone was dark. "How can I act as your interlocutor if you do not trust me, Your Highness?"

He stopped as abruptly as if he'd been brought up short by a wall. "Luviara, go to the chamber of records in the tower. See what you can find. Any correspondence from the palace. Any messages that might offer a clue to where the wardens and their menials have gone."

No one could refuse a direct order from a prince. Luviara hesitated for one breath, then took and lit a lantern. With several backward glances, her expression too shadowed to be visible, she went up the ramp and into the tower. Seen through the glaze of the tower windows, the light slowly ascended.

The haunt said, "I am going to the latrine."

Kem set down the full bucket he was carrying. "Your Highness, you're meant to stay here in the courtyard. That's what Captain Simo said."

"Where I am a target of opportunity for anyone creeping up on either side, under cover of darkness? Do your duty, Kem. I shall return soon enough." He paused, thought over his words, and added, "But your concern is understandable. I must, indeed, be guarded at all times from threats both grand and insignificant. The deputy courier will accompany me. She has a knife."

64

THE BEAT OF ITS HEART

Instead of heading into the barracks, where the latrine was out back, the haunt took the road under the tower and headed toward the outer courtyard that overlooked the Pall. Elen hustled after, ignoring Kem's startled exclamation except to call back, "Keep your eyes open."

So many questions crowded her mind she scarcely noticed the sting of the road through her boots.

She and the haunt emerged from beneath the tower onto a wide terrace paved of holystone. An embankment rose on the northern rim of the terrace as a barrier between the pavement and the shoreline. The road ramped up to the top of the embankment.

Avoiding the road, she climbed the side of the embankment and halted on its flat top. The embankment's north face pitched steeply down to a ragged shoreline where rocks met the foggy white substance of the Pall. The road turned into a causeway that proceeded north into the darkness, Pall on either side. She recognized this place, remembered it vividly, although it had been about twenty years: the well-kept pavement of the roadbed, the semicircular holystone terrace, the great Vigil tower with its heavy base and a peaked roof so many stories above that it had seemed like a dream to the child she had been that night when she and Ao had made it across the Pall, miraculously both alive although Elen was, arguably, no longer fully human. If she had ever been fully human. The viper hummed inside her, wide awake, stretching as if it wished to slither away into the Pall.

The haunt scrambled up beside her. "Ah," he said on a gasp. "Can you hear them?"

She listened. The Pall did not lap against the rocks as if it were water, but the *shush-shoom* kept on at a steady, fluid cadence.

"What makes that sound?" she asked him, although she kept her voice low.

"The beat of its heart."

"The Pall is alive? A living being?"

He smiled, canting his head to look at her. The moon had set.

In the darkness, his face was shadowed. Yet his gaze held a tender sweetness. His presence settled like balm on her restless heart. Even the viper relaxed, as if enchanted.

"Not living as you and I are, or as the prince's body is. I sense the pulse of currents beneath its surface. I hear a rustle of souls swirling in its shallows. There. Do you see?"

He pointed, his arm a dark line against a darker night.

A ways out from the shoreline, firefly lights drifted, manifold sparks winking energetically in and out of existence, so many more than in the faded exhaustion of Flat Pall. A soft, bell-like tone shivered through the air. He shut his eyes and dipped his chin as if the sound hurt him.

"Are you all right?"

"No," he said harshly, and then hoarsely, again, "No."

"Is this what you heard from the Spires? This Pall?"

"Yes." A man in pain might speak so curtly, unable to voice more. "I believe this is what called to me."

She didn't know what to say because it hurt too much to realize. He had reached the end point of his journey.

He said, in an intimate whisper, "You told me you knew the exact moment it happened?"

"What happened?" she asked, but then remembered what she had been about to tell him when Xilsi had ridden up and obliviously interrupted them. A very Xilsi thing to do. "Oh."

"You needn't tell me, if you do not wish it," he said, too quickly, but she heard a different message. He wanted to know. Or he wanted an excuse to keep her talking. Or he wanted a reason to stand here a while longer.

She glanced back at the tower. "They might see our figures from the windows. Let's go down."

Together, they descended the outer slope of the embankment and halted on the stones a body's length from the misty Pall. Ripples stirred and faded in the fog, as if an unseen creature had come prowling close to shore.

"This is where Ao and I crossed. We came from the north. We were just children."

"If children can cross, then why does everyone say there is no land north of here?"

"Because the road is broken. Both here, and on the other side of the Pall, it seems like a causeway that ends, as might a pier. The people who live in the nameless land believe they live on an island, with the ocean to the north, and the Pall a poisonous sea of mist to their south. But in both cases, the break is really a massive collapsed bridge across wide, and mostly dried-up, watercourses. One is probably a river, and I think the other could once have been a strait. The stones are so scattered it's easy to not realize it was once a very long bridge. Quite a remarkable feat of engineering. I can't imagine what could have done that much damage to such a solid stone structure."

"There were once sorcerers who devised spells specifically to shatter the things other people had built. Or . . ." His mischievous smile flashed. "A dragon would have the power."

She smiled, shaking her head. "There aren't any dragons left in the world."

"None but me," he said in a teasing voice.

"Wings, shine, and all," she murmured.

He raised a hand as if to halt this line of conversation. "Yet, you are entirely correct. There *are* no dragons left whose wings will flash through the sky, whose claws will churn a flood into a wall of water, whose beauty will enchant their prey so they may gobble them up. The last of them were shorn from the world in order to save the world and guard the world. For you see, El, the worst of the sorcerer-kings of ancient days were greedy, hoarding dragons. They devoured the lives not just of humans and aivur and swalters, and the animals who roam and even the plants that grow, but of their own kind. Those of their kinsfolk who did nothing to stop them were shamed into this final act, so the wicked ones might never rise again."

She stared at him, dazzled and disturbed in equal parts.

He pressed a hand to his heart. "But that happened long in the past. I beg your pardon. You were explaining why two girls would attempt to cross the Pall when no one else had ever tried."

"I don't know if no one else tried. I just know we attempted it because we had nothing to lose but our lives, and our lives were already forfeit. But it's a long story."

"There is so little time remaining," he murmured, pressing a hand to his face as if wondering if he were still there.

"What do you mean to do?"

"I mean to hear your story, so I may take the memory of your voice with me."

The haunt caught her hand in his and laced his fingers through hers. The gesture struck Elen breathless. His skin was warm and hers cold. His grasp was firm, and she held on, wishing she need never let go. But he was leaving, and she had always known he could not stay in a body he had only borrowed, and even then, borrowed under false pretenses.

It took her a few inhalations to get her breath back. He waited.

Finally, she said, "I thought we were walking to our deaths and I was content to do so as long as it was by our own choice, and of our own mastery of our selves. I would have stopped at any time and laid down and closed my eyes, but Ao kept going, and I would never have left her. We were so young, you see. My menstrual bleeding started about a year later, so maybe I was thirteen or fourteen, and she was about the same. It's so wide, this Pall. We walked along the causeway until we could no longer see the nameless land. The world was nothing but the road and the mist. I began to understand the world was different from how I had thought it was. For one thing, there is land beneath the Pall, not an abyss. Just ordinary land, with the Pall a low-lying mist stretched over it. But it wasn't just that. It was something I felt in my bones. Or maybe in the egg that nested in my heart."

"The viper."

"I felt something vaster than the sky. Something that reached into places I couldn't touch, that no one could touch. The world echoed, and it was silent. It was small, and it was beyond measuring. And a whisper reached into my heart."

She remembered the exact moment. Standing on the road with the sea of deadly Pall around them and yet somehow in a cocoon woven of peace. Ao asleep, curled up on the roadbed, with her head on a sack now empty of food. Dear Ao, smiling in her sleep, because even in the midst of this lonely, doomed passage, she was the happiest she had ever been.

The stars had shone in all their brilliance, beautiful but out of reach. Sparks had glittered in the Pall like the welcome lights of villages where a hungry, tired person might find a meal and a bed. A warm wind had spun a draft along the stubble of El's scalp, where her hair was starting to grow out and itch. And the itching was funny, really, because she hadn't expected it. In all her life that she remembered, her hair had never gotten even this finger's width long. The shadow of a wide-winged sea bird had sailed overhead, gliding north with majestic ease. A waning half-moon shouldered up over the horizon in greeting. Ao gave a little snort of a snore, then a sigh as she settled back to sleep. It was all so miraculous. It was beautiful. It meant beauty was reachable if a person thought to see what was right around them.

The voice whispered, *Joy is your calling.*

All this, Elen said, and then she fell silent. By the ache in her heart, she couldn't be sure whether a wound had been ripped open or healed shut.

The haunt pressed his other hand atop her fingers. "You were touched by the heart which is yourself. This grace of yours was always inside you, dear one."

He had called her "dear one." The words struck her like a blow, and yet they lifted her up.

"I'm sorry," he muttered, pressing her fingers tightly between his hands. "I'm sorry."

"Sorry for what?"

"The longer I tarry, the more it hurts that I must leave you, when I have come to see what a jewel you are."

"I'm no jewel. More like a weed that has survived being trampled on."

He laughed, although perhaps more with pain than delight. "I love what you are, whatever you may choose to call yourself. To me, you are the cloud whose rain nourishes, you are the star whose effulgence sparks dreams of better things that may yet come, you are the moon whose stubborn light offers hope in darkness and the sun whose golden rays bring life to all that lives in this world. Well, or at least to my heart."

He fell silent. They stood together as the cold wind curled around them, cocooned by the night and by the weight of the feeling between them, like an egg that has finally cracked open to spill an unexpected gift into the world.

He shook his head as if answering a question he had asked himself. "I cannot with honor remain in this body. Nor would you want me to. Anyway, this prince has his own schemes and ambitions. I must leave him to them. I'm sorry for him, though."

Throat thick, she said, "Sorry for him? Why? He has everything."

"He will not recall you, this you, the person you have trusted me to know. I suppose I pity him, for he will never comprehend the precious spirit that is the soul of you."

He pressed his hands, with hers still clasped in them, to his chest, as if to imprint her in his heart. Then, he untangled their fingers and raised one of her hands to his lips. With a kiss, he placed a seal upon her palm. His lips on her skin were sweet. Their touch made her shiver with longing.

She leaned toward him, thinking to kiss him with the whole heart and soul of her being, for it was the moment. They had risen into love, risen without meaning to pass the boundary beyond which there were no more questions.

But he did not shift toward her, lips parting to welcome her advance. He simply held her hand, so she held back. She would not force him to compromise his honor.

Yet she couldn't help but ask, desperately, "Do you have to go now? Right now?"

A shout rose from the compound, answered with another.

"Your Highness! *Your Highness!*"

"This way!"

"El," he said, all of his heart in her name. He released her and took a step away. With deliberation, sorrow creasing his face, he placed a single booted foot into the Pall.

"I love you," she said.

A shadow crossed his face. The light in his eyes snapped out. The body collapsed.

Elen grabbed the prince under his arms and dragged him free from the Pall. He was a dead weight, entirely limp. She staggered back, dragging him up the embankment to get him away from the shoreline.

The Pall churned into a violent whirlpool beneath the pale mist. A shadow darker than night rose like sinuous smoke out of the blanket of fog. The shadow had the sleek face and long body of a dragon, whiskered, winged, but entirely without substance. It twisted and turned as if seeking but unable to see her.

A gust of wind tore the smoky vision to pieces. It spilled back into the mist, where it thrashed as if in agony until it finally coalesced into a long, slender, winged form visible beneath the surface as glittering light. Only then did the haunt race in a tight circle, as if with a final message, and at last, with lightning swiftness, flash away out into the Pall and disappear.

65

THE DISTURBED VIPER

Elen's legs gave out. Everything in her heart and soul fled, torn out of her.

"Your Highness!" Footsteps on the embankment above. A chaos of frantic voices.

She slumped beside the unmoving body where it sprawled along the slope.

A rough hand fell on her shoulder. "What happened? What did you do?"

"I pulled him free," she gasped, covering her face. She couldn't bear to look on the prince's unconscious body, to see that dear face. Not now. It was too cruel.

The hand shook her harder. *What did you do?*

"Captain! Let her go," said Xilsi. "Kem said the prince ordered her to attend on him. It looks like she saved his life."

Elen had survived too many close calls not to reflexively defend herself. In a dull, numbed voice, she said, "He had a foot in the Pall. I pulled him free."

Jirvy said, "Shouldn't we get him inside?"

"I'll check him for Spore first," said Simo. "Her, too. Ipis, do it."

The flat of a shrive-steel blade pressed against her cheek, held by the young warden. It was like bitter ice burning. It stung like the road on her feet. The viper writhed at her heart and uncoiled, desperate to free itself from her body, to seek safety elsewhere, but if the wardens saw the viper, they would cut off Elen's head right then. Breaking into a sweat, she gritted her teeth and brought the viper up short. The struggle between her and viper went unseen by the others except as the tension in her body, the grimace on her face.

"That's enough, Ipis," said Xilsi sharply. "If she had Spore in her, it would have wriggled free by now."

The sting of the blade ceased as it was pulled back and the sword sheathed. "What was he doing down here?" Ipis said in a frustrated tone.

"Some kind of spell," said Simo. "He's been acting strangely this entire journey. Do you think Prince Astaylin could have had him bewitched at Orledder Halt? Could there have been an illegal theurgist hidden amid the Duenn Manor entourage?"

"A theurgist?" Ipis said in a startled voice. "Manors aren't allowed to have them. Theurgists all have to go to the Heart Temple."

"That doesn't mean some don't skulk around, does it?" said Xilsi in a dry voice, as if she knew of a couple.

"But what could a theurgist do? They control elemental spirits, not people. Unless you're saying elemental spirits can be used to control people."

"I agree it seems unlikely," said Xilsi, drier than ever, "but if they could, then you can be sure the emperor knows how it is done."

"This reminds me of what happened to His Highness at the Spires, the way he fainted," said Jirvy. He added, "I see no Spore, Captain. He's clean."

"Let's get him into the tower. Warm him up. Ipis, run ahead. You and the interlocutor get a fire going. Heat water. Go! Jirvy and Xilsi, carry him between you. Gently!"

Still fighting the disturbed viper inside her, Elen shuddered convulsively, barely registering their movements, their footfalls, their departure, their absence.

He was gone.

He was gone.

She had never sought a person who would see the heart of her and love her for it. That wasn't a dream meant for the likes of her. She was a worker, a guardian, a protector. A courier. Someone whose life served others, and that was enough. There was joy in her ordinary life, and incandescent sunrises and blazing flowers and laughter and good wine, sometimes, and cheese so salty it brought tears to your eyes, and a hearty song shared with others, and good boots to walk the path of life. She really cherished good boots.

But not this.

He was gone.

A sob broke, heaving her body. A flood tide of grief rushed through her, and she couldn't hold it back. All her life funneled into this moment, huddled on the shore of the Pall that in its own way had saved her and Ao, and yet taken him from her. A cruel exchange.

She could not stop the gusts of weeping that wracked her over and over. Once she lost control, the viper probed and pushed and finally slipped, burning, out of her wrist, nosing past sleeve and hem to tumble, writhing, to the ground. It sped downward, the final broken piece of her, racing away, abandoning her. Or returning home. The viper slithered into the Pall. And then it, too, was lost to sight. *Gone.*

Soon, Kem would be gone, too. He was already halfway out the door. As he needed to be . . . and yet, how could she bear it?

All of them gone. Gone. Gone. All she could do was sob, she who had never shed a single tear. Shaking, shuddering, crushed, hands covering her face because she could no longer bear to look at the world.

"Aunt?"

She imagined Kem's whisper—ignored it, because the idea of his voice was just a pointless craving. It was the whisper of the Spore, the bait that drew you in. Kem hated her now. She'd lied to him, and he'd turned his back, and she couldn't even blame him.

"Aunt Elen." No, he was here. He crouched beside her and draped a blanket over her shoulders. "You can't stay out here. You need to come inside where it's warm."

Her heart was cold. It was dead without the viper. The monster was part of her, woven into her. Without it, she was withering, emptied, no longer her full self.

What did it matter anyway? The haunt was gone because he'd made the honorable choice. If he hadn't, if he'd decided to stay in the prince's body, then that would have been worse. The doors shut in both directions. He'd done what he had to do.

Even knowing this, she couldn't bear to move. What if the shadow reappeared and she wasn't here to greet him? To just see him, even if they two could never speak to each other again? What if the viper had gone to find him? What if? What if? What if? Hope was a liar, so she'd trained herself to love what was present around her and let the rest go. To live where her feet were placed.

Why would these tears not stop? Had he heard her last words to him? Did it matter if he hadn't?

Kem sighed, plopped down next to her, and rearranged the blanket so it wrapped around the two of them together, snuggling them in tight, the way she and Ao would snuggle their little child between them on a wintry night and sit peaceably to watch the snow fall.

"It's all right," he said. "I'll wait out here with you until you're ready to come in."

She sobbed, tried to catch a breath, tried to say, "Kem," but all that came out was snot and tears. He took his sleeve and wiped the slimy mess from her face, and that made her break down again. And then she started laughing wildly.

Kem said, "The laughing is scaring me more than the crying."

On a sob, she said, "Why?"

"I mean, you never cried when Mama died. I'm not saying that to fault you. I knew why. You were being strong. You're always the strong one. So, it's kind of comforting to know you can cry. Not that I want to see you sad."

"Don't you hate me now?"

"Hate you!"

She could feel him roll his eyes.

He hitched the blanket back where it had slipped off her shoulder but he said nothing. She wiped her nose, swallowed, blinked. Her eyes were awash with tears. The world looked blurred, confusing, impossible to bring back into focus.

"Can you tell me what happened?" he asked, in the same intonation and with the exact same words she'd used on him more than once when he'd come running home all upset over some disappointment or slight or, once or twice, a fight. Not that he was a belligerent youth, not at all, but he tended to jump in when he thought someone else was being treated unfairly. How she loved his sense of justice and fair play.

In a changed tone, he said, "What is that?"

A slight movement stirred the edge of the Pall below them. The viper wiggled back into view, curving along the rocky shore until it found purchase on the stony-built slope to begin its ascent.

Kem tensed, making ready to jump to his feet and draw his shrive-steel sword.

She tightened an arm around him and said, "Don't move."

"What is it?"

Circumstance had forced what she'd never offered freely. She thought, *Let him walk away while he has the chance, while he has a safe haven to escape to.* She deserved nothing. No one deserved anything except her beloved child.

"The secret I couldn't tell you. Wouldn't tell you. It's why I can always find Spore and kill Spore. If you trust me, don't move."

The viper ascended like a wave toward her. It wasn't that it gleamed, but that its essence made it as visible at night as it was during the day. Darkness didn't hide it. Only her flesh could.

Kem shifted nervously, but he didn't jump up and run. He watched as she pulled off her glove, folded back the hem of her sleeve, and set her hand on the ground, palm down. The palm the haunt had kissed, but her skin was as cold as it had ever been, cold as the tomb.

The boy made a noise, clutching at her as if he meant to haul her away after all.

"Wait," she said. "Movement alarms it."

A body's length from them, the viper lifted its head and flicked out its tongue to smell the air, to taste his presence. But Kem did not interest the viper; he wasn't its prey. It lowered its head, unconcerned, sensing no threat in him. As it crawled closer and closer, he tugged on her arm. "Aunt! Move!"

"Trust me. It won't hurt me, or you."

He stared in stunned disbelief as it crawled up to her hand and dissolved into her arm. Into her body.

"What?" he gasped. "*What?* How? Your arm. Is that why you always rub it? Have you always . . . Of course. Of course! It explains . . ." He trailed off, panting.

"Explains what?" She swallowed her fears and hopes and dreams, all useless. She had to stay calm as she rolled down her sleeve and pulled her glove back on. She was prepared for him to reject her now.

"Something Mama said once that I didn't understand and she wouldn't explain. I thought it was just her way of phrasing things but now . . ." He touched the ribbon that tied back his hair. "Is that the only way in and out?"

"Yes, my wrist is the only way in and out. It's not going to attack you. It only hunts Spore. Not people or animals."

"B-but is it poisonous? If it eats Spore, if it can go into and out of the Pall, why doesn't it infest you with Spore?"

"I don't know. I've never known."

"Have you always . . . had it?"

"I think I was born with its egg in my heart, and then eventually it hatched."

He pressed his fingers against his eyes, sighed grievously, looked at her. "And Mama?"

"She was no different from you or any other person, Kem. It's just me."

The Pall shone gauzily beneath the sky. The wind had died. In the quiet, they heard the clop of horses' hooves as someone moved them into the stable, then silence.

"They'll burn you," he said softly. "They'll chain you to an iron pillar inside a shrive-steel cage and burn you on the burning ground."

"That's why I never told you. It wasn't fair to burden you with this secret. But now you know."

"Oh!" he said angrily. "So now you think because I'm a novice warden, I'll just betray you to others and give you up for some kind of reward? Is that what you think!"

"No! Of course that's not what I think! Why would you say that?"

"You've been so awful to me on this journey! Barely speaking to me! Like you're mad at me!"

"Mad at you! I just wanted to give you space. You're the one who is mad at me."

"I have every right to be mad at you!" he shouted.

"Yes! You do!"

He flinched, then winced, then pressed a hand atop his head as if he was trying to stop his skull from blowing off.

"Oh, Kem. I can never be mad at you. Well, except that one time with the turnip—"

"Don't remind me! That was so embarrassing."

"Yes, it's true your apology was so cringing and pathetic even your mother didn't scold you."

Again, silence fell. The Pall lay like death, unmoving. But it wasn't dead, was it? It had tides and currents and maybe souls alive inside it. The haunt was out there somewhere, somehow. She would never know where the end of his journey lay. But it wasn't with her.

He said, "You're crying again. What happened with you and the prince?"

"Nothing happened with me and the prince, Kem. He wasn't the prince. I'm telling you this so you'll know, but I'm asking you to never tell the others. They mustn't know."

He stared at her as he put the pieces together. "By the High Heavens, are you saying there really was a haunt, and it really did possess the prince?"

"Yes."

"It was the haunt all along?"

"Yes."

"Then what? And how?"

"He borrowed the prince's body in order to get here. To this Pall."

"Why?"

"He's one of these people called the Shorn. They were part of an ancient fight against the sorcerer-kings. He went into the Pall to look for others like him, to seek out traces of sorcery so they can eradicate it again. The Pall doesn't affect him because . . . I'm not sure, really. I don't understand quite how it all fits together."

He gazed first at the Pall and then at her. "This is a lot to take in."

She waited, wiping her cheeks. Her heart ached. It would always ache. But Kem sat next to her, clutching her arm as if he was afraid that if he let go that she would get washed away into oblivion.

He looked at her keenly, studying her with the affection of a child who trusts the person beside them. He had always had the instinct to care about others enough to make a good guess as to how they felt.

"You fell in love with him, didn't you? And him with you. It wouldn't hurt so much if he hadn't cared. That's what happened, isn't it?"

She looked away because she couldn't trust herself to speak.

"It explains everything." He sighed again, as if the weight of the world had settled onto his shoulders. "All right, then. You're chilled through, and you've had a shock. We're going to go into the stables. There's a fire and a place you can bed down for the night, or for however long until the prince wakes up. He will wake up, right?"

"Yes. Apparently he won't remember anything that has happened since he walked into the Spires."

"That will be awkward."

"I suppose so." She let him help her to her feet, let him guide her back across the terrace, under the tower, each step on the road a pinch of pain. But it didn't hurt nearly as much as the pain of losing the haunt and knowing there had been no other way.

Inside the stables, by the light of a lamp, Jirvy was settling the horses. He looked up. "Oh, good. I was just about to come out and look for her. I know they're angry, but it wasn't right to leave her out there alone. Kem, have you seen any sign of the garrison, or the garrison's horses, for that matter?"

"I haven't."

"I'm headed back out to scout, then. Can you stay with the horses?"

"Yes, that would suit me," said Kem. "My thanks."

By the door, Jirvy looked back. He brushed fingers over his face as if tracing the tracks of the tears he saw on Elen's. Then he shrugged and went out, shutting the door.

It was cozy in the stables. The horses were content to be inside, watered and fed, with other horses nearby. Safety in numbers. A fire burned in a brick hearth at one end, beside a stall fitted out with bunk beds, a table, and a bench. Kem led her to the lower bunk. She sank down, too exhausted to stand, she who was never too tired to care for those who needed help.

She folded forward over her legs and laid her head on her arms. She couldn't find the energy to move. Kem hustled about, whistling under his breath. Eventually, he went out, then returned a little later. The smell of hot soup brought her head up. Even stricken as she was, she never rejected food.

"From the kitchen," he said, holding a tray with two covered bowls and a platter of sliced, steamed turnips. "Xilsi is cooking. She's a funny one. So high and mighty, like she's used to parading around the palace in the company of the exalted palace-born, but then she goes and cooks for the rest of us, like any ordinary person might do."

"Feeding people is a great blessing, not ordinary at all," Elen said reflexively.

"If you say, 'I know what it's like to wake up hungry and go to bed hungry,' I'm not giving you this bowl." He set the tray down on the table. "Do you need help getting over here?"

She tested her strength, standing as she held on to the upper bunk, but her legs held, although they were unsteady as she walked over and sat. He handed her a warm, damp towel to wipe her face and hands. When she had finished he spoke the words of blessing: "May the Tranquil Emperor live in peace, our spear and our shield." He uncovered her bowl to reveal a spicy barley soup, something quickly cooked while turnips steamed.

She began eating. The peppery spice was pungent enough to make her eyes water. A good dish for a cold night. She ate carefully, one spoonful after the next, really concentrating on it because suddenly she was ravenous. Only when she had emptied the bowl did she realize he hadn't touched his.

"You should eat it while it's hot," she said.

There was a new maturity to the steadiness of his gaze, the determined tilt of his chin, his willingness to confront her not with anger or with avoidance but with love.

"You have to tell me," he said.

"Tell you what?" she grumbled. But she knew.

"You have to tell me the truth. I understand, I really do. Well, I understand a little. And I'm still angry. But you've waited long enough. I've seen too much. Are you even really from Duenn Manor or some isolated upland village in Woodfall Province?"

"We aren't from the empire at all," she said quietly. "Duenn Manor was the place we escaped *to*, only then we had to escape from there too."

"Where are you from, then? Who are you, to have a viper inside you? Who was Mama really? How can I understand who I am if I never know who you and Mama were?"

She thought of the dragon made of smoke, and she wondered if Kem's forgiveness was the gift the haunt had given her in the end. Sniffing, she wiped her eyes.

"If it's going to make you cry again, then it can wait."

"No. You're right. It's long past time. Before you go off into your new life, you should understand a tiny bit about your mother, what a courageous person she was and why she could be so hard to get along with at times, when the old memories took hold. But . . ."

"But?"

She smiled, although the gesture hurt like poking a bruise, and uncovered Kem's bowl to release the soup's savory scent. "But you have to eat while I'm telling you. This will take a while."

66

IMAGINE THERE IS A NAMELESS LAND

Imagine there is a nameless land that lies beyond this uncrossable Pall, beyond what the mapmakers say is the end of the empire, and maybe even the end of the inhabitable world.

Imagine two young girls who live in that nameless land. They call each other sisters, but there's no telling who birthed them and who lost them. They don't know how old they are. They can't know. There is no record-keeping, not the way there is a regular census in the empire. There are just masters, retainers, outlaws, and atoners.

Masters rule. Retainers work for the masters and, in return, the masters protect and feed them. Outlaws refuse to serve, so they are hunted. What do atoners do? They die so the masters may live.

In the nameless land, the masters and their households and courts are on the move most of the time, traveling from one royal villa to the next. If they stay too long at any one place, there will not be enough provisions to feed the court, so they never stay more than a month at a time in any one place, except for the midwinter layover. In the nameless land there is no holystone, no hallow-wood, no shrive-steel, no surveyors and couriers and wardens on patrol. A Pall may rise anywhere. Spore may sprout anywhere, with no warning. So, atoners walk at the front and back of their master's cavalcade. If they spot Spore, then they warn the main procession. If they don't spot it, if drifting Spore hooks into them or they set their foot in a puddle of Pall that has gathered on a dim path in the forest the way water gathers after a rain, then their agonized death warns the main procession.

Imagine the two little girls who have spent all their childhood walking as atoners, from as far back as they can remember. Children make the best atoners. They're rarely strong or fast enough to run away, and they wouldn't know where to go if they did. There are things worse than Spore in the world, they are told. There are violent outlaws who take slaves, inhuman raiders who are unspeakably cruel, and ravening monsters who crave human flesh. Also, there is the righteous anger of the white-haired god who will smite them if they do not obey the master.

Somehow the two girls have survived when most atoners die long before they reach adulthood.

Don't pity the two girls. They are better off than every other atoner. One of the girls has a nose for Spore that is unrivaled. Uncanny and a little disturbing. Witchy, if you will. But it means the household and court of young Lady Eleawona, to which they are attached, is well protected when they travel off the holy road to the royal strongholds and villas.

Therefore, the lady's chatelaines slip the two girls extra rations. The lady herself knows their names and allows them to kneel behind her every month, after their heads have been shaved, when the holy fire of cleansing is lit, and prayers are said thanking the white-haired god for another month of blessed life. The household and court hangers-on have come to believe the white-haired god has anointed the very young Lady Eleawona by giving her two such favored atoners. Their presence has kept the lady safe, even during the dark winters when Spore sometimes gets inside buildings. Winter is always the worst. One terrible year the Highmost—the master who rules over the other masters—and his entire court and entourage died in an irruption that swept through a royal stronghold.

The disaster left a land divided between competing factions. The Highmost left five adult children. The girls knew this because every day the household said a prayer to honor the masters. Lady Eleawona was the daughter of the dead Highmost's eldest child, a daughter. In the nameless land, a son will always inherit before a daughter, so after a quarrel with his younger brothers, the oldest son became Highmost in his father's place.

The only thing that really changed in Lady Eleawona's life, then, was that her cousin, Lord Thelan, began to travel with her court. He was a few years older than her, maybe fourteen. He was the son of the new Highmost, but his mother had been a lowly retainer, not a royal wife. Thus, Lord Thelan was not eligible to become Highmost, even though he was *his* father's eldest child.

Yes, it makes no sense. It works differently here in the empire.

All the two girls knew was that there was a ceremony of betrothal between Lady Eleawona and Lord Thelan, a promise they would marry once they came of age in four or five years. No one was quite sure if Eleawona was pleased with the arrangement, but it wasn't up to the young lady anyway, was it? Everyone said it was the bargain the new Highmost made with his elder sister to get her to agree to acclaim him as Highmost. Anyway, during the betrothal festivities even the atoners were given freshly baked bread and a slice of salted meat, so that was something to celebrate!

Lord Thelan was a most unusual individual in the nameless land: a royal child who talked to everyone. He trained with ordinary soldiers. He rode alongside the household staff. He even asked the names of the atoners. He was particularly curious about the nose-smart girl, the one called El in honor of Lady Eleawona. Occasionally he would ride at the front of the procession as if, by watching El walk, he could figure out her secret.

In this way, life went on for a year after Lord Thelan's arrival. The court traveled on its usual itinerant route.

Now, imagine that one of the two girls, the pretty one called Ao, discovers blood between her legs one summer morning. A master's soldiers are allowed to keep bed retainers—the lowest rank of retainer. It is a reward soldiers demand in exchange for fighting. They've all had their eye on this girl. But she's an atoner, and atoners are off-limits, everyone knows that. Atoners are sacred. Or at least, they're called sacred because no one wants to touch them, so they're also called cursed.

However, if an atoner reaches the age of adulthood, it is seen as a sign of the white-haired god's forgiveness. Such an atoner may ask to be cleansed by holy oil and holy water and thereby be elevated into the ranks of the retainers. An assistant chatelaine, who is in charge of the atoners' pen, discovers the blood and reports it to the head chatelaine. That evening, the head chatelaine requires the two girls to kneel before her in her office. She tells Ao that the happy day has come. On the Feast Day of the Holy Waters, when the court will be at South Ring, the girl will be declared an adult, cleansed of the burden of atonement, and elevated to the rank of retainer. The girl trembles. She knows what is in store for the likes of her, and she tremblingly tells the head chatelaine she would rather stay an atoner with her sister El.

The chatelaine is shocked by the girl's defiance but also can't understand. Who would want to stay an atoner? Anyway, it is already decided. The noble lady has heard about it and will stand as sponsor. It's an incredible honor for a child whose birth is shrouded in mystery and thus in disgrace. When the two girls are sent back to the atoners' pen, walking hand in hand as they always do, they see how the household guards stare at Ao. They know what it means.

Imagine one more thing. It's a lot to take in, but surely not more complicated than palace politics in the heartland.

There is a holy road in this nameless land, one that is said to run north from the shore of the White Sea—what we call Far Boundary Pall—all the way to the seat of the Highmost, on the shore of the Blue Sea, a true ocean. But the girls don't know for sure. Lady Eleawona's court has never traveled any farther north than the Haywold Hills. North, far past the Haywold Hills, is where her uncle, the Highmost, resides. North is where the raiders roam the coast, and where the Highmost burns alive the Sea Wolves he captures or, indeed, any outlaw or traitor he wants to make a lesson of, should anyone in the land think to rebel against his authority.

The southlands lie under the gentler stewardship of his beloved older sister. This part of the holy road still has many long, straight stretches and also a few intact holy "rings." In the empire, we call these Halts, but in the nameless land, they have all become royal strongholds, like South Ring.

At the moment, Lady Eleawona's court is in residence at Hazelberry Villa, where the recent harvest of nuts, berries, grain, and root crops has kept the court splendidly fed for an entire ten days. The lady plans to meet her mother's court at South Ring for the harvest gathering.

But first, they have to get there.

At dawn, the advance party of twelve departs with El and Ao walking in the lead along a well-trammeled dirt lane. An advance party is sent ahead to alert the next villa's caretakers and to help them get the extra hearths burning, an evening meal for two hundred started, and the royal chamber swept out and sweetened with herbal scents.

At the beginning of a long day, Ao usually chatters about food, which embroidered dress she saw the lady wearing, the gossip she overheard when she was using the latrine, but today, she is silent. El can always tell when Ao is scared because she rubs her fingers around and around the wooden badge, carved in the shape of a bear, that marks them as belonging to Lady Eleawona's court.

"I don't want to," she whispers finally. "They say such ugly things to me. 'I'll stick my pig in your trough and you'll squeal' or 'I like the fresh ones best but I suppose the sergeant will get first poke.'"

"You never told me they say those things."

"I didn't want you to worry. There's nothing you can do. But I don't want to." Tears spill from her eyes, but she doesn't cry out loud, in case the first rank of retainers, the four guardsmen riding behind them, might hear.

El thinks all day about the problem. It's a clear, clean, hot day, muggy and windless. The dusty lane is easy on their bare feet as it winds in and out of shade. They ford two shallow streams, the water curling soothingly around their feet and calves. Ao snatches ripe berries from a laden bush, but they can't pause to eat their fill since they are always in sight of the rest of the advance party. They've learned to savor what they can. The purple berries are sun-sweetened and delicious. Ao gobbles her handful all the way up in just a few bites, while El eats hers slowly to let the pleasure stretch on as long as possible. She gives the last berry to Ao, who hands it back and says, "No, I won't take yours. You eat it." So El does.

Summer garb is a cast-off wool tunic, heavily worn and much mended, that falls past their knees. Because the tunics are too big for them, Ao has woven them belts from dried reeds long enough to wrap several times around their torsos and keep the extra fabric from blowing. In recent months, Ao has taken to adjusting the strapping of her own tunic to pouch up and hide her budding breasts that seem to keep swelling larger every month. Elen's chest has a scant new contour, but she can still pass as a boy with her tall, lanky frame and shaved head. Not that the lowest-born retainer youths of any sex are safe around the northern soldiers who came south with Lord Thelan. They don't respect Lady Eleawona's rules of decorous conduct.

It's a good day, as days go. No sign of Spore, nothing that makes El's heart squeeze and her nose tingle. A good day, right up until midafternoon, when they reach the night's halting place.

Their destination is a moated villa. A patrol band of the lord's soldiers has arrived ahead of them, down from the hills. They've brought a prize to hand over to Lord Thelan: a nest of outlaws they flushed out of a cave, deep in the forest. In fact, the advance party from the court arrives while the soldiers are still raping and abusing their captives, and so the little cavalcade enters the villa to the horrific sounds of screams and sobs and the hopeless moaning of one poor soul saying, "Just kill me. Just kill me and be done."

Ao runs to the atoners' pen and shuts herself in, but El follows the deputy chatelaine. After speaking to the local caretakers—who are hiding in the kitchen wing and very upset that such unpleasantness has been visited upon their peaceful villa—the chatelaine marches to the guards' quarters and shouts for the sergeant to show himself.

He emerges from the building, buttoning his trousers and looking annoyed. "What is this? Who are you?"

"I am chatelaine lieutenant to Lady Eleawona's household, as you ought to know."

"Yeah, you lot don't know how good you have it here in the south, without Sea Wolves nipping at your balls day and night," he sneers.

She ignores his crude tone. "Her ladyship and his lordship will arrive before nightfall. Get this cleaned up. It would be ill fortune for them to arrive hearing such wailing and weeping. As it is said, 'The white-haired god causes the wicked to weep and the sinful to hear the weeping, but the godly shall hear only song and smiles.' I assume you've set aside any children for the atoners' pen. Untouched."

"I know the rules," he says irritably. "There's a toddling babe and one small fry, that's all. We fed them sleep-mane tea to shut them up because they wouldn't stop crying. We put them in the atoners' pen. They should sleep until morning."

"Very good. The adults will be burned tomorrow, after the court moves on. The lady and lord shan't have their evening sullied by the stench."

"Nay, nay, of course not, Honored Chatelaine. But there's talk that the men want more sluts. There aren't enough to go around, and there ought to be. We of his lordship's troop don't like to be treated like we don't deserve what you fancy Southerners take for granted. We made a good haul today, all six young and healthy enough. We tested them all. More than once. Haha!"

"It's not my decision to make." The look in the chatelaine's eyes makes her seem disapproving but also wary.

The sergeant's gaze settles on El, standing behind the chatelaine. He grins in a way that lets El know he is a man who likes to hurt people. He says, "Isn't this the nose-smart atoner we've heard so much about? Tell you what, Honored Chatelaine, why don't you let this witch-sprout decide. Half to the pyre and half to the bed. Wouldn't you like that, dearie? It's a rare wine to drink, to hold the knife of life or death over a man's throat. What do you say?"

She raises her gaze to the soldier. She isn't afraid of him, not with the chatelaine beside her, and she won't be cowed. "If you force someone weaker than you into the jaws of a wolf, then you have become the wolf. Anyway, it's just a game for you."

He lunges forward and slaps her. She sees the blow coming and rocks back, so it doesn't land with the full force he put behind it, but he's grinning in delight and doesn't notice, not as long as she looks like she's hurt. She rubs her eyes, so he'll think she's crying.

The chatelaine gasps in anger and yanks El back out of his reach. "The lady's protection rests on this atoner's head. So does the protection of the white-haired god. Do that again, and I'll see you whipped."

"You Southerners," he mutters contemptuously to the chatelaine, then slams a look at El and says, "I hear that sister of yours is up for auction. I've been saving up my pay; say what the lady's sergeant will, he doesn't just get to grab first poke because his daddy was sergeant before him. I'm a sergeant, too. We have our rights, Lord Thelan's rights."

He goes back inside.

The chatelaine mutters, "They say only bastards serve bastards."

El says, "Don't you like Lord Thelan?"

The woman flushes. "He's charming enough, and he's almost as smart as our blessed lady. But he's still a bastard, and she's a proper heir, so don't you forget it."

"What difference does it make to me?" El asks, not angrily, but out of curiosity.

The chatelaine gives her a long look over. "You're a strange one, that's sure. Get on, now, go back to the pen. I feel that bad for your sister. She doesn't deserve it, and they'll treat her roughly. She's still too young, for one thing, as anyone ought to know. And she's got that fey look about her that makes men like him want to make her cry. And the other thing too, of course, such a cruel thing. But there's nothing any of us can do about that."

El doesn't argue with her. In the chatelaine's mind there is nothing she can do, so therefore it's true there's nothing she can do. If anyone is going to save Ao, it's going to have to be El.

Inside the pen there's a shed fitted with crude bunks. Ao is seated on a lower bunk, stroking the head of the older child who is maybe four or five and deeply, almost disturbingly, asleep.

She looks up as El comes in. "The poor mite has clean hair, El. Someone cared for this little child."

"What about the baby?"

Ao shakes her head with a frown. "Those fools gave it too much sleep-bane."

The baby is quite thin but, like the older child, it looks cared for, with a clean face and a little wrap of a tunic, into which someone has stitched the symbol of a flying dragon as a sigil of protection against the evils of the world. But the poor infant is dead, no longer breathing.

El picks up the body. "We don't have anything to feed it anyway. Better the poor thing burns with its people."

"I could have . . . traded myself, for goat's milk," says Ao in a whisper. "A few have offered already."

El presses a knuckle into her sister's head. "No! Nothing we can do for this one. But maybe we can help the other one along."

"Maybe it would be better off dead too," Ao mutters, but she keeps stroking the child's head. "It's got a cut on its foot that will go bad without treatment. Fetch me wound-seal from the garden. You know where."

After a detour to the herb garden to gather wound-seal, El takes the dead baby to the kitchen entrance. She isn't allowed to enter, but she knows the old charwoman, Elda, who handles ashes, waste, and death. Ao once helped Elda with a concoction of herbs for a lung ailment, so the woman takes the little body with a nod and brings El a ceramic mug of hot water. Ao steeps the herbs, mashes them into a paste, and applies it to the child's cut foot. The child stirs but doesn't wake. The girls doze in the drowsy heat, enjoying the rare luxury of a quiet rest broken only, now and then, by a wailing cry from wherever the captives are being held.

Late in the afternoon, the main party arrives with the other four atoners. One is an old man with a crippled hand and a face so scarred by burns he can no longer speak; he was sent to the lady's court by her blessed lady mother, last year, before Lord Thelan arrived, because the old man could no longer do his retainer's work. The fellow is slow, which is why he walks with the main party and its wagons. The others are three younger children, called Nep, Nap, and Nup, all so weary they can barely gulp down the shared bowl of parsnip and cabbage soup that is their day's meal and which Ao had made sure to hide in a corner until they arrived so no retainer would steal it. Afterward they talk the little ones and the old man through their day, discussing in basic terms what they saw and what they should be looking for and how to deal with Spore should they encounter it. If atoners don't help each other, then they will all die, one after the next.

Later, once the little ones and the elder are asleep, Ao and El stand at the pen's gate looking toward the main hall. They can see lamplight and hear feasting, smell the glorious scent of meat and honey. That night, the two girls sleep, safe, in the pen with the others. In the morning, the child is awake but drowsy, even a little stupefied, which is a mercy. As the advance party leaves, they hear the begging cries of the outlaws as they are chained to the execution pillars. The fires will be set once the lady and lord depart. Outlaws no longer count as human, and any person who isn't human must be burned. That is the law of the white-haired god.

Ao is carrying the child, braced on her hip. She whispers, "I'd rather burn."

"No, you wouldn't," says El.

But she's not sure. Burned is dead, and on the one hand, a bed retainer has a chance of being elevated out of bed service and into the ranks of the scullery and cleaning retainers, or even trained in a skill if they're fortunate, if they survive that long. But on the other hand, the ones who don't last turn into tortured shadows who wither and splinter into a drawn-out misery that always ends in death.

The chatelaine's words chase El all day as they walk. She's not sure what "the cruel thing" means, but she does understand about the fey look that makes men want to hurt her sister. Ao is pretty in the way Lady Eleawona is pretty, not that anyone would ever make the comparison out loud. She's like a jewel thrown into the garbage heap for anyone to grab.

El's got to find a way. And there are only two ways. Death, or escape.

Escape is impossible. Everyone says so. The captured outlaws show so.

But what if there is a way?

She wonders about the Sea Wolves, the dread raiders in the north. Everyone knows they aren't human, even if they look mostly human. It can be hard to tell. She's never seen the ocean, but she swears she remembers a great water dragging on her tiny body, back when she was so young, not even really a memory but more a physical sensation woven into her bones. Once she heard a visitor tell the lady there are traitors to humankind who join the Sea Wolves and murder their own brothers and sisters. Maybe the Sea Wolves would take her and Ao on to work for them.

That would be better, wouldn't it?

What if they could escape to the north, to the coast, and join the Sea Wolves? But . . . it is so far. She doesn't know how far it is, except she heard one of the northern soldiers say it took them a month to ride south. Yet she and Ao have no food of their own, no knife, no spoon, only the tunics they wear, which don't even belong to them but to the lady. In the winter, they're lent a pair of boots and a cloak that are taken away again in the summer.

They walk in silence. Birds sing, which is a good sign. Birds mean safety.

The child keeps its head pressed against Ao's shoulder. After a while, it murmurs, "Where is Mama? The bad men took her into the other room, but I fell asleep."

"We're going to find her now, dearest," Ao lies. "Can you walk yet?"

The child clutches her more tightly.

"It's all right," Ao says in her sweetest voice. "I won't let go of you."

They walk on. The child falls asleep.

"Are you okay?" El asks Ao in a low voice. "I can take a turn."

"The poor mite barely weighs anything. I'm not a weakling, you know."

"I know you aren't a weakling. I didn't mean that."

A pause, then, "Let me do it. You always take the hard jobs. I can do this."

They walk past a harvested field of wheat, straw drying in the sun, then through an orchard of walnut and quince. El watches everything: the dirt on the path, the flying bugs, the birds flitting from branch to branch, the undergrowth beyond the orchard, the rough outline of a long-abandoned stone building at the edge of the woodland.

She whispers to Ao, "Don't look, but someone is pacing us. Hiding. I wonder if they didn't catch all the outlaws."

They exchange a glance. Atoners and retainers get a special reward of extra food if they alert the guards to the presence of an outlaw. The two girls keep walking. Nothing is worth what will be done to those captured, not even an entire loaf of bread all to themselves, not even a precious slice of meat roasted in honey.

They keep walking through the pretty landscape, pleasant until they reach one ruin of a village destroyed by Spore soon after they came into the lady's service. El had sniffed it out. She'd saved everyone. After that incident, the people in Lady Eleawona's household had started calling her the nose-smart girl. The ground is still cleared around the abandoned village, and it's burned off every season, just to make sure.

At midday, the advance party pauses to rest the chatelaine's horse at the ford at Eelwise River. The girls cross first and wait on the other side, in the shade of an ancient yew tree whose spreading branches reach across the shallows. The child won't let go of Ao, so she patiently spoons up water with a cupped hand and lets it drink. All the while Ao also sings soft nonsense songs to keep the child distracted from asking, again and again, about the mother it doesn't know is dead. There'll be time enough for that bad news later.

El scavenges lantern-berries from bushes that have used the yew's low-growing canopy as a trellis. The court's kitchen-folk won't touch these berries because their vines are entangled with the branches of the yew, whose bark is deadly. But El and Ao have never sickened from them. She ties up as many as she can fit in the hem of her tunic, for later. They share more of the berries with the child who, despite everything, is hungry enough to eat.

Ao says, "Do you have a name, little one?"

It doesn't answer.

"Can I carry you?" El asks the child, but Ao snaps, "No! I'm fine!"

The child flinches, and Ao sings again, petting its head.

The horn blows. A guardsman shouts at them. They start on through the woods, the meadows, the slow rise and fall of the land. It's hot as they trudge onward into the hazy afternoon. They've walked this route every summer. El knows each stately oak and towering pine as if it is an old friend. She sees where the current has finally cut away a stream's deep bank in whose shadow fish would idle. She smiles as they climb past a copse of beech and ash to the top of a long ridgeline. From here, a beautiful vista opens up, and on a day such as today the holy road is clearly visible on the downlands below. It's too far to reach before nightfall, but tomorrow they'll make the holy road and turn north toward South Ring, where the lady's blessed lady-mother bides for the winter, if she can supply her court for that long. To that end, Lady Eleawona's wagons bring casks of oil, baskets of pulses, bags of grain, and crates of parsnips and carrots.

"It looks so peaceful," says Ao. "Nothing but soft, white fog."

She's looking beyond the downlands, her gaze following the straight line of the holy road to where it reaches the shore of the

White Sea. The sea isn't really a sea. It isn't water at all. It's a low-lying fog that never lifts. If you touch it, Spore will get into you, and you'll die, eaten away from the inside, twisted into a monster. Even though people stay away from the White Sea, Spore can still find them. No one really knows how. Maybe it drifts on the air like dandelion seeds. Maybe it roots through the earth like worms. Maybe it sleeps, hidden in the earth for months or years, and then wakes up and sprouts.

"The White Sea doesn't touch the road, so that means the fog is shallow, not deep like a river or a lake," says El. "I wonder what lies out there."

"Peace," says Ao with a dreamy smile. "A road has to go somewhere. There has to be a reason it's there, even if we can't see the other side."

"I've heard the soldiers talking. They say it goes for a while and then is broken, cut off, and it's just the White Sea after that. So it's a dead end."

"Wouldn't you like to find out if it's true?" Ao asks. "Maybe it goes to a secret island, where there is food all year round and no snow and ice in the winter. Maybe it goes to the fortress of the white-haired god, where warriors feast all day and drink all night. Maybe it goes somewhere else."

"Where else could it go?" demands El.

Ao gives her a sharp look. "Somewhere that isn't here. Wouldn't that be enough?"

El doesn't answer. She's spotted dandelion growing in a sunny spot, and she scrambles off the path and starts digging for the roots.

"Hey! Hey! Get moving!" The advance party is coming up the slope, two guardsmen in front and two behind, with firepots hanging from their saddles in case of Spore. Between them rides the chatelaine with her flowing robe draped over her horse and, walking after her, the four royal retainers assigned to today's advance party. The retainers carry firepots too. Even the chatelaine does. The advance party's duties are simple: scout the road for Spore, and to make sure that, in the villa ahead, there is a chair ready for Lady Eleawona to sit in, fresh herbs to sweeten the air, and drink and food to refresh herself after the day's journey.

El tugs up one clump of dandelion roots, all there is time for. The girls walk on. El constantly scans the lane and the surrounding vegetation for signs of Spore, but nothing alarms her. The path stays atop the ridge for a while, then descends into a valley. The sun slides westward. There's no wind. It gets quiet except for the flutter and song of birds. The two girls reach the turnoff to the next royal villa. It's a rutted path, up and over a little hill and through a stand of royal yew. Trees and shrubs grow so thickly here that the girls can't see the buildings they're headed to. Briefly, they fall out of view of the advance party.

In the shade, El halts, putting out a hand to stop Ao. "Listen."

Ao tilts her head, then whispers, "I don't hear anything . . . Oh." The birds have fallen silent. The child stirs in her arms, raising its head.

Movement darts like a skittish deer. A young man breaks out of the foliage. He wears a desperate face, and is clad in the animal skins of an outlaw. He approaches, anxiously checking the path. *Clip-clop,* the horses' hooves ring through the silent woods, but the guardsmen haven't come into sight yet.

In a low, frantic voice, he says, "That's my child. I beg you."

The child squirms in Ao's grasp and says, "Daddy! Daddy!"

"Hush, little wolf," he says urgently, and the child obeys, used to this command. "I beg you," he repeats.

El shakes her head. "I'm sorry, but we'll be beaten or worse if we give the child to you. We can't—"

Ao sets the child on the ground and gives it a shove. It stumbles to the man, who swings it up on his back, where it clings. El's thinking frantically. *What to do? What to do?*

They'll be punished for losing the boy but maybe they can say he died like the baby did, given too much sleep-bane. Will that convince the chatelaine? Do the soldiers know they didn't capture all the outlaws? *Clip-clop,* the horses' hooves. Shapes appear on the path behind, amid the shadows cast by the leafy trees.

The man says, "Run!" and throws something at them. No, not at them—at the path behind them. Before the objects hit the ground, he's whirled and vanished into the tangle of trees.

Two small, sealed ceramic jars slam onto the dirt. One cracks while the other rolls, intact.

Curious, Ao takes a step toward the objects.

The world around El sharpens. Her instincts flare, a whisper in her heart: *Come to me.*

"Stop!" she says.

Ao stops.

A scent like rose oil brushes as a tingle to her nose. Pale filaments ooze out from between the cracks in the broken pot.

Spore.

The filaments shiver as they catch wind of the breath of life. Twisting, they writhe toward El . . . then pause. Almost as if they are hesitating. She's seen this behavior from Spore before, although not with other people. But her chance is *now*.

She darts in and grabs the intact pot. She doesn't shout a warning to the guardsmen. Instead, she drags Ao along the path toward the villa. They emerge out of the trees and into view of the moat to discover the outlaw has been here before them. He's flung a pot, or two, over the protective water moat and into the compound. Death for death.

The rose-oil scent floods the air. Spore can't cross the water, but now that it is inside the moat's ring, it will devour everything alive. Everyone alive. Two guardsmen and a retainer have scrambled to the top of the watchtower, but the retainer is covered in a bristling, thorny white growth sprouting all over her body, flowering out of her mouth. Screaming, the guards shove her off the tower. She falls. Smacks onto the stones below.

That's all El needs to make her decision.

"Run to the grandfather yew," she yells at Ao. The grandfather yew is a big tree outside the moat, grown through the ruins of a fallen structure.

She doesn't wait to see if Ao obeys. She dashes over the bridge into the compound. Her senses are as honed as a fine blade. She's learned through bitter and terrifying experience that Spore avoids her, as if she repels it; that's why she keeps Ao close to her. The filaments of deadly Spore seek better prey: the guardsmen in the tower, the yapping dogs, the frightened cook, and a scullery girl scrambling toward the pool at the center of the compound.

El runs into the kitchen, which is filled with dead things that don't interest the Spore. She stuffs all the food she can easily gather into two sacks, grabs a knife, a pot, two leather flasks and, best of all, a tinder box and a small glass jar filled with precious salt. Then, she runs out, ignoring the garbled, shrieking noises of dying people, ignoring the hysterical screaming of the scullery girl, who has reached the safety of the pool but without the cook, who by now is a shambling monstrosity of howling pain as her body transforms itself into something huge and terrifying.

El turns her back on it all. She runs, just as the outlaw said.

The grandfather yew lies at the back edge of the clearing. Yew trees are considered a holy sign of the honored ancestors. Their wood is said to fend off Spore. Ao is pressed up against the massive trunk, standing on a big branch that's grown out along the top of a half-buried stone wall. She's staring, hand over her mouth.

"Can you hear it?" she moans. "It's speaking to me."

El swings a sack into her sister's grasp. "Don't listen to it. Come on."

"Where are we going?"

"They'll think we are dead."

"But where can we go?"

"Anywhere." She pats the sealed pot, which is attached to a cord now slung around her neck. "We've got a weapon."

Imagine two girls running through the forest and then, after El judges it is safe, cutting back to the lane. They make good time and, even when the sun sets, El keeps them moving. There's a gibbous moon with enough light to guide their feet on the road. Night is dangerous because you can't see the pale glimmer of Spore before it overtakes you, but El has better instincts than most. She trusts the night, so long as it keeps speaking to her. The night birds call. The air smells only of late summer, cut straw, and a distant thunderstorm. No rose oil.

Very late that night, they reach the holy road.

A fortlet stands up on the road, constructed so as to use the road's elevation to oversee the countryside and to block traffic. That's how the masters stop people from using the road without permission. Forts, gates, and executions. A small village huddles to the south of the lane, protected by a yew hedge and a ditch filled with muddy water. Everyone is asleep there, although a sentry light burns where guards watch the road day and night.

But the girls are small, and they are silent as clouds sweep across the moon, drenching the world in deeper shadows. El hops over the ditch and steals a cloak hung out on the back porch of one of the little cottages. There's a pair of boots too. They're too large, but she can't resist, so she grabs them and slings them by tied laces around her neck. Behind her a dog growls. She turns to see a big hound staring at her. It backs up, head lowered and ears down, but it doesn't bark. She dodges around it and jumps back over the ditch.

Ao waits beneath another grandfather yew. Every community has one, usually growing outside the ditch or moat amid the ruins of an ancient building. While El was stealing the cloak, Ao rigged up their woven belts to turn the sacks El pilfered into packs they can sling over their backs instead of clumsily hauling in their arms.

"Now where?" Ao whispers as they shoulder their supplies.

"North, to the Blue Sea. We'll join the Sea Wolves."

"I thought they killed people."

"The masters kill people too. Do you have a better idea?"

Ao rubs her face nervously. "I'm scared."

"So am I."

"I don't think you are," says Ao with a resentful shake of her head. "You never seem scared. I wish I was like you."

El grabs her sister's hand. "You are fine as you are. Peace? We need to go."

"Peace," Ao agrees, trembling.

They don't climb up the embankment. For one thing, the sentry would spot them, but for another, it's forbidden by the white-haired god. The road itself will destroy any blasphemous retainer or atoner who walks upon it. The one time Elen had a moment of solitude to test a foot upon the holy pavement, it did sting her as if it were filled with angry bees, although she's still alive, whatever that means.

But the girls don't need to walk *on* the road. There's a tramped-down throughway that runs parallel alongside it, used by locals and lowborn. They'll travel at night, El thinks, and hide during the day.

They are about to turn north when they hear the rumble of horses from the east, the way they came. The moon slides out from behind the clouds. A shout rings out. They've been spotted. A horn blasts to alert the sentry in the fortlet, followed by a voice that carries easily across the quiet night.

"There! I told you! The scullery girl said she saw them taking off like thieves and leaving the rest to die! Come on, lads! We'll teach those girls a lesson they won't forget!" El recognizes the cruel cackle of the Lord Thelan's northern sergeant.

Lamps spring alight in the fortlet. Voices startle awake in the village. Dogs start barking. It's too late to circle around the village and head north. So, El turns south. She and Ao run alongside the embankment as she scans the area for a place to hide. This close to the road, the land is striped with grain fields, which are divided by black-thorn hedgerows and rows of hazelnut and walnut trees. The dogs will sniff them out in a heartbeat.

"A little farther," she says as they run. "Then we can cut east and circle around."

But they've never turned south at the fortlet. The lady's court never goes that way. It turns out they are much closer to the White Sea than El realized. The last field is bordered by a hedge of yew, beyond which lies graveled ground and a second yew hedge grown as a protective wall. Beyond the second hedge, there's only burned ground and a jumble of stones, the discarded bones of a long-abandoned village. A white-needle pine grows in the middle of the village clearing, the white-haired god's sign that Spore has killed in this place. Beyond that lies a long stony slope and then—visible at night with the same pallor as a ghost—the shore of the White Sea.

The troop roars, thundering up behind them, howling in glee.

Ao gasps, "Give me the knife. I'll kill myself."

This is the moment when El becomes a murderer.

"Keep running. I'll be right behind you," she says.

She stops and she turns, yanking the cord holding the sealed jar over her neck. She waits one breath, two, three, five. When the front ranks are a stone's toss from her, too close to easily shift direction, she flings the jar hard at the ground and stomps on it for good measure.

It cracks.

She sprints after Ao, toward the shore of the White Sea.

The screaming begins.

Spore moves fast when it senses a rush of vibrant animal life. A horse has bolted in a complete panic and, rider clinging to its back, plunges straight toward the White Sea. The soldier sees his doom coming. He tries to throw himself off the horse, but his boot gets stuck in the stirrup and so he is dragged, bumping and twisting, into the mist. How quickly it happens.

The horse rears up as its head stretches and tears apart, sprouting two heads, then four. The soldier shrieks, high and higher still, until the register of his voice turns into a whistle. He is elongating, as if the Pall is trying to turn him into a giant worm, body collapsing into segments, then dissolving, as if eaten through by a cloud of invisible locusts.

"El!" Ao's voice is frantic.

El runs. The agonized cries of the dying stab like claws trying to get their hooks into her. She's done this to them. She's killed them. But it is only the horses she regrets.

By the time El reaches her sister, Ao has scrambled up the embankment. From the road, she beckons to El. "Come on! We'll follow it across the sea."

El climbs the embankment but hesitates before setting foot on the roadbed. "It doesn't sting you?"

"No. You don't believe that story, do you?" Ao scoffs. "About the white-haired god building the road for the masters and so it stings anyone else? The masters didn't build the road."

"They didn't?"

"Well, it doesn't sting *me*." Ao grabs El's arm and pulls her onto the roadbed.

Bees sting through the bare soles of El's feet, and she skips and hops and says, "Ouch, ouch, ouch. It stings me."

Ao loves El. She does. But she has a mean streak that emerges at odd moments.

"I guess you're a blasphemer after all! Come on. Let's get out of sight before sentries or guardsmen come looking down the road."

They run south. It isn't so bad as long as El's feet don't press against the roadbed for long, but they won't be able to keep up the pace forever. Desperation pushes them on into the night. The gravel-strewn shoreline recedes behind them. The road has night behind and night ahead and the White Sea to either side. They can't go back, so they must go forward.

The screams fade. A horn shrieks. Eventually, even that sound is lost. All they hear are the slaps of their own feet as their running slows to a jog, and then to a walk, and finally Ao staggers to a halt and bends over and says, "I . . . have . . . to . . . rest."

El hops from foot to foot. The White Sea does not touch the embankment itself, so she slides off the roadbed and sits on the stone revetment.

Ao sinks down beside her. "I'm thirsty," she says, almost a whine.

They share a few swallows from one of the flasks. It's cider, biting and alcoholic. There's a loaf of bread at the top of one sack. They eat half of it.

"I have an idea to help your feet," says Ao.

By moonlight, Ao uses the knife, fabric cut from El's tunic, and a bit of leather cord to bind cloth around El's feet, so the too-big boots will stay on. The touch of the roadbed still stings but El can handle this level of pain. It's still better than what they're running from.

"You're so clever," El says.

Ao shrugs, then leans close, suddenly serious and deadly solemn. "We can't go back. Promise me, El. I'd rather die than go back."

"I promise," says El.

Ao takes off the bear badge and throws it into the mist. "Go on," she demands.

It feels strange to unpin the badge. El wonders if it wouldn't be smart to keep the needle, but she can't dig it out of the wood, and Ao is glaring at her.

"Do it! You promised!"

So El throws her badge into the mist too. The moment it vanishes into the darkness she's glad, even though it meant losing the needle. They're free, whatever comes next.

They walk as the moon sets and the stars wheel. By now it isn't just her feet that sting but her chest as well, a restless ache that won't ease even when they rest off the roadbed, on the embankment.

The sun rises. South lies only the road and the White Sea. They can still see the rise of the nameless land to the north. It's too close, so they trudge on and on into the heat of the day. They hear a distant horn. Ao cries in fear. El thinks that probably soldiers will come after them because atoners must not be allowed to break their covenant with the masters. If atoners can escape, then who else might think to rebel?

Sometime later, they hear the horn a second time. They pick up their pace but, all too soon, they reach the end of the road, where both roadbed and embankment are severed as if by a flood or an earthquake. They are trapped on a dead end. Just as El feared.

The roadbed rises a bit here, the embankment built up beneath it, and then it just . . . ends, as if someone snapped off the next bit. Ao sits at the cleft with her feet dangling over the edge. She sighs, letting go of her hopes. "Oh well. It will be the knife, after all."

El sighs too, at first. But then she really studies the scene before them, because it's odd. The road is broken, yes, but the White Sea changes here in a way she doesn't understand and hasn't seen before. The White Sea lies heavy on either side of the roadbed they stand on, so thick a fog that the ground can't be seen beneath it. Beyond the broken edge of the road, ahead of them, a gap of lower ground extends off in either direction, exactly like a river's channel if it had run dry rather than being full of water.

Along this "channel," the deadly fog lies lightly and unevenly in a patchwork of lazy puddles and slippery threads that move westward in misty currents. Some of the ground is visible, mostly bizarre stacks of rubble and scattered heaps of bricks, all arrayed more or less in a straight line from the end of the road where they sit. Beyond the gap, where the ground rises as it would if it were the far bank of a big river, the fog again settles so heavily over the land that the land is no longer visible beneath it. Just like everywhere else in the White Sea.

Why is the gap different? Why is it mostly free of Pall?

"It looks like a riverbed that's run dry, but there's no road across," Ao says wearily. "There never was a way across, was there? It always ended here."

El shakes her head. "I don't think the roadbed ever ran straight across. Because I think you're right. I think this was a river. Look at all that rubble."

Farther out, blocky stacks of bricks rise from the ground like the pillars and piers that hold up old stone bridges, although no bridge she's ever seen is this long nor the rivers they cross this wide, as far as a man can shoot an arrow. Threads of mist like watery streams trickle along the ground, snaking their way between fallen pillars of stone and scattered islands of brick.

"Look," says El, pointing across, "see that dark smear there, on the other side? Almost like a pier? There's a narrow line beyond it, like a lane through the fog. What if that's where the road starts up again? What if it used to be the other side of a bridge, where the bridge comes down to the shore to meet it?"

"What difference does that make to us since we can't reach it? We can't walk through the White Sea."

"Why does the White Sea not fully cover this channel like it covers all the rest of the land? Why can we see patches of ground? Why doesn't the fog engulf all of the stone and even some of the heaps of bricks? What if the stone is the same stone that the road is built of?"

Ao sits up straight, searching the scene as she thinks it over. She says slowly, "In the summer, when it's really hot and there hasn't been rain, some streams run dry. But there's still water beneath the mud, isn't there? What if . . ." She presses both her hands to her face, squeezes her eyes shut as she thinks, and then lowers her hands. "What if this is a summer channel? It has been hot and dry this year. Spore hates water. What if the mist doesn't want to touch the muddy parts, the wetter parts?"

Spore hates water. And it can't touch the road.

The horns sound again, closer. They hear the barking of dogs. They look at each other.

"I think we can get across if we are careful where we step," says El.
"They'll just follow us."

"Only if they think of doing it. If they want to take the risk. And
their dogs and horses can't be as careful as we can be. The soldiers
would have to leave the dogs and horses and walk across. I don't
think they'll do it."

Ao gulps several times, wipes tears from her cheeks, and nods.
"All right. Why not? If Spore gets me, kill me. Do you promise, El?
Promise!"

"I promise."

Spore doesn't get them. Years of walking as atoners has made
them keen observers. The threads wind in patterns, perhaps avoiding subsurface concentrations of water. Rocks provide safe stepping
stones. The big brick pillars hold them up above the fog for gasps of
rest. A pale haze over the dry riverbed doesn't lift, but when they
get far enough across, they clearly see the continuation of the road.
From behind they hear shouting and arguing, but the haze hides the
girls, and the sounds fade.

The pursuers have turned back, believing the criminal atoners
have met their ordained end, by the command of the white-haired
god. No one can survive who enters the White Sea.

The girls reach the new section of road and climb up to the roadbed. Safe. For now.

They walk south as the sun sets and the moon rises, and as the
moon sets and the sun rises, and the moon sets again, full and bright.
Another day and night pass. They run out of cider but, miraculously,
reach a swift-flowing river running beneath the White Sea's blanket
of deadly mist. Amazingly, the bridge crossing this river is intact.
The White Sea does not enter water, and the embankment beneath
the first pier runs right down into the river. El crawls down the embankment. While she is filling the flasks, a broken yew branch floats
past on the current, wrapped in a vine studded with lantern-berries.
She snags it, dragging it back to shore.

"Do you think this is from Eelwise Ford?" Ao asks as they pick
the berries off one by one, savoring this unexpected delight.

"River water has to come from somewhere," says El. "All the rivers and streams we cross with the lady flow south into the White
Sea. Maybe they flow into this river?"

Thus fortified, they walk on for another day and another night,
and yet one more, dividing the remaining food into ever smaller

portions to make it last longer. But their pace slows. They stop to rest more and more often, and they sleep through the hottest part of the day. They mostly walk at night now and through the early morning, when it's cooler. The world is eerily silent except, once, when a wide-winged bird sails past above, croaking.

"That bird has to land somewhere," says El. "There's got to be an end to the White Sea."

"I'm so tired," whispers Ao. "Is there any water left?"

El gives her the last swallow.

They have run out of food when they see a light shining in the south, out of the haze. The light does not waver. It's a beacon calling to them. It's the burst of hope they need to keep plodding forward with the last of their strength. Maybe there really is a land where two girls might . . . might what?

Might live.

Ao cries out, clutching her belly, and stumbles forward. El's eyes had been lifted to the light, and half her mind was on ignoring the constant, stinging pain in her feet and the dull ache that feels ready to crack in her chest. She's startled when Ao flings herself down and collapses into hopeless, exhausted sobs.

The road is broken. Before them lies another collapsed bridge across a dried-out river channel. The ruins lead to what appears to be an island of rock, like a monstrous turtle's back, that blocks their view. They can't see the other side of the channel, how much more of it lies beyond the rock, and if the bridge goes onward past the rock. Maybe the rock is the end of the road. Some distance beyond this, though, they still see the shining light, up on high. The light suggests there is something tangible, physical, rising beyond the haze. Yet unreachable, because the problem is that, this time, there is a wide and steady stream of mist pouring along the dry channel almost like water. Which means there is no way to pick a route across. Ao sprawls on the road, sobbing, each tear a gleam of hope lost. The sun sets. Ao weeps until she falls asleep.

But El has been changed by this journey. Her heart has cracked, and what is meant to emerge, she does not yet know. Stars twinkle overhead. The air is clean, and they are free. For the first time in her life, she feels unrestrainedly happy because they have escaped, and that is enough, even if this is all the freedom they will know. If they die or live this night, it will be because of their own will and their own decisions.

The world is beautiful and precious. Even the White Sea is beautiful. Sparks like fireflies wink in the mist. The shallow currents of mist that run along the channel pulse with an iridescent glow, like living rainbows. She has witnessed this unexpected splendor. That alone is something she never dreamed of. So, if this is the end, if death awaits them alongside grief at the loss of what she and Ao briefly hoped for, then she can yet smile.

Time passes. Slowly, she realizes . . . the threads are thinning. Growing more shallow. Bits and pieces of rock are emerging into view. It reminds her of a story one of the lord's chatelains told about how the ocean has *tides*.

What if the White Sea has tides, too?

She shakes Ao awake. "Up! Up! We can get across if we go right now. The tide is going out."

Ao has slept long enough to muster a final burst of determination. They sling their empty packs over their backs.

"Hold on to my hand," says El.

They run across the barren ground, feet slapping as they skip atop rocks and clamber over heaps of fallen brick. They reach the great turtle-like rock. It's a longer distance than it seemed. They're both panting, struggling, as they drag themselves up the big granite outcropping. Only when they reach the top, where the road builders long ago hammered iron stakes into the rock to anchor the middle section of their bridge, do they discover the horrible truth.

The rock is an island, or was once an island, in the middle of an astoundingly wide river or perhaps a strait. The beacon light looms closer. For the first time, as the predawn light brings color back to the world, they can see land—actual land—rising above the White Sea. A tower, like a spear, stands against the sky. The road leads right there.

Or it would, if the bridge on this side wasn't also collapsed.

That isn't even the worst of it. The "tide" hasn't gone out on this side. There is no obvious path across, no places where "dry land" emerges, no heaps of bricks and collapsed piers to create stepping stones. Just the slow slip and slide of deadly mist, the dense, impassable fog.

Ao stares as if she can't believe life could be so cruel, when they have tried so hard. This time, she doesn't even have the energy to cry. She slumps to the ground, defeated.

El never weeps. She's not even angry, precisely. Anger has left her body, and something else is writhing in her heart. A memory assails her: the broken pot in the woods. Spore can move at an astonishing speed, so why has it never swiftly and ruthlessly attached itself to her? Pure luck? Or something she doesn't understand?

"It's shallow. I swear the mist is no more than ankle deep, you can see the ground," she says.

"So what?" Ao shoots back.

"You get on my back. I'll wade across."

"But it will kill you. And then it'll kill me."

"You know Spore doesn't like me. It avoids me. Pulls away from me. I think there's a chance I can get across without Spore digging into me. What choice do we have? We can't go back. We have to go forward. We have to try. If we die, then we die, and if we live, then we live."

So that's what happens.

El hitches Ao up onto her back and walks across. The mist never gets more than knee-deep. Ao keeps her feet pulled up, out of the way, so scared that she starts reciting the names of healing herbs to keep herself from screaming.

The current tugs and drags at El, though. *Just give her to us. She's nothing but a burden to you. El. El. You'll do better without her.*

El trudges on with Ao's chatter to give her courage, pulling against the sucking pressure that tries to trap her feet. She doesn't say so to Ao, but surely even she can't endure so long a contact with the Pall. It will soon dismember her, dissolve her, as it did to the horse and its rider. But she's not concerned about that, not anymore. She needs only to get Ao across safely.

This she does. They reach the broken edge of the far causeway. It sticks a ways out into the White Sea, but it runs all the way to the grand tower with its shining light. Ao scrambles onto the embankment, keeping low.

"We have to wait here until night, so whoever's in there doesn't see us, then we can go on," Ao says. Then she gives a sob and, with an effort, stifles herself.

"There's surely Spore on me, and we ate all the salt." El strips off her pack, gives Ao the knife, the pot, the tinder box, the cloak. Even the boots. "This is all for you. I love you."

"I'd rather die than be without you," says Ao brokenly.

"I'll die if I must, and I'll live if I can, but whatever happens to me, you have to live. Promise me."

Ao is the bravest person El knows. El leaves her sister there and wades back across to the big rock. The sun is rising strong and sure into a cloudless sky when she clambers up and seats herself cross-legged at the top. She makes ready to die, to be eaten by the Spore that must be starting to consume her. The sun rises higher. She has no food, no water, not even shade beyond one tiny patch of shadow that soon vanishes as the sun lofts to zenith.

There she sits, exposed in full sun through the heat of a hot summer day. Sweating.

Dehydrated.

Parched.

Nauseated.

Dizzy.

A throb in her flesh, her bones, her very heart, a pain so intense the world darkens as she sways. This is the end.

But she doesn't die. Something else happens.

Her heart cracks open, and a viper hatches.

With a searing pain, it bores a tunnel down her arm and out into the world. It's as white as maggots. It's dreadful. It's terrifying. It's beautiful.

It flicks a cunning tongue to scent the air, and all at once it darts aggressively toward her knee. She hasn't the energy to flinch, but it isn't attacking her. It's found a filament of Spore lodged in the folds of her tunic. It unhinges its tiny jaws, and swallows the Spore, just like that.

Then it slithers down to the White Sea, where it drinks as any animal might refresh itself. After it has taken its fill, it explores the rock, then returns to her, where she hasn't moved because she's so stunned. Her hand is still pressed to the ground, bracing herself so she doesn't topple over.

The viper pokes its sharp nose into her skin and, with that same burning pain, it crawls back up inside her body, into her heart, where it curls around once, twice, and nestles to sleep.

When the sun sets, she crosses the White Sea again, this time with no fear. The viper devours any Spore that attaches itself to her, while Ao watches her approach with gleeful amazement.

Imagine two girls finding themselves in a new land, where anything might happen. Where they might even hope to live ordinary lives, with a room of their own and enough to eat more days than not. There is hardship to come, especially for Ao. They will never fully leave behind the terror of their early lives because it has woven itself into their bones, but they will live.

At first, they will live in what seems like a garden of plenty, as menials at Duenn Manor. But its walls will become a prison of a different kind for Ao. But this second time, they will know they *can* escape, so they escape again.

This second time, they will make a good, decent life in Orledder Halt, with the beloved baby who will have a better childhood than the one they suffered. This child will smile when he sees the dawn and laugh when the moon and stars delight him, because he doesn't walk every day in fear. They won't speak of what came before, so it will fade as if into background noise.

Never mistake silence for forgetting.

It's not that they don't trust the child to know. It's that it hurts so much to look back down that path.

67

THE PERFECT WEAPON

Elen woke as she always did, just before dawn. It was the one enforced demand from her childhood that she had kept and made a habit. The shutters' cracks and irregularities became visible as night lightened to gray.

The bunk was too warm because, at some point after she'd fallen asleep, Kem had crawled in with her, as he used to do as a little boy, when there was a thunderstorm. He was sprawled on his stomach, fast asleep, taking up more than his share of space. His presence eased her bruised heart. She'd told him, at long last, and he'd said nothing, no words to sympathize or to condemn, but he hadn't left. It was a start.

She eased herself over him, found a pot to piss in and water to splash on her face. After lacing up her boots and pulling on her coat, she went outside, into the empty courtyard. The Sun Chaser had been rolled into the carriage house, and its harness folded away.

The sky was cloudy, and the wind smelled of rain incoming. It was a little warmer than yesterday. The presence of the Pall brushed against her senses. The viper stirred, but it was still sluggish and sated from its feast last night.

Last night.

He was gone.

Elen set her jaw and straightened her shoulders against the weight of pain. But she didn't cry. Her tears were gone too. Tears wouldn't bring him back, so what use were they?

Yet thinking of him hurt. His mischief smile. The random statements, now easy to recognize as the thoughts of a person who didn't quite understand the human world. The delightful conversations. The pressure of his sweet lips on her lonely palm.

She knew better than to think that the grief would soften. It might dull in time, as things did that were worn and handled, over and over again. As awful as it was to have lost Ao, at least she'd had Ao for so many good years. Her mistake had been in starting to believe she could fall in love with a person who didn't truly exist in this world.

It hurt so much. Yet she couldn't regret knowing him, just as she couldn't regret a field of spring wildflowers radiant beneath the sun. It was better to have witnessed beauty, even knowing it would not last.

"Deputy Courier!" Luviara stood at the door into the tower. Her eyes were shadowed, as if she hadn't slept.

"Your Worthiness."

The theurgist started down the ramp, leaning on her cane. Seeing how stiffly the other woman moved, Elen hurried over to meet her where the ramp met the courtyard.

"You knew about the griffin scout," said the interlocutor, without preamble.

"I did."

"Did the prince give a reason he chose not to trust me with the news of this shocking murder?"

"He did not speak of the matter to me."

"Was he behind it?"

"Behind the murder? Why would he kill his own griffin scout?"

Luviara scoffed impatiently. "Griffin scouts, like sarpa, belong to the imperial army, under the direct command of the emperor. Does the prince mean to inform the emperor, or is it his intention to let the matter of the dead scout remain a mystery?"

"I am but a deputy courier, Your Worthiness. How am I to know the answer? How *could* I know the answer?"

"His Highness has been speaking to you a great deal. You can't think we haven't all noticed it. It's quite out of order."

Elen looked her in the eye, growing bored of what seemed to her like jockeying for position within a palace hierarchy that meant nothing to a mere deputy courier. Anyway, she was tired, and heartsore, and she wanted to go home. *Home.*

As a child, she had never dreamed that she might ever have a home, yet there Orledder Halt rested in her mind, waiting for her to return.

"Worthy Interlocutor, I do not have answers for you. In fact, I am surprised you would ask me. You ought to know I have done nothing but accomplish the task I was given. Which, if I may remind you, was to guide the prince-warden and his party across Grinder's Cut, so His Exalted Highness could swiftly reach Far Boundary Vigil. Here we are. I'm done. The moment I am released, I will return to Orledder Halt."

Any other worthy interlocutor and holy theurgist would have been offended by this bold statement. With a slight smile, Luviara said, "How do you mean to get back there?"

"I have two good feet, and I'm grateful for them."

Luviara snorted. "It's a long way."

"I'm used to walking. Perhaps the exalted highness and his party will be returning that way, too, since the Vigil appears to be deserted. Unless you have news of the garrison."

"Not yet. Jirvy is searching the grounds."

"I pray the missing are found alive and well. Now, if you don't mind, I'll water and feed the horses."

"That duty was assigned to Novice Kem."

"Yes. But he's asleep, and I don't mind doing it. How is the prince, if I may ask?"

Her eyebrows flashed up. "I'm surprised it wasn't the first thing you asked. Are you not concerned for his health?"

The words were a fishing line, seeking information. "I thought fainting was something His Exalted Highness does on occasion, as happened at the Spires."

"By no means. He's famous for his remarkable stamina and vitality."

"You make him sound like a horse."

Luviara smiled with a flash of her old good humor. "Never say that in front of the others. But, truly, some say he is the winning steed in the emperor's private stables." Her look at Elen was measuring, inviting confidences. Secrets.

"What does that mean?" Elen asked, struck by a sense that they had moved into a more perilous discussion. "Is this some palace cipher, to speak in riddles? Or are you talking about—dare I say—the rivalry that goes on among princes? Are influential people saying His Exalted Highness is the most promising of the princes, even including the crown prince? If the emperor could only see it that way?"

"Sometimes I wonder who you really are, Deputy Courier. There's a mystery about you I've not yet answered to my satisfaction."

"I am as you see me." Elen extended her arms to either side, belatedly realizing she was copying the gesture the prince—and then the haunt—had made when bathing. She hastily lowered her arms, although not without a smile for the remembered view.

"Are you, indeed?" murmured Luviara. "Yet I wonder what I do not see. Still, you got the prince here. I'm not sure anyone thought you could actually do it."

"My thanks. I'll accept the praise in the spirit with which it is intended."

The door into the tower opened. Simo emerged. He glanced at the sky, gauging the weather, then said, "Deputy Courier, come with me."

The door into the stable slammed open, and Kem stumbled out, rubbing his eyes.

"Oh, there you are," Kem said with relief, seeing Elen.

"Novice, see to the horses," said Simo. When Kem hesitated, Simo's tone snapped. "Was there something you didn't understand?"

Kem straightened in an instant.

"Yes, Captain!" He hurried back into the stable, casting a single glance over his shoulder as if to make sure Elen was still there.

"Is there anything I can do to help us along, Captain?" asked Luviara.

"I'll let you know. Deputy Courier? *At once.*"

Elen hustled up the ramp. Once inside, Simo led her up the stairs. They passed a map room where Xilsi and Ipis were methodically going through documents. Simo did not halt until they reached the floor below the beacon. The entire floor was a single circular chamber with large viewing slots built into the walls. Each slot was aligned with one of four standing desks, where sentries could note down their sightings. Curved benches lined the wall. Otherwise, the chamber was empty except for a single wooden chair placed in the center of the room.

"There." Simo pointed to the chair. "Sit."

She sat.

He left. His footsteps receded down the stairs.

The open shutters allowed a cold wind to whip through. Elen tightened her coat around her. From the chair, she had a view north over the road, right up to where the causeway ended in a blunt line.

Footsteps thumped on the stairs. A man walked into the room.

She gasped, heart racing. Could it be? Somehow?

He slammed shut the door with a pronounced *thunk*. She shut her mouth, seeing the whip he held.

He circled her as if she was a horse he was thinking of buying. It all came crashing in, not just her memory of the events of last night, but the arrogant way this man stalked, as if he commanded the world—and in a way he almost did. He wore the closed, proud, haughty expression of a person who expects obedience to his least whim. He examined her with condescension and disdain.

No, he looked nothing like the haunt, even if the physical features were the same. She would never mistake the two, even if, for that first instant when he'd walked in, hope had overtaken common sense.

He halted in front of her. "Stand."

No one disobeyed a prince, especially not one who used that tone. Elen stood. The chill in her flesh had nothing to do with the wind. Of course, no one disobeyed a prince using any tone. She'd known but had never fully understood: Her relationship with the haunt had been reckless beyond belief. How suspicious had it made the wardens?

"Take off your coat."

She took off her coat and draped it over the back of the chair. What was going on in his mind? Had Simo expressed how puzzled the wardens had been by his behavior toward the deputy courier? Was the prince trying to hide the blank space in his memory? Was he going to ask her questions designed to figure out what he had missed?

"Take off your glove."

"My glove?"

His lips curved up, but not in a smile. "The viper. Show me the viper."

"The viper?" Surprise left her unable to think up a lie better than *What viper?*

He nodded with satisfaction, having proved something to himself. "I don't know what manner of enchantment afflicted me, but I heard all, and I saw all. I was trapped as if behind glass. I know everything you said to him and everything he said to you."

Everything.

She was so shocked, she said the first thing that came into her head.

"He said you wouldn't recall anything."

"Yes, he did say that, did he not? He told you a passage spell leaves the host as if asleep."

"Shrouded behind a veil," she murmured.

"I wasn't asleep, nor did any veil shroud me, I assure you. I fought with all my power to retake my body. I am not to be trifled with in such a high-handed, contemptuous way. I am no weak-blooded aivur, part animal, unable to resist enchantment. I am no common-born human, but a prince risen to the Third Estate through my mother's considerable efforts and my own determined training. I had the strength to remain awake and aware for all these days. What do you have to say for yourself?"

She ought to kneel, to beg for mercy, but she just couldn't bring herself to beg.

"To say for *myself*? These events took me as much by surprise as I must suppose they took you. If you heard all and saw all, then you know as much as I do. In truth, you know far more, since you will have seen and heard all of his conversations, not just the ones with me. Not to mention the bedroom interruptions, and Lord Genia's devoted and aunty rebraiding of your magnificent hair."

The prince pressed the whip against her cheek, hard enough to make her blink as its knots ground against her skin. "It must be the viper that gives you this remarkable effrontery. We shall see how long you keep it up, now you are under my rule as a member of my personal household."

She swallowed but couldn't speak because of the pressure of the whip. His personal household! There was a threat she had no answer for. No answer but waiting for the means to escape and run.

After examining her face with a cruel intensity, he lowered the whip. "Answer my question, Deputy Courier."

With long practice, she kept her tone cool and even. *Never let them know how badly they've rattled you.* "By your expression, Your Highness, I perceive there is something specific you wish me to say. Perhaps you can let me in on your thoughts. What it is you want."

The whip twitched in his hand. She waited him out, pleased to see irritation flash across his face. Yet he didn't strike.

After a silence, he walked to the northern window slot and looked out over the Pall, tapping the whip against his thigh, his back to her.

"I have gambled everything on this," he remarked peevishly to the view.

"What have you gambled, Your Highness?"

He turned, his expression grim. "My life. Which makes yours forfeit. Yours, and that of the youth."

A chill descended. It wasn't that she feared death, for she'd seen too much of it to believe she could avoid death when it came for her. But not Kem. Not her beloved boy. Not yet. Not now.

She had to keep the prince focused on her. "Your Highness, do you mean to execute me?"

"Execute you! Of course not! You're too valuable, surely sent my way by the will of the High Heavens." He waved the whip toward the ceiling as if in salute to the all-seeing Heavens and their inexplicable workings. "You are the perfect weapon. I thought my hopes had been broken and scattered. Now, everything has changed. With your viper at my disposal, my path to the throne lies clear."

Elen's expression tightened with the impact of a fear so strong she couldn't hide it. He was going to use her viper to assassinate whoever stood between him and the throne. Prince Astaylin? The crown prince? The emperor herself? She choked, too horrified to speak.

"That's right," he said with the satisfaction of a keen competitor, one used to coming in first in all his endeavors. "Three lives hang in the balance: mine, yours, and his. Kem is smart and capable. He will be a good warden—as long as *you* don't kill him."

Raw, ragged fury spasmed through her, making her reckless. She would never give him the satisfaction of cowing her. "If you force someone weaker than you into acting as the wolf in your place, then you are still the wolf even if yours are not the teeth dripping with blood."

"A tendentiously poetic image worthy of a palace courtier," he said in a tone that made it clear he despised palace courtiers and their weary metaphors. Her rash defiance hadn't even dented his imperial composure.

"If you kill Kem, then I have no need to cooperate. That places you and me at an impasse."

"Not at all. It is your concern for him that makes you a perfect weapon for me. You will serve me, or you will die. Yet the prospect of your own death isn't enough to fix your loyalty, is it? If you die, the boy dies. If I die, the boy dies. His life, Deputy Courier. You understand."

She did understand, too well. Too much.

"Now. Sit."

She sat, struggling to rein in her galloping, disordered thoughts. The world had shifted under her feet.

"As I said before, show me the viper."

Footsteps thumped on the steps, someone hurrying up. A hand rapped on the closed door.

"Your Highness?" It was Simo.

"What is it?" the prince called impatiently, gaze gripped by Elen's fingers touching her own sleeve. He shook his head at her. Only when she withdrew her hand from her sleeve did he look to the door. "Come in."

The door opened, and the captain entered the chamber. Simo's glance took in the prince at the window and Elen seated on the chair like a prisoner being interrogated. A flash of curiosity widened his eyes but was quickly squelched as he addressed the prince.

"Your Highness, my most abject apology for disturbing you—"

"Enough! You're a warden captain, not a palace courtier. What is it?"

"The Worthy Luviara insists she needs to speak to you immediately on a matter of great urgency."

"Has she found something?" the prince asked sharply.

"I don't know, Your Highness. You ordered me not to let anyone come up, which is why I brought the message myself. She spoke more strongly than is typical for her, and hinted at dire tidings, which is why I went so far as to interrupt you."

The prince stuck the whip back into its loop on his belt. "Stay here," he said to Elen, and went out with the captain, leaving the door open behind him. No need of a lock and key. He knew what he was doing. He knew how to win.

Could she and Kem sneak away somehow? Flee? Yet how? Where? And this time, she had something she did not want to leave behind: a place she called home. People she cared about. Something to lose, besides her life.

A wave of exhaustion struck hard. She sagged forward, elbows on thighs, to rest her face in her hands. The viper stirred but settled. Her mind was a muddy field, all churned into a soupy mush that had neither texture nor contour. She could not keep a thought in her head for more than a moment before it shattered and sank beneath the murk.

Now what? Now what? If only . . .

But "if only" was how Ao had driven herself all those years into repeated breakdowns and deep despondencies. "If only" offered no way to survive.

The haunt was gone. Kem was a warden. She now belonged to the prince's personal household because His Exalted Highness had proclaimed it, and that made it true no matter what she wanted. Her viper was the weapon he planned to use to capture the throne of the Tranquil Emperor for himself.

In a heartbeat, a life changes.

"Aunt?"

Kem's whisper brought her up fast. She jumped to her feet.

He stood at the threshold scanning the chamber to make sure no one else was inside. Then he dashed forward, and she opened her arms. He flung himself into her embrace, her sweet child who had once, as a toddler, hugged her knees and shouted, with great, excited approval, "You smell like poop and worms, Auntie," after she had returned from cleaning the privies.

She sighed, holding him. He who was now as tall as she was, broader in the shoulder, strong and good-natured and clever. She breathed deeply of him.

"Poop and worms," she murmured affectionately.

"I'll never hear the end of that story, even though I don't remember it." He pushed away from her. He had that serious look he got when he was trying to figure out the hardest puzzles in his gentle life. His gaze dropped to her neck. "I know it's just a wicked old scar, but did you get it when you were an atoner? It seems like the kind of nasty thing that would happen."

She brushed her fingers along the faint indentation. "I honestly don't have any memory of how or when I got it."

He grinned. "Like me and my broken little finger."

"You and your turnip," she retorted.

He almost laughed, then sobered. "Simo said the prince has declared you are to join his household, alongside Fulmo and Luviara, and beside us wardens. Is that true? How can it be true? What's happening?"

In a low voice, she said, "He knows about the haunt, about everything that happened when the haunt was possessing his body, which he wasn't supposed to know. He was supposed to have been as if asleep. But he saw and heard everything."

She couldn't bring herself to mention the prince's ambitions and the part he meant Elen to play in them. It wasn't that she didn't want to tell Kem, but that it was all so outside of her experience of the world that she wasn't sure how to start.

"Oh, of course," he said. "If the viper is poisonous, it would be a perfect, invisible way to murder . . . well . . . someone who might be standing in your way to the position you think you deserve, if you were that sort of person."

She laughed wryly. "I see I can't put anything past you anymore, Novice Warden. Kem, this whole business has got to stay a secret between us two until I have figured out the situation we are in and where it leaves us. What we can reasonably hope to do, to be safe."

"I know that!" he said with a flash of annoyance. "By the way, I'm still mad at you."

He punched her lightly on the shoulder to make a jest of the words, but a pinch in his eyes told another story.

"We have a lot to talk about," she agreed judiciously.

He rubbed his chin, and then his eyes, before looking compassionately into her face and saying, "Are you sorry you took me to Three Spires?"

"Because of the haunt and all that happened because of him? No. Never be sorry for any moment of happiness that falls into your life, however fleeting it might be and however it may end. Cherish it. I'm glad I met him." It hurt to speak the words, even as they rang true in her heart. "I'm glad to be alive, Kem, and I miss your mother so much. I wish she were here with us now. Well, maybe not *here*, at this particular Vigil. It would have upset her so much to stand in this place again, to look back toward the north. My dear Ao. The bravest person I've ever known."

He grabbed her wrist—unthinkingly, and without the least sign of fear, he grabbed the arm that was the viper's path into the world—and pulled her to the north-facing window.

The causeway stuck out like a pier built into the deadly mist of the Pall, its broken end rimmed by a railing built of hallow-wood. Beyond the gap, almost hidden by the heavy haze, rose the turtle-back rock where she'd sat all day, under the hot sun without water to slake her thirst. Beyond the rock, the haze obscured all, which meant it wasn't possible to see the continuation of the road beyond the gap. Anyone would believe the turtle-back rock was the last piece of solid land before the Pall swallowed everything. That the road terminated at the Vigil. That this was the end of the empire, the end of the inhabitable world.

Kem stared north, his sensitive face reflecting so many emotions as he considered what he'd learned about his mother's childhood. "I want to know everything."

The weight of his words fell so heavily that, in the moment, they felt too burdensome to bear. She smiled instead and bumped a friendly shoulder into his.

"Everything? I can think of a few recent stories you claimed not to want to hear!"

He snorted, elbowing her. "You know what I mean! About you. About Mama."

"I don't think I can quite face telling you everything," she admitted. "I'll tell you as much as we can both bear. I want you to understand her. You deserve it. She deserves it."

He sighed and, with a sad smile toward the hidden north, draped an arm over her shoulders in comfortable amity. "I never thought my Declaration Week would end up this way."

"Neither did I!"

From below, heard through the open windows, Xilsi and Ipis laughed at an unknown jest. Hooves clattered in the courtyard as someone—Jirvy?—brought the horses to the trough. Closer, a tread of footsteps got louder, a person ascending the stairs.

She glanced toward the door and, firmly, back at him.

"Kem, my dear child, I don't know what is coming next, but we're here, and we're together. For now, that is enough."

ACKNOWLEDGMENTS

First, I thank my generous Patreon supporters. They got the initial glimpses of the earliest iteration of the Witch Roads universe, and even voted on several world elements, which I then incorporated into the setting. Your patronage literally made it possible for me to write this duology.

Shout-out to my writing group, Cheri Ebisu, Emma Candon, Nick Candon, and Krystle Yanagihara, who were so incredibly encouraging as they read the rough draft. To the nest, Aliette de Bodard, Vida Cruz-Borja, Zen Cho, Victor Fernando R. Ocampo, and Rochita Loenen-Ruiz. To my children and their partners, who always have my back. And to my many writing friends and acquaintances and the community that holds us up as we move forward during complex and often difficult times. I could not do this without you all.

As always, a special thank you to my brilliant editor Lee Harris, his doughty assistant (and assistant editor) Matt Rusin, publisher Devi Pillai, editorial directors Claire Eddy and Will Hinton, copyeditor Christina MacDonald, jacket artist Raja Nandepu, jacket designer Jess Kiley, production editor Sam Dauer, managing editor Rafal Gibek, production manager Jacqueline Huber-Rodriguez, designer Heather Saunders, publicists Jocelyn Bright and Saraciea Fennell, marketers Emily Honer and Becky Yeager, and social media marketer Sam Friedlander. Your professionalism shines.

ABOUT THE AUTHOR

KATE ELLIOTT has been publishing fiction for more than thirty years, with a particular focus on immersive world-building and epic stories of adventure and transformative cultural change. She's written fantasy; science fiction; space opera based on the life of Alexander the Great (*Unconquerable Sun*); young adult fantasy; the seven-volume (complete!) Crown of Stars epic fantasy series set in a landscape reminiscent of early medieval Europe; the Afro-Celtic post-Roman alternate-history fantasy with lawyer dinosaurs, *Cold Magic;* and two novellas set in the Magic: The Gathering multiverse. Her work has been nominated for the Nebula, World Fantasy, Andre Norton, and Locus Awards. Her novel *Black Wolves* won the 2015 RT Award for Best Epic Fantasy Novel. She lives in Hawaii, paddles outrigger canoes, and spoils her Schnauzer.